D0422017

A BOOK OF WIZARDS

A BOOK OF WIZARDS

EDITED BY

MARVIN KAYE

FANTASY

Compilation as a whole and introduction copyright © 2008 by Marvin Kaye

"Sorcerer Conjurer Wizard Witch" copyright © 2008 by Kim Newman
"The Day Is Ours" copyright © 2008 by Margaret Weis with Robert Krammes
"Proving the Rule" copyright © 2008 by Holly Phillips
"My Life as a Swan" copyright © 2008 by Tanith Lee
"What Tune the Enchantress Plays" copyright © 2008 by Peter S. Beagle
"Knight of the Well" copyright © 2008 by Patricia A. McKillip

All rights reserved.

Book design by Christos Peterson

First Science Fiction Book Club printing April 2008

Published by Science Fiction Book Club of Bertelsmann Direct North America, Inc., 250 West 34th Street, New York, NY 10119.

Visit the Science Fiction Book Club online at www.sfbc.com

ISBN: 978-1-58288-292-5

Printed in the United States of America

❧ CONTENTS ❧

Introduction

A Time for Wizardry?

Books and wizards—it takes no stretch of the imagination to recognize that the two go together. Where, after all, do wizards learn arcane knowledge if not from books and manuscripts? A well-stocked magician's library is so important to Gilbert Norrell in Susanna Clarke's entertaining novel *Jonathan Strange and Mr. Norrell* that he corners the market and his student-to-be Mr. Strange cannot find a book of sorcery to study throughout the width and breadth of England, except in Mr. Norrell's homes in York and London.

Though we commonly assume wizards to be adept in magical lore and practice, this is not inherent in the word itself. *Wizard* derives from the Middle English "wisard," meaning a wise man; "wisard" may be traced back to the French "guischart," which probably stems from the Icelandic "viskr," for clever, knowing.

Even if we call our mage a sorcerer, magic is not implied. The root of that word is the French "sorcier," one who threw lots. Lots were objects put in a small container, perhaps a dice cup, shaken and tossed out to provide a random answer to some public issue.

Only if we dub our wise man an enchanter do we bring magic into the mix, for that term is a descendant of "incantare," which is Latin for the singing or intoning of magical charms, spells, and similar formulae.

I suspect that wizardry's association with magic may be a gender issue, at least in part. Long before J. K. Rowling used the words as such in her wonderful Harry Potter series, wizard and witch have been corresponding labels for male and female practitioners of magic. They do not reflect the same etymological source. *Witch* is an offshoot of the Anglo-Saxon "wicce," the ancient and still extant religion that celebrates Nature and only later became associated, not altogether accurately, with black magic. (It is true that *warlock* is also linked with *witch,* but though it comes from the Old English "waerloga," one who breaks faith, by implication the Devil and his minions, in Scotland *warlock* is interchangeable with *wizard.*)

Whatever we may choose to call them, wizards are certainly popular and have been for quite some time in literature and the cinema. But while the cultural prevalency of wizardry is interesting, I am more intrigued by its significance as a social metaphor.

In *Accidie,* Aldous Huxley's great essay on the history of spiritual sloth, we are introduced to Accidie, also known as the Midday Demon, the only fiend capable of functioning in daylight. Accidie inflicted victims with boredom, hopelessness, and despair: a deadly sin that Huxley contends only came into its own with the great social changes of the past centuries—the Renaissance, the Reformation, the Industrial Revolution, the rise of the modern city, the French and American Revolutions with their ideals of freedom and the rights of the common man, the world wars, the advent and use of nuclear weaponry.

"Other epochs have witnessed disasters, have had to suffer disillusionment," Huxley wrote, "but in no century have the disillusionments followed on one another's heels with such unintermitted rapidity, as in the nineteenth and twentieth, for the good reason that in no centuries has change been so rapid and so profound."

The poetics of despair haunts important writers, composers, dramatists: Cervantes, Conrad, Dickens, Dreiser, Glass, Hesse, Ibsen, Mahler, Mann, Shakespeare, Shostakovich, Strindberg, Vonnegut, Wharton, Wilde. To this far from complete catalog, one may add French and American film noir, numerous horror movies, and in theatre, the risible nihilism of such absurdists (and fantasists) as Beckett, Genet, and Ionesco.

But a positive aesthetic of ethics and hope also exists. It is especially rich in American movies of the Great Depression and World War II: *Casablanca, The Farmer's Daughter, The Grapes of Wrath,* and Frank Capra's *Mr. Deeds Goes to Town* and *Mr. Smith Goes to Washington* (according to the late Professor Ellis Grove, who taught film at Penn State, the latter's upbeat ending was cut when shown in the USSR).

This aesthetic dominates the character and choices of the great wizards of fantasy. Hogwarts's headmaster Albus Dumbledore comes to mind, as does J. R. R. Tolkien's Gandalf (along with their real-life alter egos, the late Richard Harris, Michael Gambon, and Ian McKellen); so do Susanna Clarke's Norrell and Strange, as well as Jonathan Stroud's put-upon boy magician Nathaniel in the Bartimaeus trilogy, *The Amulet of Samarkand, The Golem's Eye,* and *Ptolemy's Gate,* and if we go back a few decades, there's Merlin in T. H. White's *The Once and Future King* and in Parke Godwin's Arthurian novel, *Firelord.* Earlier, we have magicians endlessly at war in E. R. Eddison's epic *The Worm Ouroboros;* more recently, the theme surfaces in varied guises in Paula Volsky's superb fantasies (personal favorites): *Illusion, The Luck of Relian Kru, The White Tribunal, The Curse of the Witch-Queen,* and more.

In this age of assassinations, biological warfare, environmental pollution, genocide, organized crime, nuclear meltdown, terrorism in the name of religion, and the widespread corruption of leaders both political and spiritual, it is no wonder people crave champions of justice and virtue. This need has prompted a flood of movies about comic book superheroes like Superman, Spider-Man, the Fantastic Four, and the X-Men (and -Women).

Wizards are popular for the same reason, but they possess an additional virtue that has its own potent appeal—wisdom. Father figures, perhaps, they consult books that unlock the power to resist and combat evil. What they read may not be easy to understand, but they do not shrink from the hard work of study.

It has been observed that the Harry Potter novels have contributed significantly to the cause of literacy, and this is true, but I believe they and their ilk are quite as important for the positive examples they offer of education for the betterment of a severely conflicted world.

❖ ❖ ❖

Good sorcerers outnumber the wicked in the stories that follow, but there are both, as well as some serious enchanters. *A Book of Wizards* is the sixteenth anthology I have edited for the Science Fiction Book Club over the past twenty-five years. It has been an altogether wonderful experience. Most of the credit belongs to the two SFBC editors–and friends!–who have made it possible. My deep affection and gratitude to Ellen Asher and Andy Wheeler.

–Marvin Kaye
New York City, 2007

A BOOK OF WIZARDS

SORCERER CONJURER
WIZARD WITCH

BY KIM NEWMAN

Kim Newman is a novelist, critic and broadcaster. His fiction in-cludes The Night Mayor, Bad Dreams, Jago, *the* Anno Drac-ula *novels and stories,* The Quorum, Famous Monsters, Seven Stars, Where the Bodies Are Buried, *and many other books and collections. In addition to numerous nonfiction books about fantasy literature and films, he is a contributing editor to* Sight and Sound *and* Empire *magazines and has written and broad-cast on a wide variety of topics from Sherlock Holmes and the films of Val Lewton to role-playing games and movie heroes. A Lon-doner, he has won the Bram Stoker Award, the International Hor-ror Critics Award, the British Science Fiction Award, and the British Fantasy Award. His official Web site, "Dr Shade's Labo-ratory," may be found at* www.johnnyalucard.com.

"Sorcerer Conjurer Wizard Witch" features the protagonist of "The Gypsies in the Wood," Kim's story in my earlier SF Book Club anthology, The Fair Folk. *As before, Mycroft Holmes's Diog-enes Club plays a significant role in suppressing public awareness of those dark forces that threaten Britain's security. Along the way, we hear a few things about that cantankerous old sleuth, Sir Henry Merrivale (though he is much more likable in the mystery novels that John Dickson Carr fashioned for him).*

I: 'POOLS OF POISON, MY DEAR FELLOW'

BROWNISH-GREY CLOUDS boiled low, threatening drizzle. Two keepers loomed out of the bracken, casually directing shotguns at the Bentley. Despite the overcast day, they wore heavy dark glasses. Charles shuddered, recalling the *eyes* behind those goggles. The keepers' plus-fours, Norfolk jackets and flat caps were midnight black. No brown check tweeds need apply. Spent-match stick–figures against red undergrowth, they turned in unison as the big car passed.

Charles Beauregard of the Diogenes Club was come a-calling on a long-standing rival agency. The Bentley bumped along wheel ruts carved over centuries. The carriages, carts and armoured cars that had passed this way were equipped with iron or silver bars to restrain passengers who wouldn't be making a return journey. Huntstanton, his driver, took the speaking tube to apologise for the rough ride.

'It's like the Somme, Mr B.'

'With fewer infernal devices, we trust,' said Charles.

'I'd not lay a bet on it, sir. My phantom foot's twinging. Usually means land-mines.'

Charles scanned the landscape. The 'men in black crepe' probably had littered Egdon Heath with mines and man-traps, though the unrelieved redness was more than enough to deter most hikers and cyclists. Trust the Undertaking to inhabit countryside more like Mars than England.

A lifetime in the most secret service honed a suspicious mind. Could the well-worded summons, tactfully conveyed through intermediaries, be a stratagem to lure him here for a malign purpose? He had no wish to become an 'item' among the Egdon Heath Collection. Edwin Winthrop, the Most Valued Member, advised against Charles paying this call in person. But a Name was invoked, and only the current Chairman of the Ruling Cabal would do.

These were serious times. Another War was coming. In fact, two. Winston was quite right about that little Herr Hitler, just as he had been quite wrong about that little Mr Gandhi. The new Chancellor of Germany had revived the Thule Society, but was capable of doing more than enough damage without adding dark magic to his love of Teutonic pageantry. Eventually, his Third Reich would move against encircling European nations. The Empire would have to stand against Greater Germany. Charles, heart heavy, knew mechanised mass slaughter would resume. War was unavoidable, and must be won convincingly this time. If not in 1935, then 1940, 1950.

However, that would not be Charles Beauregard's Next War. Another global conflict was in the offing, and the Club was on the front lines. Like the Second World War, it already had names: the Witch War, the Weird War, the Wizard War. If won, it would be written of only in secret histories. If lost, there would be no histories, secret or public.

The Mausoleum–by tradition, 'Mouse-o-lay-um' not 'Maws-o-lee-um'–was invisible from the track. Surrounded by a thousand acres of knee-deep bracken, it had no proud towers and flew no flags. The greater part of the keep was below ground. It had been erected–excavated?–in 1588, by Royal Decree. With Queen Elizabeth as first patron, the Undertaking claimed nearly three centuries' start on the Diogenes Club, but had broken with the Crown upon the Stuart Succession. A few maintained the 'undertakers in smoked glasses' had never truly returned to the fold. The Undertaking often acted as a supranational body, indifferent to the wishes of sovereign, parliament or people. The Club's lot would on occasion have been easier if they were accorded such a free hand, but Charles had spent a long career resisting the temptation to take liberties. When his juniors ran the show, would they continue to be as fastidious? Winthrop, the Undertaking's fiercest critic, had a certain contradictory admiration, not unhinged by envy, for their methods.

Before the War, the inter-service rivalry must be settled. The Diogenes Club must find a way to work with the Undertaking. Both operated under Royal Charter, notionally constituted as arms of British Intelligence. But Charles had seen behind the spectacles. Could any public servant truly have common cause with those who saw the world through such *different* eyes?

Mausoleum Hollow was a meteor crater, ringed by weathered standing stones. Archaeologists reckoned them the Neolithic equivalent of the 'Danger–Keep Out' signs put up at the site of a bad fire or a subsidence in the road. Something once fell from the sky and smote the land. The stones, ingeniously hauled from a quarry in far-off Wales, told folk to be wary of lingering dreadfulness. The long-ago meteorite merely seeded the earth with iron enough to redden bracken until the end of time. The undoubted dreadfulness was of more recent vintage.

It took a *significant* invocation to bring Charles here. The War was closer.

Signs had been there to read for a generation. Five years ago, a Bureau of the American federal government (the so-called 'Unnameables') conducted raids in the coastal town of Innsmouth, Massachusetts. Officially, they were after violators of the Volstead Act but the actual target was a peculiar, un-Christian sect, the Esoteric Order of Dagon. In the end, dynamiting certain offshore structures forestalled an invasion from the Deep. Charles had lent Captain Geoffrey Jeperson, a Valued Member, to the Yanks, though a transatlantic alliance in these matters was resisted on both shores. The American tendency to address problems with high explosives and machine guns was admittedly worrying. When the Club had to act against the likes of the Esoteric Order, there was rarely necessity for a cover story. Gentlemanly discretion meant avoiding loud bangs.

In 1903, an ab-human entity came close to committing the most colossal crime ever contemplated–the murder of space and time. Charles, then Most Valued Member, assisted Mycroft Holmes, the Club's founder and original Chairman, in a procedure that saved that day. No fewer than fifteen of the world's premier magicians, occult detectives, psychic adventurers, criminal geniuses, and visionary scientists set aside profound differences and worked under Mycroft's direction to avert the rending-asunder of the entire universe. Yet the only allusion to the affair in the public record was an aside by the biographer of Mycroft's more-famous, frankly less perspicacious brother, concerning the 'journalist and duellist' Isadora Persano, who was found 'stark staring mad with a matchbox in front of him which contained a remarkable worm, said to be unknown to science.'

That unique annelid wriggled still, with a silver pin stuck through it, within the Mausoleum. The contents were referred to as 'the Egdon Heath Collection', as if it were a museum of ancient curios or a menagerie of uncatalogued fauna. It was both, but, as envisioned by Good Queen Bess, primarily a prison. The 'worm unknown to science' was designated a permanent detainee at His Majesty's Pleasure. So, come to that, was Isadora Persano. Along with others too dangerous to be let loose, too valuable to be thrown away or too singular to be stifled and interred in the adjacent cemetery.

Huntstanton steered between two stones, under a heavy archpiece. Within the circle, protected by the inward slope, the wind dropped and watches stopped. Charles wondered if the cylinders would seize, but the superbly-made Bentley was proof against magics whipped up to coddle the Mausoleum. The car purred to a dignified halt outside the squat, greystone block. It had started raining.

Mr Eye, the Warden, stood by the front door, top hat doffed. An attendant shielded his hairless skull with a black umbrella. When Charles came with Mycroft to hand over the wretched worm, he had waited in the carriage while the Chairman went into the Mausoleum. Now, the keep was open to him.

He had a momentary stab of pain. Huntstanton had to get out of the car, limping, to open the door. Charles hoped Mr Eye would assume protocol was being followed, but his arthritis was bad at the moment. He *could* open the door from the inside, but only by fumbling the handle. Showing even tiny weakness to the Undertaking would be a mistake. Ignoring cramps in his legs, he unbent to step out. He put all his weight on his sword-cane. Blooded too often for his taste, it was now more for support than defence.

'Beauregard, good day,' said Mr Eye, thin lips parting to show entirely black teeth. 'I trust you have had a pleasant journey, yes?'

'Quite, quite,' Charles responded. Catching himself sounding irritable, he opted to play the game. 'You've a bracing climate here,' he said, genially. 'Excellent for the circulation.'

'Indeed. Care for a pick-me-up?'

The umbrella-wallah offered a flask.

'Not at the moment, thank you very much. If we could proceed to the *lady,* I would appreciate it. I've had a long drive down, and it's as long going back.'

The black smile curved. Mr Eye's teeth weren't rotten, just ebony. Was his whole skeleton like that?

'Ah, the *lady,*' said the Warden. 'An unusual item. We're not much on the distaff side, you might say. We've the Angel Down Changeling, but that's an it, not a she. Most of the time, it looks like little lost Rose Farrar, but it's not her.'

Mr Eye was referring to one of Winthrop's finds. The Most Valued Member hotly resented the Undertaking's assumption of authority in the matter. Years earlier, Charles had allowed something similar to retreat rather than become an 'item'. The slight had not been forgotten. He trusted 'Rose' did not suffer on his account, though the Changeling constituted a significant threat. It would not have lost its venom sacs in captivity.

'But the *lady* is a lady,' continued Mr Eye. 'Whatever else she might be, she is that. I needn't tell you to be wary, Mr Beauregard. Watch your throat and don't look into her blue, blue eyes. Pools of poison, my dear fellow. She's bitten three we know of, lately. One fatality. Be wary around all our, ah, items, come to that. You have been briefed, yes?'

Mycroft had been privy to the inventory and left memoranda in the files Charles inherited when he took the Chair. Now, the Diogenes Club was routinely apprised of Egdon Heath acquisitions.

Don Felipe Molina and Sir Timothy ffolliott, the original

items, were still here, bodies strapped to racks. Their tongueless heads were kept separately, in leather buckets. As Charles understood it, the sorcerous nobles–who might have changed the course of history–still whispered inside keepers' skulls. If beheading had been the end of them, Elizabeth wouldn't have needed the Mausoleum.

Mr Eye ushered Charles into the hallway. A nine-foot *mi-go,* or 'Abominable Snowman', dominated the vestibule, stuffed but snarling. According to a plaque, it had been shot by a Jesuit in 1802. Its claws still looked sharp.

'You'll have to leave the pig-sticker with Mr Arrh,' said Mr Eye, indicating the sword-stick. 'And your loaded revolver, yes. The fossil in your hip-pocket, hmmn. The note-book with the backward writing, I fear. The scarab amulet on your watch chain, a-hah. The watch itself–with those intricate little crystal workings–*most especially.* And the silver scalpel in your note-case. Have I missed anything?'

Mr Arrh, whose glasses were a visor-like attachment to a bowler hat, stood ready to take custody of the weaponry. Instead, Charles handed everything over to Huntstanton, who had a valise ready. Mr Eye tutted as the watch was in view. How the Undertaking would like to tinker with that particular timepiece!

'So much distrust,' Mr Eye lamented, satirically.

'I understand the need for precautions,' said Charles.

Mr Arrh patted Charles's pockets deftly and gave Mr Eye the nod.

'Let us proceed,' said the Undertaker.

Huntstanton and Mr Arrh remained in the vestibule, regarding each other with suspicion. If it came to blows, Charles would lay bets on his driver. In tight spots, he made wicked use of his tin foot.

Mr Eye led Charles to a cabinet, which opened to reveal a spiral staircase. A rope banister provided support. Charles was not too proud to avail himself of this. A nagging concern was that he would find coming up a deal more difficult than going down.

'The *lady* turned up in Weymouth, of all places,' said Mr Eye. 'It was your classic story. Bites in the night. A pick-pocket and a drunkard. Then, a corpse drained of blood, stuffed into a bathing machine. Traditional holes in the throat. A footpad, according to the local plods. They nearly let the case slide, thinking he'd got what he deserved. Our bad lad had burked more than one holidaymaker, it seems. We owe this catch to the coroner. The item wasn't hard to track to her lair. I say lair, it was more of a boarding house. I suppose *nosferatu* take seaside holidays, too. More fool they. Harder to get rid of the empties outside a city. Still, she could have done a *little* more to hide among the teeming crowds. She might as well have dripped splotches of blood along the seafront and pinned a black bat to the door of her room.'

Charles knew most of this story. It sounded even less credible from Mr Eye.

'Vampires aren't supposed to exist any more,' said Mr Eye. 'Van Helsing claimed he hunted them to extinction.'

Charles paused to catch his breath. 'There've been unsubstantiated, out-of-the-way reports in the last few years. The Club was never entirely convinced by the little Dutchman.'

'Didn't you black-ball him?'

'Not me personally. I wasn't on the Ruling Cabal then.'

Membership of the Diogenes Club was by invitation only, and invitation was rarely extended to foreign nationals. Charles understood Abraham Van Helsing had dropped a brace of freshly-severed heads on a table in the Strangers Room and had the temerity to *make an application*. The specialist's achievements were noteworthy, but the Club wasn't comfortable with his tendency to issue type-written press releases and pose for victory snaps like some Great White Hunter in front of burning crypts or piles of fresh ashes.

'I doubt Van Helsing's stalwart little band bothered to comb Weymouth for the blood-drinking undead,' said Mr Eye. 'Their quarry preferred the Northern resort towns. No, the *lady* came as quite a surprise. If vampires are officially extinct, we'll have to class her as a living fossil. Like the cedar wood wasp, the tuatara, and the Lake LaMetrie elasmosaur.'

They were–at last!–at the bottom of the staircase, in a chilly passage with a flagstone floor and brick walls. Water ran nearby. A string of electric lamps lit the area, poorly. A woman under-taker sat at her post, in black skirt and riding boots, veil over her dark glasses. She was perusing a fan magazine with Jean Harlow on the cover. When Mr Eye stepped in view, she swiftly slid her reading matter under a blotter and stood.

'This is Miss Jeye,' said Mr Eye. 'She participated in appre-hending the item.'

'The *lady* came quietly?'

'Yes. That's unusual, too. We approached with the usual cau-tion. Wafers and crosses and sharp sticks, yes? Inky string and sticky rice, which works wonders in the Far East. She showed her wrists for the silver cuffs. She more or less said "it's a fair cop, guv". Miss Jeye was disappointed. You'd boned up on slaying skills, hadn't you, dear?'

'Tumbling and Japanese wrestling,' explained the woman, adopting a stance, then shrugging.

'We barely got a flash of teeth and a hiss out of her,' said Mr Eye. 'Bit of a let-down, you might say.'

'When did she invoke the Name?'

'Not until she was here, in her new quarters. That's a puzzle, too. If she had the Name, why not use it earlier? Save herself a bother.'

Charles wondered if the Warden wasn't talking theory, rather than practice. The Undertaking was capable of pretending not to hear, especially if the Club was involved.

Miss Jeye pulled open a drawer and took out a calling card. She handed it to Mr Eye, who glanced at it, and presented it to Charles.

'She was thoroughly searched, of course, but this got through. Mr Arrh was most displeased. She got to her quarters, sat on her, ah, sleeping contraption . . . and conjured it seemingly out of the air. As you see, it's not *her* card.'

Charles looked at the white oblong. Heavy, gilt-edged, expensive, more like an invitation than a *carte de visite*. On one side, over a sigil few would recognise, was stamped 'Mycroft Holmes, the Diogenes Club, Pall Mall.' On the other, written in a hand he remembered well, was his own name.

He felt a touch of ice between his shoulders and in the small of his back.

'You have been *named*, Mr Charles Beauregard,' said Mr Eye, reappropriating the card before Charles could slip it into his pocket. 'You and your, ah, distinguished predecessor. Two Chairs for the price of one.'

'Let's see her,' he said. 'And fathom this.'

Miss Jeye took a ring of keys from her belt and unlocked a stout, silver-bound door. The room beyond was also lit by electric bulbs, burning behind grilles. Charles expected bare dungeon walls, but the room was papered (cream with violets) and carpeted. Against one wall was a long wooden box, like a packing-crate for a grandfather clock.

The lady sat at a writing-desk, playing patience. As her visitors stepped in, she swept the cards together and performed a lightning-fast shuffle, then tapped the deck. Kings in succession levitated from among their fellows. The fourth king turned out to be a jack. She frowned and shuffled again.

'Whenever you're in prison, learn something new,' she said, in a pleasant, clear voice. Sharp little teeth showed in her small, pretty mouth. 'Another month and I'll have this down pat. Stage magicians have an unfair advantage. They're all men. With big hands. I have to make do with dainty little digits.'

The kings rose again, all four this time.

'Eh, *voila!*' She smiled, showing her sharpest teeth.

Mr Eye laid Mycroft's card down on the desk in front of her. Charles put one of his own beside it.

'I know who you are, Mr Charles Beauregard,' she said, dropping a black ace on the cards as if taking a trick.

He knew her, too. He had seen her twice. In the year of Queen Victoria's Diamond Jubilee, he had noticed her one afternoon in the British Museum's Hall of Egyptian Antiquities. A pale girl wearing blue glasses. Twenty years later, no older, she had been in Kingstead Cemetery at Mycroft's funeral. Both times, Charles had been preoccupied. He had not spoken with her, but her face–among so many seen on the street or at the theatre–stuck in his mind. He knew she was part of the great story of the Diogenes Club. It did not surprise him that she was what she was, though he had not considered the possibility. There were other ways of not ageing, none of which he had availed himself of.

Even before his second sighting, he had thought of her, often. Somehow, she was among the women of his life–his wife Pamela, dead twice as long as she had been alive . . . Pamela's cousin Penelope Churchward, who'd once set her cap at him . . . Kate Reed, his loving companion of decades, now a busy, elderly gadfly for constitutional reform in the Irish Free State.

'You have the advantage of me,' he said.

'I'm Geneviève,' she said. 'Geneviève Dieudonné. Geneviève Sandrine Ysolde Dieudonné. I'll be in Mr Mycroft's precious files under that, though I've more often used "Jennifer Dee" lately.

'We have her as "Geneva Deodati",' put in Mr Eye. 'She is named as such in a writ of excommunication, dated 1638, on record with the Roman Inquisition.'

Geneviève poked her tongue out at the Warden, and seemed for an instant younger even than her face.

'They tried Galileo around then,' she said. 'It was God's work to make him recant. Do you know why it's put about that vampires shrink at the sight of the cross? Because we have long memories. Holy Inquisitions, crusades, Borgia popes, wars of religion, burnings of heretics, sale of indulgences. Live more than a century or two and you lose respect for anybody's church. I'm not afraid of the crucifix. It's afraid of me.'

She made a fangface at Mr Eye, then winked at Charles. Cooped up here, she had grown bored. Tweaking her gaolers was too much of a temptation.

She was light blonde, with unfashionably long hair. He would still have taken her for eighteen or twenty. She wore a white cotton summer dress with navy trim. He imagined a straw hat went with it. Without her tinted spectacles, he saw the blue, blue eyes the Warden had warned him of. Threaded with the tiniest veins of scarlet. Aside from sharp teeth, she showed little outward trace of her condition. No talons, no pointed ears, no rat-nose, no wings.

'Might we have privacy?' he asked Mr Eye. 'Miss Dieudonné and I have confidential matters to discuss.'

The Warden had known this was coming. He began to babble about the danger of leaving visitors alone with the item.

Geneviève held up her hands. Her wrists were shackled with leather-padded silver handcuffs. Her ankles were similarly restrained. Additionally, she was chained to the wall.

'Quite clever,' she said. 'The leather means I don't burn, but the silver means I can't break the cuffs.'

She dabbed a forefinger against an unpadded link. There was a tiny hiss. She withdrew quickly and showed the small, fast-healing weal where flesh had touched metal.

'Has anybody worked out why that happens? It's always puzzled me. Like the thing with mirrors. And garlic. The rest of it's nonsense, though. Or I'd be a pool of mist seeping out under the door and flowing upstairs.'

Mr Eye grunted irritation and left the small room.

'Now, now, Mr Beauregard,' said the vampire, raising an eyebrow, 'we're unchaperoned. What will become of my reputation, tralala?'

Charles looked around. There would be an eavesdropping hole somewhere, probably with a wire-recorder at the end of it. He was here because the item hadn't been forthcoming. She might open up if they called her bluff and presented the Named individual.

'I'd offer you a chair, but there's only one and, as you see, I'm chained to it. Would you like to drag over the crate? Don't worry. I've not slept in it. That's nonsense, too. I've always preferred soft beds. Not that I need to kip more than once a month. An afternoon nap and I'm set for weeks. Honestly. I told Mr Face-Ache I needed my native soil and tried to get them to send to Burgundy for it, but they saw I was joshing. I've never had a coffin or a grave. Most *nosferatu* die and come back, but I just *turned*. You must think I'm a chatterbox. I've had no visitors and the black hats aren't much for chit-chat. Except Miss Jeye. She is quite enthusiastic about Mr Clark Gable.'

Charles was irritated at himself: without his stick and after all those stairs, he really would like to sit down. He was worried that if he plonked himself on the crate, he'd be unable to stand up again unassisted. So he leaned against a wall. He mustn't let his pains distract him.

'Mr Charles Beauregard,' she said, savouring his name, 'I know something you don't. Two things, in fact.'

'I shouldn't be surprised. The older I get, the less I seem to know.'

'Now *that's* being overly modest. As a former Most Valued Member and current Chair of the Ruling Cabal, I daresay you know a great many things the rest of the world doesn't. Part of your duty is to keep most people in the dark. Mr Mycroft's motto was "don't panic the populace". The first thing I know that you don't you must have a tickle of suspicion about.'

She held up Mycroft's card.

'Yes,' she said, 'I am a member of your Club. A unique auxiliary, off the books, inducted even before you were. The young Mycroft–sleeker, not quite the corpulence he became–saw a need for me. It was the beginnings of the Great Game. In the 1860s, I was not in one of my more personable phases. I blame the gin. Everyone was soaked in it. Little children as young as . . . though, of course, I never took my sustenance in that manner. That strangler in Weymouth was only my third killing-by-feeding in five centuries, you know. And the other two were worse than him. I may be a *creature of the night,* but I avoid murder. Mr Mycroft's primary talent was to know everything and everyone. He found us–you, as well as me–and cultivated us to serve. I've seen you six times, Charles, and let you see me twice. But we're cousins in service. I am your shadow. You are not a public figure, but you are acknowledged. You'd have a knighthood if you hadn't quietly refused the honour. Twice. You–and the Valued Members you've brought along–are known about in the circles, called on in circumstances. In many ways, you are a policeman. Better-spoken, of course. A Harley Street specialist among policemen. Me, I can't be a policeman, woman, matron, whatever. I am the other thing Mr Mycroft made. I am a *secret* agent.'

She pulled the Queen of Spades out of thin air.

'I'm tired, Charles,' she said. 'I've been in the cold for sixty years. All the things I avoided for centuries–and you know who and what I mean–I have had to associate with. Mr Mycroft needed me to be a monster. To be in the society of monsters. To gain their trust. To learn their plans. When he died, I was set free of an obligation but had no way back. And nothing to come back to. That's the joke of it. In sixty years, I was no use. As a rule, monsters are dull, petty folk. I learned few plans and those fizzled. While you and Mr Mycroft and Carnacki and Dr Nikola and the rest were saving the universe from Persano's Wriggling Horror, I was posing as a Limehouse opium addict to infiltrate the Tong of Weng-Chiang. They were wiped out in a turf war with the Si-Fan before their High Priest posed a danger to anyone but his tailor. Oh, I knew Dracula was coming, for what it's worth. Terrible gossips, *nosferatu,* as you must be noticing. Some lesser leeches had inflated expectations of their self-declared King. They said he'd elevate them to their proper position, and you warm fellows would be naught but cattle. "Naught but cattle." That's the sort of thing they always said. No wonder they're all gone now. Mr Mycroft categorised the Count as a minor nuisance and left him to that Dutch madman. So that's another report I needn't have bothered with. But I stuck with it. At the funeral, I was given an envelope by Mr Mycroft's adjutant, Dravot. The card was in it, with your name on the back. Before we proceed to the second thing I know that you don't, the really frightening thing, I don't suppose . . .'

He took out the card Mycroft had left, clipped in an empty file. It had the single name 'Geneviève' written on the reverse.

'Snap,' she said. 'I don't suppose it would have hurt to tell you who I was and what I was about, but it would have broken the habit of a lifetime. Mr Mycroft didn't mention he had a brother until the fellow became famous. He liked to keep us all in our holes until we were needed.'

A tiny glint showed in her eye. A red tear. She wiped it away.

'Mustn't get emotional,' she said. 'It offends the English.'

'I miss him too,' he said. 'I sit in his chair . . .'

'Lots of room, then.'

He laughed. 'It is rather wide for my behind. That's my situation entirely. I sit in his chair, but can't hope to fill it.'

'Too modest, the English, too. Which is alarmingly attractive.'

It occurred to Charles that this creature was flirting with him. Age difference ought to have made that absurd, but he found it rather warming. He remembered to be cautious. She was still what she was. With Mycroft's imprimatur, however, he trusted her. In a tight corner, he'd choose her over an Undertaker.

'When he was alive, Mr Mycroft sent me little notes. Never anything as obvious as an order. Hints, as it were. News clippings, sometimes. Puzzles and acrostics. He loved them. He indicated avenues I might pursue. There was also a retainer, deposited annually at Coutt's. Most of it's still there. I have few expenses. Three weeks after the funeral, when I called at the bank, I was given a post-dated note, in his hand. Another direction to pursue. I've heard voices from the grave, and this startled me more. Since then, there have been seven more notes. I've destroyed them all. I assume you're not responsible for sending them?'

Charles spread his hands.

'Mechanisms set in motion,' she said. 'Even without the prime mover, the clockwork ticks. I'd look to Dravot.'

'Retired.'

'No one retires from the Diogenes Club.'

'And dead.'

'That wouldn't stop Dravot. Mr Mycroft saw the great patterns of history, the secret patterns. The Witch War, the Weird War, the Wizard War.'

Charles felt a chill. He had never spoken those words, only thought them.

Geneviève smiled. She tapped her temple, rattling her shackles.

'He's still in our minds, Charles. He shaped us, how we think, how we act. He wanted us together.'

'Was this in one of your notes?'

'No, those were the usual clues. I was directed into an abyss. An underworld. I have lived among our enemies. Otherwise, I wouldn't have killed to get your attention. It's too easy to give in to the red thirst. The last note came as I was on the point of changing. It was a reminder–not a clue or a name, but a wake-up call. To stay myself. For a second time, Mr Mycroft saved me. A third, if you count the time he saved everyone. I know how the War is supposed to start. By now, you know who you'll be facing. This era's Great Enchanter. Colonel Zenf.'

Charles was familiar with the name. 'All indications tend to suggest him.'

'I can confirm it. I've looked into the eyes of that Austro-Hungarian nobody. I've seen them before, in other times, other faces. The eyes of a Great Enchanter are always the same. Beside him, Dracula and Napoleon and the Beetle are petty thieves. The plan is that London should fall, smashed entirely. Not just the physical city, but its shadow, its *idea*. Then they'll all come up

from the depths and the outer darkness and it'll be on. The Weird
War. But it can be stopped. The great danger comes from a traitor
in our ranks. Not just an ordinary rat, but a King Rat. Someone
you rely on, Charles. Someone who can hand a city to the enemy.
Find this traitor and the black tide can be broken. This is what Mr
Mycroft made us for, Charles. He knew he wouldn't fight this battle himself. He left us this trust. We don't have much time before
the Thames starts boiling with lepers' blood and a rain of screaming severed heads stops play at Lord's. That's speculation, by the
way, but *informed* speculation.'

Charles looked into her blue, blue eyes and saw fire. The chill
returned, all over his body. But his other twinges fell away. He
felt as he had in 1881. A hollow youth back from India, knotted
into an agony of grief for Pamela and their son, he had been
drawn into the Diogenes Club by Mycroft Holmes. His first case
had been the Purley Horror. Then, as now, he had been terrified,
but alive. Strengthened by the confidence an extraordinary man
had in him. Determined not to disappoint.

'I know what to do,' he said.

Geneviève rattled her chains, as if applauding.

II: 'THE REALM OF RAVENS AND RATS'

LATE IN THE afternoon, Edwin Winthrop returned to the Bloomsbury rooms he shared with Catriona Kaye. The flat was above an
artists' supplies shop. With his clientele too busy arguing about cu-
bism to buy brushes, the proprietor had avoided bankruptcy by
turning half the shop into a café and selling watery coffee and hard
biscuits. Most of the artists looked as if they subsisted solely on this
fare.

As Edwin climbed the hallway stairs, he didn't hear the clack
of Catriona's typewriter. She was working on a book provision-
ally entitled *Howling Hags,* about the Mexican *llorona,* the Irish
banshee and the Welsh *gwrach-y-rhibyn.* He hoped she had written

her pages for the day, since he wanted to apply her sharp mind to the problem the Old Man had shared with him. Half in and half out of the shadow-world of the Diogenes Club, Catriona brought a valuable, commonsense perspective to affairs that would drive most people to the bottle or Bedlam.

She met him at the doormat and kissed him on the cheek. 'Hot Voodoo' came from their big-belled Victrola. She shimmied back into the flat, shaker in her hands.

'Cocktails before sunset,' he observed. 'This is a decadent turn of events.'

'Judge not till you know all the facts,' she said, with a twinkle. 'Pick up a glass.'

Edwin followed orders, taking a cocktail glass–an inverted funnel with an octagonal base–from the cabinet. Catriona made a final shake, placed a tea-strainer to catch the ice and decanted. He raised the glass to his lips.

'Hold on a moment,' she said. From a bowl, she took a cherry–which she dropped into his drink. 'The final touch,' she said.

Edwin wondered what the occasion might be. They were no great drinkers, or concocters, of cocktails. Otherwise, they would un-doubtedly own a purpose-made ice-strainer and Catriona wouldn't have to cadge vital equipment from the tea-service.

'Go on,' she said, eagerly. 'Take your medicine.'

He took a sip. It was a Manhattan. 'Very nice.'

'What do you taste?'

He took another sip. Then a gulp.

'Two parts Irish whiskey to one part vermouth. Two dashes of Angostura bitters. A cherry. And a twist of lemon. Perfect, Catty-Kit. The bartender at the Algonquin couldn't do better.'

'You don't taste anything else?'

He took another gulp.

'Ice shards?'

She smiled. 'No hint of . . . burnt almond?'

He swilled the liquid around his tongue. 'No, not a trace. I assume you're *not* trying to poison me? There's no cyanide in this?'

'No, but there *is* burnt almond. I burned it myself in a crucible.'

He finished the Manhattan and still couldn't taste any added ingredient.

'What's this about?'

'Glad you asked, Ed,' she said. 'I'm demonstrating that Olivia Gibberne, Countess of Chelm, *could* have made away with her husband last season at Monte.'

'Didn't the Earl of Chelm fall from a hotel balcony? After staggeringly ruinous losses at the table?'

'Dead before he went over the rail, if I'm any judge. Would you believe it, there was no proper post-mortem! Methinks, the slyboots widow spread some of her inheritance around. I understand a coroner is cruising those famously winding roads in a new Hispano-Suiza.'

One of Catriona's hobbies was finding out folk who think they've got away with it. She would worry away until the Countess answered for her crime, if not in court then in an appropriate alternative manner. Some people were more upset if left off guest lists than sent to the gallows.

'Is there any more poison?' he asked. 'I'm about to bring you something more momentous than the third-dullest society murder of 1932.'

Catriona refilled his glass, and poured the last of the mix for herself. She popped in the cherries.

They settled on the divan that dominated their reception room. Catriona lifted the needle from the gramophone record and took up her pad and pencil. Note-taking was a habit with her. She also kicked off her shoes and slipped her feet into his lap. He stroked her tendons.

'We're in the realm of Ravens and Rats,' he said. 'We have to bone up on four eminent personages. One of them's no good and it's up to us to spot the ringer. The King Rat. A high degree of diplomacy will be called for. The fate of–well, everything, as usual–is in play.'

'Thrilling,' she said, satirically.

'Mountebank, Mesmerist, Warlock, Mage,
Sorcerer, Conjurer, Wizard, Witch . . .'

'What's that?' she asked, dotting and dashing shorthand.

'A mnemonic for our *dramatis personae.* Sorcerer, Conjurer, Wizard, Witch. Easier to remember than the names.'

'Which are . . . ?'

'Rennes, Stone, Drake, Device.'

'Spelled Da*vis* or Da*vies*?'

'Spelled, and spelling is important in this case, De*vice.* As in "infernal device". But pronounced "Davis".'

'How obstreperous of him.'

'Her. She's "Witch". Margery Device, the Hag of Harrod's.'

'The society hostess?'

'The very same. Squiffy Oates-Haldane got tossed out of one of her shindigs for tipping a bowl of punch over Lady London-derry. Witch–so they say–turned him into a toad. Actually, Squiff came down with a tropical disease, hitherto unknown in Kensing-ton, which causes a toadlike skin condition.'

Catriona chewed the end of her pencil. Edwin considered telling her she was adorable, but decided to raise the matter later. There were facts to be set out.

'Who are your other mnemonised individuals?' she asked.

He ticked them off on his fingers.

' "Sorcerer." Marcus Rennes. Not as in Wren, the bird or the architect. R. E. Two Ns. E. S. Deputy Astrologer Royal.'

'Astronomer, but never mind. I know who he is and how to spell his name. I half-followed a lecture he gave last year, refuting the late Professor Moriarty's book about the dynamics of an aster-oid. Rennes says the planet *isn't* doomed to be knocked out of or-bit like a billiard ball. Which is a relief. Though, if you say we're in peril again, possibly not true. That flags him up as a suspect, does it not?'

He tweaked her little toe. 'We suspect everyone. And no one. Remember how it works?'

'Indeed. Proceed.'

' "Conjurer." You'll know him, too. Robert Edmond Stone. He really is a conjurer, in the sense of prestidigitator, as well as . . . ah, raising demons and that sort of palaver. The Great Edmondo. Twice nightly at the Astoria.'

'So he's real pretending to be fake pretending to be real?'

'Such are the circles we move in, Catty. And "Wizard" is what you'd expect. White beard. Pointy hat with astronomical symbols on.'

'Astrological?'

'Both. Connaught Drake. Bet you've never heard of him. He doesn't go on the halls or give lectures or throw parties.'

'In this field, I assume *lack* of notoriety implies a degree of achievement in excess of his fellow magical practitioners?'

He slid along the divan, under her legs, put an arm around her waist, and kissed her on the nose. She was appreciative, if a little impatient.

'So who is Mr Drake?'

'Officially, Keeper of Ravens at the Tower of London. They're supposed to stay put because if they ever flap away, the kingdom will fall.'

'Don't the Yeomen Warders clip their wings to make sure it never comes to that?'

'A calumny, a rumour and a lie. The clauses of the legend are quite specific.'

'A legend has *clauses?*'

'Afraid so. The Old Man has a copy in the files. The "ravens" aren't just the birds. They're the mystic guardians of the city. Sorcerer, Conjurer and Company. When the legend says "kingdom", by the way, it means London. It's possible that, say, Birmingham might stand after whatever deluge affects the capital.'

'Is this all to do with the Tower?'

'So far as we can tell. I went there once with a school party.'

'So did I. Some years *after* you.'

He passed over the tiny dig. Catriona was a Century Baby, a 1900 birth–but he'd been around for most of the last decade of the 1800s. She sometimes twitted him for supposed Victorian attitudes.

'Like most people who live in London, I've not been back since,' she said. 'Have you?'

'Once, my love. With some Crown Jewel or other in my pocket. You know how often they go missing and have to be retrieved.'

'I do, most people don't.'

'Then the anecdote will spice up my memoirs when I persuade you to write them.'

She smiled at that. 'They'll never let you publish. You'd have to deposit the book in the Secret Files with the Mycroft Memoranda and Charles's Worm War Diaries.'

Edwin had an idea she was far ahead of him. Had the Old Man laid this out to her before talking with him? She had split a pot of Lyons Corner house tea with Beauregard before he set off for Egdon Heath.

'According to Mr Baedeker's estimable guide,' he began, 'the building now known as the Tower of London was begun in 1078. The White Tower was erected on the orders of . . . ?'

'*Guillaume le Salaud.*'

'Too easy. Yes, Illegitimate Billy, William the Conqueror, the last person to whom the city fell. Since him, the ravens have been in residence, and London has survived plague, fire, stench and motorised omnibus. Neither Napoleon nor the Kaiser dared so much as set foot on the beach at Hastings. Charles the Second once got fed up with ravens leaving "presents" on the lenses of his telescope and decreed they be removed. Reminded what happened to his father, he changed his mind. Since then, the birds have relieved themselves where they want. They are important, their Keeper more so. He's also a Raven.'

'Capital R.'

'Double-underlined Capital R. The Four Ravens are constituted in accord with the legend. William of Normandy's court wizard made castings from the top of the White Tower. He established wards and protections that, mercifully, are still in force. William's Wizard was the first of a line, and his descendant is . . .'

'Connaught Drake?'

'No, surprisingly. It's Marcus Rennes. I wonder if that causes friction among the Ravens. Does our "Sorcerer" resent the fact that "Wizard" has his *grand-grand-père*'s old job? Could this festering resentment lead to dark places? Worth thinking on?'

Catriona made a shorthand hieroglyph.

'What do our Ravens *do,* exactly?' she asked. 'Stand at the top of the tower, scanning the horizon for fires?'

'In a manner of speaking. That's "Sorcerer" 's job, mostly. He spends his days inside a large clockwork model in Greenwich. It represents our universe and its environs. Imagine a chicken-farmer who has a hundred miles of ribbon strung around every inch of his property, hung with bells. Rennes has to listen for the tell-tale tinkle of foxes. Foxes with tentacles, as it happens. Or horns. Lots of the blighters have horns. And more eyes than we find reasonable. You know what I mean. The Deep Old Dirty Ones.'

Catriona shuddered. 'Pray continue. What about "Witch"? I've met Miss Device. All I got from her were impossible-to-confirm tid-bits about the private lives of an overrated poet, a very *active* bar-maid in the Spaniards and the current King of the Cats.'

'Margery Device knows all, tells all,' he explained. 'A city isn't just stone. It's people. And *doings*. Whether we like it or not, we all want to know the other fellow's business. Witch tattles the tales. Don't mistake her for the Queen of Trivial Things, though. Think of her as a safety valve. A city can have only so many secrets before it explodes, like a stoppered kettle. She lets the steam out as *gossip*.'

Catriona whistled. 'Fair enough. Now, why do we need a "Conjurer"? Does London, perhaps, have a shortage of rabbits?'

'Stone is our artilleryman. An attack magician.'

'Don't like the sound of that.'

'Frankly, me neither. He's supposed to terrify the other lot. One way to stay safe is to have a bigger sword. Remember, the Ravens were constituted by someone who liked to be known as "the Conqueror". Stone's the youngest Raven, a recent recruit. "Wizard" has been looking for someone with his Talent for thirty years. We lost the last "Conjurer" in the Worm War. Janus Stirk, formerly "the India-Rubber Boy". Trust me as someone who's *read* the Beauregard Diaries, we needed an attack magician then and need one now. Stone blunts scissors. Stone tears paper. Stone smashes other stone. If he's our King Rat, we'll be in hot water, indeed.'

'So noted.' Catriona made a mark. 'We don't want it to be him.'

'But if it is him, we'll need to know. Just don't expect anyone to be happy.'

'What about the Keeper himself? Connaught Drake? "Wizard"?'

Edwin sighed. There was no easy answer. 'That'd be calamity, too. If anyone can wrap Stone, it's Drake. He holds London's shadow. That's something all cities have. It's supported by the specialties of the other three–spiritual barriers, the doings of men and beasts, trickery–but it's a world entire and to itself. You know all the stories of London . . . Dick Whittington's Cat and the Temple of Mithras, Jack Shepherd's buried fortune and the black swine in the sewers of Hampstead, the curse on Mitre Square and the ghost of the Little Match Girl, the Invisible Theatre where Shakespeare put on the Secret History plays. Those are all wrapped up in the city's shadow. Drake can pass between here and there and keeps everything in shape. He has to polish the

London Stone every few months. Some shadows can exist without their cities. Troy is still pretty much with us, for instance, though the physical place is long gone. But without a shadow, no city can stand. Terrified yet?'

'Since I met you, my love, I have dwelled in a state of perpetual fright. I dyed the first white streak out of my hair on my sixteenth birthday. When the horrors go away, I miss them.'

'If you'd seen the Old Man's expression when he brought me into this, you wouldn't joke. I know we're always in some peril or other. This is the King Peril we've been building up to.'

She saluted, fingers crossed. Edwin had an inkling he'd be grateful for her levity before this thing was over. He held her more tightly, feeling warmth through her dress. At bottom, Catriona Kaye was a Very Serious Person. It was why she didn't let the terror take over. To her, there were more important things to worry about.

'If one of our Ravens has gone over to the Enemy,' she said, 'then my next question will be . . . who or what exactly *is* the Enemy?'

'Our best intelligence is that we're facing a retired Austro-Hungarian soldier.'

'*Him?* Isn't that too obvious? I've been boring everyone stiff for five years about Herr Hitler.'

'Ah, not him. Not yet. The Old Man says he's the war after next.'

Catriona went limp in his arms and hung her head in mock despair.

'This fellow is Colonel Zenf,' he told her. 'No first name listed. Which is sinister in itself, I think you'll agree. Some call him "the Great Enchanter" . . .'

'The perhaps-imaginary arch-enemy of Don Quixote?'

'Perhaps not-imaginary. Other aliases include "the most dangerous man in Europe", if you'll pardon the expression–"His Satanic Bastardy", "the Big Eater" and "the Crack of Doom". He's either the Devil in the flesh or the Devil's Best Chum. "Sorcerer" says he registers on his model of the universe as a white nothing. The worst people you can think of are either his friends or more afraid of him than we are. Disciples, past and present, include Declan Mountmain, Oliver Haddo, Adrian Marcato, Hamish Corbie, Anselm Oakes, Hjalmar Poelzig and Pius Mocata.'

'I know who most of those people are. Quite a few met nasty, well-deserved fates. Usually in fires or the madhouse. Being friends with the Devil hardly helped them.'

'They did a great deal of damage first.'

'I'm supposed to be impressed?'

He did kiss her nose.

'No, you're supposed to be cowering under the sofa. The fact that you aren't is why we're elected to find out who's cosying up to Zenf. Here's another name you know, Julian Karswell.'

Catriona twisted in his arms. She had written a book on Karswell, *The Biter Bit.*

'*Him*,' she said, with disgust. 'The greatest modern-day exponent of rune-casting, which–as he must have realised in the last few seconds of his life–is quite the stupidest, most dangerous method of magical assassination on the books.'

'Colonel Zenf is a great admirer of Mr Karswell. The unsigned review of *The Biter Bit* in the *Neue Wiener Tagblatt* was almost certainly by him.'

'And you haven't had him killed for that? You are slipping, my love.'

'Sadly, though there are plenty of other reasons for having the Colonel killed, the Old Man hasn't yet authorised that measure. It's one of the things that makes our side better than theirs, remember?'

'Still ... "poorly researched" ... "childish inability to grasp profound truths" ... "overuse of ellipses"! The man's a beast.'

'Can you quote from all your *positive* notices?'

'No, they tend to blur together. It's only the bad ones anyone remembers.'

Catriona settled in his lap. She had covered several pages with hieroglyphs. They might be Karswell's runes for all he knew.

'My last question . . . at least for this session . . . is, of course, how do we *know* we have a Rat among our Ravens?'

'We've a whisperer in their ranks, dear,' he said. 'It's how *espionage* works. The Great Game. You might say a little bat told us.'

III: 'A COURTESY CALL'

R OOMS OPEN TO Ordinary Members–those tiresome, dusty fellows who maintained the pretence that the Diogenes Club was merely a haven for the unsociable–enforced strict silence. Fifty years after the Club's heyday, only two or three OMs were present at any time. They sat in deep armchairs, radiating disapproval, trying not to doze for fear their fellows might expel them for snoring (such things had happened), determinedly ignoring the comings and goings of the Valued Members. Charles wondered whether he should take the effort to recruit a new generation of crotchety (preferably deaf) buffers or abandon entirely the fiction that the Club was not an arm of British Intelligence.

In most gentlemen's clubs, a Quiet Room was where noise was discouraged; in the Diogenes Club, mere *quiet* meant unavoidable talk was at least tolerated. The Quiet Room was dominated by a Hallward portrait of Mycroft Holmes. The painting was fully four-fifths voluminous waistcoat, buttons shining like extra eyes. Charles was always conscious of his late mentor gazing down at him–though he felt that the artist had not, in this case, truly caught his subject's soul. In Mycroft's lifetime, the picture was relegated to the Club's store-house in Clerkenwell, but after his passing the Ruling Cabal felt it should hang on the premises, in honour of the first great (in every sense of the word) Chairman. Charles had abstained from the vote. He worried future holders of his office might also feel dwarfed by this unavoidable reminder of the colossal position he–or, in more enlightened future times, she–was expected to fill. Now Charles looked up and wondered–as he had often during his tenure as Most Valued Member–whether he was anything more than an especially shiny cog in a mechanism confidently set in motion by Mycroft Holmes.

Geneviève had told him she was 'off the books'. Even in Mycroft's most confidential, triple-ciphered files, there was no trace of her association with the Club. Charles expected as much but still made the effort to go through the paperwork.

How many other 'secret agents' were out there, in the cold? Or had lived whole lives without being able to show their true colours?

Yesterday, he had briefed Edwin Winthrop. By now, the Most Valued Member would have told Catriona Kaye.

Already–assuming the Undertakers had eavesdropped on his tête-a-tête with the pale lady–too many people were in the know. Investigating the Ravens was a tricky proposition. If one was indeed a King Rat, it was vital to determine which and take immediate action. But the Guardians of the City were a sensitive, powerful group. If they thought they were indivicually under suspicion, there was no telling how they would react. Charles could count on Edwin and Catriona to snoop with a high degree of tact, but they were still carrying flaming torches into the powder magazine. A traitor among the Ravens was a calamity waiting to happen, but unless the matter were handled with finesse, the whole flock could easily take flight. Then, the Kingdom would fall.

The Inner Chamber, where the Ruling Cabal convened, was dimly-lit to emphasise the secrecy of the business conducted there. Charles's routine involved a great deal of reading and the Quiet Room had large windows of extra-thick glass, so he made it his office. Sunlight poured in as Huntstanton brought him Bill Owen's Long Box, a daily miscellany of newspaper clippings with scribbled annotations. The Club retained Owen to pore through the press, tearing out items which might fall within their purview. Getting on in years when Mycroft put him up for membership in '97, Owen was nearing his full century and could not be relied on much longer. Another pillar in need of shoring up or replacing.

Charles broke the seal and opened the Box. The papers were musty, as if stewed in tea. For decades, Owen had sat in a corner café, ripping up newspapers, tying and untying complicated knots. Most who saw him took him for a harmless lunatic. It was possible that, undoubted genius aside, Owen *was* a lunatic, though at one time not harmless. His *life* was an allowance from the Diogenes Club. Mycroft could have seen Owen hanged for a murder no one else, including Mycroft's brother, had suspected. Now only Charles knew the secret. Every time he looked over a Long Box, it nagged him. It had often been Mycroft's way to make use of criminals rather than see justice done. Charles hoped to be different.

The first clipping was a tiny notice about an inquest on the Weymouth exsanguination. After what Charles intuited must have been undue influence from Egdon Heath, a coroner's court had brought in a verdict of natural death. If Charles followed his instincts and trusted Geneviève, he was making use of a murderer, too.

Next came humorous items from yesterday's evening dailies. Pranksters had stolen wax figures from Madame Tussaud's Chamber of Horrors and treated them to a night on the town. Photographs showed effigies of Charlie Peace, Mrs Manning and William Corder stiff among blurred crowds in Piccadilly Circus, jammed into seats on a Number 1 omnibus to Canada Water, or convivial around a table in an upstairs room at the Newman Arms. Charles would have assumed a circulation stunt, but the items were in rival papers.

Normally, Charles would have had a Valued Member call on the waxworks. With Edwin occupied and Captain Jeperson in New York, he didn't have anyone first-rank to spare. Oh well, there was no shortage of titled busybodies eager to poke noses into any mystery that afforded an opportunity to make the police look foolish. Let one of their lordships tackle the Perambulating Horrors.

Otherwise, Owen had turned up a report of the doings of the Thule Society. They had been involved in the construction of a vast electrical device either to predict the future or manufacture gold from sea-water, which had thus far resulted only in the electrocution of several acolytes. Then came shudder pulp business about a ring of mad surgeons abducting Philadelphia debutantes for unholy purposes. Charles bundled these away. At the moment, he was concentrating on matters closer to home.

If London falls . . .

A discreet cough brought him out of a reverie threatening to become an afternoon nap.

Huntstanton brought in a familiarly-dressed visitor.

'I am the new Mr Hay,' announced the young man in mourning clothes. He doffed his top hat.

Charles stood up to receive the Undertaker.

It was as rare for the first of the alphabet men to pay a call upon the Diogenes Club as for the Chairman of the Ruling Cabal to visit the Mausoleum.

Huntstanton eyed the Undertaker with suspicion, but withdrew.

Charles understood there had recently been a succession, but was not sure how the Undertaking went about cultivating new recruits. Talk was that they were grown from seed, mulched with the remains of their predecessors. Mr Hay still had a shiny freshness to his pallor, and red scratches across one cheek and his forehead.

The undertaker's entire body swivelled and his head angled up at Mycroft's picture. Then he paid full attention to Charles, who saw himself reflected twice in dark glasses. As always when he caught sight of himself in a mirror, his reflex was to wonder who that strange old person was.

'You may be proceeding under a false assumption,' Mr Hay told him, flatly. 'An item has gone missing from the Collection.

We have cause to doubt her–its–provenance. I fear you've been the victim of an elaborate deception.'

The words slid into Charles' chest like a jack-knife.

'How . . . ?'

'We hoped you might be able to shed light on the matter. A day after your interview, the *lady* went missing. Shackles neatly fastened but empty. Door firmly locked. Guards undisturbed and unmolested. But the cupboard bare. She was under constant surveillance, of course. In a matter of seconds, she was not where she was supposed to be. The expression that comes to mind is "spirited away".'

'You think she had outside aid?'

'As a matter of fact, our first suspicion was that you were responsible. Upon reflection, it is too deft a trick for the Diogenes Club. Quite beyond your capabilities. Beyond ours, too, which is not an admission we make often.'

The 'how' was beside the point. The 'why' troubled Charles. Why would Geneviève escape? If escape she had–there was always a possibility of abduction, or assassination. He didn't doubt Mr Hay was telling the truth but he hadn't doubted Mycroft's 'secret agent,' either.

'We shall, of course, take steps to reacquire the item. You may leave the matter to us. But, and I cannot stress this enough, you should weigh most carefully any action you take upon information passed from this source. The Undertaking believes it tainted. We presume the vampire Geneva Deodati to be a creature of Colonel Zenf.'

Charles had not thought the Undertaking aware of that name.

'Her sole purpose in letting herself be apprehended was to talk with you, Mr Beauregard. To gull you into setting on a course that leads to the disaster we hope to avert.'

Charles fought hard to keep his hands from trembling.

'This has been a courtesy call. We shall keep you informed of our progress. That is all.'

Mr Hay put on his hat and left.

Now, Charles had trouble breathing. Huntstanton rushed in and fixed a medicinal brandy and soda. Charles took the drink.

His breathing difficulty passed.

But his troubles were compounded.

IV: '*EVERYONE* IS INVITED'

CATRIONA WORE A breathtaking gown–mid-length, clinging and silver-white; matching cape, pumps and a cap that fit perfectly over her bobbed hair; blood-red rose pinned to one shoulder. Like every other man in the room, Edwin had to make do with white tie and tails.

Harry Roy's Band, on loan from the Mayfair Hotel, played 'We're in the Money'–which, in this company, was hardly front-page news. Lord Kilpartinger, the railway magnate, shot back his cuffs to show off ruby links prised from the eye-sockets of a little yellow idol purchased at auction last month. He must feel protected. Edwin held up an alchemist's eyeglass which passed as a green-tinted monocle and confirmed his suspicions. A purple-black aura throbbed around Kilpartinger. Wisp-things battered themselves to pieces against it.

He passed the glass to Catriona, who peered at His Lordship.

'Those wards won't hold forever,' she commented. 'I'd rather receive one of Karswell's *billets douces* than wear blood-cursed stones.'

'Everyone's luck runs out, Catty-Kit.'

'Except ours.'

'We don't have luck, dear. We have *caution*.'

'Then remind me why we're here.'

' "Witch" is the easiest of our Ravens to get close to. She's usually in public, on display. Think of her as a figurehead.'

Margery Device held court in a corner of the ballroom. This season–after experiments with dirigibles, barges and trains to

Scotland–her party was held in a conventional mansion fronting Hyde Park.

'Good grief, what *is* she wearing?' said Catriona.

Tonight, their hostess was bright green, with real vines threading through a diaphanous gown with an eight-foot train that had taken root. Her red-dyed hair was sculpted into a thicket of shrub, blooming with corpse-flowers. A bodice of bark was bound tight around her torso. Miss Device had to be the most outrageously-dressed woman at her party, and some of her guests set the bar high.

A thin woman in a cream dress approached Edwin and Catriona. She wore eggshells as earrings.

'Darling Cat,' she shrieked, kissing the air six inches away from Catriona's cheek, 'what delight to run into *you* here! That dress . . . very thrifty. Admirable in these hard times. We all must watch the pennies.'

Catriona smiled sweetly and said, 'Hello, Ollie. What odd earrings.'

'Do you like them? Dodo eggs.'

Ollie primped the fragile ovoids. They were more distinguished by scarcity than appearance.

'So sorry to hear about the Earl,' Catriona sympathised.

Ollie adopted a tragic face. 'It's been trying, but people have been *so* kind. Only those beastly newspapers have thrown dead cats.'

'If there's anything I can do . . .'

'I'll give you a tinkle. You're still in that dear little slum in Bloomsbury?'

'Yes, and you still own Norfolk?'

'As far as I know, darling. It's hard to keep track of one's *portfolio*. That's my word for the day.'

'That's funny. Mine's *apnoea*.'

'What does that mean?'

'Look it up, Ollie. Or you'll never learn.'

There was a glint in the woman's smile. 'I'll do just that. Now, must dash, Cat. Have to circulate. Wouldn't want to monopolise you. Toodle-oo.'

'See you in court, dearie,' said Catriona, after Ollie was gone.

Edwin had an inkling what that had all been about. 'That was . . .'

'Ollie. Olivia Gibberne, the Countess of Chelm. I was just talking about her the other day.'

'So you were. The cocktail-mixing minx. *Apnoea* is the primary symptom of death by cyanide poisoning, isn't it?'

'Literal loss of breath. Does a Countess rate the silk when she's hanged? Or is that only peers of the realm?'

'Not my field of expertise, love. The Old Man would know.'

'No matter. So long as justice is done.'

Across the room, Olivia Gibberne waved a long ivory holder with an unlit cigarette stuffed into it. Three smart young fellows produced flames. She smiled back at Catriona, who waved cheerfully.

'I had no idea you knew the Countess,' said Edwin.

'Didn't I mention it? We were at school together.'

'Gal pals, eh?'

'Not exactly.'

Edwin scanned the room and clocked fourteen murderers that he knew of. He thought it best not to mention them to Catriona. Then he glimpsed a pasty face, lurking beyond Noël Coward and Ivor Novello.

'Hey up,' he said to himself. 'Fifteen.'

Catriona snagged unpoisoned cocktails from a passing tray-bearer–a gilded youth in a loin-cloth and turban.

'Don't stare,' he said, 'but you see the famous folks over there?'

She looked at him askance.

'The *very* famous folks. West End.'

'Oh, *them*. Stay between me and Novello. He always pretends he wants to fetch me away to some little chalet. It's not very flattering. He thinks I look like a chorus boy from Cardiff.'

'Look without looking at the fellow just behind them. Round-faced cove with thinning hair. Listening to the Duke of Emsworth's pig stories.'

Catriona did a little twirl.

'Got him,' she said. 'That can't be right.'

She looked again, blatantly this time. The Duke's auditor didn't notice. His eyes were glassy, anyway. He was a little man with a drooping moustache and Teddy Roosevelt spectacles.

'Speaking of hangings,' she said. 'He was.'

'You agree with me, then?'

'Hawley Harvey Crippen.'

'Let's drift over,' he said, putting his empty glass and hers on a passing tray. 'I know Miss Device boasts everyone who is any-one comes to her party, but even for her this is out of the ordinary.'

'Don't let him give you a drink.'

'Ha Ha.'

'I'll see your "Ha Ha" and raise you a "Tee Hee".'

'I'll take your "Tee Hee" and trump it with a "Chortle".'

As they passed, Novello opened his mouth to speak to Catriona. Noël Coward tossed the olive from his cocktail into it. The matinee idol swallowed like a trained seal.

By the time they got to Emsworth, Crippen had moved on.

'B—y queer little b——n' c–t,' grunted the Duke. 'Shows no f——n' interest at f——n' all in pigs. Probably b——s goats in his spare time, the s–t-headed weasel-f——r! What a f——n' stupid f–k-faced b——d!'

It occurred to Edwin that Plum Wodehouse considerably worked over the Duke's country language when writing about him.

Their quarry had plunged, alone, onto the dance-floor, jostling packed couples.

Harry Roy was leading a lively 'Puttin' on the Ritz'. Crippen got buffeted.

'He's heading for the punch-bowl,' said Catriona, urgently.

Edwin took her in his arms and danced her in the murderer's wake, whisking between less-coordinated folks.

At the edge of the dance-floor, they bumped against two implacable bodies. Above immaculate evening dress, they had beefy, brutal faces–swollen noses, open pores, tufty side-whiskers, worked-in dirt, glittering eyes. They were Burke and Hare, Old Edinburgh's most notorious suppliers of fresh cadavers for anatomy lectures. Their heads didn't fit their suits.

Crippen took something like Catriona's cocktail shaker out from his shirt-front. It must have been in his chest cavity. He poured into a cauldron-sized bowl.

The brutes blocking Edwin's way wouldn't let him pass.

Catriona slipped out of his hold and, with a skirl of silver, got round the long-dead miscreants. She laid a hand on Crippen's shoulder and pulled his arm off. At this, people took notice.

'B––r me!' exclaimed the Duke of Emsworth.

A dowager raised a just-filled glass to quaff away astonishment. Catriona used the severed arm to bat the drink from her lips. Liquid fizzed on the floor and ate into the varnish. Other would-be poisonees poured their glasses back into the bowl.

Edwin adopted a pugilist's stance.

Burke and Hare came for him. In the popular imagination, the pair were remembered as resurrection men–but they hadn't the stomach for the honest work of exhumation, and took to suffocating folks, then pretending they'd been found dead or dug up. Few things were lower than a bogus body-snatcher.

He landed a solid right on Burke's chin and the head flew off. A mannequin body fell to pieces. Then he rounded on Hare–the slimiest of the pair, who peached on his brother-in-law to escape the gallows. The bounder pulled a dagger from his trousers, but Edwin knocked it away. He punched Hare square on the nose. His wax face cracked across and fell away, showing a pair of glass eyes (one milk-white) and a set of false teeth on a wooden frame.

Panic and commotion spread through the crowd.

'Look to "Witch",' Edwin shouted.

Catriona nodded and let a couple of young bloods pull Crippen apart. Once the heads came off, the murderers were incapacitated.

Edwin knew where he had seen the malefactors before. In the Chamber of Horrors at Madame Tussaud's Wax Works.

Catriona slid through the crowds towards their hostess, who had realised this was more than the usual fun and games. Determined wax guests were taking the same route. Louis Bauer, the Pimlico poisoner. George Joseph Smith, the 'Brides-in-the-Bath' murderer. Rodger Baskerville, the damnable dog-trainer. Amelia Dyer, the baby farmer of the 1890s. Sir Francis Varney, the vampyre.

Edwin had a loaded revolver in a special pocket inside his tail-coat. Too many people were blundering about for him to use of it.

Smith got to Miss Device first. She plucked a thorn from her hair-piece and darted it into his face, which melted and froze into a shapeless mass with eyes. Then she took a length of vine from her train and used it as a switch, whipping Bauer and Dyer to segments.

Many of her guests applauded.

'It's another turn,' commented Noël Coward. 'One is humiliatingly upstaged again.'

Some foolish fellows, a little the worse for drink, set about Ivor Novello and began pummelling him. He swore at them in his original Welsh accent.

'It's bloody Jack the Ripper,' said a rugby prop forward. 'I'd know that face anywhere. Saw it in the flickers. Twice.'

'He only *played* Jack the Ripper, you utter idiot,' said Coward. 'In *The Lodger.*'

'Silent and talkie,' grunted Novello. 'And I was innocent both times, boyo.'

'He's right, you know,' said the rugger player, calling off his team-mates. 'I remember now. This is the fellow who was *mis-*

taken for the Ripper. Fearfully sorry, old son. It must happen to you all the time.'

'Funnily enough, no,' said Novello, straightening his coat. His collar was exploded and he'd have to cake powder over black eyes if he went on stage in the next week. He kneed the prop forward between the legs, doubling him over. 'I must apologise,' he said. 'Sheer reflex. It must happen to you all the time.'

'Steady on, old chap,' said the forward's least-intoxicated friend. 'Play the game and all that.'

Catriona was by Miss Device, standing in a pile of broken dummies. She had her little pearl-handled automatic out of its inner-thigh holster.

The crowds stood still to applaud and Edwin made his way to the dais. Harry Roy struck up 'Don't Bring Lulu' and many revellers joined in the refrain.

He wasn't sure all the wax murderers were weeded out.

'This is a pretty pass, Mr Winthrop,' commented Miss Device, flexing her willow-switch. 'I thought the Diogenes Club was in the business of nipping these bothersome trifles in the bud.'

Catriona sorted through the pile of mannequin parts. She found something inside a coat pocket. A card. She passed it to Edwin.

'It seems they were invited,' he said, giving it to the hostess.

'*Everyone* is invited,' she said, airily. 'There's a list.'

The card had a name and address in copperplate. Rodger Baskerville, c/o Beryl Stapleton, Merripit House, Dartmoor.

The party swallowed the excitement and got on with revelry. There were always unadvertised occurrences. Most guests would think an attack by waxwork horrors was part of a sparkling array of entertainment.

'You, Mr Winthrop, Miss Kaye, have cocktails. Consider it an order.'

Miss Device snapped her fingers. An attendant stepped out of a plume of red smoke with a tray. Edwin took a glass for Catriona and one for himself.

'Now,' said their hostess, 'what is all this nonsense?'

The cocktail was sweet yet tart. For a moment, Edwin feared he had been slipped waters of truth at precisely the moment he most needed to be evasive.

'We have worries, ma'am. About the Ravens.'

'Well, *don't*. It's our business to have worries about you. As you see, we're not in danger. That's your lot. We keep *you* safe.'

Under her penetrating gaze, Edwin couldn't doubt it.

'Still, *quis custodiet ipsos custodes,* Miss Device?' put in Catriona.

'*Quis* indeed?'

'*Nos,*' said Edwin. 'Sorry about it, but there you are. Someone has to.'

Attendants discreetly took bits and pieces of the Chamber of Horrors escapees out of the room.

'Robbie Stone said this sort of thing was happening all over town,' said Miss Device. 'He's supposed to be here, but cried off. Rather pull artificial flowers out of real rabbits for the one-and-nines.'

Was that suspicious? None of the other Ravens was here. Except under extra-extraordinary circumstances, the four were never in one place at the same time. It was a precautionary measure. Still, one or two of the others would be admissible.

'Might we have a talk with you, ma'am?' asked Edwin. 'In private.'

'You sound like a policeman, Mr Winthrop. Am I to help you with your enquiries?'

She might almost be flirting. Then again, her calling involved flirting. And diplomacy.

'That's a stunning gown, my dear,' she told Catriona. 'How did you pull your little gun out of it?'

Catriona smiled slyly. 'There's a slit, but you can't see it. Hooks and eyes.'

'Very ingenious. You must give me the name of your dressmaker. By the way, did you see Ollie Gibberne earlier? Cream's not a good colour for her. I understand she has an appointment with the silk rope.'

Margery Device, of course, knew everyone's secrets. And none were safe. She doled out gossip the way other hostesses dispensed drinks.

'Look at Wallis Simpson, by the way,' she said. 'Now *there's* a threat to the kingdom. Trust me, that horse-faced American gold-digger will crack the throne.'

'If you say so, ma'am.'

'But you're not here about that crisis a-brewing, are you? I've heard *whispers*. A veritable stormcloud of little birdies have been chirruping in Mama Device's shell-likes. I've had word from your Mr Beauregard on the subject. The Great Old Ones. Writhing Chaos in the Outer Darkness. All God's Chillun Got Horns.'

She tugged a rope and a curtain parted. Beyond was a small reception room, with comfortable chairs and a low table. A silver service was laid out.

'Now, join me in a pot of tea and tell me your troubles.'

'Miss Device,' he said, 'you really are the perfect hostess.'

'Did you doubt it? How disappointing. I must be slipping.'

V: 'SILVER SHOT WILL FIT ANY WEBLEY'

TRADITIONALLY, THREE OFFICE-HOLDERS constituted the Ruling Cabal: two Chairs and a Chairman. The Cabal convened in the Inner Chamber and sat at the High Table. The Inner Chamber, a windowless room, did not feature on the registered building plans. Behind oak-panelling was armour plate. The High Table was exalted in significance rather than stature—in point of fact, it was no higher than an ordinary dining table. Up to seven Chairs had crowded around the Table, and—in certain unlikely-to-be-repeated circumstances—the Cabal had consisted solely of a Chairman (Mycroft, of course). Charles had taken a Chair when he stepped down as Most Valued Member and become Chairman upon Mycroft's death. He had served two non-consecutive terms.

The Inner Chamber was threaded with cigarette smoke. Charles was tired and his temples throbbed.

The other Chairs were the voluminous Sir Henry Merrivale and the rake-thin General Lord Hector Tarr. H.M. had succeeded Charles as Chairman but resigned in 1928, outvoted on the question of admitting lady members. The diehard was still not reconciled to women having the vote, let alone joining the Diogenes Club. Tarr was a veteran of Military Intelligence under Mansfield Smith-Cumming and the Royal Society for Psychical Research under Sir Michael Calme. A canny, practical man, he was all for 'modernisation', an adherent of 'the scientific approach' and the sort of person who habitually drew up detailed contingency plans.

Charles had apprised the Chairs of recent developments. Sir Henry responded by telegram, claiming to be too caught up with a knotty locked-room mystery (he was a noted amateur sleuth, i.e.: pompous busybody) to attend the emergency meeting but wishing to be kept informed.

So, Charles was closeted with Tarr and his adjutant, Captain Giles Gallant. The junior officer stood at hand with a thick buff folder of papers. Tarr puffed methodically, as if under orders to transform a certain number of cigarettes into smoke and ash before dawn.

Sir Henry's absence was strategic. H.M. was letting Charles have enough rope, trusting Tarr to hang him. Two Ruling Members formed a quorum, and could make decisions for which the third could not be held accountable. In differences of opinion, the Chairman's vote decided. Charles would have to answer alone for any ensuing disasters. Sir Henry planned graciously to resume Chairmanship, sweeping away all that nonsense about letting in women. If it were up to H.M., electric wires would be stripped out of the building and gas-lamps put back in to get things back to the way they were 'in Mycroft's day'. He didn't take Tarr and his typewritten, triplicate reports and memoranda seriously. It didn't even occur to him that Tarr would make a play for Chairman. Charles assumed there was an 'eyes-only' memo in Gallant's folder, outlining post-Beauregard stratagems for the Diogenes Club. In this utopia, General Lord Hector Tarr ran the Ruling Cabal, with every report rubber-stamped and acted on. There wouldn't be much room for windy old H.M. in such an efficient organisation.

'I've framed a plan of action, Beauregard,' announced Tarr, as if he were doing the Chairman a favour. Gallant gave him a sheet of paper. 'We must track this vampire down, put it to the question, and have its head off. Your man Winthrop is chasing his tail round the Ravens. He's too compromised for the mission. These are my suggestions for suitable operatives. Good men, all of 'em.'

Charles looked over the list. He knew the names.

Dennis Rattray. Hugh Drummond. Dr Jonathan Chambers. Michael Bellamy.

'Four Just Men,' he observed. 'You've a whole Black Hand Gang here.'

'If that's what it takes, Beauregard. We can find the bloodsucker before it does any more damage. Get answers.'

'Isn't Captain Rattray *hors de combat*?'

'His medical condition is in check. He is highly motivated, needs to make a name for himself again. 'Blackfist' always got results.'

Of Tarr's list, only Jonathan Chambers–better known as 'Dr Shade'–was even an Associate Member. Charles had worked with him on several cases, and they had a guarded mutual respect. Dr Shade kept well-appointed lairs around London, including an apartment inside the Clock Tower of the Houses of Parliament. Mostly, he flapped about the night on a near-silent autogiro, terrorising 'evil-doers' with 'shadow gas' and 'dark matter'. The doctor's style–his usual get-up consisted of black slouch hat, ingenious night-sight goggles and flaring black coat–was closer to the Undertaking than the Diogenes Club, though he was more of a scientific than a mystic bent. For Charles's taste, he tended to leave too many corpses lying about.

Dennis Rattray, formerly of The Splendid Six, had once been black-balled by the Ruling Cabal. Also, Catriona had pinned an ordinary murder on his band of heroes. Rattray was at least out of the ordinary. He possessed the Fang of Night, a gem which endowed great strength upon anyone who held it in a closed fist. However, overusing the jewel gave rise to an embarrassing medical complication that was the frequent subject of indecent jokes. During a messy divorce action, Rattray had been hauled over the coals in court and the press. Tarr's other nominees were little more than posh thugs. Bellamy liked dressing up as Robin Hood and calling himself 'the Green Archer'. Drummond was a loose cannon with a penchant for thumping tradesmen and blaming the Jews.

If Charles wanted anyone dead, he might have called on any of these volunteer public servants. He rarely did, however. That sort of thinking led to the other camp.

Charles slid the list of head-breakers back across the table.

Tarr's tactic was to get him to discuss *which* of his proposed 'operatives' should be turned loose in pursuit of Geneviève, not *whether* . . .

'I don't think we need to let slip the bulldogs of Britain yet.'

'We can't afford that sort of woolly thinking, man,' said Tarr, pluming smoke from his nostrils. 'If you're wrong, we could lose the Ravens. And then . . .'

'You don't need to tell me, Hector.'

'At least, call off Winthrop and Kaye,' insisted Tarr. 'Who knows what damage they'll do in Mayfair!'

'They have proved their discretion in the past.'

Catriona Kaye was the first of the Lady Members who so incensed Sir Henry. A generation ago, Charles had offered to sponsor Kate Reed, but she'd refused the 'honour', responding with choice words on the subject of the Club's occasional anti-Fenian activities. And Geneviève Dieudonné had been a Member all along. Charles would have given ten shillings to see H.M.'s face when he had learned the sainted Mycroft Holmes covertly extended membership to Geneviève–a woman, a vampire and French.

'We should have people around all the Ravens at all times,' said Tarr, tapping his list. 'Trained men. Skilled operatives.'

'I don't disagree. However, we require tact and discretion, not a show of force.'

During the Worm War, Mycroft Holmes had dipped into a desk drawer and withdrawn a sealed envelope. Inside was a plan, drawn up years earlier: it did not precisely fit the situation, but was a starting-point for an ultimately successful course of action. There were other envelopes in the drawer, for other potential crises. These contingencies, framed after consultation and speculation, were Mycroft's legacy to the Ruling Cabal. There was even an envelope, in another desk drawer, in the event of the Cabal being suborned by hostile elements. Mycroft had commissioned this plan from his brother, whom he could trust to be suitably devious. As Chairman, Charles had only once had recourse to one of the contingencies. In 1926, opening the sealed envelope marked 'in the event of a General Strike', he'd found a single sheet of paper inscribed with Mycroft's copperplate handwriting, advising the Club to stay out of it as much as possible. That, he conceded, was a good idea.

There was no envelope marked 'Rat Among the Ravens', though there were contingencies for an occupation of Great Britain by a foreign (i.e.: German) army, an aggressive visitation by beings from another world, the marriage of the sovereign to an evil consort with supernatural powers, and the rising from the sea of a malign lost continent. He had shuffled through the private files, in the hope Mycroft had considered a situation even slightly similar to the present crisis.

If the Diogenes Club–and the kingdom–weathered this storm, Charles would commission fresh plans. He would gather the most imaginative pessimists in the land and have them consider every possible, or even impossible, disaster. Then, he would have experts plot courses of action for each dire circumstance. He would not find himself in a room with Tarr and Gallant, or even H.M.–and having to make up strategy on the hoof.

'What about the *thing*?' queried Tarr.

'The thing has a name,' Charles reminded him. 'Geneviève Dieudonné.'

Tarr did not respond. He had signed up to exterminate creatures of the night, not get on first-name terms with them.

'From what we can gather about her bloodline,' said Giles Gallant, 'she should be susceptible to these.'

The adjutant put a box of cartridges on the table.

'Silver shot,' he said. 'Will fit any Webley.'

Charles looked at the wall. Geneviève's face floated in his memory. He instinctively put his trust in her (and, even more, in Mycroft), but weight of evidence was piling up. Whether she stood with the Club or (the thought chilled him) Zenf, she was out of her cage. He had thought to get her free of the Mausoleum. Perhaps he should have demanded the Undertaking turn her over? Now, she was running loose.

He picked a shell out of the paper box and rolled it between his fingers.

'I thought these were for werewolves,' he said.

'According to field tests,' said Gallant, 'they'll bring down vampires, zombies, your common shapeshifters, ghouls, sundry revenants, and some of the more physical species of ghost. People, come to that. Bloody nasty thing to be shot with. Silver is a soft metal. Fragments on impact.'

Charles came to a decision, and held the silver bullet like Blackfist gripping the Fang of Night.

'We let our money ride on Geneviève,' he said. 'Edwin and Catriona stay on the Ravens. *I* can be fooled by a pretty face and a sharp mind. Mycroft Holmes could not. He made our choice.'

Tarr smoked. He was saving his shots.

'Business is settled,' concluded Charles.

VI: 'NO BUMP OF DISCRETION'

BEFORE EDWIN HAD finished his first cup of tea, Margery Device explained in credible detail exactly how Wallis Simpson had ensnared the Prince of Wales ('good luck to her,' he thought). She also dropped footnotes about Haile Selassie, Simon Templar, Peggy Hopkins Joyce, Pandora Reynolds, Roderick Spode and Gracie Fields, most of whom ought to be ashamed of themselves.

'Anthony Zenith . . . Zenith the Albino? Dyes his hair, my dears. Naturally, he'd be yellow as old newspapers.'

Witch had inside information about the deaths of prominent folk, which varied considerably from the newspaper accounts. Arnold Bennett, who drank the water in Paris to prove it safe, was poisoned by a jealous rival . . . Roger Ackroyd was murdered, but not by the fellow who owned up to it . . . Geli Raubel was shot in the head on the orders of her devoted Uncle Adolf . . . Rebecca DeWinter committed spiteful suicide by nagging her husband to murder her . . . and John Thomson, the goalkeeper whose neck was broken during a Celtic-Rangers match at Ibrox Park, was victim of a Papist plot of Machiavellian intricacy.

Disappointingly, Miss Device drew a blank on the escapees from the Chamber of Horrors.

'I'm in the dark, *mes amis*,' she said.

She lifted the lid of her teapot and stirred a Sargasso of leaves with a long spoon.

'Nope,' she concluded. 'No augurs as yet. Of course, tea-leaves are gypsy piffle. But signs and omens are everywhere for those who can see.'

'Wax murderers *en masse* are fairly significant,' said Edwin.

'And ominous,' added Catriona.

'As you know, you can't pull the wool over my eyes any day

with a 'd' in it,' continued Miss Device. 'You represent yourselves as protectors, but come here looking for suspects, not witnesses.'

Edwin tried to waffle the insight away, but was skewered.

'Don't bother to deny it. Charles Beauregard was always too transparent for this business. And the situation has changed since the little leech gave the funereal fellows the slip . . .'

Edwin sensed another shift in the playing field.

'Either one of the Ravens is your King Rat or we're all being painted black to undermine the defence of the realm. It's down to you to determine, eh? If I were you, I'd suspect me. I'm so open and considerate and helpful. People like that always turn out to be the murderer, don't they? Ask Lord Peter Wimsey or that appalling American upstart Vance. Of course, I haven't got a motive, but you'll ferret one out. I did seem to be the intended victim of tonight's little business, though.'

'You expertly warded off the attack,' Catriona observed.

Miss Device gave her one of her penetrating witchy looks.

'Indeed. I was merely being tested. Serious stabbing will come later. More tea?'

'Yes, thank you,' said Catriona.

Miss Device did the honours. 'If I'm out of the running, which of the others do you suspect? Mark Rennes seethes inside his mathematical construct, you know. On the wall, eternally vigilant. Must be tiresome, waiting for a war? And Robbie Stone's a common theatrical until the spelling starts. It's the eternal dilemma of the weather man. Make ready for the deluge and eventually you can't help wishing the clouds would open so you can show how clever you are. When it's dry, you're so unappreciated you start thinking. Do you have more in common with your opposite numbers in the dark than the dreary, trivial happy folks you're supposed to fight for? Rennes and Stone might well feel mothballed.'

'What about Drake?' Edwin prompted.

'Keeper of the Ravens? I don't know how Conny can have common cause with *anyone*. But if resentments, temptations or imps of perversity tug at his starry robes, I don't know about them. And I know about *everything*.'

'Isn't that, in itself, suspicious?' asked Catriona.

Miss Device looked at her again, almost showing doubt.

'Yes,' she said, candidly, 'I suppose it is. Then again, he *is* a Wizard. I'm only a Witch. Long ago, before Prince Albert had his uncomfortable alteration, Conny and I were . . . well, I'm not here to gossip about *myself*, fascinating as I'm sure it would be. Safe to say, I know Connaught Drake better than anyone and I know next to nothing about him. Robbie Stone has this invisibility trick–he's there in front of you, but you don't see him. It's not that you can see through him, it's that he makes you look the other way. Conny doesn't need to bother with that. He's nobody. Seven eighths of him is always out of sight. Do you have any idea of the lifelong commitment that takes? A man who can do that could do anything. The reason I don't believe he's in league with all the Devils of all the Hells is that I think he'd have to lower himself to deal with a mere Prince of Darkness. Give him my regards, by the way.'

As they left the party, while he was settling her wrap on her shoulders, Catriona told him Witch wasn't a Queen Rat.

'How do you work that out?'

'The mouth on her, Ed. You said it yourself. Madame Device "knows all, *tells* all". She has no bump of discretion. If she were in the least bit ratty, she'd have squeaked on herself. She couldn't help it.'

They stepped out into the street. A red omnibus drove by. Two pale, familiar faces looked down from the upper deck. Guy Fawkes and Captain Macheath. There were still waxworks on the loose.

'You're right, as always,' said Edwin, kissing her nose.

'Did you . . .'

' . . . see the Horrors on the bus? Yes. They'll be a nuisance for weeks. This gets murkier and murkier.'

They walked towards Hyde Park Corner to pick up a taxi.

'My head is stuffed full,' said Catriona. 'The Witch stirs so much into her cauldron it's impossible to tell the tittle from the tattle.'

'I didn't like that remark about "the little leech",' said Edwin. 'Almost an aside. It was something we're supposed to know. She must have meant Charles's informant. The vampire.'

'I noticed it, too,' said Catriona.

A chill wind blew down Park Lane. Cold air rippled across his face.

'Where to now?' she asked, shivering. 'Bloomsbury and bed?'

'Sadly, no. Pall Mall and an elucidation.'

VII: 'AN INFINITY OF MIRRORS'

A FRESHLY-DECIPHERED report from 'Karolyi', the Budapest Affiliate, sat on Charles Beauregard's desk in the Quiet Room. Next to a pot of strong coffee Huntstanton had sent in.

Colonel Zenf had been at the Opéra two nights ago, in full view of an audience of five hundred. That evening, two men in different quarters of the city died in locked rooms, looks of stark terror plastered on their faces. One corpse was found in an apartment above a stables. Every horse in the place was dead, also a cat and–close examination showed–every mouse, rat and even fly on the premises. At the end of the opera (*The Temptation of Faust*, of course), a mystery clique insisted Zenf, who had no obvious connection with the entertainment, take a bow. Charles didn't know, either, of the dead men, but they had both been inconveniences to the Great Enchanter: a retired officer who wrote to the newspapers questioning Zenf's right to military rank, stating that the Regiment in which the Colonel claimed to have served had been cut down to the last man during the War; and a coachman in Zenf's employ who had lately been talkative. The Club's Man in Budapest–he had bribed the coachman, of course–was worried. 'Karolyi' no longer noticed swarthy men pretending to read newspapers while eavesdropping on his tête-a-têtes, as if someone he was less likely to spot had scared off the regular Secret Police spies.

Appended to the report were recent cables, reporting that Zenf had left for Vienna, Zurich and Brussels. The most recent wire was not from 'Karolyi' but his second, standing in while the Affiliate was indisposed. The Great Enchanter was getting near. He was the Most Dangerous Man in Europe, and maybe more than that.

Charles drank strong coffee. The fug of Tarr's cigarettes was still in his head.

There was *always* someone like Colonel Zenf. Mycroft had reckoned the financier Leo Dare the Worst Villain of the Age. Dare had fallen off the map around the time of the Boer War, then Isadora Persano popped up with a portal to another universe inside his box of Swan and Edgar. Others through the ages had earned the title of Great Enchanter. The mountebanks, charlatans and self-publicists–the Cagliostros, Rasputins and Crowleys–might be hailed the wickedest, most darkly powerful of their ages. The Great Enchanters were less obviously voluptuaries or crackpots, more likely to tear pages out of history books than inscribe their names there. Who knew, or remembered, Nicholas Goodman of Mildew Manor? Mrs Mary Braxton, who quietly slipped out of the net that hauled in Don Felipe Molina and Sir Timothy ffolliott? Cardinal Silencio, who never rose to the Papacy but cast votes which elevated five other men, then called in dreadful debts?

Charles wondered if these people didn't crawl full-grown out of filthy water, bereft of a past, suddenly gifted with great fortune and greater influence. These dark whisperers were sworn to the ruination of man's higher works. Leo Dare, it was said, invented the advertising circular. Silencio celebrated Black Mass in the heart of Vatican City.

Zenf first appeared in Vienna in 1919, around the time of the global influenza pandemic. Bill Owen argued that there was a connection. Suddenly, the Colonel was *everywhere,* if only in the shadows: buying into Czech and German munitions firms, and patenting features of the automatic pistol; photographed shaking hands with Lindbergh at Le Bourget, though public records insisted he was at an angry stock-holders' meeting in Turin on that famous day; visiting Trotsky in Prinkipo, with a personal message from Stalin; reaping a third of Performing Rights Society royalties on comical odes to self-abuse made popular by George Formby (though Zenf's contribution, if any, to lyrics or music was hard to determine); refusing to extend bank credit to Ernst Röhm in 1925, but providing sweatshop labour (ironically, Jewish) to manufacture brown shirts for the Nazi SA; smoking a cigar in the lobby of the St Francis Hotel in San Francisco as Virginia Rappé collapsed after attending a party thrown by Roscoe 'Fatty' Arbuckle; hands stained with purple ink at the disrupted Paris premiere of *L'Âge d'Or,* pointedly not slashing surrealist paintings alongside the League of Patriots; sitting quietly in court during the trial of Nathan Leopold and Richard Loeb; allegedly fathering a child upon Magda Lupescu, mistress of the King of Romania; giving a private audience in Cicero, Illinois, to Al Capone, from which the racketeer emerged with his old scar freshly bleeding; financing the first all-talking pornographic pictures, *What the Butler Said* and *You Really Ain't Heard Nothing Yet;* facilitating the export of farm machinery to Turkey; meeting in Georgia with the Grand Imperial Wizard of the Ku Klux Klan.

The Colonel had never been charged with a crime by any government. He held high honours from most European countries, including Great Britain. H. G. Wells said Zenf was a 'samurai of science with a good, clear head'. Charles had tried to apprise the Cabinet of as much of the Zenf File as they could read without going mad. Robert Vansittart, the Permanent Under-Secretary with Responsibility for Intelligence, gave word to soft-pedal criticism of the Colonel. Officially, Zenf was a good friend to Britain. The Prime Minister cited him as 'one of the greatest agitators for peace in the world today'. If the Diogenes Club pressed the point, they risked being written off as cranks.

Charles looked up at Mycroft's portrait, wondering how much things had changed in this century. Zenf was a scientific samurai. A good friend to Britain. An agitator for peace. Yes, and James Moriarty was a humble professor of mathematics . . .

The door opened. Huntstanton was stationed outside.

'Anything we ought to know, Charles?' asked Catriona Kaye.

She sat down in one of the armchairs, dress shimmering. Edwin Winthrop stood like a schoolboy in the Head's study.

They both looked at him. Pointedly. It was about Geneviève.

'How the *deuce* have you heard?' Charles asked. Then the penny dropped. 'Margery Device.'

'Knows all,' said Catriona, making mesmeric gestures.

'. . . tells all,' said Edwin.

'Doesn't she just? Here are the facts. Our well-placed source is absent. Some argue she's playing a triple game, and your present investigation is founded upon a false premise.'

'Nice of you to let us in on it, Charlie!' drawled Catriona.

'A coded telegram awaits you at your flat, summoning you here,' said Charles. 'To be let in on it, as you say.'

'Fair enough,' said Edwin. 'Are you saying there's no King Rat?'

Charles shook his head. 'No. Others are.'

'How did the vampire fly from the Mausoleum?' asked Catriona.

Charles opened his hands.

'Aren't the Undertakers known for not letting this happen?' she continued. 'Items from the Egdon Heath Collection seldom come on the open market?'

Edwin grinned, with little humour. 'The black hats must be fuming. This is one in the eye for the Hays, Bees and Seas. I'm surprised they admit they've lost her.'

'To be frank,' said Charles, 'so am I. Something else to be suspicious about.'

'So there's a fearful bloodsucker on the loose,' said Catriona. 'Any more corpses?'

Charles shook his head.

'She couldn't have been destroyed in her cell? Turned to dust and swept away? Sunlight directed in by mirrors?'

Charles was momentarily concerned, surprisingly bereft. Not just at the notion Geneviève might be truly dead, but that he hadn't considered it.

'Disappearing acts are in the Great Edmondo's line,' said Edwin. 'We've a box at the Astoria for tomorrow night. Unless you want to call us off.'

Charles considered. 'No. Stay on it. An agent provocateur sending us on a false trail would try to be as unsuspicious as possible. Disappearing is the *most* suspicious thing Geneviève could do.'

'Unless she wants to avoid further quizzing,' put in Catriona. 'Now she's seen you in the flesh, she might doubt her ability to fool you for long.'

'Six of one,' said Edwin, 'half a dozen of the other. An infinity of mirrors.'

'Indeed, Edwin,' said Charles. 'Nothing is clear. Except that Colonel Zenf has been busy. He's in Brussels. He could be in London within hours. He's a great believer in air travel. A few of his recent endeavours could be construed as warnings aimed in our direction.'

'Is it true Karolyi's off his oats?'

Charles admitted this was so. Edwin swore.

'Good man, Karolyi. Cat and I wouldn't have got out of that business at the Café Mozart without him.'

'You've heard about the ambulatory waxworks?' said Catriona.

'Bill Owen had it before anyone else. Not that he saw where it was going. The Yard's Department of Queer Complaints are on it.

They've issued descriptions of murderers thought long-hanged, and are quietly hauling them in. The cells in Holborn Central are full of broken mannequins. Sir Percival Glyde was found in Seven Dials this morning, importuning a "soiled dove" with a bottle of laudanum.'

'I should think soiled doves have changed since Sir Percy's day,' said Catriona.

'Indeed. Jenny Maple, a person well known to the police, kneed the wicked Baronet in the, ah, middle-parts, dashed his own medicine into his glass eyes and made off with his topcoat. Sadly for her, Tussaud's exhibits rarely carry cash.'

'According to Witch, other omens are indicative of a storm in the offing,' said Edwin. 'If it's any help, Margery Device thinks one of her fellows is a Rat.'

'She makes convincing cases for all of them,' added Catriona.

'Lord forbid,' said Charles.

Edwin shook his head, reassuringly. 'If things were that bad, we'd be knee-deep in burning filth already. We must have weight of numbers on our side or the Great Enchanter wouldn't have to be so infernally *sneaky*. It's got to be just one King Rat.'

Charles agreed with the Most Valued Member. Edwin's wartime background was Intelligence: he was used to thinking deviously and expecting everyone else to do likewise. Young Winthrop might well be better suited to the coming war than Charles was–though he needed Catriona, as a moral tether. Deviousness was all very well, but they all needed to be reminded that they served a just cause. Men of Edwin's generation could not believe in Crown and Country as Charles and his contemporaries had done, but women like Catriona had found other, stronger values–they would not let an injustice persist. Any injustice. He hoped Edwin would always have Catriona, as a conscience, a partner, a guide. The Club needed them both.

'One thing might be to our advantage,' Charles told them. 'This is a horribly important business. The people we're dealing with look down on us from a great height. And, in our own secret world, we're not inconsiderable.'

'We're tip-toeing around giants' feet,' observed Catriona. 'Trying to stay out from under their boot-soles.'

'Our King Rat, whichever of the Ravens he might be, is the Great Enchanter's foremost Asset. His most prized piece. Not an informant or a minion, but a near-equal. And steeped in treachery, or he wouldn't be a Rat. So Zenf can't fully trust him. The Colonel will need, especially when the situation is developing fast, to look into his Asset's ratty eyes. They have to meet.'

'You mean we should put a shadow on Zenf?'

'As you know, Edwin, that's no easy proposition. No, I mean you should *look out* for the Colonel. He displaces more water than a rabble of wax horrors. He's coming to London. For him, this is a long-nurtured scheme, about to pay off. He hopes to exceed the achievements of all the Great Enchanters before him. He knows about Isadora Persano and the Worm War. He will be mindful. Like all commanders, he will have a sense of his position, and how suddenly it can change. Anyone who can be a Raven and a Rat at the same time could contest the title of Great Enchanter.'

'You think they'll do for each other? That'd be a happy outcome.'

Charles sighed. 'Too much to ask for, Edwin. But there's no reason we can't sow dissent in their ranks, let suspicions fester. They do it to us all the time.'

'What about your vampire?' asked Catriona.

'Until firmly established otherwise, Geneviève is in our camp. She is an Asset. One of Mycroft's. I don't worry about her.'

'If you say so, Chief.'

'Yes, Edwin, I do.'

Charles saw Edwin was not convinced. Catriona was, though. Good. That balance made sense.

Where was Geneviève now? A long way from Egdon Heath, certainly.

VIII: 'UNIQUELY UNHAUNTED'

THE GREAT EDMONDO'S act featured mannequins dressed exactly like him–in tail-coats, top hats and red-lined capes. The magician kept disappearing into his posed crowd, and a different mannequin seemed to come to life for each trick. The figure the audience took for the magician turned to show a blank where its face should be, then an apparent puppet darted up to reveal animated, moustachioed, punchinello-nosed features.

Edwin and Catriona had a box at the Astoria. Most magic acts insisted the boxes not be sold for their performances, because side-on views give away secrets. Robert Stone made a point of letting the audience close, even encouraging some to wander backstage and in the wings. He could still achieve all his marvels without anyone seeing the trick.

Conjurer repeatedly proved his puppets had no strings by whirling a scimitar where they should be. The wax chorus danced in lock-step, moving exactly like the murderers at Margery Device's party.

'So he can make mannequins do his bidding,' Catriona whispered. 'Either he's innocent of the attack on Witch or arrogant beyond belief.'

'Arrogance beyond belief rather comes with the profession. Perhaps someone else wants us to put "Conjurer" under the grill. Everyone in this game is a trickster.'

'I'm bored with magic, Ed,' Catriona explained. 'It makes my head ache.'

The mannequins came to pieces but kept dancing to Tartini's 'Devil's Trill'. Stone swung his blade through the gaps between shoulders and arms and necks and heads, demonstrating again that no strings were involved.

'It's magnets and mirrors,' said someone, loudly, from the stalls.

'No,' responded another voice, 'it's compressed air and trained midgets.'

'Mass mesmerism.'

'Witchcraft! Warlockery! Burn him!'

The hecklers stood up, each in their own follow-spot. They were all no-face puppets.

Edwin tensed, expecting another attack.

But it was part of the act. The Great Edmondo gestured with his wand, and the hecklers vanished. In each seat was a squirming animal–a rabbit, a pig, a dove and a kitten.

There was applause. Catriona joined in.

'Conjurer' took a bow, with a flourish of his enormous cape. The curtains closed, then opened again–each puppet was replaced by a live, fleshy chorus girl in spangly tights and tight blonde curls. They tap-danced to 'It's the Talk of the Town'.

Edwin looked at his program. The Great Edmondo was due back on in the second half. Before then there was a patter comedian, 'Mr Memory', a dog act and a woman who tore paper into amusing shapes.

'Let's take advantage of the invitation and venture backstage,' he suggested.

'What fun,' said Catriona, dryly. 'Perhaps this time we can get to the interview without witnessing an attempted assassination?'

Edwin stepped out of the box and led Catriona along the corridor. He tugged a Victorian sconce and a small door opened, affording access to a walkway above the stage. He made an 'after you' gesture, and she squeezed through, setting ropes and pulleys rattling.

'This is where the ghost of Harry "Brass" Button, tragic clown of the 1890s, is supposed to walk, telling his famous joke to anyone he comes across. They say his victims start laughing and can't stop. There's a madhouse ward full of cackling stage-hands.'

'I know the story,' said Catriona. 'I also know Harry Button was cast out of this place in 1905 by Sandersby Scott Dignam, dramatic critic and exorcist, waving bell, book and bad review. Among London's theatres and music halls, the Astoria is uniquely unhaunted.'

On the stage below, the comedian recited a lengthy verse

about a family of Yorkshire holidaymakers unwisely attending a political rally in Berlin. Edwin feared 'Little Albert' would wind up eaten by Goering.

They crossed the walkway. Edwin showed his card to a stage-hand, who helped them into a large wicker basket which lowered on ropes. The Astoria wasn't one of the larger, more labyrinthine houses, but had been built with magic in mind. One of the dogs waiting in the wings yapped as they sank through the floor, putting the comic off his patter–but allowing him to get a cheer with his catch-phrase 'shoot that blessed hound oop!'

Below stage were layers of dusty machinery. Stone's mannequins were bent and crammed into the works. They hadn't yet been collected. Eyeless heads seemed to turn to follow their progress.

'That's a trick,' said Catriona. 'He knows we're coming.'

Edwin hoped she was right.

At last, the basket touched ground. Edwin lifted Catriona up and out of the wicker. She took the opportunity to nip his ear.

'Remember, we're being watched,' he whispered.

'I'm putting any spies off their guard,' she replied.

He quieted her with a long kiss. Then clambered out of the basket.

They were in a below-stage cavern, stacked with rolled canvas backdrops and left-behind props. In one corner, a collection of crushed bird skeletons was jammed into a big bin. Casualties of magic.

Edwin pulled a door open, and found himself in a tuppeny harem: a corridor packed with squealing chorus girls in states of dishabille. Artistes strategically covered themselves as he and Catriona passed through.

Catriona, rather surprisingly, met someone else she was at school with.

'All the best husbands are going to chorus girls these days,' Catriona explained. 'Lucia's adopting a policy of "if you can't beat 'em, join 'em".'

'So, is she engaged to a viscount yet?'

'No, she's "walking out" with Mr Twisty, the Contortionist. He's fifth on the bill.'

'I don't want to think about that.'

'Me neither.'

Once out of the chorus quarters, they came to a door emblazoned with a large gold star. Inside the star was a sunny face.

'The Great Edmondo, I presume,' said Edwin, opening the door.

He felt a stickiness under his shoes, and instantly recognised the coppery smell of freshly-spilled blood.

Catriona crammed behind him.

Robert Edmond Stone, the Great Edmondo, lay face-up on the floor, hissing through bared teeth, blood-soaked cloak spread around him. He pressed both hands to a gouting wound in his neck. A lithe blonde woman in a green dress knelt on his chest, her own hands trying to unpick his grip as if to unstopper the flow. Her lower face and chest dripped with gore.

The woman looked at Edwin and Catriona. She had sharp, pointed eye-teeth.

'You probably think this looks suspicious,' she said.

IX: 'PEOPLE OF HIS SORT DON'T EXPIRE IN ACCIDENTS'

IN THE FOYER of the Diogenes Club, attendants politely but firmly barred entrance to Franz Beckert, the German child-murderer. He was not a member, of course. The mannequins were still a nuisance. A rash of second-storey burglaries in the manner of Charlie Peace was bothering residents of Fitzrovia. No waxwork had successfully recreated the more appalling crimes of their originals, but that could come.

Returning from an evening constitutional that had not settled his mind, Charles was handed a report by Huntstanton. He glanced over it as he climbed the stairs.

A two-seater plane had taken off from Belgium this afternoon, and crashed in the Kent countryside two hours ago. Pilot and passenger were killed instantly, burned beyond recognition. Documents on the passenger–a large body–identified him as Colonel Zenf.

In the Quiet Room, Charles found General Lord Hector Tarr in a huddle with Mr Hay of the Undertaking. Giles Gallant was by the tickertape machine, reading off news Charles had from his own sources.

'We had nothing to do with this,' Mr Hay told Charles. 'Mrs Elle was there, but as an observer.'

'Have you heard from her?' Charles asked.

The Undertaker gave nothing away.

'You won't. And you'll have another black topper to fill.'

'Now's the time to strike, Beauregard,' said Tarr. 'While they're in disarray. Why, without the Great Enchanter . . .'

' "They" are not without him, Tarr. Zenf isn't dead. People of his sort don't expire in accidents.'

'Good God,' said Gallant, threading the latest report through his fingers. 'The passenger . . . it's a woman.'

'My condolences,' Charles said to Mr Hay.

Charles sat down. His sanctum was now a War Room.

'Colonel Zenf is in the country,' he announced. 'As of now, we have no idea what he is up to. Mr Hay, do you consent to make Common Cause?'

The words echoed. Tarr bit his lip. Tape chattered through Gallant's fingers, unread.

Common Cause was seldom invoked, and more seldom made. The Diogenes Club and the Undertaking more often acted apart than in collaboration. Charles habitually kept a wary eye on the men with smoked glasses. In 1770, Nicholas Goodman, the Great Enchanter, contrived to become Mr Zed and twisted the Undertaking's purpose. He had fetched the heads of Molina and ffolliott from the Mausoleum, intent on carrying out their long-thwarted scheme. On that occasion, only blind chance–in the shape of Eithne Orfe, Goodman's dagger-wielding fiancée–saved the crowned heads of Europe, and several of them not for long. The taint had never been entirely expunged. There was a deal of the night about the Undertaking.

One of Mycroft's contingency plans was entitled 'In the Event of the Undertaking Assuming Control Over the Government of the Day'. Charles suspected the envelope contained a stratagem for completely dismantling the organisation and breaking any power they might have. More than once, he had been tempted to break the seal and weigh up the options–it was easier to deal with the likes of the Great Enchanter or the Order of Dagon or the Lord of Strange Deaths without having to watch one's back.

However, during the Worm War, an earlier Mr Hay had taken a Chair on the Ruling Cabal and Charles had himself worn hat and goggles as the acting Mr Bee. Stranger alliances were made in those tense weeks.

'No,' said Mr Hay. 'Not yet.'

Charles nodded. 'An exchange of liaisons, at least?'

Mr Hay ruminated. 'That is acceptable.'

'Giles, would you accompany Mr Hay to Westminster?'

Gallant was surprised to be asked. He was Tarr's man. He would have expected Charles to put forward Huntstanton. Charles saw the adjutant rapidly considering the matter–was this a tactic to separate Tarr from his most loyal supporter, or could be it be to the advantage of their faction to develop ties with the Undertaking? Wheels went round in his mind as visibly as the cogs inside the glass dome of the ticker-tape machine.

'I'm asking you because you're in the room, man,' Charles said, letting Gallant off the hook. 'And qualified. You were in signals. Your job will be to keep open lines of communication.'

Gallant looked to Tarr, who gave him a curt nod.

'Honoured to accept,' said the adjutant.

'Who do we get in exchange?' asked Tarr.

A thin smile spread across Mr Hay's face. He snapped gloved

fingers and a homunculus detached itself from the shadow under Charles's desk.

'How the devil did he get in?' blustered Tarr.

Mr Hay's thin smile stayed even, like a healed wound.

'This is Master Wuh.'

The shadow was a child, dressed in a miniature version of undertakers' habit: top hat, gloves, dark glasses, mourning clothes, patent-leather shoes. His face was black–not like an African but a sweep, covered with camouflage soot.

'Wuh?' said Tarr.

'It's W,' explained Charles.

Wuh grinned, showing even white teeth.

'That settled, I shall be on my way,' announced Mr Hay, standing up. 'Mr Gallant, if you will follow . . .'

The Undertaker led the adjutant out of the Quiet Room.

Tarr looked at Master Wuh.

'What shall we do with this little blighter?'

'Get him supper, I imagine,' said Charles, pressing the silent buzzer. 'Then turn our minds to the problem of Colonel Zenf.'

X: 'RATHER WRITTEN IN SCARLET'

SUSPICIOUS" DOESN'T SAY the half of it, dear,' Catriona addressed the gore-spattered creature kneeling on top of the bleeding magician. 'Pardon the observation, but you take the concept of "red-handed" to a ludicrous extreme.'

Edwin knew better than to accept anything at face value.

'I know it seems rather written in scarlet,' said the vampire. Her esses susurrated through the blood bubbling in her mouth. She had a trace of accent. 'But if you'll lend a hand, I think we can stop your Conjurer from bleeding out.'

Stone bucked, as if going into seizure. His white-gloved hands flapped like landed fish. His eyes were open, but unseeing.

The blonde vampire nearly had his hands away from his neck.

'Geneviève Dieudonné, I presume,' observed Edwin.

'Call me Gené. Be careful about getting the red stuff on you. It never washes out. I ought to know.'

Edwin and Catriona knelt either side of Robert Stone, holding his arms.

'You might not have seen anything like this before,' said Geneviève. 'Please not to be alarmed. And not to make a fuss, *hein*?'

She lifted Stone's hands from his wound. The deep cut could have been done with a straight razor. Not teeth. Richly red blood welled.

'Ugh, nasty,' said Geneviève, bending over as if putting her mouth to a drinking fountain.

The vampire didn't bite or suckle. Instead, she stuck out her unusually long tongue and–with a single, cat-like slathering–licked the wound clean.

At her wet touch, Stone stopped kicking and swooned.

Geneviève wiped her mouth and swallowed a little, like a cook apologetically taking a lick of cake-mixture from a used spoon. She pulled a scarf–the first of an infinite string–from Conjurer's top-pocket and dabbed the slash in his throat, which glistened with her saliva. Edwin didn't think the procedure was recommended by any physician he knew. But, visibly, the wound knit.

'Think about it,' said Geneviève. 'You have to turn off the tap after you've had a drink. A peculiarity of vampire physiology is that our saliva glands secrete a natural coagulating agent. And a mild euphoric, too. A perk of being kissed by me.'

She used Stone's scarf to wipe herself off. As she fixed her face, her fang-teeth receded into gumsheaths and her smile closed.

Catriona nudged Edwin, jarring him out of astonishment.

'You know who I am,' said Geneviève. 'You must be friends of Charles Beauregard.'

'Edwin Winthrop,' he said, 'of the Diogenes Club. Most Valued Member. And this is Miss Catriona Kaye.'

'The authoress? I enjoyed your monograph on Martin Hesselius.'

Catriona was taken aback. Pleasantly.

They stood. Stone seemed to be sleeping peacefully. Thanks to that mild euphoric, Edwin assumed. The dressing room was cramped for all of them at once. Behind Geneviève was a mirror, in which she cast a shadow rather than a reflection.

'If we're past introductions,' said Edwin, 'I'm obliged to ask if you have any idea how the Great Edmondo got his throat cut?'

'I bumped into a waxy-faced fellow with a razor,' said Geneviève. 'I thought London had seen the last of Sweeney Todd, but I'd swear it was him.'

'How do you come to be in the dressing rooms of the Astoria Theatre?' asked Catriona. 'Do you, perchance, have a trained bat act?'

'My standing orders are to make myself useful.'

'Standing orders?'

'Yes, Edwin. Standing orders. From the Ruling Cabal. Well, Mr Mycroft.'

'Weren't you supposed to be in the Egdon Heath Collection?'

Geneviève shrugged. 'I'd been useful there. As much as I could. Now, I'm better off out of the Mausoleum. You know what it's like being a police informant in gaol–locked up with the felons you've squealed on. Several "items" wouldn't be above bidding for the favour of the Great Enchanter by slipping a sharpened wooden spoon through my ribs. They all think Zenf will set them free to ravage and revenge, you know. Don't worry, the means by which I got out aren't available to the rest of the inmates. They're all locked up safe and snug.'

Catriona made sceptical gestures. Edwin understood her caution, but for the moment this undead woman was an Asset.

'The Old Man would like to hear from you,' he said.

'The Old Man? Charles? He's not old. I know old, and he's not, really.'

Edwin fully realised–a few minutes into their acquaintance–the implications of Geneviève being what she was.

Catriona bent over again to look at the sleeping magician. He was breathing steadily.

'Here's a funny thing,' said Catriona, unpeeling false moustaches. They brought away a bulb of nose and stretched a patch of skin. 'There's more.'

She detached a wig from the prone man's head, disclosing a mostly-bald skull.

'So, Conjurer is vain?'

'Ed, this isn't Conjurer. This is Sorcerer.'

She rubbed more make-up from the face. It was Marcus Rennes.

'Another Raven?' inquired Geneviève.

'The wrong Raven,' Edwin explained. 'Our Conjurer has made a switch.'

'It *is* part of his act,' said Catriona.

'Are you sure it was Sweeney Todd you bumped into?'

Geneviève's brow furrowed. 'His face was wax, but now I think of it he was *warm*–you know, a live person.'

Catriona exaggeratedly mouthed 'not like her' and pointed at the back of Geneviève's head.

'I might not have a proper reflection,' said Geneviève. 'But you do, Miss Kaye.'

A mirror was above the dressing room door. A smudgy column of vaguely woman-shaped smoke stood between Edwin and Catriona and the magician. He would never get used to that.

'Also, it's not true. I'm undying, not undead. Death drives *nosferatu* cuckoo, by the way. It accounts for the stories you hear. Millie Karnstein, dear little thing but a total imbecile. Lord Ruthven, complete ego-maniac. Count Dracula . . .'

'Sorry if I was rude,' Catriona interrupted. Geneviève could be as chatty as Margery Device. 'It's been a trying few days.'

'No need to apologise. I'm used to it. After you've had six or seven mobs come for you with burning torches, you can put up with a lot.'

Catriona redirected her attention to the sleeping man. 'If Sorcerer is in Conjurer's place, where's Conjurer got to?'

'Do you think Robbie Stone is twitching like a King Rat?' he asked.

Catriona shrugged. 'We've not met all the players yet.'

'I don't think Wizard would deign to come out of his tower and run about with a razor,' said Edwin. 'He'd have familiars to do that sort of thing.'

'Nothing is beneath anyone in this game, Ed.'

Catriona slapped Rennes a little, but he only snorted and turned over.

'He'll be asleep a while longer,' said Geneviève. 'Sorry.'

XI: 'SOME DIFFICULTY BETWEEN US'

AT MIDNIGHT, CHARLES'S presence was requested at Margery Device's *après-soirée*. In time of open war, he might have tendered his excuses–but no lesser crisis relieved him of the obligation.

The venue was Mekka, a vile drinking hole popular with criminals and off-duty policemen. Like other pubs that catered to trades that kept unconventional hours, it was exempt from licensing laws. Behind a deceptively small, honestly shabby frontage on the Embankment, Mekka was cavernously huge. A perpetual throng of boozers packed into a warren of underground taprooms which had once been smugglers' store-houses and still afforded secret access to the Thames through trap-doors and unofficial jetties.

The occasion was the Pick-Pockets' Ball, one of Margery's long-established annual events.

From the Bentley, Charles saw shifty characters crowded out onto the pavement. A sad-faced fellow had false arms in his sleeves, and a huge fake paunch. Light fingers could stretch from his waistcoat pockets and filch watches and coins from anyone he got close to.

'This lot'd have the gold out of your teeth and the pennies off your eyes,' said Huntstanton.

Charles emptied his pockets of anything valuable, dangerous or pertinent, then distributed worthless items about his person–gift-wrapped stones, an old wallet stuffed with strips of newspaper, a broken tin watch. A traditional courtesy at the Pick-Pockets' Ball.

He got out of the Bentley, cautiously made his way through the crowd, and eased into Mekka, keeping track of a blur at the corner of his eye. Master Wuh was his shadow. That lad had little to fear from pick-pockets. He could amuse himself by redistributing stolen items around the company, even returning them to their original owners.

Inside, the air was thick with smoke, steam and chatter, and the room filled with warm bodies. Charles negotiated a way towards the bar. Someone began to assault an upright piano. Searchlights converged on a black curtain that whipped aside to disclose Margery Device dressed as a comedy burglar–striped jersey, battered cap, domino mask, black tights, handbag marked 'swag'.

'And the shark has pretty teeth, dear,' she sang in a thirty-cigarettes-a-day-washed-down-by-six-pints-of-gin voice, 'and he keeps them in his face . . . *und Macheath, der hat ein Messer,* hidden in another place . . .'

Margery drifted from table to table, warbling 'Mack the Knife' in a melange of cockney English and gutter German, improvising verses about notable crooks in the room. At every table, someone reached into her swag-bag and ostentatiously stole something which bit their fingers–a snapping mouse-trap, a struggling shrew, a small fizzing firework. Outrageous (but all too true) accusations raised laughter from those exposed. Betrayed confederates, unpaid mothers of wronged girls, and inspectors cut out of profits by sergeants found the verses less amusing.

By dawn, everyone would know everyone else's sins–and it ought to even out. Every year, one or two knived bodies floated down-river after the Ball. As with dropped glasses or stained carpets at other parties, a certain amount of breakage was expected.

Charles felt fingers in his pockets. He slapped them away with good humour.

'H'awfully sorry, guv'nor,' said a bright-eyed, loose-limbed fellow with an enormous beaky nose. 'Force of 'abit. Didn't see it was you, sir.'

'That's quite all right, Nosey. How's your mother?'

Alfred 'Nosey' Parker looked stricken, and held a hand to his chest. 'A martyr to 'er feet, Mr Beauregard.'

'Aren't we all?'

'True, true. As Mum h'always says, "h'it comes to us h'all in the h'end". Pardon me a mo, guv'nor . . . H'I've just seen a cove 'oo owes me h'eight quid.'

Nosey slid away, intent on surreptitiously reclaiming the debt.

Margery concluded her turn, to vigorous applause. Post-song fights broke out and had to be stifled.

For a moment, Charles feared he would have to talk with that dreadful bore Colonel Sebastian Moran–how had he avoided the gallows all these years?–but Margery took his arm and whisked him past the gasping old reprobate.

'There's someone you should meet,' she shouted over the hubbub.

She steered him into a less-crowded backroom patronised by a better class of criminal. Or, at least, a better-*dressed* class of criminal. A duchess might look down on a dishwasher, but such mild snobbery paled beside a bogus clergyman or a Mayfair bag-snatcher turning up their noses at a safe-cracker or a strong-arm johnnie. Some villains needed to imitate perfectly their prey, assuming haughty mien, conservative attitudes and impeccable couture. When not trying to get widows to invest in non-existent diamond mines, these people had one topic of conversation–the shocking state of crime today, especially when it came to sturdy beggars and rabblesome dirty-faced urchins.

The hostess indicated a short, very fat man whose back was turned. He wore a tight coat with a forked tail and had too much pomade on thick, black, wavy hair. He waved stubby beringed fingers as he talked with Ivy Petersen, a hideously respectable old strumpet. On a famous night in 1887, she had reputedly serviced the entire Preston North End team to commemorate their record-setting 26–nil cup tie victory over Hyde United.

Margery tapped the fat man on the shoulder.

He turned, flashing a smile beneath a waxed moustache. A Napoleonic kiss-curl was slicked to his forehead. Were it not for his adder's eyes, he might have been cherubic.

'Charles Beauregard, this is Colonel Zenf.'

The Austro-Hungarian clicked his heels, striking sparks, and extended his hand.

Charles took the offered paw and shook.

Zenf's hand was soft and moist. Charles took care not to scratch himself on any of the rings.

'My good fellow,' said Zenf, who had a high-pitched voice, 'I am much pleased to make your acquaintance. We have many ... associations ... in common.'

Charles let Zenf's hand go. 'I did not think to find you here,' he said, weakly.

'You may think to find *everyone* here,' said Margery.

'So it seems,' said Charles.

'One or two matters intrigue me, Beauregard,' said Colonel Zenf, pin-points of fire in his eyes. 'I should like soon to have a long, private conversation with you.'

'I too would appreciate such an occasion,' Charles responded.

'Perhaps I might call on you at your Club?'

The mild suggestion set Charles's heart pounding.

'I'm not often there at present. Where are you staying in London?'

Zenf's moustache-points quivered. 'I am tending to be in different places at different times.'

Charles held Zenf's reptile gaze. 'It seems some difficulty is between us,' he said, 'in ordering our diaries.'

'Indeed,' said Zenf. 'This is . . . a pity.'

Margery's eyes flicked between them. She knew what was going on under the surface of chat. Surely, if she were a Queen Rat, Zenf would not be on her guest list? Unless she had a surfeit of bare-faced cheek, which—as it happens—she certainly did. Besides, this was a ball for criminals: the company would not be complete without the Great Enchanter.

Charles looked at Zenf, who seemed completely relaxed. The Colonel reached into an inside pocket and took out a cigarette case. A tiny razor-edge stuck out of the catch, smeared with blood.

'Some larcenous soul seems to have attempted to steal this keepsake,' said Zenf, carefully working a stud which made the blade recede. 'I trust he takes his regular dose of anti-venom.'

An elderly man who represented himself as the Bishop of Matabeleland fell as if his knees had been chopped out, face black and swollen, foam pouring over his chin. A young, dark-haired, violet-eyed woman dressed as a governess tried to loosen his dog-collar. She was swatted away with a rattle of unepiscopal oaths. In this company, no one liked having their clothes touched.

'A mild strain,' purred Zenf. 'Scarcely fatal.'

The bogus bishop kicked, gaiters scrabbling on the floorboards, and his entire body jack-knifed. Then he settled down and commenced snoring. The woman who had come to his aid carefully sorted through his inside pockets, making a collection. She found a gold ring, which she respectfully returned to Colonel Zenf, who screwed it onto his left little finger.

'My thanks to you, Vivian,' he said. 'I wondered where this had strayed.'

Zenf opened his cigarette case and offered it to Charles.

The cigarettes were custom-made, with symbols embossed on the paper.

Charles politely declined. Burning them might have more unpleasant after-effects than smoker's cough.

Zenf selected a cigarette. Vivian, the sham governess, produced someone else's lighter and flicked a flame. Zenf lit his smoke, and exhaled plumes through his nostrils.

'Beauregard, you are familiar with the practice of "casting the runes"?'

'I read Karswell's obituaries.'

'Ah yes, Julian,' said Zenf, dreamily. 'He was . . . unwise.'

Zenf opened the back of his cigarette case. He peeled out some small strips of paper, neatly-printed with symbols. Charles recognised one or two runes–fire and frost. Catriona Kaye, who had made a study of the Karswell case, would have known all of them.

'I took the precaution of preparing these earlier. Most potent, you understand. To each rune is bound a . . . how does your poet Mr Coleridge have it, "frightful fiend". By sunrise, anyone in possession of any one of these slips of paper will suffer unpleasant consequences. Would you care to take them from me?'

'Thank you, no.'

Zenf giggled. He rolled and twisted the papers into individual swirls, which he slipped into his various pockets.

'Now, as possessor of these highly dangerous shreds, I am fated to be torn apart at dawn. That would be a happy outcome for some, would it not?'

Charles regretted that he had left his sword-stick in the Bentley. He could save a lot of bother with one swift heart-thrust.

Perhaps instinctively, people in the room backed away from the Colonel, making space around him.

'I trust merciful providence to ensure my safety,' he announced. 'If even one of these charms remains upon my person a few hours from now, my number is up. Our business shall be at an end.'

Blithely, he turned and waddled out of the room, bumping into as many people as possible.

Charles opened his mouth to warn the guests, but Vivian chose the moment to faint in his arms. She locked wrists behind his neck and dragged him to the floor. His trick knee, an old wound, went out. Hot pain shot through his nerves. He bit down on an unmanly scream.

When he had disentangled himself, with the help of several guests who took the opportunity to purloin mock valuables, Zenf was out of the room. So was Vivian. Charles would remember her. Dark, pale, pretty, dangerous.

Margery helped him up. He dragged her to the door. Zenf was gone. The path he had made through the throng was closing. It was important to learn who had jostled the Colonel on his way out. Master Wuh, up on a bar with an empty glass, wiped off a milk moustache and raised both hands. Seven fingers.

Charles's head throbbed.

'What did you think of the Great Enchanter?' asked the hostess. 'Nasty little person, but he didn't seem much of a threat.'

'He's killed seven people while leaving this party, Margery.'

The hostess looked about, puzzled. The Bishop of Matabeleland snoozed peacefully, face almost normal. No one else seemed dead.

'He put runes in his pockets,' Charles explained. 'Then just walked through the crowd. At dawn, seven of these dips will get their collars felt . . . and not by the police.'

'Scarcely the behaviour of a gracious guest,' said Margery. 'Still, he *is* foreign.'

Charles made fists. Zenf had put him in a thorny position. He *could* go round the party, affronting the etiquette of the occasion by grilling pick-pockets about their hauls. If, by some miracle of explanation, he convinced the nimble-fingered victims of their peril, they'd likely spend the hours till dawn pressing paper dooms on other unsuspecting folks. If he browbeat the marks into parting with their runes, he would call sevenfold doom down on himself.

Margery wasn't happy, either. This was too much breakage.

XII: 'DON'T CALL ME "DOC"'

EDWIN SLUNG MARCUS Rennes over his shoulder and carried him out of the Astoria. Witnesses would take him for drunk and incapable.

Catriona and Geneviève giggled conspiratorially, like schoolgirls. Had Catriona fallen victim to the vampire power of fascination? More likely, she'd taken an instant liking to the centuries-old girl. In theory, they were hailing a taxi. Several cruised by, with their lights on. One even stopped, but Geneviève threw it back into the stream like a too-small fish.

Sorcerer's deadweight was getting to be a strain.

This business was turning into a run-around. Typical 'intelligence' work–leaping through flaming hoops, tripping over gnarly branches in thick forest, too busy with the little problems to get perspective. Edwin had a nasty feeling they were all part of someone else's game, or magic trick.

Finally, an acceptable cab was secured. The driver was slightly put off by Rennes, but Catriona and Geneviève charmed him into taking the fare. Edwin gave an address in Harley Street.

'I should hardly be the one to say this,' ventured Geneviève, 'but aren't we outside regular surgery hours?'

'Dr Chambers doesn't have a regular practice,' said Edwin.

'Not *the* Dr Chambers?'

'Actually, no,' said Catriona. 'That's *Jonathan* Chambers. Dr Shade keeps night-hours, but isn't often in his office. This is his sister, Dr *Jennifer* Chambers. She's more approachable. Slightly.'

It wasn't a long ride.

Catriona paid the cabbie, while Geneviève helped Edwin

with Rennes. She hefted him as if he were a papier-mâché dummy. Of course, she was stronger than she looked. Which she might have mentioned earlier–though showing off by carrying Sorcerer out of the theatre like a six-foot-six fireman would have attracted unwelcome attention.

Catriona nipped round them and pressed the door-bell.

The ring was quickly answered by a wide young man in a nurse's tunic.

'Hullo, Winthrop,' he said. 'Who's this?'

Edwin angled Rennes's face into the light, tipping up his chin to show the scarf knotted around Sorcerer's cut throat as a makeshift bandage.

Simon Pure, Dr Chambers's nurse, whistled through his teeth. 'Better come in, old son. I say, who are these pretty fillies?'

'Down, boy,' said a woman from inside the hallway. 'Miss Kaye, you know. Our other guest must be Mademoiselle Dieudonné . . .'

Jennifer Chambers was a tiny, fine-boned, fiftyish woman with short black hair, thick brows, sky-blue eyes and purple lips. The hem of her pristine white coat touched the floor. A stethoscope hung around her neck, business end tucked into her top pocket. Her speciality was injuries folks would be unwise to take to their general practitioner–either because of their unique nature or the unusual circumstances under which they were sustained. Her patients were drawn exclusively from the night-world that her family had been involved in for generations. Her practice extended to the Diogenes Club, the Undertaking, the Splendid Six (though not lately), most of the London-based lone wolves, and even factions on the Other Side, including the Seven Dials Sewing Circle, the New Red-Headed League and the Black Quorum.

Edwin and Geneviève heaved Sorcerer over the threshold. Dr Chambers directed them to dump Rennes on a gurney which Simon Pure wheeled into a large, well-appointed surgery. Two other patients were in the room, a shapeless lump on a cot, with a sheet over his or her face, and a little girl with an arm (too big for her body and covered in thick reddish fur) in a sling.

Dr Chambers angled a light onto Marcus Rennes's throat. She snapped on surgical gloves and delicately prodded his healing wound.

'Not a vampire bite,' she said. 'Which you know. Nice work, mademoiselle. Without your clever tongue, this man would be dead.'

Simon Pure stood by the gurney.

'Get some strong beef tea brewed,' Dr Chambers ordered, 'and pour it into him when he wakes. Take good care of him. He's one of the Ravens. If he pops, the city wobbles.'

'No worries, doc.'

'And don't call me "doc".'

Simon Pure grinned.

'You three,' said Dr Chambers, 'I want a briefing. My brother was in earlier, dropping off the Cunning Little Vixen.'

The girl with the peculiar arm looked glum.

'He was talking up a streak. Half hell is breaking loose in the city and I'm the one who has to get out the sticking plasters. It wouldn't kill Charles Beauregard to give me an idea what to expect.'

Edwin wondered how much he was allowed to tell Jennifer Chambers. She was respected within the community of the night, but anything she knew might get passed to her brother. If Dr Shade thought one of the Ravens a Rat, his usual course of action would be to kill all four and apologise to the three innocents at the funerals. Just now, Edwin saw the appeal of such Alexandrine knot-cutting tactics, and if anyone in town was up to facing the Great Enchanter . . .

A telephone jangled, saving Edwin from a dilemma.

'Jenny Chambers here.' The other party spoke for a few moments. 'Charles, I thought I might hear from you,' she continued. 'Some of your strays are in my surgery . . . no, none of *them* is a patient. They brought in a Raven . . . the Astronomical one. You want me where . . . ? Good grief, you *are* calling out the reserves . . . Yes, I know, I'm fed up with hearing it. "Don't bring

Johnny." The way everyone carries on, you'd think he batted for the Other Side . . .'

Dr Chambers listened for a full minute, concentrating. Her brows touched over the bridge of her nose. She jotted notes on a pad, muttering 'anti-venom . . . tana leaves . . . penicillin'. Then she handed the receiver to Edwin.

'Your master's voice,' she announced.

'Charles?'

'Edwin. Who hurt Sorcerer?'

'Conjurer, we think. He's looking like the Rat. Your lady leech has showed up.'

'Geneviève? Good. Keep her close.'

'No problems there. She could be another of Catriona's long-lost chums. One Cat *doesn't* want to see hanged.'

'I need Jenny here. Mekka, on the Embankment. Catriona and Geneviève, too. And more Ravens.'

'Sorcerer's *hors de combat*.'

'I've got Witch. If Conjurer's loose, that leaves Wizard. Get to the Tower and prepare him.'

'For what?'

'A scrap at dawn, probably. We're bringing him some difficult customers.'

'The Tower of London. You'll be there at sunrise, with company. Got it.'

'Edwin, watch out for Zenf. He's in a mischief-making mood. I wouldn't put it past him to show up and watch how his little joke plays out.'

'Joke?'

'You'll find out. Put Cat . . . no, *Geneviève*, on . . .'

Charles gave the telephone to the vampire.

' *"Allo,"* ' she said, kittenish. 'Don't be angry with me.'

Geneviève turned and talked low into the phone, so Edwin couldn't hear.

Dr Chambers had put a bulky tartan car-coat over her whites, with a matching tam o'shanter. She packed a medical bag, while issuing instructions to the nurse about the three patients.

'There are silver bullets in the revolver if Johnny's pet gets frisky,' she told the nurse. Simon Pure pulled a face at the Cunning Little Vixen, who made a rude gesture with two stubby, hairy, clawed fingers.

Edwin told Catriona she was going to Mekka.

'It's the Pick-Pockets' Ball tonight, isn't it?' she said, lightly. 'That's so much tamer than it used to be. In 1915, I dressed as a boy and sneaked in, and . . .'

'It might not be tame this year, Cat. Zenf showed up.'

Catriona was serious and paid attention. Edwin tapped two fingers against his wristwatch and pointed them at Geneviève.

'Watch . . . her,' Catriona mouthed, then nodded.

Dr Chambers was ready to set out. Geneviève was off the phone.

'Charles has sent a car for us,' she announced.

'What about me?' Edwin asked.

Dr Chambers took a key-ring out of her pocket, and detached a key.

'One of my brother's toys,' she said, handing it over. 'It'll get you to the Tower. If you crash it, I advise you to die instantly. There'd be no way to protect you from the wrath of Johnny.'

Edwin hoped it wasn't an autogyro.

'When's dawn?' Edwin asked.

'A little more than an hour and a half,' said Dr Chambers. 'You better get a move on. You know where the garage is. You can't miss the Night Flier.'

Edwin kissed Catriona, waved to the others, and left.

XIII: 'LIGHT-FINGERED IDIOTS'

CHARLES CONSULTED HIS real watch again. In the subjective minute or so since he last looked, half an hour had sped by. Towards dawn. He didn't like the oranginess of the lamp-light along the Embankment. It wavered, as if fog were rising from the river.

Runes summoned entities who killed the unfortunate possessors of the fateful scraps of paper. Though there was debate as to what exactly the entities were, it made sense to call them demons. Seven would converge here in just over an hour. They might come out of the sky, from under the water, detach from the shadows, simply manifest . . .

Margery Device had winnowed the seven fated pick-pockets from her other guests, drawing them onto the street with a promise of something special. She kept the crooks entertained with rapid-fire, unverifiable gossip about famous crime-fighters.

'Sir Dennis Nayland-Smith can't keep his hands off little yellow bottoms,' she said. 'It's the real reason why he's always haring off to the Far East. Jane Marple is the most dreadful lush. Almost every murderer she exposes gets off because evidence gets lost among all the gin-bottles when she turns up blotto at the Old Bailey . . .'

The only dip Charles recognised was Nosey Parker, of the long-suffering mother and the h'added h'aitches. There were five men and two women. One of the men was either a police constable or wore the uniform as a disguise. One of the women looked like a bare-knuckles boxer in petticoats. The rest were middling-to-anonymous, ideally suited to their profession.

While Charles was concentrating on this, what was Zenf up to?

The Bentley reappeared and parked by Mekka. Out came three women: Jenny Chambers, Catriona, Geneviève. The vampire looked, surprisingly, as if she were enjoying herself.

Master Wuh crossed himself. Seeing the miniature undertaker, Geneviève did a double-take.

'He's a liaison,' Charles explained.

'Pleased to meet him,' said Geneviève. 'Should he be up this late?'

A long van parked at the kerb behind the Bentley, and a top-hatted, goggled figure got out. Mr Esse, the collector. The Black Mariah could–under certain circumstances–be used as a hearse. Before calling Jenny, Charles had alerted the Undertaking. He hadn't known Geneviève would be invited to the party and run into her former gaolers.

Geneviève ignored Mr Esse and took Charles's arm, soliciting his protection. He patted her chilly fingers.

'Is that them?' asked Catriona, indicating Margery's audience. They were intent on the inside details of a titled-but-stony-broke amateur sleuth's racket–charging guilty parties fat fees to be exonerated, and innocent parties even fatter ones not to be perfectly framed.

Charles nodded.

'They don't look doomed,' Catriona observed. 'Well, no more than anyone else.'

'Undooming them isn't difficult,' he said. 'You just have to ask them to surrender the runes. Of course, whoever's holding the parcel when the music stops gets torn to the proverbial shreds.'

'Light-fingered idiots,' said Geneviève. 'No one asked them to be thieves. Why would anyone steal useless pieces of paper?'

'Professional pride, Geneviève. Traditional behaviour at the Pick-Pockets' Ball. They don't even expect valuables, just the challenge. These people have been stealing from each other all night. Some runes changed pockets several times before we extracted the current holders . . .'

Master Wuh tugged his sleeve, and pointed.

'Ah,' said Charles, 'even within the group, the blessed chits are in circulation.'

Master Wuh made finger gestures. Nosey had two runes now, the constable three. The other rune-holders were an effete-seeming man about town and a soberly-dressed woman with a Temperance sash and pince-nez.

'That's progress,' he said. 'Three are out of the game.'

He signalled to Margery like a racetrack tout–three fingers, individual jabs at the currently safe parties, a dismissive wave.

Margery drew the four remaining pick-pockets closer, and said something that sent the others packing without offending them. As the city's presiding hostess, she was a seventh-degree master of diplomacy.

As she left, the big woman took something from the constable's pocket. Charles saw the situation getting out of hand again–but the prize was not a rune, just the constable's whistle. The anti-drink campaigner clucked near the man about town, and got his rune from him. Margery saw at once, and asked him 'be a dear' and fetch her a gin fizz.

'Now prying ears have departed,' Margery stage-whispered, 'I can reveal all. It was Sexton Blake who pushed Sherlock Holmes off the waterfall that time . . . being the *second*-cleverest detective in Baker Street drove him round the bend.'

'No more games,' said Charles. 'I want these three isolated, as if they were carrying a disease. We can't take chances on losing track of the runes.'

He strolled over to the little group. Geneviève sauntered with him, taking his arm. He still wanted to have a conversation with her about her disappearance from the Mausoleum.

He handed his card to the policeman, eliciting a salute.

'Constable,' he said, 'arrest these two criminals.'

'Well, H'I never . . .' exclaimed Nosey.

'I'll have you know I'm a respectable woman,' said the temperance lady.

The constable was taken aback. Making an arrest at the Pick-Pockets' Ball would violate agreements and truces dating back to Magna Carta. But the card of the Diogenes Club was universally recognised.

Red was in the sky, not acting like pre-dawn light. A scarlet question-mark was forming, somewhere over the river. Tower Reach.

Mr Esse and Huntstanton had the rear doors of the Black Mariah open.

'If you'll get in, Nosey,' said Charles. 'I'll explain.'

'Whatever you say, Mr Beauregard,' said Nosey, complying at once. He had good cause to trust the Diogenes Club.

'Miss . . . ?'

'Leticia Hesketh-Stafford,' said the eminently respectable woman, bristling with practiced indignation.

'In the van, Letty,' insisted the policeman.

'I shall be writing to my Member of Parliament,' she said, clambering in beside Nosey–then cringing in horror and withdrawing her skirts, expertly sorting through several hidden pockets. If she understood what her swag meant, she wouldn't be so keen to hang onto it.

'It would be best if Constable Ottermole went with you,' said Margery.

The policeman looked suspicious but was keen not to defy authority.

'Yes,' said Charles, 'I agree. Constable, what's the time?'

Ottermole searched through his pockets and came up with three watches, all giving slightly different times.

'That's mine,' said Huntstanton, claiming one timepiece.

'Ah . . . evidence,' said the policeman, weakly. 'My sergeant is very particular about hanging on to evidence.'

Huntstanton gave Ottermole a shove. Mr Esse locked the doors behind the three rune-bearing miscreants.

'That won't protect them,' said Margery, meaning the van.

'Or keep them in,' commented Catriona. 'Look, Nosey's jiggling the lock already.'

'This isn't an ordinary Black Mariah,' said Mr Esse. 'The lock is trickier than usual.'

Sparks came out between the doors. Bad language was heard.

Some sober pick-pockets formed a deputation to protest. Margery had to soothe them.

'This isn't a police van,' she said. 'It's an ambulance. Nosey, Letty and P. C. Ottermole have been overcome by a mystery ailment. This woman, as you can see, is a doctor.'

Jenny undid her muffler to show her stethoscope.

'Never seen no black ambulance afore,' said a pick-pocket.

'Now you have,' cooed Margery.

Mr Esse stood beside Jenny, cracking black-gloved knuckles. His presence intimidated the deputation, who decided they'd be better employed somewhere else.

'Is that what I'm here for?' asked Jenny, impatient. 'A cover story? No one, so far as I can see, needs a doctor . . .'

'Yet,' said Charles.

Geneviève pointed at the sky. The question mark was a spiral now.

'Margery, I am sure you can be counted on to bring the ball to a successful conclusion with no one any the wiser. We shall leave now.'

Catriona, Geneviève and Jenny got into the Bentley. Huntstanton and Mr Esse took to their driving seats.

Margery bade Charles good night.

'Not much night left,' he said, looking at his watch again.

Master Wuh sat up front, next to Huntstanton.

Charles got into the back of the Bentley. The ladies made room for him. He pulled the speaking tube and gave an order.

'To the Tower.'

XIV: 'GUINNESS IS GOOD FOR YOU!'

THE NIGHT FLIER turned out to be a Norton motorcycle, an all-black, 600cc, 4-gear exemplar of British precision engineering, custom-built for Dr Shade. A prow-like steel cowl welded to the front column would ram through anything less sturdy than a brick wall and usefully turn aside projectiles or pedestrians. Extra tanks under the pillion, containing a noxious mix of petrol and brimstone, fed either the CamShaft One engine or a flexible nozzle fitted above the fishtail exhaust. An oily machine-gun, like a fighter plane's, was built into the prow.

Edwin would have to be careful which switches to throw.

It was a kick-start model. The key Dr Chambers had given him unlocked an ingenious hobbling device he assumed was to prevent unauthorised persons driving the beast away. What a wary, suspicious soul Dr Shade must be! Edwin couldn't imagine thievery of such hard-to-fence vehicles would ever become an epidemic problem. If such conditions ever came to pass, this odd contraption–three iron bars and a padlock, which disabled the engine and locked the wheels–might find a market.

He straddled the bike and stamped down on the starter-pedal. The engine growled instantly to life. He bent low and aimed the throbbing bike at the slope which led up from the underground garage to the street. The machine seemed to know what was required and tore off, prompting Edwin to hang on tight. The Night Flier crested the slope and leaped across three feet of pavement, landing smoothly on the road. He leant into a sharp turn, and drove down Harley Street, startling cats and a courting couple.

The Norton handled better than a Sopwith Camel.

Apart from lorries carrying the early editions and a horse-drawn milk-cart in Cavendish Square, there wasn't much other traffic about. Edwin sped across Oxford Circus, down Regent Street, into Piccadilly Circus.

A few all-night waifs and strays huddled around Eros, in the dazzle of eternal neon. Two or three fellows in bedraggled evening clothes stretched on the pavement, at the frazzled end of a rag which must have begun with a tipple at the Drones and ended with forced ejection from the Criterion Bar. Their natural predators would be at the Pick-Pockets' Ball–so this was the safest night of the year to lie drunk in the centre of town, with a note-case full of fivers, pockets overflowing with small change and grandfather's gold watch dangling on a chain. It had rained earlier. Slick, wet tarmac glittered with reflected highlights from advertisements for Bovril, Sandeman's Port, Schweppes, Gordons London Gin, Army Club cigarettes and C. B. Cochrane's annual review. By the Guinness Clock–*Guinness is Good for You!*–it was nearly four o'clock.

He ought to be at the Tower before dawn.

In Haymarket, something like a scarecrow clung three-quarters of the way up a lamp-post. It turned to stare as the Night Flier passed. The roughly human figure was wrapped in an over-sized ulster that hung like folded wings. The face was a scowling leather mask, eyes blazing with blue light. For a moment, Edwin thought it might be Dr Shade, wondering who was warming his saddle. The creature leaped from its perch, coat-skirts flaring to show long, grasshopper-like legs. It slammed onto the pavement, body concertinaing like a coiled spring, then launched into space with a mighty hop, arms outspread, kukri knives flashing in each gloved hand.

It was another fugitive waxwork–Spring Heel'd Jack, the Terror of London. A bad one. Last time the original had bounced around town, it had taken all of the Splendid Six, plus Granite Grant and the Green Archer, to bring him down to earth–and the Splendids weren't in business any more. Surprisingly, the Night Flier didn't seem to be equipped with a bow and arrow.

The demi-demon soared overhead, aiming heels against a wall, and bounced off–flying well ahead of the Norton, landing, arms outspread, in the middle of the road. He tossed the kukri knives and Edwin weaved to evade the blades. Jack drew a brace of pistols from holsters under his arms. Closer now, Edwin tucked his head down and drove straight at the villain.

Edwin's thumbs were against switches. He aimed the bike and pressed the right switch.

A burst of controlled gunfire, strangely quiet, struck the road. Jack had jumped above the fire.

As Edwin drove under him, Jack seemed to hang in the air, calmly aiming his guns.

A bullet spanged against the Night Flier's prow, striking sparks. When Jack landed, he was behind the bike, with a clear shot at Edwin's unprotected back.

If the right switch was the gun, then the left must be the nozzle above the exhaust. Edwin pressed.

A jet of flame coursed out of the rear-nozzle.

He looked back and saw Jack's mask burn away from his face, which melted. His ulster caught fire, but that didn't stop him leaping, on whatever mechanisms were really built into his heels. On wings of flame, the Terror of London flapped in the Norton's wake, following Edwin into Cockspur Street and across Trafalgar Square. Wherever he touched ground, he left burning pools of wax and cloth. He bounced erratically, then exploded against a Landseer lion, falling to flaming pieces, startling a flock of drowsing pigeons.

Edwin hoped that was the last of the waxworks. Then he remembered Sweeney Todd was still at large, or at least whoever–Conjurer, presumably–had dressed as the Demon Barber of Fleet Street to slash Sorcerer's throat.

The motorcycle was a perfect machine.

He made a mental note to get in touch with the Norton Company. One of these things could come in handy.

He didn't see why Dr Shade should have a monopoly.

In the moment, he felt considerably better. Wind rushing his face, a downed enemy in flames in his wake, the thrill of speed in his water.

Violence and victory cleared his head.

XV: 'THIS IS ABOUT DRAWING A LINE'

THE SKY WAS red. The Bentley sped towards the Tower, the Black Mariah close on its rear bumper.

This was another instance in which Charles would have welcomed one of Mycroft's contingencies–an envelope with easy-to-follow instructions, a sheet of paper to trump the runes. Again, sadly, his mentor had failed to foresee this specific eventuality. However, he had a carful of lively minds at his disposal.

'So, ladies,' said Charles, 'suggestions?'

The three women all hesitated, thinking. They knew the

problem. At dawn, whoever held any of the seven runes would be killed by whatever Zenf had taken the trouble to summon and bind. To judge from rusty threads in the gutters, these parties were set to appear from the sky in a welter of blood.

'We shouldn't rely on Wizard's counter-spells,' said Catriona, who had made a study of rune-casting for her monograph on the late, unlamented Julian Karswell. 'It's easier to let the dogs loose than call them to heel. No one has ever beat the runes through dispersion, banishment or holding charm. And it's been tried. In '26, Frank Chandler cast a spell to stop time. He simply froze the poor rune-bearer in her place, but scarcely slowed the demons, who happened to be the Devourers From Outside Time. The victim was, well, devoured. Chandu didn't broadcast *that* in his radio memoirs. Last year in Marseilles, the Duc de Richleau managed to *kill* the demon before it got its claws into its appointed victim. I don't want to think about how he managed that. The operation was a success but the patient died. Demon, rune and rune-bearer are mystically linked by the initial summoning. Slay the demon and the rune-bearer goes up in flames. The Duc made a valuable discovery, but looked even more of an idiot than usual. Connaught Drake can spell rings around lightweights like Chandu and de Richleau, but I still doubt he has anything in his tomes to counter a serious rune-casting. Our Great Enchanter is taking his first, best shot.'

Charles took in Catriona's summation. Don't hope for too much from Drake. Yet, this was all about the Ravens–the business with the runes was supposed to make him take his eyes off them.

Their best course still led to the Tower.

'Couldn't the vampire take the runes?' suggested Jenny Chambers.

Geneviève looked aghast. 'I'm not *that* expendable,' she protested.

'No, but technically you're dead already. If the demon is dispelled with the death of the person holding the papers, might the curse not apply to you?'

'I see your point, doctor, but I'm not that sort of vampire. Sorry.'

'Precedents there are unpleasant also,' said Catriona. 'In Alte Strelsau in 1408, Iohannes Meister cast a rune and passed it to a merchant who'd rooked him. However, before his time was up, the merchant was conventionally stabbed to death by another dissatisfied customer.'

'What happened when Meister's demon manifested?' asked Jenny.

'Cheated of its prey, it . . . well, it was a hundred years before they started work on *Neue* Strelsau.'

'Fair enough. Scrub that. It was an idea, though.'

'Yes, thank you, Jenny,' said Charles.

'Here's a thought,' said Catriona. 'We gather the runes and give them to, say, Ollie Gibberne. She's going to hang in the end, for murder. Being rent limb from limb by fiends isn't *much* more than she deserves.'

'There are practical difficulties, Catriona,' said Charles. 'We've half an hour at the most. Finding your murderess and persuading her to accept a suspicious envelope is liable to take longer.'

'I could do it in two hours. She's frightfully thick. I could tell her it was a mash note from, say, Ronald Colman. Or the King.'

'We don't have two hours.'

Geneviève peered out of the window, looking up into the sky.

'Those clouds are drifting *against* the wind,' she said. 'The red ones that seem to be boiling over.'

'Someone has to say it, so I will,' began Jenny. 'Didn't these three ask for it? They are all petty crooks. Even if one of them is a jolly old bobby . . .'

'"If you want to know the time, ask a policeman . . ."' warbled Catriona.

'Yes. "Every member of the force has a watch and chain, of course." Remember what the song is about? Victorian constables were famous for rolling drunks. That's how they got the watches.'

Jenny shared some of her brother's merciless attitudes to law-breakers.

'I was once arrested by Jonathan Wild, the London Thief-Taker,' said Geneviève. 'Now, *he* was a bigger crook than Fantô-mas, Arsène Lupin and John Dillinger rolled together.'

'We should get them out in the open, then,' said Catriona. 'Limit the damage. Anyone who gets in the way is liable to suffer. A shame about Nosey Parker, though . . . his mother will be grief-stricken.'

'He doesn't have a mother, Catriona.'

Catriona's eyes goggled. 'It's all lies . . . !?'

'Not exactly,' he explained. 'It's part of his *act*. Pick-pockets are like music hall turns. They have patter, embroidered through-out their careers. Nosey's mother is more like an imaginary friend. Or a comedian's mother-in-law.'

'If one of them–or anyone–ends up with all seven runes, the rest go free,' said Catriona. 'If we can't get someone who really deserves it here, we can at least save two of the three. Despite the mother rou-tine, which I'm still *appalled* by, I vote for Nosey and . . .'

'Go on,' said Charles.

'Can't decide,' said Catriona. 'Letty's just as obnoxious as the type of fanatical annoyance she poses as . . . and Ottermole regu-larly betrays the public trust. I'm sorry. I can't make those deci-sions. You need Edwin for that. Or Dr Shade.'

'Jenny . . .' prompted Charles.

'I am, of course, familiar with the concept of triage. Save who you can.'

'Here, we can save almost everyone but must pick one to die,' said Charles. 'Doesn't have to be one of the three dips. Anyone in this car, or the Black Mariah, or at the Tower, or on the streets will do . . .'

Jenny spread her hands and shook her head.

'I thought so,' he said. 'Good for you, Jenny. You're not your brother.'

Charles saw the Tower up ahead. The bloody clouds were

above it, taking solid shape. Wherever the rune-bearers might be at dawn, Southwark or Samara, their deaths would be waiting.

He was determined.

'Ladies, it is decided. We will *not* let this thing happen. It doesn't matter who these people are. It didn't matter to the Great Enchanter when he scattered his runes. Zenf wants to show he can hurt *anyone*. That we can't protect our people. Purse-snatcher or Prince of the Realm, they're all the same to him–and they should be to us. Few may know it, but we're here for the people. We preserve this country from this species of hurt. This is about drawing a line and saying it shall not be crossed.'

Geneviève, Catriona and Jenny looked at him, eyes wide, mouths slightly open.

'What?' he said. 'What is it?'

'It's just . . . it's just *you*,' said Catriona.

Geneviève leaned over and kissed him on the mouth.

'What was that for?' he asked, bewildered.

'Someone had to,' she explained. 'I elected myself. "Drawing a line." It's so perfect. I see what Mr Mycroft meant about you.'

Charles feared his face was flushed.

'Don't worry,' Geneviève whispered in his ear. 'In this red light, no one can tell.'

She kissed him again, on the cheek, and sat back. Catriona squeezed his knee. Even Jenny Chambers, who usually only smiled during surgery, was on the point of simpering.

Charles still had no idea what it was all about.

He had puzzled out many mysteries in his long life, but was still on the lower slopes when it came to women.

XVI: 'PEREDUR CHAFFINCH THREEPENCE'

ANY SHEPHERDS IN London would have been served severe warning by the dawn skies. From the excessive redness of the clouds, it was to be a bloody, bloody day.

89

Edwin startled two Yeoman Warders on the early watch. They crossed pikes and braced themselves as the Night Flier roared towards the visitors' gate. He executed a smart turn and used the brakes. The Norton halted smartly.

'Peredur Chaffinch Threepence,' he said.

The code-words signified direst peril to crown and country. The beefeaters stood at once to attention, pikes parted. A trickle of fear-sweat dripped onto one man's ruff.

'You've two more parties arriving,' he told the guards, 'in a Bentley and a Black Mariah. Let them pass. Then lower the portcullis and be ready to defend the Tower.'

'Yes, sir,' said the Warders.

Some thought the duty merely ceremonial, standing about in fancy dress for tour parties, posing for picture post-cards. But the Tower of London was a Royal Residence, a national treasure store, a prison and the old stone heart of William the Conqueror's city. All this made the place a target. Only the best long-term service veterans were eligible to become Yeoman Warders, men proved in battles all over the world.

As Edwin wheeled Dr Shade's bike into the courtyard, there was activity. The full complement of Warders were roused from beds and took defensive positions. It was odd to see beefeaters in their embroidered velvet tunics, knee-britches, floppy hats and half-capes deployed with Thompson sub-machine guns instead of pikestaffs and ceremonial swords. A few of the famous ravens flapped lazily into the air and found perches. Edwin hoped they were used to the chatter of tommy guns. He didn't want to be responsible for scaring off the blessed birds and bringing down the kingdom.

The Keeper of the Ravens was quartered in the White Tower, the oldest part of the fortress. Edwin wondered if he'd have to hammer on the huge mediaeval door to wake up the Wizard.

'Don't like the look of that sky, Bert,' a Warder told a comrade. 'It'll belt down, sure as eggs is eggs.'

A mild little old fellow in tweeds and an apron, who was scattering feed for the birds, paused with a handful of breadcrumbs, looked up through half-spectacles, and clucked.

'It won't rain,' he said. 'Dear me no. Rain would be a blessing, weather we've been having.'

This was Wizard.

Edwin had expected starry robes and a conical hat, as advertised. Connaught Drake sported a white beard, close-cropped rather than waist-length. His hat was a battered trilby, with a small black feather in the brim.

Edwin opened his mouth to speak.

'Yes . . . yes . . . Peredur Chaffinch Threepence,' said Drake, waving away the bother. 'Why we have to make the men learn such rot by heart is beyond me. If it's come to *Peredur Chaffinch Threepence,* then you might as well shout *Woe Calamity Doom.* So, what manner of catastrophe threatens, eh? My birdies have been off their seed for days. So peril must be dire indeed. Tentacles? The Deep Old Damp Ones? No, no, that'd be rising waters, not red skies. The Thames is behaving itself for a change. Bat-wings and scaly tails? It'll be Zenf, then. Continentals think too much of their gargoyles. They think we're still scared of pantomime bogey men with stuck-out tongues and the flaming pitchforks.'

As far as Edwin was concerned, he *was* still scared. In this business, it wasn't cowardice–it was clearheadedness. Black shapes were in the clouds now. Flapping wings were involved, presumably bat-like.

Something about Wizard rubbed Edwin wrong. He was prepared to concede that he, and everyone he cared about, fell into the category of 'lesser mortals'–but it wasn't quite cricket to rub it in with such high-handed, dismissive irritation. They all had jobs to do, even the Keeper of the Ravens.

Charles Beauregard's Bentley cruised through the main gate, followed by a Black Mariah. When they were in the courtyard, the portcullis came down.

'It's well before visiting hours,' said Wizard. 'We can't be having this, you know. Your Ruling Cabal have a lot to answer for. And the other shower with the black hats.'

It occurred to Edwin that if Wizard was the King Rat, they were now locked in with him.

Huntstanton got out of the Bentley and opened the passenger door. Catriona and Dr Chambers helped Charles out, another indication of the situation's seriousness. The Old Man rarely let anyone treat him like an invalid. Geneviève emerged into dawn light. She didn't shrivel to dust, but hid from the sun with a large green scarf over her hair and blue-tinted tortoise-shell glasses.

A pair of Undertakers were here, too, one a half-sized specimen. He supposed that was inevitable, though he didn't have to like it. The Undertaking were mystery-wallahs of the worst kind, and Edwin didn't like the way they went about things.

With Yeoman Warders added to the party, everyone gathered round the Black Mariah. A heavy rock whistled down from the sky and smashed nearby, exploding to flinty shrapnel. A beefeater was wounded, shards stuck into his cheek and shoulder. Dr Chambers got close to him, tweezers out. With distracted irritation, Connaught Drake snapped his fingers. Black fragments extracted from the Warder's wounds and flew past the startled doctor. The beefeater's tunic was ragged where he'd been blasted, but his skin healed over instantly. He put a hand to his face in disbelief. Dr Chambers clacked her tweezers. After whirling around ostentatiously, the splinters reassembled into a well-behaved stone cherub's head.

Everyone was impressed, but Wizard didn't take applause.

'Which of you is Beauregard?'

Charles stepped forward, leaning heavily on his stick, extending a hand that Drake didn't take.

'Surrounded by women, I see,' said Drake. Edwin was astonished that the Old Man looked sheepish. 'Says something about your character.'

Geneviève bristled a little, like a French cat considering where best to scratch. Good for her. Dr Chambers harrumphed.

'Margery Device speaks highly of you,' Wizard admitted,

testily. 'And she speaks lowly of everyone. Now, what *is* all this *bother*? Why have you trooped here in force at the crack of dawn to disturb the birdies and haul the beefeaters out of bed? Zenf's raised some imps, I presume. Do you perchance have *runes* about your person?'

'Not me, Keeper,' said Charles. 'We have three afflicted souls in here.'

Everyone shrank from the van, except Connaught Drake.

'Let's have them in the light, then,' he said. 'Take a look at them. Chances are they won't stay long, so we should get to know them while we can. Horrid business, rune-raising. Underhanded and cowardly. Not British. *Merlin* never cast runes.'

Mr Esse, the adult Undertaker, unlocked the back of the Black Mariah. A beefeater subtly pointed his tommy gun at the doors, as if expecting hungry lions.

'The *event* is set for dawn,' said the Old Man.

'Best be quick, then,' said Drake. 'Get it over with before breakfast. This being Thursday, it's kedgeree.'

The doors opened and three miserable people climbed out. Edwin assumed they were pick-pockets, though one was a police constable and another a pinch-faced woman wearing an 'Abjure Strong Drink' sash. The third was Alfred Parker–who certainly *was* a pick-pocket. Everyone knew Nosey. His larcenous fingers had been used in the service of the Club. Once, by purloining an Eurasian courtesan's deadly steel fan, he had saved Edwin's neck.

'How's your mum, Nosey?' he asked.

Nosey shook his head, in sorrow. 'H'it's 'er h'arches, Mr Winthrop. Fallen like h'ancient Rome.'

'I'd like to talk about Nosey's mother,' said Catriona, in middling-high dudgeon. 'According to Mr Knows-All-Tells-Little here . . .'

'This may not be the time,' interrupted Charles.

Catriona shut up, which–as far as Edwin was concerned–was another Sign of the Apocalypse.

'Now, you three,' said Drake, sternly, 'turn out your pockets . . .'

None of them looked happy, and no wonder.

'Come come,' said Drake, 'I'm not a policeman or a schoolmaster. I wish to save you discomfort.'

His tone of voice was convincing.

'You can keep all your loot except some scraps of paper with funny writing. Of no value whatsoever. Nothing you could fence. Yes, Miss Strong Drink, those are what I mean, hand them over . . .'

The woman parted reluctantly with three runes. They were twisted into little shapes.

'Congratulations, you're not doomed any more,' said Drake, rolling the runes together.

'Hey, that's mine,' said Dr Chambers, reclaiming her stethoscope.

The temperance woman looked as if she were the victim of a severe affront, and about to set the law on an impertinent false accuser. That must be her act.

'I have no idea how that came to be upon my person. It must have been planted by a malicious individual. Almost certainly in the employ of the perfidious purveyors of alcoholic beverages.'

'Give it up, Letty,' said the constable. 'It's a fair cop.'

The policeman and Nosey came up with two runes apiece. Nosey seemed fascinated by his little strips of deadly paper.

Catriona pointedly took back her silver retracting pencil, without comment. She was in a pet with Nosey Parker.

'That's the lot?' Drake asked.

Charles nodded.

'Such *fuss* over so little,' mused Wizard.

Nosey was the last to part with his strips.

There were shouts from Yeoman Warders, about hostiles in the skies. Mr Esse looked up, staring into the sun. In the twin dark mirrors of his specs, Edwin caught doubled glimpses of something angular and swift. It hovered like a large locust with too few legs and too many wings.

Connaught Drake held up a fistful of runes, letting the trailing edges flutter. It was as if the papers were trying to fly away, but Wizard had a firm grip. Large, thick shadows fell on the court-yard.

Edwin didn't know whether to look up or keep his eyes on the ground. Catriona was by his side, clutching his arm. She clutched her silver pencil like a stiletto–it might do for a vampire, but he was doubtful it'd even annoy the coming predators.

Beefeaters on the battlements began firing into the sky.

Wizard made an exasperated, irritated face and nodded an order, which was relayed upwards. The gunfire cut off. Spent bullets pattered on gravel.

'Now,' said Connaught Drake, holding their full attention, 'you're expecting me to be rent limb from limb by seven demons, aren't you? Well, as Robbie Stone is wont to say rather too often, "for my next trick", I shan't be.'

Edwin looked up and wished he hadn't.

XVII: 'NO H'END OF GRIEF FROM ME H'OLD PLATES'

CHARLES HELD HIS sword-cane in both hands, several inches of steel showing, catching the red light. It was instinct rather than sense. The sword would be no more use than the beefeaters' bullets.

Connaught Drake, Raven and Keeper of Ravens, held all the runes. Zenf's creatures were coming from the skies, all teeth and talons. They would not return to their infernal aerie until they had shredded the rune-bearer. Yet Drake had announced that he would *not* suffer the consequences. If he could get out of this fix, he'd be a Wizard indeed.

Someone else was with them in the courtyard.

'Mr Parker,' said Drake, mildly, 'isn't this your mother?'

Nosey, goggling, spun round.

Charles was scarcely less astonished. Here, wincing with each step, was Nosey Parker's mythical mother. There could be no doubt of the relationship. She had the same beak, the same oddly-jointed gait, the same oversized eyes. She wore a hat with gauze and dead flowers around the rim and a cloth coat with a fur collar. Her famously troublesome feet were in carpet-slippers.

Catriona was aghast again, but puzzled.

'Mum,' breathed Nosey, tears in his eyes. 'Mum . . .'

'Close h'up your mouth, H'Alfred,' she said, 'h'or a bee will fly h'into h'it.'

Something large and sinewy landed on the side of the White Tower, stinking of sulphur, claws digging into old stone.

Geneviève showed her fangface. Her nails had grown to knifepoints. Master Wuh was crouched at her feet, holding a stick like a Chinese fighting monk.

'So this is the Tower of London, then,' said Nosey's Mum, looking around. 'H'I 'ope you h'ain't gettin' ideas h'above your station, H'Alfred. We've always been true blue in h'our family. H'ever since your H'Uncle Charlie, 'im what was relieved at Mafekin', was h'awarded by the h'old Queen. So, no stealin' of the Koh-I-Nor or any h'other of them Crown Jewels. Those sparklers belongs properly to 'Is Majesty the King. You find somethin' h'else to nick, or don't come 'ome with your washin' h'at the h'end of the week.'

Nosey was shame-faced, which suggested he *had* seen an opportunity in this irregular visit to the Tower.

'Mrs Parker,' said Drake, 'if you will take these off my hands.' He offered her the runes.

'Certainly, ducks,' she said, opening her purse. Drake folded the papers into it, and pressed its catch shut. 'H'I'll willingly take responsibility.'

She patted the purse and slipped it into her pocket.

Drake snapped his fingers and a comfortable chair appeared

behind Nosey's Mum. A padded, red-flock armchair with gilt feet.

'Would you care to sit down?' he suggested.

'Cor, thanks, luv,' said Nosey's Mum, sitting down with relief. 'H'it's me feet, you know. No h'end of grief from me h'old plates . . .'

'It would be best if we all withdrew to a safe distance,' said Drake, to everyone but the old woman. 'It was a pleasure to meet you, Mrs Parker.'

'Don't mention h'it, dearie.'

Geneviève pulled Charles away. He couldn't help but look at the new arrival. She was no illusion. He thought he understood how she had come here. Drake was guardian of the *stories* of London and Nosey's Mum was one of those. Wizard had opened a doorway to the city's shadow, and invited this woman to step through, to be real for a few brief minutes.

They all gave Mrs Parker a wide circle. She raised a cheery hand and flapped it at Nosey.

More creatures alighted. They were big, red-black and indistinct, as if they had their own personal clouds. These things weren't supposed to be seen even in dawn light.

Warders had to put out fires.

Mrs Parker wasn't at all concerned by the seven creatures stalking towards her. She got out some knitting and hummed. The first demon prodded her with a long, triple-segmented finger.

Then, they were on her. In an instant, she was rendered into a red cloud. The chair was torn apart, too. In another instant, their purpose fulfilled, Zenf's imps popped out of existence, leaving behind a stench that made Charles choke.

Nosey howled and fell to his knees.

Catriona had a hand over her mouth, horrified.

Most of the warders–and Letty and Ottermole–didn't even know what had happened. It had been too quick.

Wizard pottered about, walking onto the red, white-flecked

patch where Nosey's Mum had been. Ravens gathered, settling on his shoulders, pecking at scraps from the ground.

The immediate danger was over. Wizard had bested the Great Enchanter.

'No,' said Catriona, firmly. 'That wasn't fair. That didn't count. You cheated, Drake. You passed the runes. To a real person. An innocent. That's not what you were supposed to do.'

'She took them willingly,' he said. 'She sacrificed herself for the city. She was a true cockney.'

Edwin held Catriona's shoulders. She was furious.

'What about *him*? Nosey? He's broken. If he hadn't believed, deep down *believed,* you wouldn't have been able to fetch her from storyland.'

'No. But it wasn't just him. You *all* had to go along with the stories. And look at him, Miss Kaye. Look.'

Nosey blinked in the sunlight, more baffled than anything else.

'The story is gone,' explained Drake, not unkindly, 'as if it were never told. For him, the pages are blank. For the rest of you, it'll take a few more minutes–until the sun is fully up.'

Charles slid his sword-stick shut.

Dr Chambers took a look at Nosey. 'Doesn't seem to be shock,' she reported.

'H'what's all this about,' said Nosey, deftly extracting a bottle of pills from Jenny Chambers's pocket. 'And h'why are you all lookin' h'at me like that. H'I'm a poor h'orphan, H'I am, h'what never knew 'is Mum and Dad. H'I suffered somethin' h'awful in that 'orrible h'orphanage. H'it'd make a grown man weep . . .'

A new story was taking shape, to fill the blank page.

The ruin on the cobbles was all wood and cloth and padding and gilt. No other matter. In this world, all that had been sacrificed was a chair.

Catriona was not yet mollified. Charles squeezed her shoulder. At times like this, Edwin's friend reminded him of Kate

Reed. Someone had to count the cost, and she was ready to step up—no matter if important persons took offence.

'You'll have to reissue *The Biter Bit*, Miss Kaye,' said Mr Esse. 'With a new appendix. Someone has finally beaten the runes.'

Catriona looked at the Undertaker with disgust.

'Now,' said Drake. 'About this Rat . . .'

XVIII: 'THE RAVENS MUST BE FED'

THE GHASTLY LETICIA Hesketh-Stafford was made to give up a cake of soap into which she'd accidentally pressed some keys a beefeater had 'dropped' in all the excitement. After that, the pickpockets were packed off home.

What had they made of this morning's happening at the Tower? Far-fetched tales would spread through the underworld, refilling the story-pool depleted by Wizard's sacrificial gambit. Edwin knew Mrs Parker had looked exactly as he always imagined her, but the exact image was blurry in his memory now. Wizard had said she would fade. A few minutes ago, he had shared Nosey's hot spasm of grief, but now there was only an after-tingle. He was disturbed at the absence of feelings that had momentarily been real.

An alert came from the guards watching the Thames.

A motor launch approached, piloted by a tall girl in a reddish-brown body stocking and moth-winged domino mask. She was an occasional associate of Dr Shade's, and went by the name of Kentish Glory. Margery Device stood next to the woman of mystery, in a tailored sailor suit, ribbons streaming from a jaunty cap. The black, shark-finned boat—presumably another loan from Dr Chambers's brother—slid almost silently up to Tower Dock. Miss Device stepped ashore as, on Drake's nod, a gate was raised.

The launch sped away from the dock, Isinglass carapace unfolding to enclose the skipper. When Kentish Glory was sealed inside, the boat became a submersible and knived under the waters of the Thames.

Miss Device entered the Tower through Traitor's Gate, formerly the Water-Gate.

'You found a way around the rune-casting,' she said with mild congratulation, as if noticing he'd filled in the *Times* crossword double-quick. 'Well done, Conny. I knew you'd spell up some fresh cleverness.'

Wizard looked at Witch and said, 'Who is this at Traitor's Gate? Margery, I don't suppose you've been betraying the Kingdom?'

She seemed delighted at the accusation. '*Moi*? A Queen Rat? You know me better than that, dear.'

'I suppose I do,' he said. 'Still, you had to be asked to your face. At least, to one of your faces. Or aren't we talking about that in public?'

At last, Miss Device was shocked. Edwin had thought she was unflappable.

'You'd all better come into the White Tower,' said Wizard. 'The ravens must be fed, and you can tell me what little you know.'

Connaught Drake rarely had to deal with other people. He was not very good at it. He was probably better with the birds.

Yeoman Warders opened doors and saluted, and Drake led them up a cramped circular staircase to a large room with niches in the walls, straw on the flagstone floor and open vents in the glass ceiling. The Raven-Cote was airy and sunlit–Geneviève had to find a shadow to shrink into. A shallow drinking fountain burbled pleasantly. Birds arrived in an orderly fashion, and found individual perches and nooks. Wizard unlocked a cabinet and took out several cups, into which he poured birdseed from a packet. He handed cups to Dr Chambers, Catriona and the Junior Undertaker.

'You're the trustworthy ones,' Drake told them. 'Don't give too much, or they bloat.'

He showed how to dribble seeds into smooth depressions in the stone, and his appointed deputies followed suit. The birds came and pecked, not caring whose hand tipped their food.

With a set of long tweezers, Drake doled out special treats–maggots and caterpillars–to favoured ravens. In 1903, he had fed three of the birds with the grubs of the notorious 'worm unknown to science'–they hadn't shown ill-effects and, if rumour was to be believed, were still here at the Tower, having long outlived their contemporaries.

'I have *news*,' said Miss Device. 'It's why I hied myself here . . .'

'Not more *gossip*, Margery . . .'

'No, hard information. Marcus has been abducted from Harley Street.'

Dr Chambers was alarmed, and startled a raven with an over-generous spill.

'I had this from a sweet little fox-child who has lately been cruelly treated,' continued Miss Device. 'Don't fret so, Jenny. Your nursie man was only bopped over the head and rendered unconscious. The Sorcerer-snatcher didn't feel a need to make a point by stringing entrails around the room like Christmas deco-rations.'

'It has to be Conjurer,' Edwin said. 'He's tried once already.'

The Old Man looked doubtful. 'If Stone could get into the surgery, why not murder Rennes in his sleep without incurring the trouble and risk of spiriting him away? Are we certain it was Conjurer who attacked Sorcerer at the Tivoli?'

'If not Stone, who?' asked Catriona. A raven perched on her knuckle, cooing like a dove. The bird had taken a shine to her.

'Zenf?' suggested Edwin. 'He's kept us busy with runes and pick-pockets. It could have been a deliberate diversion as much as a show of strength.'

'Zenf is the Rat-Master,' said Catriona. 'Stone is his creature.'

'So it seems,' said the Old Man.

'Conjuring tricks,' said Wizard, with disdain. 'All look-here-at-my-waggling-fingers-while-I-stack-the-cards-under-the-table. Scarcely magic. Just an elevated form of *cheating*.'

'Don't mind, Conny,' said Miss Device. 'He's an old fusspot.'

Drake looked as if he was thinking about siccing his ravens on Witch.

Mr Esse stood by the fountain, like a scarecrow in mourning cast-offs. Ravens landed on him. One deposited white birdlime on his top hat.

'So, the Diogenes Club has *lost* two of the Ravens,' said the Undertaker, ignoring the birds. 'This was to be expected. Firmer protective measures should have been taken. Rennes should have been given over into our custody.'

Before Dr Chambers could protest, Beauregard spoke up for her. 'As you well know, anyone who can get past Simon Pure could certainly get into the Mausoleum.'

'It's not that hard to get *out* of,' said Geneviève, teasing a little.

Black fire burned behind Mr Esse's glasses. In daylight, with droppings on his hat and (now) shoulders, an Undertaker wasn't quite so fearsome. Or maybe it was because in this business, they weren't the most frightening players. In that race, the Undertaking would have a hard time placing. Zenf, the Rat, the Ravens, Spring-Heel'd Jack, the waxworks and Dr Chambers's brother (if he counted) were making all the running for the Top Three.

More ravens landed on the Undertaker, overcrowding his shoulders, spreading onto his arms.

'How many birds are there supposed to be?' Catriona asked Drake.

'Fewer,' said Wizard.

Edwin looked up. Black, mean eyes met his gaze. Many more black birds flocked around the vents.

'What's the difference between a raven and a crow?' he asked.

'Strictly speaking, very little,' said Drake. 'They're all *corvidae*. Ravens *are* crows. So are rooks.'

Birds flew in through the vents, and settled on the drinking fountain, the floor and in niches, crowding out the natural tenants with wing-shoves. Catriona protected her new friend from a pecking intruder.

'Ouch,' said Mr Esse. A red flap of skin hung on his bone-white cheek. The bird closest his face pecked him again, cracking the lens of his glasses. He shook his shoulders. The birds lifted off, flapped a little, then attacked him in concert.

Beauregard and Geneviève went to help the Undertaker. Edwin pulled out his revolver–useless, he instantly realised. He shielded Catriona with his body, pressing her against a wall.

He knew she was about to complain.

Then the general attack began.

XIX: 'PEST CONTROL'

MR ESSE ROLLED on the flagstones, trying to be rid of the pecking blackbirds. He opened his mouth, and a crow fastened a determined beak into his tongue. The Undertaker squawked, tears pouring from under his dark glasses, but the crow hung on grimly, wings battering his face.

Charles and Geneviève knelt, frantically picking birds off Mr Esse and batting the creatures away. Charles took hold of the crow which had the Undertaker's tongue in its razor-grip and, at first gingerly, pulled. Mr Esse managed a scream, as if a dentist had just drilled into a nerve. Charles tried squeezing the bird, hard. His wrist took a blow from a wing, which landed as heavily as a police truncheon, and he let go.

Geneviève grasped the raven with fingerpoints, and then extended talons through its feathers into the red meat. That killed it, and it let go of Mr Esse's ragged tongue. The Undertaker's head flopped back, his broken glasses lost. Charles clamped a hand over the open eyes, not wanting them in his mind for the rest of the year. The vampire girl had to remove the dead bird from her fingers, while slapping away its vengeful comrades.

'This isn't how I expected the Diogenes Club to deploy me in the Great Game of Good and Evil,' she said. 'Pest control!'

Charles felt the Undertaker's neck. No pulse. A big, filthy bird on his chest had pecked straight into his heart. Charles took his hand away from the cold face. In death Mr Esse's eyes were ordinary again.

The Raven-Cote was a blizzard of shrieking birds, sharp-beaked, barb-taloned, thick-winged. Charles had been pecked about the ears. Blood dribbled into his collar.

Margery whirled up some defensive spell, hiding inside a personal tornado, and ravens slammed into hard air currents that spun them away from her. Winthrop shielded Catriona, the back of his tuxedo in shreds. Jenny was under the fountain, hands over her eyes, coat up over the crown of her head. Connaught Drake, Keeper of the Ravens, showed concern for his original birds, stepping in to slap away any intruders who dared molest them.

Some vampires have, or are reputed to have, sway over night-beasts. Crows, at least by their plumage, were as night-associated as wolves or bats. Sadly, Geneviève wasn't of that bloodline.

Her face was torn open from cheek to jaw, to the bone. She pressed a hand to the wound. It closed and healed without a scar even before she had wiped the blood off. The same happened to scratches on her hands and neck. She at least had that useful trait.

Unlike him.

A crow nipped his already-bleeding ear, several times. He couldn't shake it.

Geneviève reached out to him, but the flock–a murder!–of crows was like a thick, thorny hedge between them. Charles felt more shallow stabs. He drew his sword and slashed, not quite at random–several bisected or beheaded birds fell. But his strained knee gave out, and he found himself sprawled over the Under-taker's limp corpse–more immediately pained by his leg and back than the harrying birds who could kill him. His mouth was full of foul, wet feathers.

A thump came on his chest. The heart-eater bird regarded him with malevolent, quick-blinking black eyes. Its claws hooked into his waistcoat, and its beak aimed at his starched shirt-front. He tried to raise his sword, but a thousand pecks at his hand made him lose his grip.

'Charles!' called Geneviève.

For one quick blink, the heart-eater had Zenf's eyes. Charles knew this killing blow was personal.

Then the crow's neck kinked, broken as if by an invisible whip, and its head hung sideways. Talons relaxed, and the heart-eater fell off his chest.

The other birds on him and Geneviève were suddenly less troublesome. He struggled to sit, ignoring his pains, intent on not being completely useless when she got to his side to help him.

What had happened to the heart-eater?

A niche in the Raven-Cote was entirely filled by Master Wuh, who held the great offensive weapon of generations of British boys, the home-made catapult–a stout forked stick, home-polished, with a length of supple black rubber between the tines. In an Indian hill station, more than sixty years ago, Charles had been a deadly expert with an identical contraption–as many curs, windows, bullies and an *ayah* knew to their cost. With a single pebble, the child had avenged Mr Esse and fulfilled his obligation to protect Charles's life–he doubted Mr Hay was finding Giles Gallant half as useful.

Margery's tornado grew to encompass the whole of the Raven-Cote, spiralling birds up and out through the vents, tearing them away from their intended prey. Her scarf unpicked by beaks, Geneviève's long hair lashed across his face, and she had to gather it up to keep it out of their eyes.

Edwin relaxed and let Catriona free. There were rents scratched in Edwin's overcoat, but he and Catriona were otherwise unharmed. A bird pulled out of Catriona's hand and she snatched it back. It was the bird that had taken a shine to her.

'Don't throw the baby out with the bath-water,' she told Margery Device.

Margery clucked at such ingratitude. She was enjoying her show of weather-witchery.

'Miss Kaye makes an important point,' said Charles. 'If you get rid of the original ravens, the Kingdom is in peril.'

'Oh, pish,' said Witch, in a pet. 'The Kingdom is *always* in peril.'

Nevertheless, Margery shut off the wind. Several birds fell dead. One splashed legs-up into the fountain. A few hardy ravens, mostly with bloody scratches, survived and were not cast out.

Jenny composed herself, opened her doctors' bag, and set about treating scratches. First, she examined Geneviève–whose criss-crossed face healed completely before the doctor could so much as dab at a cut. Unflapped by this miracle, she proceeded to Charles and took a look at his ear.

'Nasty,' she said, applying something that stung to the wound. 'But you won't need stitches.'

Catriona restored her raven to its prime perch.

'I say,' she exclaimed, 'where's the Wizard?'

XX: 'A DISAPPEARING ACT'

IF MR ESSE weren't too busy being dead, the Undertaker would doubtless have gloated over the Diogenes Club managing to lose another Raven.

Edwin looked around the Raven-Cote.

'Did anyone see . . . ?' he asked.

Heads shook. 'Someone was in my way,' said Catriona. 'Providing unasked-for-shielding, and practically crushing my poor Hugin.'

Her new special friend was named after one of Odin's attendant birds.

'Next time, I'll let your dressmaker suffer as much as my tailor,' he responded.

He picked his dinner jacket off in ragged strips. He was left with the sleeves, which had to be unpeeled. Catriona helped and tidied his hair while she was about it.

'He was just talking about conjuring tricks,' pointed out Geneviève. 'A distraction of birds, to cover a disappearing act.'

'You think he did this?' Edwin asked the vampire. 'Drake?'

Geneviève gave an unhelpful gallic shrug.

'Do you think something like this could be done to *him*?' asked Miss Device. 'If I can snap my fingers and see off the murdering murderer, with only my poor witch ways, then surely Wizard–the *Keeper* of the Ravens, who is *fabulously* gifted when it comes to our feathered friends–could have done better?'

Everyone tried not to look at the dead Undertaker.

'Colonel Zenf is arrogant enough to send birds,' said the Old Man, wincing as Dr Chambers fit a large sticking plaster around his gashed ear. 'He wants to best everyone at their own games.'

'I know this isn't going to be a popular observation,' began Catriona, 'but are we *sure* Robert Stone is the Rat?'

Everyone looked at her. Hugin squawked, indignant at the suggestion. She had to chuff neck-feathers to restore herself to the bird's affections.

'Someone had to say it,' she apologised.

Connaught Drake displaced more air by his absence than his presence–like an unnoticed linch-pin suddenly pulled. At least his ravens were still here. Without them, Edwin would have feared the Tower might tumble and drag the city down with it.

'You can never tell with Conny,' said Miss Device. 'He could have stepped into storyland, written a happy ending–with Zenf turned into a pig and fed to the Royal Family at Christmas–and be back in a trice muttering about the high price of seed and wondering why we're bothering his blessed birds . . .'

They waited just a few moments longer than a trice.

'Sorry,' said Miss Device. 'Wishful thinking. Bad habit. Still, wishing can make it so. Sometimes.'

Part of what Witch said made sense. Wizard could have stepped into the city's shadow. Storyland. Catriona had called it that, earlier. Mrs Parker–melted from his memory like ice in the sun–had lived there, and the original Spring-Heel'd Jack. The city's shadow was under attack, too, and Drake was its appointed guardian.

'Is it easy,' he asked. 'Stepping into storyland?'

Miss Device was surprised, more at the temerity of the question than its practicality.

Edwin did not miss the flash of pride in Charles Beauregard's eyes as he followed and approved his train of thought. That tiny nod meant more than any medal or honour.

'Not *easy*,' said Miss Device, 'but it's done often. More often by accident than design. Here, in the Keeper's Tower, there are portals and keys. You find others dotted about the city. The London Stone, if used properly. One of those "not for the use of the public" telephone box affairs, I'm told–though that comes and goes. A Highgate antiques shop called Temptations, Ltd. has a minor specialty in permanent doors. You can install them anywhere, and they'll always open into the same place. Some mirrors work like that, too. Always risky propositions, though. You never know what's behind a door before you open it. You know the parable of the Lady or the Tiger? It simplifies the situation. In storyland, you might find a tame tiger or a ravenous lady . . . no offence, Mademoiselle LaVampire . . . and sometimes there are hungry big cats behind both doors. No, I wouldn't recommend such an expedition to . . . and again, no offence intended . . . *amateurs*.'

Miss Device shook her head.

'It's settled, then,' said the Old Man, setting aside everything Witch had said, especially that patronising nonsense about *amateurs*. 'Margery opens a Door. Edwin goes after Wizard . . .'

'I'll want a change of clothes.'

'Huntstanton has anything you need in the car. I want to borrow Catriona for a few hours, to help me track down Colonel Zenf and, perhaps, one or other of our missing Ravens. If Geneviève would volunteer to accompany you, she might come in handy . . .'

The vampire girl gave Beauregard an ironic *vive-la-France* salute.

'Jenny,' the Old Man addressed Dr Chambers, 'thank you for your help. You'll want to get back to your surgery and see to Simon Pure. I'll have you chauffeured. It is always a pleasure to see you and I regret–again!–that the circumstances of our meeting should be so troublesome.'

Dr Chambers gave a tight little smile but was grateful to be excused.

Edwin and Geneviève looked at each other. Should he still be wary of the vampire? Charles Beauregard plainly trusted her.

'What should we do in this storyland?' Geneviève asked the Old Man.

'Find Drake and render him what assistance he needs, if he needs it. Then accompany him back here. *If* you judge him to be the King Rat, get him here as soon as possible using whatever means you can. I needn't say that you are stepping into a dangerous world and should exercise utmost caution for, as you know, you are also stepping *out* of a dangerous world. Both planes are in peril, and must be saved.'

'Will do, sir.'

'Good man, Winthrop,' said Beauregard.

XXI: 'A JUICY TID-BIT'

MARGERY DEVICE BUSIED herself finding Drake's Door. Winthrop was kitted out with a padded coat and other sundries, including the flying helmet that came with Dr Shade's motorcycle. Geneviève lingered, expectant.

Charles left them to it and sat in the back of the Bentley with Catriona.

'Among our little group, you're the best detective,' he said. 'Which of our Ravens do you think is a Rat?'

Catriona was surprised. She shouldn't have been. She was

good at finding things out and, more important, working things out. Charles often set her loose on businesses that came under the category of 'mystery'. Unlike the general run of amateur or professional sleuths, she wasn't just a thinking, puzzle-solving machine. She empathised with the people caught up in the conundrum, and sought justice more often than a solution. No wonder Sir Henry Merrivale went purple whenever she was around.

She angled her head in what he recognised as a thinking position.

'Something about this riddle has troubled me ever since Edwin set it out,' she said. 'It's too pat. Four Suspects. One Guilty Party. I mean, it's a bit Green Penguin . . .'

'Go on,' he said.

'You got this intelligence from Geneviève? She passed on the question–which? Not whether?'

'Mycroft trusted Geneviève.'

'So do I, for what it's worth. But . . .'

Catriona hesitated. Charles prompted.

'From my experience,' she said, 'you and I are in a minority. Edwin trusts you the way you trust Mycroft, so he has no trouble *accepting* Geneviève–though our first meeting was startling, to say the least. But the rest of the Ruling Cabal *must* be wary of her, if only because they desperately don't want to believe what she's told us. The same goes for the Undertaking, who can't be happy about her escape from the Mausoleum.'

Charles allowed that she was on the money.

'And–have you noticed?–this business of Rat among the Ravens has gone from a state secret whispered in hushed tones among a tiny circle to being general knowledge. Everyone we meet knows what we're up to and what we suspect. That includes all the Ravens, and a widening circle of our acquaintances. Dr Chambers wasn't surprised. I think she heard something from her brother. It's as if some *gossip* were spreading the word all over town . . .'

As if on cue, Margery Device popped up at the window and said, 'Did you miss me?'

Catriona bit her tongue.

'Are you flirting with Charles, young lady?' reproached Margery. 'He's old enough to be your grandpa. And aren't you walking out with that nice Mr Winthrop? Such a juicy tid-bit. No one will believe it.'

Catriona was momentarily horror-struck.

'A little joke,' said Margery, blithely. 'I've found Drake's Door. Opening's in a minute or so. Better get a move on. Portals can get shifty if left to themselves.'

Margery flitted off.

'So,' Charles asked Catriona, '*is* there a Rat among the Ravens?'

'I don't know, but this isn't just Zenf sowing suspicion in our camp. There are big brutes in this jungle, shaking the trees. Geneviève tells us we have *a* Rat, but I'm beginning to wonder—judging from the way the Ravens have acted in the last day or so–whether there's just the one?'

'Two Rats?' he said, thinking it over, chill seeping up his spine.

'Why not three? Or four?'

XXII: 'OUR MAN IN STORYLAND'

BEYOND DRAKE'S DOOR was a sea of white fog. Real London pea-soup was yellow-green and foul. The fog of Shadow London was more like thick mist, odourless but damp, arranged in artful drapes.

Edwin kick-walked the Night Flier through the Door. Geneviève sat on the pillion, hands on his shoulders, nails sharp but sheathed. He let the engine growl, but kept the motorcycle on a leash.

When they were through, the Door was gone.

He had never visited Drake's domain before. Shadow London had roughly the same geography as the real city, but famous or infamous buildings and streets were more solid, more defined, than lesser-known byways and districts, which blurred behind thicker curtains of fog.

'I didn't know it was so easy to come here,' said the vampire. 'Or I'd have considered moving. Sometimes, I'd feel happier as a story than a real person.'

'Our Witch makes the near-impossible seem easy, and she only kept open the door Drake made. Usually, there's a high cost to passing over. Jack the Ripper got here by committing five murders . . .'

'A ritual?'

'Not exactly. The point was to become part of the fabric of *story*. That he managed.'

'Who was he?'

'No one. That was his problem. He had a name once, and Mycroft at least knew it, but with his final murder, it was wiped out of our world completely. The files are blank. A pathetic, vicious little man became a legend. Even that was an exchange. This place got the Ripper, but Spring-Heel'd Jack crossed the other way. I ran into a fair simulacrum of that bounder last night. Leaping Jack began as a whisper and drunkards' tales, but took on substance when Bloody Jack joined the company of phantom fiends.'

They were still in the courtyard of the Tower of London. Ravens the size of condors nested on the battlements. A wailing sounded through the fog. A wide-skirted, child-sized figure slushed across cobbles towards them.

Edwin turned on a searchlight-bright head-lamp.

A screech came from a mouth located somewhere to the side of the figure's hip. A white, pinched, angry face shrivelled and a seven-fingered hand clapped over the eyes.

'It's Anne Boleyn,' Edwin exclaimed.

' "Wiv 'er 'ead tucked underneaf 'er arm",' Geneviève quoted. 'She waa-aa-alked the Bloody Tower!'

The butchered bride had seemed child-sized because her head wasn't on her shoulders. Blood wept from her neck-stump, staining her enormous ruff like some unknown species of chrysanthemum.

The poor spectre was no threat, and simply kept wailing as she shuffled out of the light. Other, bulkier figures walked through the fog–mostly dead traitors, he assumed, unrepentant or penitent, lugging severed noggins. They might well be in a mood to do some harm. One loose-limbed shadow tumbled and tinkled, whipping streamers of fog with each caper. It wore a belled, three-pronged hat and curly-toed shoes. It was Jack Point, the melancholy fool from *The Yeoman of the Guard*. A keening song shrilled through gloom, 'heigh-dee, heigh-dee, misery me, lack-a-day-dee . . .'

A rasping sounded, as of a giant, rusted chain unspooling. A portcullis was coming down. Back in the real world, the chains were oiled and Edwin had barely noticed the noise as the gates lowered. Here, the portcullis sounded as he imagined it would.

'Hold on tight,' he told Geneviève, gunning the bike.

Flame shot from the exhaust, which was alarming, and Edwin drove for the gate. He saw the sharpened spear-points of the portcullis, glinting as the Night Flier's beam fell on them.

There was not enough head-room, and it was diminishing by the second.

Trusting to Dr Shade's design, he leaned to the left with all his body, taking the bike and Geneviève with him. His sleeve scraped cobbles and the Night Flier rode on the edges of its tires. At an unnatural angle, they passed under the points and were out of the Tower a second before the portcullis-spears dug into the gravel.

He hauled the Night Flier upright, and the bike did what it was supposed to. He assumed counter-weights and gyroscopes and balances inside the works assisted stunts like this.

It was exhilarating, bombing through the fog–it was impossible to tell if it were day or night here–on the marvellous machine.

He shot a look back at Geneviève. Deep parallel scratches on her cheek sliced to the bone around her right eye, tearing her mouth away from glistening fang-teeth.

'The portcullith caught me,' she explained, slushing through her wound. The torn flesh reassembled and healed smoothly. There wasn't even blood, though she licked her lips as if there were. 'That's convenient. I seem to be different here.'

'Careful,' he cautioned. 'I'm told it's addictive.'

As the Night Flier throbbed, he knew he should take the warning himself.

'Where to?' she asked.

'Over Tower Bridge. We've got to liaise with Our Man in Storyland.'

'Who?'

'You'll see.'

Driving almost blind, he took the turn onto the bridge and cruised under the gothic arch of the North Tower. There was little other road traffic in Shadow London, though a man on a penny-farthing bicycle pedalled the other way across the bridge, lifting a tall hat as he passed.

'Can you hear that?' said Geneviève.

Tiny bells tinkled above. Jack Point had followed them. Edwin wondered whether the embittered jester–'a merryman moping mum, whose soul was sad and whose glance was glum, who sipped no sup and who craved no crumb as he sighed for the love of a lay-dee'–might not be the sort of malcontent easily swayed by the blandishments of the Great Enchanter. Where better to find a treasonable sort than behind Traitors' Gate?

Point had fellows with him–ghosts? traitors? storymen?–on the high-level walkways between the Towers. Back in reality, this section had been closed to the public since 1910. It once had a bad reputation as a haunt of cutpurses, petty thieves and harlots. Here, the bad elements still held that particular high ground.

Now, the road underneath the Night Flier was sloping upwards.

Jack Point was raising the bridge. He must have command over the hydraulic mechanisms that could lift the two hundred-foot, thousand-ton leaves to let shipping pass through.

The bike sped on, forward momentum overcoming the increasing tug of brute gravity.

Through the fog, Edwin saw the edge of the bridge-leaf. The masts of an old schooner, hung with rags, were passing slowly through the gap. Something gigantic thrashed in the waters, making vast eddies in the fog. A sucker-lined tentacle the size of Nelson's column scythed through the masts.

They had bigger things to worry about than a treacherous jester.

The bike slowed as it neared the lip of the bridge. The drag increased as the incline bested forty-five degrees. At maximum elevation, the leaves saluted each other at eighty-three degrees.

'We're too heavy,' said Geneviève, pressing cold lips to his ear. She let go and her weight was whipped from his back.

The Night Flier surged forward, cresting the lip of the bridge-leaf. On instinct, Edwin pressed two red buttons and more flame burst from the exhaust.

Below, a ship was crushed in the thrashing coils of a leviathan, sailors dragged towards a many-toothed beak. A huge, salty eye swivelled as Edwin rocketed across the gap between the two leaves of Tower Bridge.

He didn't have time to mourn Geneviève.

The front wheel landed on the near-vertical incline of the Southern bridge-leaf, and he pulled the bike around. It skidded down on its side, wheel-rims striking showers of sparks. Edwin tucked in his knee. The bike was designed to allow such a manoeuvre–his leg neatly fit into a groove in the metal carapace, and his trousers weren't even singed.

At the Southwark end of the bridge, the bike landed with a thump, but kept upright.

He really must write a note of thanks to the Norton Company!

What about the vampire woman? He would have to explain to the Old Man that he had lost her.

He stalled the Night Flier under the arch of the South Tower and looked up.

The bridge-leaves were lowering now. Something hung from the upper walkway.

Laughing, shrieking figures–cutpurses, petty thieves, harlots?–swarmed towards Geneviève, who dangled upside-down like a bat, knees crooked over a cable, hair streaming. Hands reached down and scrabbled at her legs, trying to dislodge her from her perch. Down below, the leviathan still hungered. Maybe only a stake through the heart or a silver bullet in the brain could *kill* a vampire, but Edwin had a notion that being diced by the beak of a monstrous imaginary cephalopod and soaked in its digestive juices might at least severely inconvenience the woman.

From the Night Flier's saddle-bag, he took a bulky, black-painted Verey pistol and shot up a flare. The result wasn't what he expected, which is what he got for using borrowed gear. A purple cloud burst above the bridge, casting a sickly violet glow and forming a shape like a black skull wearing goggles. The gimmick was supposed to terrify those who dared defy Dr Shade. It did the trick on Geneviève's persecutors, who properly cringed and left her alone.

No, only the lesser shadows were seen off. The crooked, bell-tagged Jack Point clung like a gecko to the bridgeworks, spidering under the walkway, teeth bared in his clown grin, working inexorably towards Geneviève Dieudonné.

Edwin drew his Webley and tried to sight on the jester. Jack Point zig-zagged, to avoid being a target or because it was the only way it could move. With a rifle, Edwin might have made the shot. With a pistol, he could as easily shoot Geneviève–and he was loaded with silver.

Gracefully, the vampire swung herself off the cable as if leaping from the trapeze. Jack Point made an ill-judged grab for her and lost his grip. He plunged through the fog, bouncing and breaking against the guardrail, then sailed, limp, into the thick surface-mists of Shadow Thames. Edwin hoped that was the end of the fool.

Geneviève hung in the air, not clinging to anything.

Edwin was astonished.

She held out her arms and drifted towards him, smiling broadly, enjoying herself too much.

The air was different here.

Dr Shade's giant skull illusion laughed—the Devil knew how that trick was worked!—and evaporated.

Edwin caught Geneviève as if she were his partner in an acrobatic act and set her down.

'Can we do that again?' she asked, breathless. '*C'est incroyable!* Here, I think I can do all the things they say vampires can do . . .'

She held up her hand and turned it to mist. The effect spread quickly up her arm, and the shape threatened to drift in the breeze. She had to concentrate to make herself solid again.

'*That* I didn't enjoy,' she said.

'Focus, Mademoiselle,' he said. 'Remember what I said. It's dangerous here. You can end up as one of the stories. Trapped in one. Like Anne Boleyn, trudging around with her head because it's expected. Or Peter Pan. He lives here, too.'

She snapped her fingers and sobered up.

They got back on the Night Flier and drove cautiously through almost-familiar streets. It was a mistake to assume the topography here was exactly what they knew. Shadows lingered long after buildings fell.

They arrived at the building the Old Man had told him to find.

'There's something I never thought to see again,' said Geneviève. Edwin felt her shudder before she hopped off the pillion. 'It's the Clink.'

'Burned down in the Gordon Riots of 1780. London's most

notorious gaol, used for the detention of heretics from the 12th Century, then for the rabble and riff-raff of Southwark. It lingers here because its name is still used as a slang term.'

He got off the Night Flier and propped it up against a horse-trough. He unstrapped his flying helmet. His body still thrummed from the ride.

'I wonder if my cell is still here,' said the vampire. 'I scratched my name on the stone.'

He looked at her as anyone looks at someone who's just admitted to serving a term in prison.

'What were you in for?' he asked.

'Not what you're thinking,' she said, turning with a shy smile. 'No blood-drinking involved. It was *debt*. Twelve shillings, owed to an apothecary. I go by the rules, too. Fifty years of needlework, paying off all those pennies. And the interest. I wasn't so accomplished an escape artist back then. And the other prisoners needed me.'

'For what?'

'Doctoring. It's what I've done, mostly. My father before me. I've a couple of medical degrees, taken centuries apart. I knew about blood-types before Jansky and Moss.'

Edwin was surprised. He hadn't considered vampires might need careers.

'Where's your mysterious contact?' she asked. 'I hope it's not one of those dreary English Jesuits who were clapped up here. Or, worse, a gaoler. The turnkeys were bigger bloodsuckers than me.'

'Our fellow should be *outside* the Clink.'

There, on a bench, sat the Man. A neatly-dressed, nondescript personage in an 18th Century coat and hat, half-leaning on a stick.

'Ho there,' he called. 'Who approaches?'

'A friend,' said Edwin. 'From the Diogenes Club.'

'I've been expecting ye,' said the Man. 'The Wizard came by earlier. There've been wild rumours. Signs and wonders. Imps and sports. A two-headed calf born in Clerkenwell. Tommy Atkins tells me he's orders to muster in. That's never good news.'

'Geneviève, this is the Ticket-of-Leave Man,' said Edwin.

'Delighted to make your acquaintance,' said the Man, doffing his hat to show a ringlet-fringed bald pate.

'He runs straight now,' Edwin explained, 'but still knows everything that happens in this city, straight or crooked.'

The Man smiled, sadly. At one time, he was a familiar London character: a convict, not exactly released, but trusted enough to be at large; indeed, in such a precarious position, he could be reckoned the most trustworthy man in the city, for he had most to lose from the slightest step off the path. A sentence in the Clink was not something anyone would wish to resume.

'As a lad, I fell among bad companions,' the Man confessed. 'I chased after the baubles of the wicked world. But I have now repented of that, and serve only the Crown and the cause of Justice.'

The Man set his hat back on his head, which now boasted flowing, grey-gold locks. His nose was longer, with a twist to the side. Now, he had whiskers swarming up his cheeks; now, he was shaven clean. Beauregard had told Edwin about this, but seeing it was another matter. This wasn't any particular Ticket-of-Leave Man, but *all* of them–whether transported to the colonies or lately freed from Clink. There had been a popular melodrama titled *The Ticket-of-Leave Man,* in which the central figure was a put-upon innocent conspired against by a hypocritical villain. This had transformed the Ticket-of-Leave Man in the popular imagination, taking away an edge of possible menace and setting in stone the notion of a redeemed soul doing his best to make up for past wrongs.

Many citizens of Shadow London were like this–composites of types, rather than individuals. The incarnation of many, many stories, ballads, smoking room jokes, bedtime yarns or fondly-held rumours. The Wretched Child Chimney Sweep, the Friendly Bobby on the Beat, the Soho Tart with a Heart, Burlington Bertie from

Bow, the Roaring Toff, the Fathead Farmer Lately from the Country (and Ripe to be Rooked), the Mother Ruined by Gin, the Sailor with Six Months' Pay in His Pocket, the Unscrupulous Anatomist, the Irish Labourers Pat and Mike, and other types, archetypes or caricatures.

'Things have not been right round these parts,' confided the Man, talking like a melodrama. 'We have had a Visitor, unwelcome by most, but a dangerous friend to some. You know who I mean?'

Edwin could guess. So, he was sure, could Geneviève.

He saw another layer to the Great Enchanter's gambit with the runes. To keep Connaught Drake busy while he was trespassing in Wizard's realm. Zenf could evidently gain easy access to Shadow London. Edwin wouldn't put it past the Great Enchanter to manage in an evening as many murders as Jack the Ripper in a long, busy autumn, though he suspected Zenf could conjure up a Door by other means.

'The Visitor has made allies. Unfortunates, mostly. The unrepentant.'

'We met one at the Tower,' said Geneviève. 'A clown.'

The Man shivered. 'Never could abide clowns,' he admitted. 'Don't see why they're supposed to be funny. Grimaldi's all right, mind. More a weeper than a mocker.'

'What about the Wizard?' asked Edwin. 'Connaught Drake?'

'He's here,' said the Man. 'North of the river. In the City. I've a whisper from a certain Woman of Pleasure that Wizard comes to parlay with the Visitor. He has already offered a sacrifice . . .'

Nosey Parker's Mum.

'There's great uncertainty in the city,' continued the Man.

Edwin didn't like the sound of 'parlay'. Surely, Drake *couldn't* be the King Rat? If Wizard were in league with Zenf, the war would be over.

'Do you know exactly where Drake is?'

The Ticket-of-Leave Man nodded, and said 'Thomas Farriner's Bakery.'

Geneviève rolled up her eyes and groaned, 'not again.'

It took Edwin a moment to make the connection.

To the north of the Clink was the river, and beyond that the City of London. London Bridge was nearby, the ramshackle span that fell down in the rhyme, and beyond that was a bank of pink-tinged fog, as if a giant sun were rising. Shouts and alarums came through the fog, and red-orange plumes darted.

Farriner's Bakery was in Pudding Lane. It was where the Great Fire of London started.

The cries carried over the water, 'City on fire! City on fire!'

'Drake's sold us out,' said Edwin, despair thumping in his chest. 'He's burning the city's shadow.'

'What'll that do to the real London?' Geneviève asked.

'Turn it to ashes and cinders,' said Edwin, '*ashes and cinders*.'

XXIII: 'ABRACADABRA!'

THE QUIET ROOM was anything but.

General Lord Hector Tarr argued the toss with Mr Hay. The alliance of the Diogenes Club and the Undertaking was strained near to breaking.

Charles called 'order'. During the Great War, he'd listened to too much squabbling in operations rooms while ranks of brave men were mowed down in the field. Tarr and Hay were momentarily cowed.

Reports came in from all over London, especially from the area of the Old City. Buildings had collasped. Ghosts that walked to a regular schedule failed to appear. Every psychic, swami, seer, fortune-teller, spiritualist medium, prophet, visionary and palmist in the city was struck with raving horrors. At Colney Hatch Asylum and the Purfleet sanatorium, the insane were rioting. Sewer workers and a museum night watchman were missing. A spate of 'tong suicides' had broken out in Limehouse. A backbench MP had spontaneously combusted during a debate on dog licencing;

Special Branch and Military Intelligence were scurrying down blind alleys looking for bomb-tossing, black-bearded anarchists. This, Charles assumed, was overspill from what was happening in the Shadow City.

He looked up at Mycroft's portrait. As usual, he saw something in the eyes, a secret held back. How would the Great Man have handled this?

Catriona rattled the telephone, cut off in mid-call, and tried to get connected again. Charles had her following leads on Rennes and Stone, the missing Ravens. He needed everyone else to cope with small fires and do their best to limit the damage, but it could be that her job was the most important.

Earlier, it had seemed certain Robert Edmond Stone was the Rat. Now the question was open again. Catriona had suggested there might be more than one bad apple in the barrel.

If the Ravens, the city's protectors, stood with Zenf, could they be bested?

Catriona hung up, after another call.

'Simon Pure's recovered from his knock on the head,' she said, 'but has no idea who or what hit him. Dr Chambers is still somewhat short-tempered, and her practice is overwhelmed. A stream of minor casualties has flowed into her surgery. She wonders if we could spare any specialists, but they're all working flat out as it is. Margery got hold of Dr Silence, and he's on his way. I don't suppose it matters whether he sets up shop here or in Harley Street. Harry Dickson promises to get the boat train. The others on the reserve list are casualties, I'm afraid. All our sensitives are screaming. Morris Klaw complains of nightmares. Taverner, Chard and Scarfe are *hors de combat.*'

Charles didn't like relying on the reserves anyway–most were dilettantes and cranks, though he'd be glad of John Silence's help. Jenny Chambers could do with another 'physician extraordinary' on site.

'There is *some* good news,' said Catriona, bitterly. 'The blessed Sir Henry sends his excuses. Apparently, a mystery death in Rutland intrigues H.M. more than the fall of the kingdom. Such a comfort that a few still value the high art of detection above passing expediencies.'

'Anything from Margery?' Charles asked.

'She has her ear out for word on Rennes and Stone,' Catriona continued. 'No luck yet. She hears everything, normally. We have to assume Zenf is deliberately drowning out the usual background chatter. There is currently no echo in the Whispering Gallery of St Paul's. And the Town Crier tried to poison himself with some noxious stuff that burned out his vocal cords.'

'The Ravens must still be in London.'

'Or else things would be worse? I agree. I have a splitting headache, by the way, but I'm putting that down to being awake for thirty-six hours without having eaten.'

Charles realised how tired he was. And hungry.

'I thought so,' said Catriona, diagnosing his condition at a glance. 'I'll send your chimney-sweep down to the kitchens, and have sandwiches and tea sent up. I'm sure even the Undertakers need regular meals.'

Catriona scribbled a note and gave it to Master Wuh, who scuttled off.

As the young Undertaker left the Quiet Room, noise leaked in—a commotion from the supposedly hallowed, silent precincts. Where a rustled newspaper was cause for expulsion and a post-prandial burp once led to a duel with pistols, there was now un-holy commotion, with raised voices and a sound horribly like rattled sabres.

The commotion made its way into the Quiet Room.

A gnarly-faced gent in evening dress, complete with silk-lined cape and opera hat, stood there, supporting an identically-dressed, insensible fellow whose throat was bandaged.

'Alakazam,' announced the Great Edmondo, tossing Marcus Rennes into the room. He held up empty, white-gloved hands, showing that there was nothing up his sleeves. 'Abracadabra!'

Choking red smoke filled the room.

XXIV: 'FETCH THE ENGINES'

As THE NIGHT Flier crossed London Bridge, the whole structure shook. They had to drive between the tall, rickety, mediaeval houses that edged the span, encroaching aggressively on the public right of way. The buildings shook like jelly on a platter. Some collapsed backwards into the river, their fronts floating a moment, doors and windows popped open, before sinking into the Thames.

This was the proverbial London Bridge, the one which was *falling down, falling down.*

A zig-zag crack appeared in the road, showing foaming waters beneath. Edwin jumped the motorbike over the gap, playing hopscotch with the abyss. Geneviève held on tight.

The air was filled with tumult and clanking as iron and steel bent and bowed, wood and clay washed away. Thieves stripped silver and gold from vital support structures. Vikings ravaged the houses–the rhyme dated back to the destruction of a London Bridge by Danes, Edwin remembered–and a long-dressed, white-robed 'fair lady' was dragged by a mob towards an open tomb on the North Embankment.

'Build it up with stone so strong,' Geneviève quoted the nursery rhyme, 'stone so strong will last so long . . .'

Once they were off the bridge and in the City, fog turned to smoke. Giant towers of flame roared. Many fire-fighters were busy, big red engines with shiny brass trim and human chains of suddenly homeless folk with buckets. A cadre of dancing fanatics threw themselves into the fires.

It was another rhyme, 'London's Burning, London's Burning'.

'Fire fire, fire fire,' quoted Geneviève, 'fetch the engines, fetch the engines, pour on water, pour on water . . .'

Through great black ropes of smoke, Edwin saw long-destroyed buildings burning again. This wasn't just the Great Fire of 1666, but all of London's fires, past, present, future, historical, legendary and imaginary. Guy Fawkes wriggled atop a burning pyramid stuffed with casks of gunpowder. Along the river, his once-thwarted scheme paid off as the Houses of Parliament exploded in a great, thunderous puff of flame as if a sleeping dragon had belched in its cellars. Obese Zeppelins and vulture-like Gotha bombers soared overhead, dropping incendiary bombs stamped with black eagles as presents from the Kaiser. One of the Martian War Machines from Wells's book waded three-legged through the silt of a dried-up stretch of the river, heat ray ranging against the stock exchanges, law courts and rookeries of Old London. Maddened lamp-lighters, faces clown-like from savage smears of soot and blood, ran from home to home, touching firebrands to dry wood, babies' bedding, curtains, and pots of oil. Cathedral after cathedral fell as if dismissed by an ungrateful or aggrieved deity, spires collapsing upon praying crowds, vast stones raining on the grounds, the honoured dead rudely thrust out of their tombs.

Edwin heard again the big guns of the Somme. For a moment, Dr Shade's Norton was his old Camel. He ached to take to the skies and tear through the whale-hide of a Zeppelin.

Instead, he drove into the heart of the inferno.

Dangerous paths threaded through the burning district. Geneviève patted out flames before they could take hold on their sleeves. Grime built up on his goggles, which Geneviève wiped with her handkerchief. Did vampires have ordinary use for hankies? A watch-tower collapsed behind them, barring the road. Up ahead was Pudding Lane, where the fire started, where Connaught Drake was. The Keeper of the Ravens in league with the Great Enchanter. From now on, if there was a 'from now on', Drake would be known as the Great Traitor.

They halted at a burning traffic light, waiting for curtains of flame to die down so they could pass.

'What are we expected to *do*?' shouted Geneviève.

'Find Drake. Stop him. Take him back. Save the city.'

'Fair enough. How?'

'I'm sure we'll think of something. Ready?'

'As I'll ever be, *mon brave.*'

The fire ahead burned *green,* which he took as a signal to go . . .

The Night Flier shot forward, punching a hole through flame, into an oasis of calm within the city-wide holocaust.

At first, he thought this was an eye of the hurricane, an untouched clearing . . . then he saw the black buildings. They were charcoal and ash constructions, barely holding the ghost of their former shape. Ash-coated Londoners lay on black cobbles, curled into Pompeii-mummy foetal shapes. Other blasted skeletons, coated with black rags of meat, were Medusa-struck, staring statues.

Connaught Drake sat on a bench outside Thomas Farriner's Bakery, nibbling a currant bun.

'Hello, Winthrop, mademoiselle,' he said, genially. 'Either of you care for one of these? I saved a tray from the flames. Much better than Mrs Lovett's meat pies.'

Wizard indicated a plate on the bench, piled with sweet-smelling, fresh-baked London Buns.

Fire-shapes, phoenix-shadows of Drake's ravens, hopped about. One alighted on the Keeper's shoulder without burning his tweed. He fed it crumbs.

Edwin took off his flying helmet. He drew and pointed his Webley, declaring 'Connaught Drake, I arrest you in the name of the law . . .'

Wizard chuckled. Edwin had expected as much. Was there a glint of malevolence in the man's mild eye?

'Dear boy, you've grasped the wrong end of the stick.'

Geneviève stood at Edwin's shoulder, showing her best fang-face and talons.

'Didn't your mother ever tell you not to pull faces, young lady? You know what'll happen if the wind changes.'

A breeze riffled through Pudding Lane. Charcoal corpses crumbled. Shops and houses fell to pieces.

Geneviève wisely pulled her teeth and claws.

'That's better,' said Drake.

'You burned the city,' Edwin accused.

Drake waved the observation away. 'The city is *always* being burned. It *needs* to be burned, just as the bridge needs to fall down. Fire is one of the great forces of London. Once, fire ended plague, cleared the way for . . . well, the rather overrated St Paul's, but that's by the by. Heed these words: London Can Take It. You'll hear them again, when the air-raid sirens shriek. Indeed, London Must Take It. Taking it is what London is *for*.'

Edwin lowered his gun. What did Drake mean?

'Pay attention, Winthrop. We are close to the final working of a clever trick. Better than any of Robbie Stone's, I assure you–though he has helped in a minor sort of way. We've all had our parts to play, including you two. Just now, you need to do what Beauregard told you to . . . render me any assistance.'

Fires were dying all around. A parade was coming–rescuers or an invading army? Edwin heard the stamp of marching feet, and cocked his gun. At the head of the parade was a giant nag, which clumped through the embers on huge hooves. On its back sat an imposing figure in a big hat.

'Just the fellow we need,' said Drake. 'Have you met Colonel Zenf?'

The horseman rode into the light, followed by a rabble of Vikings, French infantry, Roman legionaries, ragged cavaliers, fire-spreaders, shaggy Anglo-Saxons, Martian squid-vampires, rowdies from the country and Prussian Uhlans. The Great Enchanter was dwarfish and pot-bellied, gussied up in a too-large uniform with gold epaulettes and a sash. Attached to his sideways-worn hat was a domino mask and a huge, crooked, cardboard nose.

At first, Edwin thought Zenf was dressed as Napoleon . . . then, he saw this sham did not represent the historical Buonaparte, but a caricature of the Little Corporal. This was the dreaded *Boney*–a recurring threat, any foreign commander who might boast that his armies would swarm across the Channel, sail up the Thames and put London to the sword.

'Boney was a warrior, way-ay-aye,' he breathed.

'Boney was a warrior, Jean François,' Geneviève completed.

Zenf took off his mask and hat. He looked inordinately pleased with himself. He was waiting to accept a pre-arranged surrender.

Edwin thought he could manage a single shot before the mob got to him. Who best to take out? Drake or Zenf?

'A "very clever trick", you say,' Edwin accused, aiming his Webley. 'Can you manage a bullet-catch?'

'A volunteer from the audience,' Drake told Zenf. 'As for the bullet business, I think that might best be left to my, ah, *lovely assistant.*'

A swift pinch came at Edwin's wrist, paralysing his arm. He dropped his gun.

In a whirl, he was held by cold, strong, fast arms and forced painfully down on his knees. A mouth close to his ear exhaled numbing iciness.

'Sorry,' whispered Geneviève.

He hadn't seen *that* trick coming.

XXV: 'THE WORST POSSIBLE OUTCOME'

WHEN THE SMOKE cleared, Conjurer was on the floor, arms wrestled behind his back and bound with his own cloak. Master Wuh sat on the Great Edmondo.

'Get this incubus off me,' snarled Robert Stone. 'I'm not your Rat.'

'You are the *attack* magician,' said Charles. 'You must expect us to put up a defence.'

'I am addicted to dramatic entrances,' muttered the magician. 'Do I deserve a broken back for it?'

Catriona examined Marcus Rennes. He was unconscious. Slapping didn't wake him up.

'It's not Sorcerer, either,' insisted Stone. 'I had to whip him out the back door of Chambers's clinic while Zenf's creatures were knocking at the front. Good man, that nurse. Stood his ground like Archaeopteryx at the Bridge . . .'

'I don't think that's the name,' said Giles Gallant. 'If I remember my Classics . . .'

'B——r your Classics!' said Stone. 'Let me up.'

Charles nodded, and Master Wuh got off his back, then helped him upright–without untying him.

'I do this for a living, you know,' said the Great Edmondo, shrugging free of his makeshift bonds with a flourish. He tried to bring up his hands and found they were still cuffed. Piqued, he shrugged again, and gave the handcuffs to the young Undertaker only to see his wrist now shackled to the boy's. 'This is most irritating and unnecessary,' he said, disappearing the cuffs and pulling coins out of Master Wuh's ears, then dropping them as if they were filthy.

'I've been playing hide-and-seek with Sweeney Todd and Charlie Peace,' said Conjurer, 'all the way from Harley Street to here. They're both broken now. They weren't wax, by the way. Just wearing wax masks of themselves. They were borrowed from Drake's place, the Shadow City.'

'So it's Wizard after all,' said Charles. 'The worst possible outcome.'

'On some level, I ought to be offended,' said Stone. 'Rennes, too, if he were awake. Both of us could do a great deal of damage if so inclined. Far more than that fathead Drake. However, I don't think you have anything to worry about from that direction. Or Margery. It's none of us. You should have checked your sources.'

'The leech!' shouted Mr Hay.

'I knew it,' said Tarr.

The two looked at each other, astonished that they agreed on something, then gabbled at once.

'That vampire bitch is in it with Zenf,' said Gallant.

Charles caught a fleeting, instantly suppressed sympathy

from Catriona. He felt a chill, a sadness he could not express. It was so *disappointing* ...

'I have your attention now,' said Stone. 'This is how magic works. Stage magic, anyway. You were looking in the wrong place. But, just this once, I *have* something up my sleeve ... another trick, a trick within a trick, as it were.'

From his sleeve, Stone produced an envelope, which he gave to Charles.

'This was given me when I joined the Ravens,' he said. 'Note the three seals. The red raven is Drake's. The white dove is Stirk's. He was Conjurer before me. Slippery b——d, he was. Could get out of anything. The other one you'll know.'

Charles saw the initials 'M. H.'

'What's it say, man?' prompted Tarr, impatient.

Charles read the legend aloud, 'The Stratagem of King Raven in Rat's Fur, With Notes Upon the Segregation of a Great Enchanter.'

Catriona clapped her forehead, seeing it at once. 'It's all been a lure–a worm on a hook! That clever, monstrous, fat old man! Dead for fifteen years, and still pulling all the strings.'

Charles looked up at the portrait, remembering what it was like to work for Mycroft Holmes, not to see what was intended until the last moment.

He still didn't know what game Geneviève was playing.

XXVI: 'NOT THE USUAL ARRANGEMENT'

STAY DOWN, EDWIN,' said the vampire, sadly. 'Let the grown-ups talk.'

He wasn't sure why he was still alive. Geneviève could have opened his throat with a kiss and bled him like human veal. Maybe in the Shadow City, killing wasn't liable to take. He wouldn't rise as *nosferatu*–for that you had to exchange blood with a vampire, drink from their veins as they drank from yours–but he might find himself playing this scene over and over, one of the minor stories attendant upon the Fall of London. The Betrayed Knight, or the Blockhead of Bloomsbury. Old St Paul's burned twice nightly with matinees Wednesdays and Saturdays. And don't forget Edwin Winthrop, starring in *Backstabbed by a Blood-sucking Biddy*.

'Don't struggle,' she said. 'It'll be all right. Trust me.'

'Trusting you hasn't worked well so far.'

Colonel Zenf was enjoying his moment. He looked about the blackened, after-fire skeleton of Pudding Lane. He poked a wall, and an entire row of bakers' shops crumbled silently, resolved to ash and cinders.

'Amusing,' he observed. 'Just the lightest touch of my finger, and ... *pouf*! A fortress of blanc-mange, scarcely worth the conquering. And yet, what a magnificent achievement. The greatest city of the world in flames, at my feet. I am humbled with delight, and quite giddy at the prospect of what to do next ...'

Connaught Drake indulged the Great Enchanter. Edwin couldn't imagine what Wizard was thinking. What could Drake possibly *want*?

'I assume you have some symbol of surrender,' said Zenf. 'A key to the city?'

Wizard shrugged.

'Of course, this is but a shadow, but when one holds the shadow, the real thing must follow.'

'That's not the usual arrangement,' said Drake, dryly.

Zenf chortled. 'I suppose not. But we are *unusual* persons.'

'Not that unusual, old thing.'

A crack appeared in Zenf's preening.

Geneviève's grip relaxed, deliberately. 'Be ready,' she whispered in his ear. 'There's everything to play for.'

Edwin could have reached for his dropped pistol. But he was interested now. How would this play out?

Like Edwin, Zenf had got it the wrong way round. When Shadow London burned, it was not weaker, but stronger.

'Feh,' said the Colonel to Drake. 'I was going to kill you, anyway.'

The Great Enchanter reached into his coat.

'Now,' said Geneviève, letting Edwin free.

They leaped on Zenf, securing his arms. A contraption like a sextant, covered in runic writing, fell from his grasp. The Great Enchanter struggled against them, but they held on fast.

Edwin took an elbow in the face, but sank a knee into a paunch. Geneviève raked nails across Zenf's piggy cheek.

Drake began to laugh, and the Wizard War was over.

Zenf took a few moments to catch up. His pomp leaked away, leaving a prissy, absurd little man in a comic opera uniform. Edwin and Geneviève held him between them.

The Great Enchanter looked about for his invading army.

In the shadows stood redcoats with muskets, knights in armour, tommies in tin hats, roundheads and cavaliers shoulder to shoulder, bloods and blades, pearly kings and queens, costers, tarts, loafers, brawlers, football fanatics with scarves and rattles, the *haut ton* and the *demi-monde*, air-raid wardens, firemen, peelers, bobbies, Bow Street Runners, Chelsea pensioners, dandies, strollers and–yes!–Dick Whittington's Cat. The unconquered and, indeed, *unconquerable* of London.

'A word about tactics, old chap,' Drake said, mildly. 'Upon walking into the enemy's camp to accept surrender, make sure it's actually on offer.'

'But you're . . .'

'A Rat? Perhaps.'

'It was *revealed*. A Rat among the Ravens.'

'A Rat to whom? A turncoat and betrayer, of course. Tell me, Colonel, don't *you* feel betrayed?'

Zenf shook his head. He still didn't see how he'd been gulled.

Edwin still hadn't completely caught up, but a picture was beginning to form. How much of this had Geneviève known?

A Pearly Queen–*the* Pearly Queen–emerged from the crowd,

a thousand luminous teardrops studding her padded jacket, flat cap and long skirts. It was Margery Device.

'Did you get *a little whisper,* Colonel? You should never trust gossip.'

Darkness rose in Zenf's face. Crimson fury stood out on his forehead. He made fists. He raised shadows from the ground. He was still the Great Enchanter, and could summon an army of fiends. Edwin remembered the waxwork horrors . . . the things that had come after the rune-bearers . . . the flock of pecking birds . . . the clowns of Shadow Tower . . . the worse things that waited.

An ogre loomed over Drake, one of Zenf's 'frightful fiends'. At his touch, it fell to ashes like the shops Zenf had puffed away.

'Not here, old fellow,' said Wizard. 'Sorry.'

'This is our city,' said Witch. 'And you are a prisoner. You came for the key, and all we have for you are chains . . .'

Zenf was done.

'Well played, Mr Winthrop, Mademoiselle Dieudonné,' Miss Device said to them. 'This couldn't have been done without you.'

Edwin burned, a little. A pat on the back seemed slightly insufficient.

'Cheer up,' said Geneviève. 'We've won.'

Edwin looked at the smoking ruins.

'You're right,' said Wizard. 'It is a mess. But that can be fixed.'

Drake gestured, in distinctly Wizardy fashion, summoning great and powerful forces. In the wake of fire came rebirth. New shops sprung from rubble, a cathedral rose, stones rearranged into fresh edifices. Streets ran straight or crooked, cobbled or tarred. And the river flowed fast and deep, a bloodstream through the heart of the city.

Wizard experimentally touched a petrified fire victim, a lad with a tray of pies. He came to life, crying 'fresh from the oven', hawking his wares. The lad was at the centre of a crowd, spreading the effect. It was like a vivid colour wash over a pencil sketch, turning shrivelled corpses to lively Londoners, fresh from the oven, hale and hearty, hustling and bustling.

Edwin's mouth hung open. Geneviève popped a slice of plum pie into it.

Suddenly, even ashes tasted sweet.

XXVII: 'FRUSTRATE THEIR KNAVISH TRICKS'

CHARLES,' BEGAN THE letter, 'you must steer the Diogenes Club into this new age. Wars will be waged on a scale scarcely imaginable. The coming conflicts between Britain and her allies and Greater Germany can not be averted. It will be the business of the whole world, fought in the open, on battlefields, in the air and on the seas. I hope you come through these particular fires, though at my age–and, frankly, at my weight–it seems certain I shall not.

'However, these "world wars" do not most concern me. As I write, the dreadful business of Persano's Worm has just been concluded. We came closer to ruin than I allowed anyone to know. The purpose of the Stratagem I have set in motion is to prevent a recurrence of such peril. Isadora Persano's wits are fled, and with them his status as Great Enchanter. Others yet unknown or unborn will assume that mantle. We can do nothing to prevent the rise of such person or persons, but we can take steps to cope with them, to–as our National Anthem has it–'confound their politics, frustrate their knavish tricks'.

'I have conferred with Rennes, the Greenwich Sorcerer. The augurs suggest a time of danger some twenty-five to thirty years hence. An Enchanter will make his debut, and the forces at his command will be more potent, aggressive and malevolent than at any time in history. Fat ticks bloated on the human misery poured out on the battlefields of Europe will swarm to his cause. Our enemies–human and otherwise–may have their Napoleon, their Bismarck, their Arthur. If this prodigy of wickedness–a successor of Mary Braxton, Isadora Persano and Leo Dare–manages a coup early in his tenure, there will be dire consequences.

'So, in consultation with the Ravens, I intend to nip that man's career in the bud. An agent, at present unknown to you, will–when certain conditions have been fulfilled–allow a rumour to spread. I regret the necessity for deception, but for the Stratagem to succeed, *you must yourself believe this rumour*–which is why this is to be delivered only after an outcome has been achieved. I know you will take actions to oppose the Great Enchanter, by launching a hunt for the Rat Among the Ravens. Our enemy–as yet unknown, and perhaps unmade!–is to be convinced that an opportunity has arisen for him to make a great pre-emptive strike against us. It is my intention that instead he will deliver himself into our hands.

'With the Great Enchanter off the board, dangers will remain– the city may still burn, again–but I am satisfied greater calamities will be prevented. If our enemy survives the affair, use can be made of him. As long as he is alive and in his right mind, *no other can rise to take his place.* Interrogation of Persano has yielded little, but it is my hope our next Great Enchanter can be taken in his right wits, then *turned* to our ends, tapped for what he will know.

'It is a matter of regret to me that I have had to keep you and my other agent apart, for your abilities and temperaments are a perfect complement. It has always been my intention that you and she should *together* carry on the work I have begun.

'Other details of the Stratagem, and the parties who will inevitably be involved, are enclosed.

'Your servant, Mycroft Holmes.'

Charles set down the letter and looked at the faces around him.

'Well . . .' prompted Catriona.

Charles riffled through the other pages, which detailed the Stratagem. Most of it he had guessed at once, from the heading.

'Geneviève's with us,' he said. 'And so are all the Ravens.'

'There was no Rat?' said Mr Hay.

Charles shook his head. 'Just a Rat-Trap.'

XXVIII: 'MAGIC, I EXPECT'

THE JUDGE HADN'T quite had the temerity to don the black cap while sentencing the Countess of Chelm, but Olivia Gibberne would be in prison until at least 1956–so Catriona was in a good mood.

Edwin, Catriona and Geneviève sat in the Café Royal.

Upon their entrance, the gentleman and ladies of the Diogenes Club had received a polite smattering of applause. Ivor Novello sent over a magnum of fizz, which even the vampire enjoyed. No one quite knew what they had done, but everyone knew it was something grand.

Even in their night-world, things had moved on. Margery Device whispered that the partnership of Dr Shade and Kentish Glory was on the rocks; now, Jonathan Chambers was running around town with a girl reporter, Penny Stamp. Edwin had received a bill from the Norton Company, for minor repairs to the Night Flier. With no reigning Great Enchanter, troublesome elements were in a high state of confusion–which served to make some even more troublesome. Geoff Jeperson was back from California, with a disturbing report on the resurgence of the Esoteric Order of Dagon. Lesser warlocks and would-be black magi were feuding and murdering each other in a contest for the unattainable title, and quite a few innocent persons were caught in the crossfire. The one and only original Spring-Heel'd Jack was back, working with Zenith the Albino–and half of Kensington was terrorised. Sweeney Todd was returned to the Shadow City Chamber of Horrors, but no one had caught Charlie Peace yet. The Ruling Cabal were officially 'very concerned' about most of Herr Hitler's ambitions for Europe.

'I'd love to have seen Ed's face when you bit him,' said Catriona.

'I didn't bite him,' responded Geneviève. 'I *held* him. Otherwise he might have shot the Wizard. With a silver bullet. Which I take as a personal slight, by the way.'

The women laughed.

Edwin still shivered at the moment. It had very nearly all gone wrong, and it needn't have.

'You must have known all along there was no real Rat?' said Catriona.

Geneviève sighed. 'Mr Mycroft preferred to complicate things. I no more knew what was in his mind than Charles did. I was told to begin the Rat Hunt. Not in so many words. I was directed to listen for intelligence, and it came to me. When I was in the Mausoleum, I believed it all–one of the Ravens was a traitor, and the city would fall. Then, I was spirited out of gaol . . .'

'By Stone?' prompted Edwin.

'Yes, Conjurer. I still don't know how it was done. Magic, I expect. Stone had a letter for me, from Mr Mycroft. Sealed orders. I was given a little more of the Stratagem, but the outcome, the purpose, was as much a surprise to me as anyone. And I thought the whole plan in ruins when Rennes was attacked. It seemed there might be a Rat after all. Robbie Stone was the only Raven not in office when Mr Mycroft drew up his plans, so he *could* have been a random factor. When Conjurer gave me the letter–and, of course, seals mean little when you're dealing with professional prestidigitators–it might have been a master-stroke, a Rat telling me there was no Rat. Mr Mycroft's Stratagem was based on convincing Zenf–whom he didn't even know–there was a Rat among the Ravens. Sorcerer was silenced because he was the Raven who scanned the horizon. Zenf would want him out of play, but so would our imaginary Rat. I was on a knife-edge of doubt and belief. But Charles tipped it for me. We are both creatures of Mr Mycroft. He never steered us wrong. And, even after his death, he hasn't now.'

Catriona whistled. 'We all did our parts,' she said, 'as if they were written for us. It's astonishing. I can't wait to look at the documents.'

'Private files, Cat,' said Edwin.

'Membership has its privileges,' she responded. 'Charles has granted a special dispensation. Of course, anything I write has to go in the private files, too.'

Edwin's champagne was a little flat. Had he left something of himself in the Shadow City? It seemed to him that slivers of ice had slipped in when he was on his knees in Pudding Lane, while the 'grown-ups' were talking. He knew Geneviève had been doing her duty, but . . .

He had not known Mycroft Holmes, though Charles sometimes said Edwin thought like the late Chairman–he, too, planned ahead, set mechanisms in motion, placed people on the board, devised contingencies. Now, he was not sure that was entirely a good thing. He hadn't cared overmuch for being a pawn or a cog.

'What *are* you thinking, Ed?' said Catriona. 'I know that broody brow. Some scheme is a-hatching.'

'It's nothing like that,' he said. 'It's the Old Man.'

'Charles?' asked Geneviève.

'She likes him,' put in Catriona. 'Cradle-snatching, really.'

'When I grow up,' said Edwin, 'I want to be like Charles Beauregard, not . . .'

'Not who?' prompted Catriona, intrigued.

'Anyone else.'

They laughed and clinked glasses. Outside, the sun was down and the street-lamps on. Londoners bustled to and fro, busy and (for the moment) safe.

XXIX: 'TO JUDGE FROM THE AUTOPSIES'

MR EYE LEFT the room. Since Charles was last here, the crate had been taken out and a cot put in.

The little man at the other side of the desk seemed absent-minded, all the wind leaked out of him. He did not look well, though Charles was assured the Undertaking made sure he got enough to eat and allowed him exercise and books. His mind was to be as carefully preserved as his body.

'Have you looked in on Isadora Persano?' Charles asked. 'I should think you'd have much in common.'

'Frankly,' responded Zenf, 'I'd rather talk with the worm.'

'There,' said Charles. 'That's your silence broken. A beginning. We trust you'll have much more to say.'

'It wasn't you, was it?' said Zenf, curiously desperate. 'It can't have been. It wasn't Drake, not entirely. There was someone else in it. Someone in deeper shadow?'

'You should know shadow.'

Zenf smiled bitterly. 'So I should.'

Charles allowed a little mercy. 'You are right, Colonel. There was a plan. A contingency. Against you.'

'I knew it.'

The former Great Enchanter was almost flattered. If a man was judged on the quality of his enemies, Zenf was still noteworthy.

'You haven't been replaced,' Charles said. 'Some have tried.'

Zenf snorted.

'Two or three of your, ah, associates have simply disappeared. Others are in morgues or unmarked graves.'

'It was expected. We, too, have our *contingency plans.*'

'Some deem it sacrilege that lesser lights aspire to your former position. You still have disciples. One particularly devoted follower, to judge from the autopsies.'

Zenf breathed a name, perhaps unconsciously.

Charles caught it. *Vivian.* The woman from the Pick-Pockets' Ball, dressed like a governess. She had retrieved Zenf's ring from the Bishop of Matabeleland. Margery Device would know her full name.

Charles didn't press the point. Zenf had begun to talk. He

might not even have realised yet, but now he would co-operate. Now, he would tell all he knew . . .

Zenf laughed, slyly. For a moment, the Enchanter believed he had power again, and needed to demonstrate it. He was the master, Charles the supplicant. This was as it should seem. In truth, he was a goose, about to be coaxed into laying a succession of golden eggs.

'I know something about those autopsies,' said Zenf, 'something that I believe would surprise you, might even shock you . . .'

Charles doubted that, but let it slide.

'You see, Miss Vivian has a peculiarity, a secret known only to the dead–and, as it happens, myself. Mr Beauregard, would you care to know what I know?'

Charles nodded, and Zenf began to share his secrets.

THE DAY IS OURS

BY MARGARET WEIS WITH ROBERT KRAMMES

Margaret Weis is the prolific author/coauthor of numerous best-selling fantasy books and series, including Darksword, Rose of the Prophet, Star of the Guardians, The Death Gate Cycle, The Sovereign Stone, *and many others. A native of Independence, Missouri, she moved to Wisconsin to become a book editor for TSR Inc., manufacturers of the* Dungeons and Dragons *series of role-playing games. At TSR, she is part of the* Dragonlance® *design team. She is currently at work with Tracy Hickman on a new six-book series,* Dragonships of the Vindras, *to be published by Tor Books.*

This is her first collaboration with Robert Krammes, a long-time southwestern Ohio member of the Society for Creative Anachronism. An avid reader, gamer and student of history, he has served as historic/military advisor for Ms. Weis's Dragonvarld *series.*

"The Day Is Ours"—which demonstrates that even in fantasy war is hell—is from their as yet unpublished book, The Breath of God.

THE THREE DRAGONS and their riders flew nearer to the location where the battle raged. They did not fly too close, took care not to come within range of the gunfire. The lead dragon's rider, Commander Stephano de Guichen, was here to observe, gather intelligence, size up the enemy. He was second in command of the famed Dragon Brigade, and he would be riding into battle for the first time. He wanted this fight to be one to remember—for all the right reasons. There were those (some on his own side) who would be happy to see the last flight of the Dragon Brigade go down in history as an unmitigated disaster.

One such was Lord Captain William Hastind, Master of His Majesty's new fleet of airships. Stephano could make out the Lord Captain—resplendent in his dark blue uniform coat with glittering gold epaulets—pacing the quarterdeck of his two-decker airship, directing the firing of the ship's guns at the enemy. Four other airships, not as large as the flagship, but equally formidable, were also taking part in the battle.

The cannons belched smoke and fire. The booming thunder of the broadsides rolled through the air, echoing off the ground far below. Cannonballs whizzed and whistled through the air. All very impressive until the cannonballs hit their target—one of the fortress's redoubts. The balls slammed into the side of the redoubt with dull thunks. The fortress's solid stone walls, reinforced by powerful magical constructs, shook a little, but took no real damage.

"Hastind might as well be throwing rocks at the enemy, wouldn't you say so, my lady?" Stephano remarked to his dragon.

Lady Cam had served in the Dragon Brigade for twenty years, and she was far too disciplined and well bred to openly criticize a senior officer in the King's military. But she glanced back at Stephano and her eyelids flickered in amused agreement.

When the smoke cleared, Stephano saw Hastind and his officers train their telescopes on the fortress to observe the results. Hastind lowered his telescope and shut it with an irritated motion. His officers clustered around him, gesturing and pointing, making suggestions.

The Estarans were returning fire, but the airship was careful to keep above the elevation of the fortress's heavy guns. The Estaran cannonballs sailed through the air, slicing the smoke, and that was all the damage they did before plummeting to the ground a thousand feet below.

After a month of both sides flinging cannonballs at each other the plains below must be hip-deep in iron, Stephano reflected wryly.

Which was why the Dragon Brigade was here, to put an end to

the rock-throwing. Small wonder Hastind was not pleased to see them. The much-touted airships—the miracle of modern warfare—had fought a single Estaran fortress for a month, and all they managed to do was knock down three small towers. The main fortress and all four redoubts were still intact, still capable of keeping the Rosians at bay.

Lady Cam gave a twitch of her shoulders and looked back at Stephano. "Is it the leader's intention to fight or are we on holiday?" she bellowed.

A dragon of strong—some might say obstinate—personality, Lady Cam disliked "lolly-gagging." Plainly they had seen all they were going to see. Stephano grinned and gave a hand signal to his fellow riders.

"If you would be so good as to take us around the fortress, my lady." He shouted to be heard above the reverberations of the cannons.

The dragon gave a flap of her wings. She was a large dragon, born and bred to warfare, with a thick neck, massive head, ponderous shoulders, and a broad, flat back. She came from a noble family of dragons who had served the Crown for centuries, and she knew what was due her rank, one reason Stephano always made his commands into requests. Lady Cam made certain Stephano never forgot that she was here because she chose to serve, not because anyone dared give her an order.

Stephano felt a sudden surge of affection for Lady Cam and with it a twinge of melancholy. Rumor had it that after this battle, she and the other noble dragons who fought in the Dragon Brigade were going to be "put out to pasture," sent back to their ancestral homelands—much like Stephano himself, only he no longer had any ancestral lands to go back to. His Majesty had seen to that.

If rumor were true, it would be the end of a glorious era—the end of the famed Dragon Brigade, the troop of gallant knights and their dragons who had won fame and fortune for Rosia. As Lady Cam spread her wings to swoop down over the fortress, Stephano patted the dragon fondly on the side of the neck.

Lady Cam's scales twitched at his touch. Such was the marvel of dragons that bullets would bounce off their scales, but they could still feel the touch of a human hand or the pressure of a human leg. Stephano's father had once likened a dragon's scales to the chain mail worn by knights of old, except that a dragon's scales were a thousand times stronger.

Lady Cam glanced back at him and nodded. Not surprising she understood his thoughts. They'd flown together a long time now, he and Lady Cam, mostly driving off pirates that sailed the Breath along the coast. This was their first time to take part in a major battle.

A cannonball whistled past them, flying in between Stephano and the dragon rider to his left. The ball did no harm—it would take a lucky shot to hit a dragon in mid-flight—but it forced Stephano to bring his mind back to the business at hand. He and his small patrol were coming within range of the fortress's fire and he needed to keep alert, think about today, forget about tomorrow. Perhaps if the Dragon Brigade accorded themselves well in this battle, tomorrow would be better than Stephano expected.

He took a moment to adjust the heavy, padded coat with its stiff high-necked collar and rows of buttons down the front. The coat had magical constructs worked into it to protect him from bullets and extended down to cover his tall riding boots. A short cape on his shoulders flapped in the wind, presumably throwing off a rifleman's aim. A metal helm and heavy leather gloves completed his uniform.

He studied the fortress and found it impressive. It was not a man-made structure, but had been created largely by magic. Though not a user of magic himself, Stephano knew enough about the art from his childhood friend Rodrigo, who was a Crafter (albeit not a very good one), to recognize the time and expert workmanship that had gone into the shaping of the fortress.

The Estarans had snagged one of the many small islands drifting in the Breath of God off the coastline of the main continent of Estara and magically altered the natural landscape, smoothing the jagged rocks of a small mountain into an inverted bowl shape, then fortifying that with walls and guard towers that ran in concentric circles from the top of the mountain to the bottom.

Four smaller free-floating islands with walls and gun batteries were tethered by heavy iron chains to the main fortress. These redoubts could be extended to provide a better field of fire and keep the enemy from landing troops on the main fortress.

Part of Stephano's orders was to try to find out if there were any enemy Crafters left inside that fortress. Knowing if there were any still inside could make a difference. If there were no Crafters to either guard it or repair it, an attack by a massed force of dragons could destroy the redoubt. Eyeing the redoubt, Stephano came up with a plan.

He and Lady Cam and his two wingmen circled the fortress. They did not use reins to guide their dragons. A dragon would have never felt a bit in its mouth, if, indeed, the noble dragons who served the king would have tolerated such an insult. Dragon riders guided their mounts by movements of the body.

"Look where you're going, not at the dragon's head," his father had instructed him. "Fly by your belly button."

This odd-sounding advice meant that the rider kept his belly button facing the direction he wanted to go. Stephano never thought about it now. He and Lady Cam had flown together so long, they were like partners in a waltz. They formed a single unit.

Having seen what he could of the fortress, Stephano and his men flew back to the airship. Hastind had quit firing on the redoubt; perhaps he'd used up his daily allotment of cannonballs. Seeing the Lord Captain staring straight at him, Stephano saluted. He had been intending to communicate his plan to the Lord Captain, but Hastind ignored his salute, turned on his heel, and stalked off.

"I think we've just been insulted," said Stephano in astonishment.

"Peasant!" Lady Cam remarked with a snort that sent small gouts of flame shooting out her nostrils.

Actually the Lord Captain was the second son of the Earl of Avaneur, but Stephano knew what Lady Cam meant.

The propellers on the airship creaked into motion. Several Crafters clustered about them, nursing the magic that kept the propellers running. When the airship started to sail away from the redoubt, the Estarans raised a ragged cheer at the sight of the enemy's departure.

Stephano had been going to wait until tomorrow to put his plan into action, but Hastind's rudeness prompted him to act now. Stephano was, after all, second in command. He could use his own judgment. By means of hand signals, Stephano communicated his plan to his wingmen. Both of them grinned hugely. Both had seen Hastind give them his backside.

Stephano gave the signal to attack, and he and Lady Cam soared off, heading straight for the redoubt. His wingmen followed in what was known as "pelican" formation in a straight line behind him.

Dragon breath has the power to deconstruct magic, something no round lump of iron can do. Airships could attack from long range and therein lay their value. Dragons had to fly perilously close to the enemy to breathe their flame on the target. Dragons flew too fast to be much threatened by cannon fire, but rifle fire and grapeshot were a threat. Neither Stephano's coat nor his helm would protect his from a direct hit, and while bullets and grapeshot would bounce off a dragon's scales, they could tear through the membrane of a dragon's wing, impairing flight—a rather dire circumstance when the ground is a thousand feet below.

Stephano gestured and his two wing dragons flew to attack the fortress on the side facing the redoubt, providing cover for Stephano. The dragons dove down one at a time, flying close to spew flame on the walls, forcing the artillery crews and riflemen to flee for their lives. The dragon flame striking the walls would have the additional effect of weakening the magic used to reinforce the stonework.

After repeated attacks, the walls would be in danger of col-

lapse. That wasn't likely to happen today, for only two dragons
were attacking, but the flaming breath would make the walls shaky
enough to rattle the nerves of those forced to stand on them. When
the cannon and rifle fire from the main fortress had all but ceased,
Stephano flew toward the redoubt.

The smoke from the cannon fire hung lazily in the still air, its
acrid smell stinging the nostrils. Lady Cam flew through the haze,
using it as cover, then burst out of the cloud almost right on top of
the redoubt, relying on Stephano to guide her to the most advanta-
geous point on which she would breath her flame.

The soldiers lined up on top of the wall could see the dragon
coming closer and closer, see her opening her enormous mouth
and sucking in a gigantic breath. They could guess what would
come next–flames that were ten times hotter than the fire of a
blacksmith's forge washing over them, causing flesh to bubble,
boiling the blood. One soldier lost his nerve and turned and
bolted, and soon nearly every man on the battlements was pushing
and shoving, trying to make good his escape from fiery death.

One man remained standing on the wall, trying to stop the
stampede. He was a big man, one of the biggest men Stephano had
ever seen–a Guundaran mercenary, to judge by his uniform.

Impressed by the Guundaran's courage, Stephano kept his
eyes on the officer as Lady Cam breathed a spout of flame on the
wall. The officer was safe from the flame, though the heat must
have been intense. If so, he braved it. He lifted his musket, aimed
at Stephano, and fired.

Lucky for Stephano he'd been watching. At the sight of the rifle, he flung himself forward, using the dragon's neck and shoulders for cover. Lady Cam was flying so fast he did not see what
happened to the bullet, whether it struck her scales or missed. All
he knew was that it didn't strike him. He glanced back over his
shoulder as Lady Cam winged her way upward from the attack,
saw the big officer still standing there. The flames were spreading,
coming closer to the big officer, and he finally descended from the
wall, though he took his time about it.

The dragon attack on the redoubt continued. The redoubt's magical constructs were now severely damaged. The Breath of God kept the small island afloat, but magic kept it stable, and that magic had been so severely weakened that the island was now bobbing erratically up and down like a duck on a wind-whipped lake.

Stephano could imagine the poor devils inside, getting tossed about unmercifully, and he was not surprised to hear the squeal of giant winches. The Estarans in the fortress were hauling the damaged redoubt back onto the main island.

Stephano did a last flyby and saw the big officer again. He was standing on the damaged wall, supervising the docking. His position was precarious; a sudden lurch could send him over the edge to a terrible death far below. The big man was an easy target. Stephano's pistol was at his side.

He urged Lady Cam closer. The big man caught sight of them out of the corner of his eye. He turned to look at Stephano. The big man's face was impassive.

Stephano was pleased with himself, pleased with all the world. His attack had been highly successful. In an hour, he and his dragons had done more damage to the redoubt than the airships had accomplished in a month. He had proven that dragons were still of use in this age of modern warfare. The king could not disband the Dragon Brigade now. As he flew past, Stephano raised his hand to salute a gallant enemy.

The big man eyed Stephano a moment, then he lifted his hand, gravely returning the salute before going back to work.

Stephano and his weary men and their wearier dragons descended through the clouds, returning to headquarters, which had been established on the ground below. The flagship and a frigate were also sinking slowly down, leaving two sloops to keep watch. With the redoubt damaged, the Rosians could land troops, seize the fortress, end this battle tomorrow. Stephano cast a last glance at the island-fort that was now high above him.

There would be no descent to the ground for the Estarans. No restocking. No resupplying. They were stuck, with nothing to look forward to tomorrow except defeat.

❖ ❖ ❖

The big man's name was Dag Thorgrimson. Guundaran by birth, he belonged to one of that small nation's famed mercenary companies. Employed by the Estarans, he was currently the ranking Guundaran officer and he was the nominal commander of the entire fortress, the Estaran captain having been slain during the third week of the siege. The next in line for command, nineteen-year-old Lieutenant Elizandro, had purchased the rank only several months prior to the attack and had no actual military experience. The Lieutenant was, however, smart enough to ask Dag for help.

Thirty years old, Dag had been in the military most of his life, having run away from home as a boy to join the army as a drummer. He fought for the Estarans because they paid well, and because Estara and Guundar were allies against the burgeoning might of Rosia. When the Estarans first decided to establish her claim to the land on the southeastern edge of the floating continent of Rosia, they knew the Rosians would dispute them. They'd fought over this small strip of arable land for centuries. Dag couldn't begin to imagine the cost in money and magic required to build this fortress and sail it through the Breath to this location, along with five thousand regular troops and a thousand Guundaran heavy infantry.

Estara had tweaked the tail of the Rosian lion to see if it would roll over and go back to sleep or if it would bite. The lion bit–and Estara had run off yelping with its own tail between its legs. Dag sighed deeply. In a way, he was glad the Dragon Brigade had arrived. The end would come sooner rather than later.

A messenger was there to meet the redoubt when it nudged up against the dock. The boy was jumping up and down, waving his hand to gain Dag's attention.

"Excuse me, sir, the commander requests your presence at your earliest convenience!" the boy shouted.

Dag nodded his head.

"Please, sir!" pleaded the boy. "The Lieutenant said—"

"I know what the Lieutenant said," Dag replied. He always spoke quietly, moved quietly. "I'll come when I can." He glanced over his shoulder at the boy's dirt-and-powder-smeared face and added quietly, "No need for haste, son. We're not going anywhere."

He made a final assessment of the damage to the redoubt, then made his way to the command room. The small room was crowded with men bringing in damage assessments, casualty lists, resupply, and repair needs. The fortress's only magician, Master Crafter Antonius Saumeraz, was endeavoring to coordinate everything, which at this stage of the siege basically meant he had to find thirty diplomatic ways to tell people "no," "sorry," "can't be done." As a magician, Antonius was not technically a part of the military, although the forty-year-old Crafter had been working for the military almost as long as Dag. Much as Dag had taken over commanding the troops, Antonius had taken over the fortress's operations.

Antonius was listening patiently to a swearing, sweating gunnery sergeant complain that yet another gun had blown up, killing the crew, all because of the combination of horse piss and rat droppings that was being foisted on him as an excuse for gunpowder and what was the Crafter going to do about it? Lieutenant Elizandro, unhappy and nervous, stood alongside the Crafter. He had a tendency to bite his nails. When Elizandro's hand started to steal toward his mouth, a sharp glance from Dag brought him up short. He jammed his hands in his pockets and tried his best to look like he knew what he was doing.

"Relief supplies will be coming soon, Sergeant," Antonius stated, lying through his teeth.

The sergeant knew he was lying. He'd only wanted to let off steam. He left, grumbling, and the room grew quiet.

An orderly brought in dinner, if rancid salt pork and weevily biscuit could be graced by the name. The orderly gave Dag and

Elizandro skimpy amounts, ladled out a double portion to Antonius, who looked embarrassed and shook his head.

"I don't feel right about eating like a pig when the rest of you are going hungry."

"You have to keep up your strength," said Dag. "We need our Crafter."

The Lieutenant shoved the food around on his plate.

"I saw the dragons," he said abruptly.

Dag nodded. "It was only a matter of time before they sent in the Dragon Brigade. I'm surprised they didn't come sooner."

"They mangled the redoubt," the Lieutenant continued glumly. "And now, with it gone, they can land troops. Lots of troops. More than we can handle." He looked from Dag to Antonius and back to Dag. "How could dragons do that much damage? The walls were magically reinforced. How could the dragons *do* that?"

The young man's voice cracked and he drew in a breath, endeavored to calm himself. "Those walls have held against cannon fire for weeks—"

"Cannon fire is not dragon fire, Lieutenant," Antonius explained, tapping his biscuit on the table to dislodge the weevils. "Cannonballs smash stone, whereas dragon fire smashes the magic itself, causing the lines of magical energy all up and down the wall to break until the entire construct falls apart."

Seeing the Lieutenant look confused, Antonius added, "If you could see what I could see, you'd know what I mean. When I look at a stone wall in good condition, I see the sigils glowing at the proper intervals with the lines of energy running straight and true between them. When a dragon breathes on that wall, it's like pouring acid on metal. The dragon fire eats away at the sigils. When they go, the lines of energy waver and weaken and eventually disappear. At that point, a child with a peashooter could damn near knock down the wall."

"But you can fix it tonight," Elizandro said hopefully. "You're a Crafter. That's what you do."

Antonius shook his head and rubbed his eyes. He hadn't been

getting much sleep lately. "How can I put this, sir? Let us say your lady mother has a lace mantilla; beautiful lace, very intricate, delicate work, thousands of threads woven in a lovely design. If a few of those threads are snipped, a good seamstress could repair them. But if your lady mother's chambermaid goes on a drunken rampage and slashes at the lace mantilla with a pair of scissors, leaving it in pieces, even the best seamstress would have difficulty stitching all the parts back together—"

"I understand," said the Lieutenant, downcast.

"Ordinarily there would be twenty Crafters employed inside this fortress to keep up with repairs," Dag added. "That's why the dragon riders attacked the redoubt. They want to determine our strength. If it's repaired and sent back out in the morning, they'll know we have Crafters among us."

"I asked for more Crafters," said Elizandro. "They're going to be coming on the transports along with the additional men and the food and water and relief supplies."

Dag and Antonius exchanged glances.

"What?" Elizandro demanded. His fingers went to his mouth. He caught himself, made a fist. "I saw that look. What does it mean?"

"No relief is coming, sir," said Dag finally. "The ground forces pulled out a week ago. We're on our own."

"Pulled out?" Elizandro gasped. "But they'll be sending ships to take us off . . ."

"Estaran frigates wouldn't stand a chance against that Rosian two-decker," said Dag. "They'd be blown out of the Breath."

The Lieutenant stared at them, pleading with them to laugh and say it was all a joke. Both men met his gaze, held it.

"But that means . . ." Elizandro swallowed. "They can't, can they? They can't leave us here to . . . to die?"

Neither man answered.

Antonius turned to Dag. "We could use grapeshot against the dragons. It's far more effective than cannonballs. Tears hell out of their wings."

"We could," said Dag, adding dryly, "except we'll run out of shot sooner than they'll run out of dragons."

"Dear God!" Elizandro groaned and clutched at his head.

"I was thinking, sir," Dag said deferentially, "that if we could capture one of their airships, we could use it to transport most of the men off the fortress."

"*Can* we capture one of their ships?" Elizandro asked, dubious, but hopeful.

"I believe we might," said Dag. "I have a plan."

"What about the dragons?" Antonius asked. "They'll attack."

"I have a plan for that, too," Dag responded.

Elizandro looked so relieved that Dag was fearful the young man might run around the table to hug him.

The young man's relief wavered. "You said 'most' of the troops."

"A small force would remain here, sir, to act as rear guard, keep the enemy occupied so the ship could have time to escape."

The Lieutenant gulped. "Would . . . would I be expected to stay here with them?"

"No, sir," said Dag gravely. "You'll be needed on the ship. I can remain to command the rear guard."

Elizandro's eyes filled with tears. Ashamed, he sat up quite straight and tall and said formally, "Very good. Let us hear your plan, Commander."

Dag smiled inwardly. Elizandro was a good kid. Someday, when he grew up, he'd make a good officer. Dag explained his idea.

❖ ❖ ❖

Stephano's dinner was far more elegant, far more delicious, and ended up being just as rancid as if he'd been dining with the enemy. Stephano and Dragon Brigade commander Jeantrou had both been invited along with the airship officers to dine with the general. A large dining pavilion had been set up on the grassy plain. Tapestries lined the walls, rugs were thrown over the ground, two chandeliers hung suspended from the ceiling. China and silver flatware adorned the table, which could seat fourteen, and there were sideboards and serving tables set up in the corners. The servants filled crystal glasses with a fine champagne chilled in buckets of snow.

Stephano had been presented at the royal court and he was accustomed to seeing things done on a lavish scale, but not on the battlefield. He gaped like a yokel at the grandeur and gave a grudging thank-you to his countess mother, who had sent him a hand-tailored and extremely expensive dress uniform coat and breeches.

Stephano had tossed his mother's gift aside in disgust when it first arrived. The uniform coat the village tailor had sewn up was good enough for him, and he chewed out his servant, Old Rodolfo, properly when he found the "dandified" uniform, as he termed it, packed along with the rest of his equipment. It was the ill-tempered old servant who insisted Stephano wear the new uniform to the general's dinner and since it was easier to do as Rodolfo said than listen to him grouse and grumble for the next two days, Stephano had put it on. Seeing Lord Captain Hastind resplendent in his own expensive coat, Stephano was glad he could match him.

The officers would remain standing until the general made his appearance. Drinking wine, they discussed the day's battle. Stephano waited expectantly for someone to bring up the amazing exploits of the Dragon Brigade, but no one did. Stephano listened to Hastind and his officers talk of the impressive showing of the airships until he could stand it no longer. Taking a glass of snow-chilled champagne from the sideboard, he walked over to one of Hastind's officers, Captain Reynard, whom Stephano had met at court.

Stephano ventured a greeting, then said, "Interesting turn of events—the Estarans having to reel in their damaged redoubt. It was listing pretty badly there at the last."

"We gave it a good pounding," Captain Reynard remarked. "Knocked the stuffing out of it, so to speak. Naturally the bastards would have to reel it in for repair."

"*You* gave it a pounding!" Stephano repeated, astonished. "It was our dragons–"

"Ah, yes," Reynard interrupted, "I trust you and your lizards had an enjoyable time playing at war today, Commander, while the rest of us did the real work. A good evening to you, sir."

Captain Reynard bowed and walked away.

Stephano felt the hot blood rush to his face. He started after the captain, scathing words on his lips.

A hand clamped down on Stephano's shoulder. "Let it go."

Stephano turned around angrily. "Commander, did you hear him! He said–"

"I heard what he said and I said let it go, de Guichen," Commander Jeantrou repeated sternly. "That's an order. Look at him. Reynard *wants* you to start something. Don't play into his hands. He's a crack shot with a pistol, you know. Killed two men in duels last year."

"I don't give a damn–" Stephano began furiously.

"But I do," Commander Jeantrou said, digging his nails into Stephano's shoulder. "And, more to the point, so does General Dennis. Don't end your career before it's begun."

Stephano shook off Jeantrou's hand. He was still so angry that he might have ignored his commander's order, but then General Dennis walked into the pavilion and all conversation ended.

General Dennis was a man in his late middle years, due to retire soon, not by choice, but because he had fallen out of favor when the new king took the throne. The general's career had been a long and glorious one. He was known as one of Rosia's finest soldiers, but he was old military, his views antiquated and out-of-date. Hastind and his airships were the future. Hastind was polite, but he made his disdain obvious. General Dennis, looking haggard and tired, kept the conversation to pleasantries until the cloth had been removed and the port handed around.

As Lord Captain Hastind drank his port, his two captains launched into a barrage of complaints about the effrontery of the dragon riders, who had ignored orders, placed the airships in danger with their reckless actions, and so forth. When Stephano would have responded, Commander Jeantrou shot him a warning look and he kept quiet.

General Dennis listened patiently, then said, "Gentlemen, I am glad we have had this chance to get to know one another. Let us remember that our purpose here is to fight for Rosia."

Captain Reynard raised his glass. "If I may be so bold, sir, I propose we drink to a victory that will echo through the ages. One to rival our glorious victory at Daenar."

General Dennis put his glass down untouched. "Captain, I was at Daenar and there was nothing glorious about that victory. Twenty thousand good men died storming that rock. Twice that number were injured or crippled." His heavy white brows came together. His blue eyes glinted. "They could never wash all the blood out of the fort. Eventually they towed it out into the Breath and sank it."

In the ensuing silence, he lifted his glass and drained it, then refilled it. "This, gentlemen, is a skirmish. Nothing more. Five years from now no one will remember it. Still, it has fallen on us to defeat Rosia's enemies. I mean to see it done. That is why I called in the Dragon Brigade."

He looked down the table at Stephano and the corners of the older man's eyes crinkled in a slight smile. The general turned back to Hastind.

"I will give us a toast, Lord Captain." General Dennis raised his glass. "To Rosia."

Hastind drank the toast, but as he put down his glass, he shot an angry glance at Stephano, who responded with a look of glittering contempt. Stephano had his mother's eyes, so he'd been told, and nothing in court was said to be more feared than a contemptuous glance from the cat-green eyes of the Countess de Marjolaine.

Hastind flushed in anger, and Stephano knew he'd made an enemy for life, but at that moment, heady with wine and victory, he didn't care.

The general rose. The dinner was ended. Hastind and his officers left at once. Jeantrou and Stephano were about to take their leave when General Dennis called out, "Commander de Guichen, a word with you, sir."

"I was going to warn you," said Jeantrou in an undertone. "Just listen to what he has to say and keep that temper of yours in check for once."

Stephano was startled. What had Jeantrou meant? Warn him about what?

"About your actions this afternoon, Commander," said General Dennis. "I understand it was you who decided to attack the redoubt. On a whim, apparently."

"A whim!" Stephano was shocked. "No, sir, I realized—"

"You do not have leave to speak, Commander," Dennis said sternly. "You attacked the redoubt without orders and, furthermore, you acted without any knowledge or understanding of my plans for this siege. You might have thrown the outcome of this entire battle into jeopardy."

Stephano knew this wasn't the case. "Sir, I—"

"Again, Commander, I have not given you leave to speak. The Lord Captain had good grounds for his complaints, Commander. You acted irresponsibly. If you ever again decide to supersede my authority and strike out on your own, I will send you back to Argonne on foot. Do you understand me?"

"Yes, sir," Stephano said, still annoyed.

"There is more going on here than you know, Commander. Your actions today made Hastind and the navy *and* His Majesty the King look bad today. Very bad."

Stephano gaped in amazement.

General Dennis sighed. "You've made an enemy of Hastind and King Alaric, as well. Son, why do you think we're wasting time and money and lives out here fighting over a strip of land that no one gives a damn about? Because Hastind was sent here to prove His Majesty's theory that the airship is the future of modern warfare, that dragons are relics of the past. Then you come along and in two hours prove His Majesty and Hastind both wrong. A fact which neither of them is likely to forget."

"May I have leave to speak, sir?" Stephano asked, now subdued. "Begging your pardon, General, I don't mean to sound like a whining brat, but you sent for us—for the Dragon Brigade."

"So I did. And if you had waited for my orders, I would have commanded you to attack the redoubt exactly as you did."

"Then, sir, why—"

"Because then the King's anger would have fallen on me, Commander." General Dennis shrugged. "I'm an old man. This is my last command. I see the face of modern warfare, and it's an ugly face. Frankly, I want nothing to do with it. I sent for the Dragon Brigade because I'm sick of the bloodshed. It's time this battle came to an end." The general handed Stephano a sealed envelope. "Here are the Brigade's orders for tomorrow. Give them to Commander Jeantrou."

"Yes, sir," said Stephano. "And, sir, please accept my apology. I . . . I wasn't thinking."

General Dennis smiled and turned to leave, only to turn back. "Commander de Guichen, His Majesty is right about one thing— the Dragon Brigade *is* rooted in the past—a time when honor and integrity still had meaning. Don't let them take that away from you, Commander. Never let them take that."

Stephano stood thinking over his words for long moments, then he shook his head and went off to give Jeantrou his orders.

Dag and Antonius worked all night, readying the trap that would, God willing, snag them an airship. Dag could see the airships out there, their running lights bobbing up and down as they drifted on the night winds, keeping watch on the fortress.

God knows why, Dag thought. *It isn't as if we're going to sneak off during the night.*

The enemy would have their telescopes trained on the redoubt, of course. They'd see lights and activity. They would figure the Estarans were working frantically all through the night, trying to repair the redoubt enough to send it back out. What they would not know is that the Estarans were setting a trap.

Fortunately, parts of the wall still stood, and Dag was able to conceal the work behind them. It would never do for Rosian telescopes to see men hauling cannons from the redoubt into the fortress or shoving two enormous ballistae into position.

The dawn brought the return of the flagship, rising ponderously up through the air, accompanied by an attendant frigate. Dag brought out his telescope, as did Antonius, who was standing on the wall of the redoubt alongside him and the Lieutenant.

"The ship is filled with marines," said Elizandro. "There must be two hundred or more."

"They'll add sailors, as well," said Dag. "And another hundred and fifty marines and sailors on the small ship."

"When will they attack?" Elizandro asked nervously.

"Not for a while yet," said Dag, snapping shut his telescope and turning away. "The Lord Captain will want to see things for himself. Take a good look at the redoubt, make certain our attempts at repairing it were a failure."

"Will the dragons come back?"

"Undoubtedly. And this time there will be a full-scale assault. Not just three having fun," Dag replied.

"Fun!" The Lieutenant gave a bitter laugh. He was fidgeting, not seeming to know what to do with himself.

"Why don't you go back to the fortress, sir," Dag suggested. "Make certain the cannon are in position and the men understand their orders. No one fires a shot until I give the signal. That is crucial."

"I'll have someone's head if they do," said Elizandro, and he hurried off.

"Everything's ready," said Dag. "Now we wait."

"That's the hardest part," said Antonius.

Dag nodded agreement. The two stood watching the sun rise, a spectacular sight, gilding the clouds with gold and splashing the dawn mists with touches of pinks and purples. The sails of the flagship were decorated with streamers and the Rosian Rose en Solet– a rose with a sunburst behind it–done in gleaming gold leaf.

The dragons flew alongside, their scales glistening green-gold. Their wings extended, they lazily rode the thermals. As Dag watched, the flagship maneuvered into position and began to pivot, bringing her guns to bear. The morning air was so clear he could hear the orders being shouted to the gun crews.

"Time to go," said Dag.

The redoubt was still tied to the dock, still listing slightly. A most tempting target.

"I want you to know, Antonius, that it has been a privilege and pleasure serving with you," said Dag as they entered the cool semi-darkness of the earthen fortress.

"Thank you, Commander," said Antonius. "That means a great deal to me." He glanced out a gun port. All was quiet now, but that quiet would soon be blown apart. "Someday, when the winds bring us back together, we'll remember this day over a fine Estaran wine."

They could hear, quite clearly, the order to fire.

"We better take up our positions," said Dag. "It won't be long now."

The flagship sent a crashing broadside into the redoubt. The enemy Crafters had apparently made an attempt to repair it during the night, but had been only partially successful. The redoubt remained afloat, though it was still listing.

No cannonfire came from the redoubt or the fortress. Stephano and his dragon riders had hit the gun emplacements hard yesterday; probably those guns were damaged beyond repair. As for the cannons in the fortress, the Estarans were undoubtedly running low on powder and shot. The airships were not yet in range. The

Estarans would wait to fire until they flew closer, when they had a good chance of hitting something.

The airship's gunners reloaded and another broadside followed the first. The officers on the flagship had their telescopes trained on the redoubt and when the smoke cleared, they saw the wall had collapsed. The Lord Captain barked an order. Flags flew up the halyards, ordering to the fleet to cease fire.

Now it was the Dragon Brigade's turn. Commander Jeantrou, riding his proud and sleek young dragon, raised his hand, giving the signal for everyone to prepare for the attack. Stephano checked to make certain the straps that kept him in the saddle were good and tight. He was eager, excited. He could feel his heart pulse in his throat. Lady Cam was excited, too; her mane bristled and she bared her fangs in defiance.

The Dragon Brigade would finish today what Stephano and his dragons had begun yesterday—they would weaken the magical constructs that were keeping the redoubt afloat. When it sank, leaving one side of the fortress vulnerable to attack, the airships would move in, land their troops, and the final assault against the fortress would commence.

Stephano wondered if there would be another dinner tonight to celebrate the victory. If so, he would apologize to Lord Captain Hastind. Not because Stephano was afraid of him, but because he had been in the wrong. He'd show Hastind that, in the Dragon Brigade, honor still meant something.

Commander Jeantrou lowered his hand. The Dragon Brigade flew to the attack.

Antonius stood inside one of the gun rooms in the fortress's interior, gazing out a gun port, watching the dragons. They flew close to the fortress, gliding on the thermals. The fortress fired grapeshot at them, but the cannons could be elevated only so high and the dragons were able to keep clear of the shot. The dragons would attack from above, Dag explained, diving down on their targets like stooping hawks. Antonius had never witnessed a dragon attack before, and he found it so fascinating he forgot the danger and thrust his head out the gun port for a better view.

"You should step away from the port, Crafter," said a soldier, plucking Antonius's sleeve. "The dragons'll come at us from the sky. You won't be able to see them."

Antonius thought this an excellent suggestion, and he was just moving away from the port when a shadow blotted out the sunlight, plunging the room into darkness. The next instant, a gout of flame roared through the window. Antonius threw himself sideways and landed heavily on the floor as the fiery blast shook the walls and floor.

Protective magic constructs he'd laid on his robes deflected the heat and flame from his body, but the soldier who had warned him took the blast full in the face. His screams were terrible to hear, but, mercifully, they didn't last long. When the smoke cleared and Antonius could see, he glanced over at the soldier and wished desperately he hadn't. The man no longer had a face or even much of a head left.

"You all right, Crafter?" asked one soldier, who had come running when he heard the screams. Antonius was on his hands and knees, heaving up his breakfast. He nodded, wiped his mouth and nose, and, with the man's help, managed to stagger shakily to his feet.

Another soldier had thoughtfully thrown a gunny sack over the corpse. Blood was running in meandering rivulets along the stone floor.

Antonius wrenched his attention back to the walls, and he gasped in dismay and astonishment. The dragon's breath had wreaked havoc on the magical constructs. Several of the sigils had disappeared completely, while others were starting to fade. Energy lines were broken or missing altogether.

"Good god!" Antonius gasped.

It was one thing to sit in the library reading texts about dragons, quite another to be under attack. He hastened from sigil to sigil, laying his hands on each, bringing most back to life again, like touching a match to a wick in an oil lamp. The lamp was the wall. The oil in the lamp was the magic that God had breathed into all things in the world, from "mountains to molehills, men to mice," as the old catechism went. The sigil was the wick dipped in the oil and Antonius's touch was the flame that lit the sigil.

Another shadow darkened a window. "Look out!" yelled a soldier, and everyone scrambled for cover.

Dragon fire struck the fortress again, this time hitting a gun port down the corridor from where Antonius crouched behind a column. Flames burst through the windows. Men screamed and died. Antonius watched the sigils blink out, including some he'd just lit, and he understood, for the first time, their deadly peril.

Usually, even if a sigil had gone out, he could see it glimmer with life, but some of these were gone for good. They could not be rekindled. Soon more and more would go out. Within hours, dragons could destroy enough magic to level this fortress and maybe even sink the floating island.

Antonius had to keep the walls standing just a little longer.

"The redoubt's gone," said someone quietly.

Antonius had been so preoccupied with his work, he hadn't been paying attention to what was happening outside. He looked through a window—keeping his distance—and saw the redoubt falling into the Breath.

Some of the men riding the dragons began cheering as the redoubt fell. At that moment, one of the gun crews got in a lucky hit. Grapeshot struck a dragon, tearing through a wing and knocking the beast sideways. The shot must have hit the rider, too, for he dangled like a limp doll from the saddle. The dragon struggled heroically to keep flying, but with one wing useless, the beast began to spiral downward.

"Here come the Rosians!" called a soldier.

One of the Rosian frigates was sailing toward the ruined dock.

The soldiers around Antonius gripped their rifles tightly. It wouldn't be long now.

Antonius hastily left his sigil-lighting and made his way through the corridors to where Dag had laid his deadly trap.

❖ ❖ ❖

Stephano did not know either the injured dragon or the rider that well, but he—like every other dragon rider—flinched as the shot slammed into the rider's body and tore through the dragon's wing.

Braving the grapeshot, Jeantrou flew to the side of the injured dragon, to see if there was anything he could do. But the commander could not reach the dragon before the beast started to "lose sky," as the dragons put it. Stephano prayed that the rider was either dead or unconscious, spared the terror of that last, horrible descent.

Stephano looked to the flagship, where they had hoisted signal flags headed by the Dragon Brigade's number. The Dragon Brigade was ordered to back off, as Captain Reynard's sloop sailed toward the fortress. The ship fired a broadside and the walls of the fortress, their magic weakened, crumbled, breaching the fortifications. Jeantrou gave the signal for two of the talons to withdraw. Others, including Stephano's, remained to keep an eye on the fortress.

Reynard's sloop nudged up to the ruined dock. Stephano could see Hastind on deck, alongside Reynard. Sailors jumped off the airship to attach lines to what remained of the dock; then they lowered the gangplank. The hundred marines marched in orderly ranks down the gangplank, along with fifty sailors.

They encountered rifle fire from the defenders, but no cannon fire. The marines fired a volley and then another. That was apparently enough to dislodge the defenders, for no more shots came after that.

The landing party marched through the breach in the fortress's outer wall. The sloop edged out of the dock to make way for Captain Fascinel's frigate, now flying the Lord Captain's flag, to land two hundred marines and one hundred sailors. They swarmed through the breach in support of the first group. Stephano saw Hastind on the foredeck, standing next to Fascinel. His air barge had been hauled aboard. The Lord Captain had transferred to the sloop, to be on hand when they delivered the final blow.

By sunset, Stephano thought exultantly, *the day will be ours.*

❖ ❖ ❖

Antonius crouched behind the barricade. Dag knelt beside him. They could hear the orders being shouted by the Rosian marine commander, the tramp of hundreds of booted feet.

"When I give the order, Crafter," said Dag quietly.

Antonius nodded. He was too nervous to speak. It was all up to him—a Crafter who had never before been in battle. And now he was responsible for the lives of all these men. He wondered, awed and a little dazed, how, from where he had started, he had come to this.

He had been born to privilege. A bright child of noble blood, he could have spent his days gracing the salons of the rich and powerful, entertaining elegant ladies with his witty bons mots. But his mind crackled with magic. He was born with a rare gift, the priest had explained to his noble parents, who could not begin to understand. He could see a world invisible to them. They looked at their castle walls and saw the tapestries. He looked at the walls and saw the magical sigils, the constructs, the flow of power.

The Church had recommended strongly—most strongly—that they take over his tutelage. His parents had little choice in the matter. Two priests arrived to escort him to the Church Academy. Knowing he was going to be allowed to study the magic that fascinated him, Antonius had left home at age six joyfully, never thinking of the hurt he was inflicting on his parents. He rarely saw them now. To this day, they still did not understand.

Antonius could remember the moment he set his first line. The nun had constructed two sigils, one on either side of the classroom, and told the students to connect them. That was the first time Antonius had attempted to control the magic that before now had been allowed to dance about aimlessly. He grasped it, briefly wrestled with it, then, having taken firm hold, he sent it where he wanted it to go. The sigils flared to life and so, in that moment, had Antonius.

And at any moment now, that life might be extinguished. Antonius gulped and swallowed hard. Dag glanced at him in concern. Antonius managed a reassuring smile.

Dag had explained how the assault would unfold, and Antonius pictured it in his mind's eye. After storming the breach, the marines and sailors would enter the main gun room. They would find it in ruins, filled with smoke. They would dimly see the large cannon in its truck tipped over on its side, the muzzle covered with rubble and debris. What the soldiers would not see was the faint glow of the magical sigil located on the priming hole.

The Rosians would secure the room and move cautiously out the door and down the corridors that led off to the left and right, connecting all the gun ports. The troops wouldn't be able to see far, due to the curvature of the walls, and they'd be expecting resistance. The barricades, manned by riflemen and small artillery pieces, would stop the first advance. The troops would retreat back to the main gun room to wait for reinforcements, which would crowd into the main gun room.

Hundreds of men crowded into that room . . .

The cannon, looking impotent, pathetic, tipped over on its side . . .

The sigil glowing . . .

Antonius found it hard to catch his breath. His bowels gripped. He was sweating and shivering at the same time, and he had to concentrate.

"Steady," said Dag quietly. "You can do this."

Antonius closed his eyes and willed himself not to be sick. He conjured up the image of the sigil on the cannon, kept it before his eyes.

"Here they come," said Dag. He sounded as calm as though announcing they were sitting down to dinner.

A hundred Guundaran soldiers stood in the darkness behind him, waiting his command. Lieutenant Elizandro was ensconced in the corridor on the left with his own contingent of troops.

Antonius could hear the sound of feet moving down the corridor, coming this direction. He swallowed.

"Wait," Dag murmured. "Wait."

The first of the enemy soldiers came into view, rounding the curve in the wall. They would not be able to see well, due to the smoke and darkness. It would take a while to notice the barricade. Dag let them get closer, and then one man stopped and let out a sharp exclamation.

"Fire!" Dag ordered.

The small artillery pieces went off, filling the corridor with grapeshot. At almost exactly the same time, Elizandro fired his artillery, catching the enemy in a deadly hail of iron. The walls and floor and ceiling were suddenly plastered with blood and gore as the shot tore into flesh, severed limbs, took off heads. Bodies crashed to the floor. Rifles clattered on the stone. The wounded screamed and writhed in their own blood, begging for help. As Dag had predicted, the survivors retreated back to the main gun room.

Dag motioned for the firing to cease. He rested his hand on Antonius's shoulder. The big man's hand was steadying, warm and reassuring.

"Now," said Dag.

Antonius closed his eyes. Touching a sigil from a distance was far more difficult than physically touching sigils painted on the wall. A teacher had likened this to a soprano using her voice to shatter a crystal glass. The soprano's voice at the proper pitch sent out waves on a certain harmonic frequency that would cause the crystal to vibrate until it broke apart.

Antonius did much the same thing. He sent out magical waves with his mind that were tuned to the sigil's magic. When the waves of magic connected with the sigil, it would glow brilliantly and catch fire.

He bent his thoughts on the sigil. He could see it so clearly. He could almost touch it . . .

The blast shook the walls and the floor and made his heart lurch. Then everything went oddly quiet. No one was screaming and for a moment he was terrified that he'd failed. Then he understood why. The cannon had been filled half its length with powder, then two canister rounds, and a load of grapeshot. With all those troops jammed into that room, many would have been killed instantly, the rest severely wounded.

Dag and his troops were up and over the barricade before the smoke cleared. Antonius stayed where he was. He was shaking in every limb, too weak to move. Something somewhere was burning and in the light of the fire he watched the blood flow over the stone floor in a red river.

The heat and concussive force of the blast washed over Stephano, causing him to duck behind Lady Cam. The dragon flipped belly-up to protect her rider and veered away from the flames that now enveloped a portion of the fortress—the portion the Rosian troops had just stormed.

Twisting in the saddle, Stephano stared through the smoke, hoping desperately to see survivors fleeing the wreckage. Out of the hundreds who had entered, only a few stragglers came limping from the blaze, and they were being cut down by Estaran gunfire.

"A trap," he said, swearing. "A goddamn trap!"

And suddenly he understood the reason.

Ballistae with sturdy ropes attached thudded into the airship's wooden hull and stuck fast. Estarans rushed out, grabbed hold of the lines, and secured them to the dock. Fascinel and Hastind on board the airship fired their handguns at the Estarans, as some of the sailors hacked at the ballistae with axes, trying to cut them loose.

A force of Guundaran mercenaries came rushing out of the fortress. They were led by a giant of a man—the very same man who had exchanged salutes with Stephano on the redoubt.

Stephano dug his thighs into Lady Cam and shifted his body to the right. She responded, carrying him over to Commander Jeantrou, who was staring, grim-faced, at the frigate.

Stephano flew alongside. "What can we do, sir?"

"Nothing," said Jeantrou.

"But they can't expect to get away with stealing an airship!" Stephano protested.

"Why not?" Jeantrou demanded. "After all, they've just managed to capture a boatload of hostages!"

❖ ❖ ❖

Dag and his Guundaran soldiers swarmed up and over the bulwarks and jumped down onto the deck of the airship.

"Remember," Dag yelled, "take as many of the bastards alive as you can! Above all, don't kill an officer!"

A small force of the airship's sailors came at them, swinging swords and firing pistols. Leaving them to his men, Dag and those with him made a dash for the stairs leading to the quarterdeck. His way was blocked by sailors wielding boarding pikes, swords, and pistols. Dag knocked aside a boarding pike with his axe and shot his attacker in the face. His gun empty, he threw it at another sailor, smacking him in the forehead. A swing of his axe took off another man's hand.

A man wearing a Lord Captain's epaulets and baldric aimed a pistol directly at Dag's head and pulled the trigger. Dag flinched, but no bullet slammed into him and he breathed a sigh of relief. The pistol had misfired. Swearing, the Lord Captain hurled the gun onto the deck and advanced with his sword.

Dag stepped onto the quarterdeck, his men right behind him. The Lord Captain stared down the barrels of at least half a dozen rifles. He lowered his sword.

Dag glanced down at the deck below. The experienced mercenaries had made short work of the sailors. The initial volley of small arms fire had wounded a midshipman and knocked the fight out of the Rosians. Dag turned back to the officers. One of them, the frigate's captain, lay on the deck, blood flowing from a cut on his head. The captain was conscious, but seemed dazed.

"Lord Captain," Dag said, politely saluting. He had never captured an airship before and he wasn't certain of the proper protocol. He decided to keep it simple. "You are outnumbered and outgunned. Do you surrender, sir?"

"I'll see you in the Bottom first!" snarled the Lord Captain.

Dag was running out of time. He could see, out of the corner of his eye, the dragons hovering near. They wouldn't attack, not with the lives of sailors and officers at stake. Dag sized up the Lord Captain, obviously some well-to-do noble, unaccustomed to defeat, for he was red-faced, trembling with rage.

Dag decided to call the man's bluff. He made a motion with his hand. "The Lord Captain has expressed a wish to see the Bottom. Very well. Throw his lordship overboard."

The Lord Captain swore viciously, then hurled his sword to the deck at Dag's feet.

Not very gentlemanly, but Dag would take what he could get.

"Strike the colors! Raise the Estaran flag," Dag ordered, adding urgently, "And make it fast!"

Growls and snarls came from both the dragon riders and their mounts as the Estaran flag sailed up the halyard. Their commander bellowed an order and they shut up and kept their distance.

"Lord Captain," said Dag, "I want only to send my people back to Estara. You and your men will be hostages to guarantee our safety, but once you reach Estara, you have my word that you will be released and returned safely to Rosia."

"Your word!" The Lord Captain sneered. "Why should I take the word of a sell-sword?"

Dag was patient. "Because it is either that or go for a swim in the Breath. I need someone from your staff to take this message to your general. My terms are these: your fleet and the dragons are to give us safe passage. They will not fire on us or follow us. If they do, I will kill the hostages one by one."

The Lord Captain was sullen, thinking. Finally he said stiffly, "I will go myself."

Dag raised an eyebrow. The Lord Captain was his most valuable hostage, but he was also the one who had the most influence. If anyone could persuade the general to go along with these terms, it would be a Lord Captain.

"I would have to have your word, sir, as an officer, that you will return to the ship as my hostage," said Dag.

"Of course," said the Lord Captain haughtily. "You have my word on it! The word of a *gentleman*," he added pointedly.

"Make the Lord Captain's barge ready!" Dag shouted.

His mercenaries knew little about launching an air barge, but several sailors, who understood that their lives depended on this, eagerly volunteered. The Lord Captain climbed in, taking with him a sailor to pilot the craft. The barge was lowered over the side and the Lord Captain sailed off, his air barge making a rapid descent toward the ground and Rosian command.

Dag settled down to wait.

❖ ❖ ❖

Stephano and Jeantrou served as escorts for the air barge. Hastind jumped out of the barge before the soldiers could secure it and walked with rapid strides toward the general's tent, where General Dennis was waiting. The general held a telescope in his hand. He was not happy.

Jeantrou and Stephano followed after Hastind, who glared at them as he started to enter the tent.

171

"You are not needed, gentlemen," he said angrily.

"On the contrary, my lord," said General Dennis. "I want them to be present. I want to hear their report."

Hastind went livid, but he had no choice. Removing his hat, he gave a fairly accurate account of what had happened. Stephano wondered what story the Lord Captain would have told if he and Jeantrou had not been present. As it was, Hastind still managed to lay blame on the Dragon Brigade.

"If they had been doing their jobs instead of flying about like daredevils, showing off, they would have seen the ambush laid for us!"

Jeantrou bristled. "General, my men and I—"

"Silence!" the general roared. "We can argue over whose fault this was later. The question is—what do we do now?"

"There is no question, General," said Hastind calmly. "We cannot allow an airship to fall into enemy hands. Their Crafters would soon figure out the new magicks we're using to keep it afloat. We must destroy it, send it to the Bottom."

General Dennis regarded him intently. "This is an extraordinary act of courage, my lord. Returning to the ship, knowing that we plan to set fire to it."

Hastind shrugged, but made no reply. General Dennis eyed him grimly, then dismissed him. Hastind motioned for Jeantrou and Stephano to accompany him back to the barge.

"I echo the general's sentiments, sir," said Jeantrou. "Your sacrifice is the most courageous—"

Hastind snorted. "What a simpleton you are, Commander. Almost as bad as that doddering old fool in the tent. I have no intention of returning to that ship."

"But you gave your word, my lord!" Stephano said, appalled.

"I gave my word to a peasant, not a gentleman."

"All the more reason—"

Jeantrou shot him a glance, and Stephano shut his mouth. Hastind was not listening, anyway. He was too busy giving the Dragon Brigade orders which would doom the officers and sailors who remained on board the airship to fiery death. Stephano listened unhappily, deeply ashamed of having anything to do with this. He thought of going back to tell the general, but he remembered Dennis's look, his grim face, and Stephano realized that Dennis already knew what Hastind intended. The general could have stopped the Lord Captain, but he didn't care any more. He wanted this war to end so he could go home.

"The other ships of the fleet will hold their fire. The Dragon Brigade will have the honor of destroying the airship," said Hastind in conclusion. He stared at Stephano, a slight smile on his lips. Then he turned on his heel and walked off.

Stephano stared after Hastind. "That bastard!" he said softly. He looked at Jeantrou. "You know what he's doing?"

"Yes," Jeantrou said shortly. He began walking rapidly back to where their dragons waited, fanning their wings gently to keep limber.

"Never mind that we only obeyed orders!" Stephano continued, his outrage growing. "The Rosian people won't understand that! All they'll know is that *we*–the Dragon Brigade–set fire to one of our own ships and killed our own men!"

It would be in all the newspapers. The masses would be in an uproar. The public outcry would give His Majesty the excuse he needed to disband them. In one fell swoop, Hastind had managed to rid himself of two enemies–the Estarans and the Dragon Brigade.

"God's Breath!" Stephano swore. "He won't get away with it! Sir, I have an idea, a way around this."

Jeantrou listened to Stephano's plan and smiled. "We'll go back and talk to the General."

❖   ❖   ❖

Dag's first intimation that his brilliant plan was going straight to the Bottom was when the Lord Captain's barge made an appearance, rising up through the wispy clouds, and sailed straight to one of the

Rosian frigates. A flag announced that the Lord Captain was on board. The second came when the dragon arrived and flew slowly toward him. The dragon rider bore in his hand a white flag of truce.

At the sight of the white flag, signal flags sailed up the airship's halyard, but the dragon rider paid them no heed. A cannon boomed out, calling attention to the command. The Dragon Brigade's commander flew over to speak to the Lord Captain, but he took his time about it.

The dragon rider kept a wary eye on the airship as he approached. The dragon flew to within hailing distance, then shifted her body, allowing her rider to see and be seen, hear and be heard. There must be no mistaking his words.

"Ahoy the ship!" the dragon rider called out. "I want to speak to the commander."

Dag stepped forward. He recognized the young man, the same one who had saluted him yesterday.

"I'm the commander. Name's Dag."

"Stephano de Guichen," said the rider, touching his hat.

"Is your Lord Captain coming back?" Dag asked.

The young man's face went rigid. He did not answer the question. Instead he said in formal tones, "Commander Dag–"

"Sergeant," said Dag.

"I beg your pardon. Sergeant Dag, I am authorized by General Dennis, commander of the army of Rosia, to accept your surrender. Be apprised, sir, that unless you surrender, I have orders to attack this ship, set fire to it, and kill every man aboard."

"The son of a bitch gave me his word," Dag said bitterly.

"Yes, Sergeant," said Stephano quietly. "I know." His eyes met Dag's. He lowered his voice. When he next spoke, it was as if it was just the two of them talking. "Even now the fleet is maneuvering into firing position. Hastind will not hesitate to kill you and the hostages. End the slaughter, Commander Dag. You have *my* word that you will be treated fairly. And my word is good."

Dag was generally a pragmatic man, slow to anger. But he was angry now, as angry as he'd ever been in his life. His anger boiled in his gut so that he was almost sick with it. He would have liked nothing better than to vent his spleen by giving his men the order to shoot every damn Rosian in sight. The Rosians would fire on the ship the moment they heard the first gunshot, but he and his men might be able to make it back to the fort . . .

Hot breath, smelling of sulphur, washed over him. He looked up, saw De Guichen's dragon gazing down. Her mouth gaped open. The dragon's eyes were narrowed. That breath had either been a threat or an impatient sigh, he couldn't tell which. He saw, past her wing, more dragons, drawing up in formation.

Dag looked at his men as they stood ready. They would fight if he asked them, and they would all die. He carefully lowered the hammer on his pistol and handed the weapon to Stephano.

The fortress's defenders stood in orderly rows on the docks. Their muskets were stacked in neat piles. Dag had insisted the men appear at their best. They might have lost, but they had put up a damn good fight and they should be proud of themselves.

The surrender terms were surprisingly generous, considering how many Rosian lives had been lost in today's attack. The airship had been returned; its wounded captain and the surviving crewmen had sailed it back to join the fleet. The fortress was now the possession of King Alaric of Rosia. The defenders were allowed to keep only personal weapons, such as family swords. All the men were to swear to never again take up arms against Rosia. Nobles, such as Lieutenant Elizandro, were to pay a ransom.

Dag stood next to Antonius. The Crafter was taking this hard. He seemed to have aged twenty years in a few moments. Dag was a professional soldier. Win a few. Lose a few. All part of the job. Antonius was a patriot, and patriots never thought they could lose. After all, God was on their side. From what Dag had seen of warfare, the minute the gunfire started, God was the first one out of town.

The Lord Captain's airship sailed, escorted by two dragons, sailed toward the fortress. Lieutenant Elizandro stood on the ruined dock, waiting to meet the Lord Captain, prepared to hand over his sword. The young man's eyes were red with tears. Weak from hunger, fear, and fatigue, Elizandro had cried like a child when Dag suggested they should agree to the surrender terms. But the young man had managed to pull himself together and now he stood straight and tall in front of his troops. Dag was proud of him.

He noticed, as the airship began her approach to the dock, that she had all her gun ports open and the guns run out. This was unusual, but Dag didn't think much of it. Perhaps they were going to give a salute when the fort surrendered.

The broadside, fired at almost point-blank range, took him completely by surprise.

❖ ❖ ❖

The concussion from the unexpected blast blew his dragon backward and nearly knocked Stephano from his saddle. Dazed, he had no idea, for a moment, what had happened. Then the wind blew away the smoke and revealed a hellish scene of carnage on the dock. The Estarans had been lined up to surrender and now fully one half of them were gone, simply blown to pieces. Those who were still standing looked stunned, as though unable to believe what had just happened.

Stephano could not believe it, either. He looked for Jeantrou, but the commander's dragon had been blown into the airship and damaged his wing on the rudder. The dragon could still fly, but he would not be able to remain airborne for long. Jeantrou had time for one appalled and disbelieving gesture, then his dragon began the slow and painful descent toward the ground.

Stephano was now in command. He thrust his leg into Lady Cam's flank. She made a tight turn, and they swept down out of the sky, flying as close to the airship and its wing-tangling ropes as they dared.

Hastind stood on the deck, calmly surveying the damage through his telescope. A few officers stood around him. One of them was Fascinel. He lowered his telescope and turned away. The man was green. He looked as sick as Stephano felt.

"Hastind!" Stephano's scream shredded his throat. He could taste the blood in his mouth. "Have you lost your mind?"

Hastind looked at him and coolly looked away. He paid no heed, just as Stephano had paid no heed to the Lord Captain's repeated commands to destroy the captured frigate. Hastind had been furious when he'd heard that General Dennis had agreed to the fortress's surrender. He had flown down to headquarters, tried to talk Dennis out of it. When that failed, he tried to make the terms as harsh as possible. When that failed, he cast a furious glance at Stephano and Jeantrou and then stalked out of the tent.

"What's the matter with Hastind?" Stephano wondered. "He won."

"He wanted to be able to claim the airships had knocked the fortress out of the skies," Jeantrou said. "This can't help but make him look bad. He pounds away at the fortress for a month and nothing happens. The dragons show up and within a day the fortress surrenders."

Stephano heard the rumble of the guns being run out again. Hastind was going to fire a second broadside.

He wasn't insane. More's the pity. He planned to do what he'd said. He was going to knock the fortress out of the sky.

Stephano looked back at the fortress. The commander, Dag, was shouting for everyone to run back into the fort. Some of the men managed to do as he said, but many were either too stunned or too injured to move. The big man did not heed his own advice. He remained by the side of a young lieutenant, who lay on the bloody ground. Dag looked straight at Stephano. The look was not one of anger, but of reproach, and it tore through Stephano like grapeshot.

"I gave my word," Stephano said through gritted teeth. "And, by God, I'll keep it." He paused, then added bitterly, "Or what's left of it."

❖　❖　❖

"Didn't we surrender, Dag?" Elizandro asked confusedly.

"Yes, sir. We did, sir," said Dag. He held the shuddering body tightly.

The young man was bleeding from countless wounds, including a gaping hole in his belly. Dag saw at once there was nothing to be done for him. Antonius appeared, knelt down beside them.

"The motherless sons of bitches!" Antonius swore.

"You all right?" Dag asked. The Crafter's robes were covered in blood.

"No," said Antonius. "But I'm not hurt, if that's what you mean."

Dag could hear the rumble of the gun carriages. The ship was close enough that he could see the faces of the gunners, furiously swabbing out the barrels, getting ready to reload.

"My God! They're going to fire again," Antonius said in disbelief.

"Yes," Dag returned. "Get inside the fortress, Crafter. I'll stay with the Lieutenant."

Antonius stared at him in dismay. "But—"

"I'm staying with the Lieutenant," Dag repeated quietly.

Elizandro's head lolled against Dag's chest. His lips were tightly clenched. Sweat rolled down his face.

Antonius's eyes filled with tears. "They won't win," he said, his voice shaking with rage. "I promise."

Before Dag could ask what Antonius meant, the Crafter gathered up his robes and made a dash for the fortress.

Dag could hear the orders being relayed to the gunners, the canisters slamming home.

"Help me sit up, Dag," said the Lieutenant, pushing him away. "And load my pistol. I won't die like a cow going to the slaughter."

"Yes, sir," said Dag.

He propped the Lieutenant up against a shrapnel-ridden fortification and loaded the young man's pistol. Picking up a musket, he loaded it for himself.

The guns were being run out. Sunlight glinted off the barrels.

Dag raised the musket. He sought a target, took aim at the Lord Captain's glittering gold epaulets . . .

An enormous body blotted out the Lord Captain, the gun barrels, and half the airship. Astonished, Dag lowered his weapon. A dragon hung in front of him, keeping her body between him and the airship, between him and the guns. The dragon was so close Dag could feel the Breath of God stirred by the wings. On the dragon's back was the young man who had carried the truce flag. De Guichen, that was his name. One by one, more dragons dropped down out of the sky. The entire Dragon Brigade took up position between the fortress and the fleet of airships.

Dag waited tensely. He would not have been surprised if the Lord Captain had ordered his men to fire, anyway. Dag had known officers like him. Officers who cared for nothing except their own aggrandizement. If he did give the order, though, would his men obey? Dag could see the Lord Captain over the dragon's shoulder, could see the man's face suffused with rage. He had to be wondering that very same thing. Giving an order that no one would obey would make him look worse than backing down.

Even as Dag thought this, the Lord Captain gave an order. The airship started to turn to leave.

Dag let out a sigh and then he saw Lieutenant Elizandro raise his pistol and fire. The Lord Captain grabbed his shoulder and fell to the deck.

"Dear God, boy!" Dag cried, aghast. "What have you done?"

There was no answer. Elizandro had slumped down, dead.

Stephano could never afterward remember if he heard an order to fire. He thought he had, though the officers all later denied it. He knew his dragon had heard the order, for Lady Cam suddenly spread her wings and flipped over, putting her body between the cannons and her rider, just as hell itself exploded all around

Stephano. Lady Cam's body shuddered as the grapeshot ripped through her wings and slammed into her head.

Stephano felt a searing pain in his leg as he clung to the saddle. There was nothing he could do to save himself or his dragon. Facing that terrifying fall, the final smash into the ground, he wondered why he was fighting so desperately to stay in the saddle. It would be easier just to let go . . .

But Lady Cam hadn't given up. A noble lady, from a line of noble dragons, she made a valiant effort to save her rider, though she could not save herself. Through force of will, she fluttered her tattered wings and half-flew, half-fell onto one of the sloops. Men on the decks saw her falling toward them and ran for their lives. Unable to control her landing, she crashed headlong into a mast and dropped heavily to the deck below. With her failing strength, she rolled her body, so as not to pin Stephano beneath her.

Sailors came running to help him. Stephano cut himself free of the straps on the saddle and, dismounting, rounded on them.

"Back off!" he shouted, and the sailors hurriedly retreated.

"Are you all right, sir?" Lady Cam asked weakly, peering at Stephano with her one remaining eye.

"Yes, thanks to you, my lady," he said.

"Tell my clan to sing my death song to the high snows and the blue sky," the dragon said. "Carry my spirit home, sir. Take me home."

"I will, my lady," Stephano promised brokenly. "I will."

He had felt, more than seen, Captain Reynard and the two marines standing over him. He did not look up, but remained with his dragon. He stroked Lady Cam's neck until the light left her eye. Then he whispered a prayer for her, and finally rose to his feet. Unable to put weight on his wounded leg, he braced himself against the still-warm body of the dragon.

"Lord Captain Hastind's orders, sir," said Captain Reynard. "You are under arrest."

"What's the charge?" Stephano asked.

"Mutiny," said Reynard.

Stephano gazed straight at the man. Reynard at least had the grace to look ashamed. As the marines were busy locking manacles onto Stephano's wrists, Reynard turned and walked off.

Stephano looked overhead. The flagship was above them and, as he watched, the ship rocked with the impact of another broadside sweeping the fortress.

❖ ❖ ❖

Antonius had run into the fort, knocking men aside in his haste. He had not seen the Dragon Brigade try to stop the madness by placing themselves between the guns and their victims. He had not seen the Lieutenant shoot the Lord Captain. He did hear the sound of the second broadside and more screams, though not nearly as many as the first time. Even that didn't register with Antonius. He was concentrating on his magic.

He ran from glowing sigil to glowing sigil, touching each one, knocking them out, severing the magic.

Its magical moorings gone, the fortress gave a lurch that knocked Antonius off his feet. He pressed his hands against the wall and fed all his magic into the stone that was soaked with the blood of his compatriots. The effort drained him and he fell to the floor. He looked out a gun port. The fortress was on the move.

His work was done. He sighed, put his back to the wall, braced for the crash.

❖ ❖ ❖

A lookout on board Reynard's ship gave a cry, shouting, "The flagship!"

The marines taking Stephano to the bridge stopped to look. Stephano stopped. Men, officers—everyone stared upward in horrified disbelief.

Lord Captain Hastind had done what he set out to do—he'd knocked the island-fortress loose from its moorings. What he hadn't expected was that the fortress would be turned into a battering ram aimed directly at his airship.

The flagship tried her best to escape the catastrophe that was rumbling ponderously toward her, but she wasn't fast enough.

Everyone aboard ship gasped and flinched in sympathy as the fortress rammed the flagship. The wooden hull splintered. Men pitched overboard and fell, screaming, into a thousand feet of nothing. Debris rained down on top of their ship. Stephano ducked as a wooden plank smashed onto the deck not a foot away from him.

The fortress was now descending rapidly, pushing the wreckage of the flagship in front of it. The order had been given to abandon ship and the survivors were running for the lifeboats. Lord Captain Hastind was already in his barge and it was pushing away, heedless of the cries of the wounded sailors left behind.

Captain Reynard sailed out to meet the Lord Captain's barge. Hastind's left arm was wrapped in a bloody sling, but he managed to take off his hat and yell out loudly, "Give three cheers, my lads! The day is ours!"

The sailors cheered dutifully. The Lord Captain sat back down comfortably in the air barge. It descended to the ground, moving slowly and gently, so as not to jar his lordship–Lord Captain Hastind, the gallant, suffering hero of the Battle of Fallen Star, so called by the daily scandal sheets, making a clever play on the word "Estaran."

Stephano stood with his hands shackled, his clothes wet with his blood and that of his dragon, and watched the fortress, wreathed in smoke and dust, sink into the clouds. A single man still stood on it, stood alone.

The big man, Dag, the Guundaran officer.

Dag's eyes met Stephano's.

A hearty cheer, my lads. The day is ours.

PROVING THE RULE

BY HOLLY PHILLIPS

*Holly Phillips, one of the most promising new writers in fantasy
literature, has already won awards and nominations for such remarkable work as* In the Palace of Repose, *a collection of short
fiction; its title story appeared in the premiere issue of* H. P.
Lovecraft's Magazine of Horror. *Her first novel,* The Burning Girl, *has been critically acclaimed, and her next novel,* The
Engine's Child, *is scheduled to appear in 2008 from Del Rey
Books. A western Canadian who lives by the Columbia River, she
comes honestly by her first name, having been born on Christmas
Day.*

*"Proving the Rule" is typically untypical Phillips: the strange
adventure of a book-loving distaff researcher into that old dead
(?) discipline, magic . . .*

A BUSY PUB at noon.

He had his pocket notebook out on the table and was flipping
past old stories, scratching out unconfirmed facts and unusable
quotes: the merest gesture toward work. Someone jogged his
table, but he saw it coming and lifted his pint out of danger. He
drank, licked his lip, set the glass warily down. Should have ordered food, he thought. The crowd at the bar was two deep and if
he got up now he'd lose the table and the chair he was saving
for her. If she didn't come he'd go hungry. But if he got up and
she came? He went on leafing through the notebook, his head
bent low.

She slipped inside like a draft through an open window. He
would have sworn that he felt her, that he looked up an instant

183

before she came into view. The crowd parted for her like curtains; she lit him up like a ray of light. Resenting it, he refused to stand, but bad manners failed to hide his open face, his pencil falling to the floor. She smiled, pleased to see him, and sat in the saved chair.

"What are you drinking?" she asked him.

"Bitter. You won't like it. Try the ale."

"All right. And food? Are you feeding me, too?"

He fed her cold game pie and apples and cheese. The apples were from somebody's cold store and under their wrinkled skins tasted of cider and old wood. They went well with the beer.

She had the knack of elegance. She was dressed well, of course, something simple in green wool that hinted at the coming spring, but that was just money. The mystery was the rest of her. The way she could hum with greed, wrinkle her nose when she took a bite, catch a drop of mustard with her tongue, and still be elegant, dainty and refined. That wasn't money, surely? Breeding, another woman of her class would say. But she was the daughter of a scandal and didn't know who her father was.

"You aren't listening," he said.

She took her time reeling her gaze in from the depths. She had darkish hair, paleish skin, eyes somewhere between gray and blue. Yet her gaze was definite. When she looked at you, you knew you were looked at.

"I am," she said. "Well, a little bit, I am."

"What did I say, then?"

She offered him a smile. "I'm inventing a riddle. The answer is 'magic,' but I haven't got the question right yet."

"If it's the one about the racehorse trainer and the greyhound, I've already heard it."

She smiled again, but her mind was still somewhere else.

Piqued, he said, in accidental parody of a jealous lover, "If you don't want the work, just say so. We both know you only do it for fun."

"Fun? You mean, I don't do it for money."

"What for, then?"

"Well, it's what I do. History. Research. All the delicious books, yum, yum, and reading dead people's letters behind their backs. Lovely, malicious sense of power. Blackmailing ghosts. It's where my money really comes from, of course." She played at mischief with a straight face, her long-fingered hands fluttering in the air.

"All right," he said heavily to drag her back down to earth. "But really. Why?"

She looked at him with those pale eyes, her pupils so black they never seemed to reflect any light. "All for love of you, my hero. Tell me again what you need?"

Another beer, he thought. He flipped back a page in his notebook so vigorously that the thin paper tore.

❖ ❖ ❖

For love of him? *Because it's my only talent, because it's the only thing that marks me as something besides my mother's daughter, because it's the only thing that's entirely mine.* But though Graham was her friend, he wasn't that kind of friend, so she didn't say it. She just took a little leather-bound notebook out of her purse and made notes, to mollify him, with her little gold pencil. He was writing a series of articles on immigration. While he was talking she jotted down a few citations, reminded herself of a private memoir that she had found in the family library; thought that she probably could have written the articles herself, and knew that she would never say so. Graham needed to work for a living. They could be friends for fifty years, she thought, and he would never reconcile himself to the fact that she did not.

No, she only needed to work to live. Because, because.

Her name was Lucy Donne. Her mother was beautiful, her grandfather was rich. She had been allowed to go to university—it was one of the done things these days—but there were no advanced degrees for women. One could study, write, publish, even tutor, but one could not lecture; one could never call oneself Professor Lucy Donne. She might have done anything, really, she had her mother's recklessness, but she had her grandfather's self-conscious pride as well. She would not trail in her mother's footsteps. Books would be her open doors. A drab compromise, she thought sometimes, though she tried not to think about it. She preferred the delicious books, the impossible hunt, the riddling obsession that kept her up late, night after night. Yum, yum . . . yawn.

The library was a rich man's pride, a set-designer's dream: a long room with a gallery and window bays, jewel-colored carpets and fat-legged tables and a globe clasped in a polished brass arm. It was real to Lucy, though, it was her province, her private realm. She knew about the mousetraps behind the bottom shelves, the silverfish like hungry beads of quicksilver, the dead moths that would fly again if you gave the curtains a good shake. She knew that in a cold winter the cavernous fireplaces could only warm the end bays, leaving an arctic space between them, and she knew that in a hot summer the very walls breathed sleep into the dusty, sun-shot air. Home.

The big clock with its gold and ivory face ticked down another hour. A brass-shaded lamp spilled its pool of light, but Lucy's mind had wandered off into the dark, and so did her books and papers, sprawling outside the lamplight. Her chin was in her hands, her elbows on the ink-splotched blotter. An hour ago she had still been chasing her quarry. Now she dreamed, tracing the route of past hunts across the map of knowledge in her mind. Landmarks, scraps of information, raised themselves up above the horizon and fell away. Yes, she knew this. Yes, she had been there. Most recently:

. . . in the "he's famous even if I don't care" category, the Marshal of Kallisfane (of ancient and dull renown) returned to the capital today after a refreshing month's holiday in the historic and terminally comfortless garrison of Denbreath. The garrison might have a

greater appeal to this writer and several other ladies of her acquaintance (the Hon. Miss H. comes to mind!) if it still featured hot-and-cold running soldiers, but as the Denbreath Fortress was recently turned into a museum, one can only wish the Chief Exhibit joy of his new vacation spot . . .

Yes, and:

From our provincial correspondent: Two teachers at the Palton Grammar School were dismissed yesterday after a recent outbreak of hysteria among the students forced authorities to close the school. The school will reopen next week and school governors say they will not be bringing charges against the teachers, saying the two women demonstrated "poor judgment rather than criminal intent."

And what has the one to do with the other? Nothing at all, except that Palton is only ten miles from Denbreath as the crow flies. What tales did the teachers tell? What tales did the children claim to encounter on their way home from school? What would the crow see as it launched itself from the highest steeple in Palton and flew over the winter-dark woods of Breadon How?

Up over the haunted trees, up over the bare brow of the hill where the Cold Hounds were once said to lair, out along the stony ridge where Denbreath Castle sits as it has for six hundred years, a fortified shell for its silent master, the Exhibit, who is older still. The breeze carries the crow to the deep sill of an archer's window, where it folds its wings and cocks its head to stare inside. A stony room. A man, or the shape of a man, stiff as a mannequin waiting for the curators to put its armor on.

The clock clunked and whirred, preparing Lucy for the mellow gong of the hour. One, two . . . Lucy waited for the rest, but the clock had said its piece. She rubbed her face, made a token gesture towards putting her notes in order . . . impossible, it would take a week . . . she put out the lamp and went to bed.

She dreamed the dream in which her house dissolved into a

muddled realm of college rooms and hospital corridors. There were a lot of doors, a lot of odd corners twisting the known world out of true. It got harder and harder to find her way, but the harder it got the closer she was to something important, some vivid presence at the heart of the maze. This anticipation was as familiar as the dream, but as the dreamer did not know she was dreaming she could not say, as she would when she woke, "Ah! *This* dream!" But she could recognize the feeling for what it was, and that recognition opened the final door. There were the heavy stones of the wall, the arch that opened out onto nothing but the air. There was the bright clear light, the taste of autumn, the memory of trees. And perhaps the dreamer woke a little in her dreaming, because when she saw the man who stood looking out on the world, she thought or said, "Maybe this time I will see his face. Maybe I will. I will."

An obvious dream; a biographer's dream. But there was nothing stale about the brightness of her will to turn him. Oh, she wanted to see! He knew she was there, he stirred. Her heart leapt. She would wake now, she always woke now and was now awake enough to know it. She held on to the dream with both hands.

And then it seemed that the dream turned and grabbed on to her. The brightness in the air was gone, there was only a warmth as oppressive as a stranger's breath. He stirred, and she no longer knew why she wanted to see his face. "Don't," she said, and the catch of sound in her throat drew her farther out of sleep.

The dream followed her.

He turned. He saw her, and she fled, a bird dashing across the room—the window was there again, his dark figure like a door—she fled, he plucked her from the air. She was a sand-colored dove between his hands, his flesh pressing her flesh as if he grasped her bare ribs, her naked arms. She cried out and woke.

She was still held.

She tore herself free from the bedclothes, flung herself from the bed to fall on her hands and knees. Awake, yes, and dreaming, yes, and still held. Her heart beat its wings. Sweating, trembling, she launched herself from the floor and caromed into the wardrobe across the room like a bird battering itself against a windowpane. Wood bruised flesh, a banged elbow barked, and she woke, finally, truly woke, with the wardrobe door swinging open and her nightgown clinging to her skin.

With a deliberate, practical gesture, Lucy reached out and swung the door closed. The latch *snicked,* and held.

Her room was dark except for the pale rim around the curtain's edge, and the house was quiet, although it seemed to Lucy that the reverberations of her thumps and cries still hung in the air. She stood and listened as if the house might mutter a response—

As if, far below, the street door might open and booted feet might begin to climb the groaning stairs.

She was found.

It was a dream, she told herself with the sweat still wet on her face. Only a nightmare version of a dream she had been dreaming since she was a little girl.

She had been hunting him since girlhood. She had finally come near enough to be noticed.

Him.

. . . the Marshal of Kallisfane (of ancient and dull renown) returned to the capital today . . .

The Marshal of Kallisfane, the Dead Lord, the Revenant, the Living Ghost, Empire's Bane: Him.

The Marshal of Kallisfane returned to the capital today.

She was found.

Lucy pried herself away from the wardrobe and crept up to the window. One finger opened a crack between curtain and frame. A gray dawn, the garden in the square still more turned earth than green, the windows in all the houses still dark. No deathless warrior on the pavement, no Nameless Regiment pulling up in big black motorcars. No one at all, in fact, except for a few sparrows and a cat digging in a flower bed. Logic, late in waking, said that even if he had found her by some arcane process in her dream, a dream does not shout out a name and an address. Her heart was still thumping, her skin still clammy, and Lucy was not reassured. Sick with fear, she walked with increasing haste down the hall to the lavatory and vomited out the residue of the dream.

Pipes thumped when she flushed the toilet and sang when she ran water to rinse her mouth, guaranteed to wake half the household. But the prosaic was reassuring and nausea imposed its own earthy fatalism. If the Revenant really had found her where she lived she was already doomed, and if he had not, then . . . then she hardly knew what. The need to do something was beginning to assert itself, but what the something was, was still obscure. Bathe, Lucy thought, smelling the fear sweat like bile on her skin.

She washed, found a skirt and jacket in sensible tweed, and put on the most sensible shoes she owned, which weren't very. Dull, ordinary, please-don't-notice-me clothes. She pinned up her hair, powdered her face—in the mirror her hands shook—put a few practical items in her pocketbook. She paused on the landing, but there was no sound from behind the family's doors. Her mother's door. Would her mother still hold her after a bad dream, envelop her in warm silk and cigarette smoke and perfume?

Lucy shook herself back into motion. Down the stairs to the grand entry hall, and did she scurry across the marble floor, wrench open the bolts, flit like a sparrow out into the square? That was the motion of her heart, but she hesitated at the stained-glass window by the door, peering through a red rose into the square. A yawning domestic was airing a pair of leashed dogs. Still no living statue (ten feet tall? lichened armor? pigeon-stained helm?) and no ominous black cars. Do what, Lucy? Go where? Seized by a sudden impulse, she left the hall and struck out for the library.

No one had been in yet to open the drapes. She pulled them open as she walked down the main room, letting in daylight the same color as the dust she shook from the brocade. The farthest bay held her table like a ship in its berth, a ship still laded with the cargo of a years-long journey: books, clippings, diaries, letters; notes sorted and unsorted, re-sorted, scribbled over, lost. No one tidied Lucy's desk, Lucy least of all. The order was all in her head, a tangled complexity that, taken all in all, built a structure as simple as a tombstone. Lucy sifted through the top layer of papers, shifted a book from one stack to another, and failed utterly to discover the source of her panic. This was scholarship. It had only been a dream.

Then the panic said: *This is evidence.*

At first she read her notes over with an eye to organization, but she gave that up almost immediately. The clock chimed the half hour and her whole skin shivered. She crammed papers into whatever folder would hold them, shook out the books and scrabbled to gather up the snowfall of torn envelopes and old letters and receipts from the dressmaker with her elegant scrawl on the back. She liberated a large portfolio from an ancestor's anatomical sketches and tied her papers inside with a faded ribbon. She took up armloads of books and scattered them about the shelves, almost dancing as she moved in and out of bays, up and down the gallery stairs. It would take her days to find them all again, these books with their damning marginalia, but it would take a stranger weeks. Finally, swiftly, she disposed of the anatomical sketches behind a rank of foreign dictionaries, tore the blotter from her desk pad and tossed it burning into the fireplace, snatched up the heavy portfolio and her pocketbook and fled for the door.

Doing what, Lucy?

She seemed to be discovering that as it got done.

Going where, Lucy?

She would likely discover that as well.

But it was only a dream.

❖ ❖ ❖

The same pub, too early for a crowd.

Resentful at being called away from his typewriter, Graham

sat at a table under the small-paned window, scribbling on a tablet of ruled paper: real work this time, distilling interviews into news. The midmorning sun fought through thin clouds and thick, old glass to raise a gleam from the polished table. He didn't notice. He did notice the brewer's dray that creaked to a stop outside, its high sides painted with the brewer's slogan–Our Best Bitter is Better! Barrels rumbled off the tailgate, enormous horses stamped iron-shod feet, and he experienced one of those hiccups in time, a flash of his childhood when horses were everywhere and motorcars were rare. Change, he thought. Would we dread it so much if it didn't sneak up on us from behind?

"What do you do," she said, "if you have a story no one will believe?"

"Don't write it." He rescued his notes from the descending bulk of a leather-bound portfolio. The thump of its landing was lost in the grumble of barrel rims being rolled across the stone floor. "You could have asked me that over the telephone."

She sat down and drank from his glass. It was an unprecedented intimacy and he watched, astonished, the tilt of the glass and the long swallow. The bitter made her grimace even as she sucked the dampness off her upper lip. Oh, Lucy, he thought. What is this, now? A barman materialized, wiping his hands on his long white apron.

"Brandy, please," she said.

"She means the real stuff, Jock," Graham said. "In one of those fat glasses that spill all down your chin."

"A snifter, sir, yes, thank you, sir," said Jock, his accent refined to the point of sarcasm. But he came back with the brandy and another pint for Graham. Graham finished off the old pint and then looked at Lucy. She was shivering from too harsh a swallow–Our Best Brandy Isn't Better–and put the back of her hand to her mouth, a fascinating gesture, but they all were, her gestures like a private conversation between Lucy and herself, and she had such beautiful hands . . . Graham gave his second pint a wary look and pushed it away. Trouble, he thought. And then looked at her again and woke up to her pallor and bruised eyelids: trouble indeed.

"But what do you really do?" she said, and lowered her hand.

He had to retrieve her initial question. "Really don't write it. What would be the point?"

"What if people should believe it? What if they need to know?"

Graham hooted with laughter. "There is no such story. Listen, love, you can't tell the glorious public anything for their own good, not unless you're in advertising. One of the great mysteries of life. Tell them snake oil cures warts and they're happy to pay a shilling an ounce. Tell them the Country Hospital Fund requires property taxes to increase by a shilling next year and consider the outrage!" He drank from his beer, then remembered and set it aside.

"Maybe outrage cures warts," she said with a smile that made him feel she was looking at him for the first time.

"Maybe snake oil does. What's your story that no one will believe?"

"Maybe magic does."

"Cut a potato with a silver knife and bury it by the light of a full moon."

Her smile grew lighter, questioning.

"Magic," he explained. "To cure warts."

"Shhh." She reached across the table and touched her fingers to his lips. "Not so loud. He might hear you."

She wasn't smiling now. He knew what he was supposed to ask, but it took him a moment, seduced as he was by a touch that lingered after she had taken her hand away. What is this, Lucy? What the hell?

"Who might hear?"

She didn't answer him directly. "Do you believe in magic?"

"Do I believe in . . . are we talking philosophy? History? Curing warts?"

"Magic," she said, as if it were a perfectly sensible thing to say in an empty pub on a day in early spring. "Here and now, curing warts, whatever you like."

"No. Never tell me that's your story." His eyes wandered to the fat portfolio between them on the table. "What is that, dispatches from a thousand years ago? Or is all this just leading up to something else?"

"Magic is real. Here and now. And I can prove it."

She had a faint smile and a tension that dared him to take her seriously, but was she serious?

"You're dead right, chicken: nobody will believe you."

"But I can prove it. I can. And it's easy, anyone can do it who's ever read a newspaper, seen a newsreel at the moving picture show. Anyone who learned their history lessons at school."

"What?" This whole conversation was the setup for an insult to his intelligence. "Can you possibly be talking about who I think you're talking about? That stuffed suit the royals haul out for parades! That dressmaker's dummy! That moth-eaten remainder from a waxwork museum! What the hell has come over you?" His gaze was caught again by her portfolio. "Oh, Lucy. Lucy, no. *This* is your life's work? *This* is what you've been chasing after all this time?"

She looked down as if she were surprised to see the battered folio case on the table. Her cheeks were flushed and her smile had fled; he felt a stab of shame, as if he'd been picking on the slow child at school; but all the same!

"Of all the dull corners of history you could have chosen," he said before he could change tack. "Well, all right. But please don't suggest the Marshal of Whatsisname is news. Really, old darling, believability is not the issue. Sheer, unadulterated boredom is the issue."

"Didn't you ever scare yourself with the stories when you were a child?" Her voice was quiet, and though there was a humorous quirk to her brows she didn't meet his eyes. "The end of an empire, the end of an age. The end of magic. And the one who did it just goes on and on . . ."

"I know. 'Don't stay out after dark, *he* might get you!' But that was just to make staying out after dark more fun." Studying her face, Graham found himself increasingly sorry for his scorn. She always looked delicate; at this moment she looked frail. "I still don't get what this is about? The story no one will believe?"

"Magic is still alive," she said, almost in a whisper. "And I can prove it."

"All right. What's your proof?"

"The Marshal of Kallisfane."

"But he ended it." He leaned forward, as if it was important to convince her. "He brought the dread empire down and put an end to magic. Hurray for the dawn of reason and the rule of law."

"A thousand years ago."

"Give or take."

"Then what's keeping him alive?"

"What . . ." Graham scratched his chin. He was on the verge of laughter, because though it was nonsense, it was clever nonsense. "Well, he's a remnant, isn't he? Sort of . . . a leftover. Wasn't it supposed to be the doing of it, whatever he did, that preserved him? Dried prunes, salt cod, the Marshal of Whatsisname?"

"Are you asking me, or telling me?"

"I am telling you," he said pompously, "what they taught us in school."

But the more he tried to jolly her out of it, the more solemn she became.

"That," she said with one of those direct, heartstopping looks, "is what he told someone a long time ago."

"There you are, then."

"And he's a reliable source, is he? Mister Newspaperman?"

"Oh, come on!" He was stung by her echo of his scorn. "It's clever, I grant you, but you don't think you're the first person ever to think of it, do you?"

"No," she said, her gaze falling again to her papers. "No, I don't."

"Even if it's a neat bit of logic, it doesn't go anywhere, does it? I mean, so what if he is . . ." (he felt like an ass for saying the word) ". . . magical. If he's the only magical thing in the world, what's it good for? He's an anomaly, the exception that proves the rule."

"That just means 'tests the rule.' The challenge to the rule. Did you know that?" This, apparently to the portfolio.

"And it's no kind of newspaper story," he forged on, though he was starting to hate the sound of his own voice. "You do know that, right?"

"Oh, yes. I know. Because no one will believe it, and no one will care."

"Well, listen . . ." By this time feeling like an utter shit. "There's nothing wrong with the idea. I mean, as an idea. Philosophy, history, all that. Very profound."

"Rest easy, my hero. I wasn't going to ask you to put it in your paper."

She smiled, finally, but she didn't quite meet his gaze. And then before he knew it she was gathering up the weighty portfolio and bending down to kiss him, which she never did, a press of her lips to the corner of his mouth, a gesture as mysterious and expressive as any of hers, warm and sad and what? What is this, Lucy? What the hell *is* this?

But by the time it occurred to him simply to ask, she was gone.

Lucy had called up Graham with the vague notion of asking for help, or perhaps for less than that, for comradeship, a shoulder braced against her own. So his contempt stung, and confused her, too, because she could have argued against it, but what if he was wrong? What if the danger was real? It *was* real, it was the crooked backward course she had been plotting all this time. So if she was wrong, if she had been chasing nothing more than a scholar's delusion, then she was a fool, but she was safe. And if she wasn't wrong, then *he* was safe, because she had taken her proof away unshared. And wasn't it just a dream? She didn't know. She could not explain the certainty of danger, even to herself. She went home.

And walking from the bus stop (the bus easier than hunting for a cab so close to noon) she turned the corner into the square and saw him.

Him.

Benbury Square was really three squares nested one inside the other: the outer square of town houses; then the square of cobblestone pavement fronting the houses; then the square of the central garden, hemmed in by palings and punctuated by trees. There were beds of turned earth, two benches awaiting this year's coat of paint, and a rounded patch of lawn already showing green. And on the lawn stood a man wearing a double-breasted overcoat of the sober, fashionless type favored by royalty. As Lucy had said to Graham, one saw this figure sometimes in the newsreels: herky-jerky frames of celluloid gray, at once luminous and drab, of the king opening the High Court or greeting a Special Envoy, with this stiff dark figure in the background. Stuffed suit, waxwork dummy, museum mannequin waiting for his armor. He stood so dreadfully still on the greening lawn. Watching Lucy's house.

Lucy drifted backwards, taking a glacial age to slip back around the corner. She felt transparent as a ghost, as if her substance had been stripped by shock, leaving nothing but the damp gray chill of the day. She drifted, and even around the corner she could feel him, as if she were a compass and he, black as iron, were a magnetic pole. Still walking backwards, she was jostled by a passer-by, and suddenly the world leapt into existence: not a ghostly arena hushed with anticipation, but a living city, busy with pedestrians, motor cabs squawking their horns and delivery van horses clattering on metal-shod hooves.

She ran until she could not breathe around the stitch in her side.

She rode a bus until the conductor turned her off at the end of its route, and then she rode another one.

She did not know where to go. The very concept of hiding was equivocal, denying as it did her passage from there to here. Hadn't her feet pressed all that ground? Didn't the tires of the bus? Wasn't there a trail?

Hadn't he, even he, left her a trail?

The buses all seemed to turn her back towards the center of the city. After a bit she realized this was no arcane conspiracy, it was simply the logic of transportation: where else would the buses go? But getting off was hard. She looked anxiously through the dusty windows, expecting that stiff, dark figure; or if not that, then the rumored black motorcars of the Regiment No One Ever Saw.

There were black cars, but they were only taxicabs. She hoped. She dared. She descended the high steps onto the curb and found herself in a neighborhood she knew, the politely shabby territory behind the national library, realm of scholars and writers, private libraries and obscure museums, bookstores and cafés. She was known here. She could not possibly go to ground here. But her feet were on pavement they knew, and they took her to one of the smaller train stations in the city where she bought a ticket for a slow suburban train leaving in half an hour.

Half an hour. A terrifying gulf of time.

She sat, her feet throbbing in her not very sensible shoes, and watched the suburban shoppers flock and scatter like pigeons. She eyed the crippled clock above the ticket booth that refused to move its hands any faster than a creep. She studied the Departures board, looking for the hundredth time for a train that left any sooner. Which means that she must have looked at that one word a hundred times before she saw it. Palton. A country town, one stop among many, so why did it swim slowly up into her consciousness like a fish rising to the hook? Palton, Palton . . .

Palton, where only last week two teachers had been dismissed to cover up the "hysteria" amongst the students of a country school. Palton, that lay tucked under the haunted peak of Breadon How. Palton, that was only a crow's flight away from the castle at Denbreath.

It was like finding a path in the trackless wood. She had somewhere to go.

❖ ❖ ❖

The last thing Lucy expected was to fall asleep on the train, but that was what she did, all but resting her head on the shoulder of the plump girl who had entered the compartment with a bevy of aunts just as the train pulled away. While they clucked over their parcels Lucy slipped gently into the murmur of voices, the swaying of the carriage, the rhythm of the wheels. Outside the window the city peeled away, diminishing into low brick districts, into gray waste grounds, into greening suburbs half-veiled by the engine's steam. The train's whistle shrieked at crossings and hooted for stations like a huge iron owl. Lucy half-slept while the train was in motion, half-woke when it crawled into one station and the next. The ladies left in a flurry of packages and she had the compartment to herself until a young man looked shyly in.

"Do you mind, miss?"

"No," she said. He had a plain, open face, and an old raincoat slung over an off-the-rack suit that gave an impression of untidiness despite the bright polish of his enormous black shoes. Perhaps it was just that men of a certain size shouldn't wear suits: he wasn't fat, but he was very large. He gave Lucy a nervous smile and tucked himself away behind a paperback book that looked small in his hands. She relaxed a little; yet as the train rolled on, she began to find the racketing rhythm of the wheels more implacable than soothing. *To Palton to Palton to Palton* and what was she going to do when she got there? Something, she thought with her hands clenched into sharp-knuckled fists. Something to oppose. Something to defy.

Unable to sit still, she got up and slid open the door to the corridor. The countryside spread over brown fields and grey-green trees to the dusky northern hills. The smoke of burning thatch rose to meet the end of the day, drawing down the clouds. Lucy leaned against the corridor window, feeling a hard, old-woman's sadness that seemed like the older sister to her fear, as if part of her knew that things weren't going to turn out well. To defy, yes, that seemed necessary. That did not mean that she, knowing what she knew, could hope to overcome. She thought of the books scattered throughout her grandfather's library. She thought of her grandfather, and her mother, and Graham. She thought of the hasty letter she had written, and of the papers she had abandoned to the care of the Left Luggage Office of Skilly-ham Station, and of the claim check that had gone into the post just as the train was called.

A woman swaying down the corridor to the end of the carriage excused herself as she bumped into Lucy. Lucy pressed herself aside, and through the window of the compartment's glass door she caught the eye of the large young man with the book, who was watching her as patiently and unfeelingly as the fox watches the brush pile, waiting for the hare.

❖ ❖ ❖

My hero,

Here is the story no one wants to know:

Two hundred and eighteen years ago, the Marshal of Kallisfane founded Madrigal College's Chair of Imperial Studies, the only one in that subject in the university. Since the founding, there have been twenty-nine Fellows, as compared to an average of sixteen Fellows in the same period of time across all other subjects. Of those twenty-nine Fellows, only six in 218 years have died peacefully of old age. Three have simply disappeared—the rest have died of suicide, un-

explained accident, or outright murder. Check the university records and local police blotters: this is fact. Also ask yourself: Why is there only one fellowship in Imperial History, when we are, today, living in the ruins of that empire? In the university, it is because every time another such fellowship has been proposed—even when the proposal includes generous funding—the University Council has declined. The only reason ever offered: such a chair already exists. Never mind that six different colleges sport research chairs in Modern History. There shall only ever be one chair in Imperial History, and the scholars who hold that chair are more likely to die violently than if they joined the army or worked in a mine . . .

❖ ❖ ❖

They waited until she stepped off the train in Palton.

The large young man, with his book in his coat pocket, followed her onto the platform and was joined by an older man, thin enough to hide in his shadow, who materialized out of the engine's steam.

"Please, Miss Donne," said the older man as he took her elbow, "let's not have a fuss."

They didn't have a fuss. It was exactly as though she had been met by friends. The large young man took her pocketbook and rifled through it, but he did it so calmly that no one seemed to notice. The ticket collector took Lucy's ticket from his hand without a flicker and they walked out into the astonishing freshness of the spring evening. There was the cobbled street of the country town, the sketch of chimney pots against the violet sky. The air was impossibly sweet after the stuffiness of the train. Instinct made Lucy look up, but clouds hid the stars. Looking down she saw the massive shape of the long black car pulling up to the station door. There was something inevitable about that car, about the dusk, about the country quiet pouring in around the wail of the departing train. She drew a long breath with a strange kind of eagerness. Whatever else happened, she was going to *know*.

"That's right, Miss Donne," said the older man as he opened the rear door. "Nothing to be frightened of here."

❖ ❖ ❖

. . . But it isn't only scholars he is keeping under his thumb. Seventy-two years ago the village of Galburgh in South Pevenshire was digging up a section of the commons at the edge of the village to widen a carriage road. In the course of the work they uncovered a stretch of old paving which, when it was taken up, proved to cover a spring that drained into the Macklebrook via an underground channel. There was some debate, reported in the parish records, as to whether to cover the spring and carry on with the road or to leave it uncovered and put it to some use. In the meantime, however, workmen who drank from the spring complained of dreams of such terrible import that one man joined an overseas missionary society and another committed suicide. The parish priest called upon the bishop for advice, but no church action was ever taken, for the simple reason that that was the month in which the Crown passed the Commons Development Act, which allowed, and still allows, the sale of common land by parish councils for the "creation or development of such industries, enterprises, public buildings, etc., to the benefit of the township." The commons was bought, the spring was paved over, and a new village police station built on the spot. According to the Pevenshire newspapers of the time, the Marshal of Kallisfane was on hand for the new station's official opening.

Graham, the king overturned a common-use law of centuries' standing so that the Revenant could pave over a spring and put it under guard. And that is one of the most harmless stories that comes to mind . . .

❖ ❖ ❖

The motorcar slid down narrow country roads, carrying Lucy into the night. Lucy's companion from the train shared the back seat with her, but with the darkness to hide his watchful gaze he was just the shy young man abashed by his own size, and then even less than that, as if he were absorbed into the car itself, just one more shade of dark. The air was chill, whistling with drafts, but it smelled warmly of tobacco and leather, leaf-mold and aging upholstery. Lucy was reminded of being chauffeured from school to her grandfather's country house, always knowing that the man behind the wheel reckoned she was no more than an excuse to take the new car, hand-built in her grandfather's own stable, out for a drive. She had never minded that feeling. It had been the real holiday between the heated friendships and rivalries of school and the equally perilous attentions of her mother, her cousins, her aunts. Tonight, as the wind whined in around the windows and the chill soaked through her sensible tweed, she felt as though she were wrapped in a ghost of that comfort. But while she acknowledged that ghost, she did not let it fool her. In the end, she thought, it was just the calm certainty of doom.

. . . for he is rarely inclined to hold his hand. Consider the fishers of Belmouth, who only two years ago complained of seals with human voices wrecking their nets and stealing their fish, but paying for their plunder with prophecy and song. The Marshal of Kallisfane, according to your very own newspaper, was granted use of the royal yacht for a late-autumn cruise ending in Belmouth harbor. Captain Ellerby, master of the king's yacht, reported cloudless skies, light breezes, and an easy sail. That same day, the entire fishing fleet of Belmouth was lost in a freak storm. We will never know if it was because those fishermen were telling stories of talking seals, or if it was because of what those seals were saying. Every man off those boats is presumed drowned. Fifty-seven men . . .

❖ ❖ ❖

The black motorcar of the Unnamed Regiment paused just long enough for an iron gate to swing open. They eased past a saluting sentry and onto a drive. It was late. They had traveled much further than Denbreath. Trees flickered in the edge of the head-lamps' glow, then fell away into blackness and an impression of rough ground. The car's note deepened as it began to climb. Then even the ground fell away, and Lucy's heart stopped for an instant of disoriented terror—but they were not flying, only fol-lowing the back of a ridge, its steep slope invisible in the dark. That moment of fear lingered, a quickening in her belly and a tightening in her flesh, prelude to the shock of arrival.

❖ ❖ ❖

. . . And if even the list of the dead is still not enough to make any-one care—and Graham, I know hundreds of these stories—then con-sider our history. Consider the holy wars in which the ancient pantheon and its temples were thrown down. Thousands of priests hanged or burned, their congregations killed, persecuted, scattered, an entire faith relegated to a footnote in the history books, because we have no ancient history, no memory, and no way to know what those priests once knew about the world or the magic the Revenant claims to have killed a thousand years ago.

He isn't a joke, Graham, he isn't a scarecrow stuffed with straw. He isn't even a walking corpse. He is a tombstone, and he has spent the last thousand years keeping magic in its grave.

My train is leaving, I must fly—
Lucy

❖ ❖ ❖

Perhaps it was the starless night they had traveled through, per-haps it was the chill and the wood-rot smell of age, but Lucy was exquisitely aware of the stony weight of the castle that swallowed her up. She felt as if she had been eaten by a mountain, as if the dark were the perfect and immutable dark of a mine. And there was the silence, too, a deep, conscious, listening silence. Even her escorts seemed reluctant to intrude; they stepped softly, spoke in undertones to the men at the door.

What must it be like to work for the Undying, to run his bloody errands, to keep his house?

They ushered her through the great hall, shadowy as a cathedral, and down a back-eddy of a corridor to a chapel. In the corridors there were electric lights strung along the plastered walls, but in the chapel there were only banks of candles burning with a honey smell. Light and warmth hovered in the narrow room, complementing rather than banishing the cold and dark. The high white walls were decked with brass memorial plaques, mirrors for the ranks of flame burning in their corner stands, and there were more plaques set in the floor. There were no pews, only a plain altar stone and the candles, and the Sacred Flame hanging on the end wall, a tapered silver oval like the point of a spear.

The room was so quiet Lucy could hear the rustle of the many candleflames, and the footsteps coming down the hall.

He still wore his overcoat, buttoned to show only his trouser hems and the neat square knot of his tie. His head was bare, his thick dark hair neatly combed, his face expressionless, lifeless . . . dead. Lucy thought his eyes were dark, but she found it impossible to meet them. She did not want to see them or be seen by them. Her heart beat with a trapped flutter, remembering the bird in her dream.

"Miss Donne," he said, "do you know why you are here?"

His voice shocked her: an ordinary baritone, a little rough, but without menace. No sullen echo of the grave.

"I dreamed . . ."

He waited for her to finish, as patient as the walls. The pause was so long it finally seemed that Lucy's fear had peaked, that she had breasted some steep rise and found herself still standing. She took what felt like her first breath since he entered the room and said, laying her cards on the table or throwing them to the wind, "I have been studying you. I have researched you, I have learned . . . I have learned some of what you are . . ." Lucy trailed off again, this time with a blush. How childish that sounded! And how intimate, with an unwarranted, uninvited intimacy.

"And you dreamed," he said, inflectionless.

"I did not dream you outside my house," she said. *You.* That was the intimacy: saying, not *him,* but *you.* You.

Lucy, is it only fear that makes your heart race?

He had stepped further into the chapel without her noticing. She drifted away from his advance.

"You looked for me. You found me." He began to unbutton his overcoat, standing before the altar, and Lucy realized there was something lying on the stone as if for consecration. She tore her gaze away, desperate not to have seen what she saw. The Marshal of Kallisfane shrugged his coat from his shoulders and bent to lay it on the floor, and Lucy closed her eyes, trembling in every bone.

This was beyond fear. This was the end of her life.

"Me, and some of what I am," he went on. "Tell me what you think you know."

And there it was, still, the magic of intimacy; of talking with him, her whole treasure store of knowledge rising in her mind. Who he was, who she was.

Lucy opened her eyes and accepted what she saw: the sword on the altar, the Marshal of Kallisfane laying his suit jacket, neatly folded, next to his coat on the floor. He looked smaller in his shirtsleeves, but she could see the muscles in his arms as he began to unknot his tie.

She was very conscious of her trembling body, her stuttering heart, the dizzying lack of air.

"I know that magic did not die with the Empire."

"True." He slipped his tie from his collar.

"I know . . ." Breath failed her. Her chest hurt, a widening pain from her breastbone to her shoulder blade, and for the first time she began to wonder if this was only fear. It felt as though he crowded all the air out of the room, pressed the blood out of her heart. Even the candles seemed to be growing dim. "I know you have been fighting all this time to keep magic out of the world. I know you have lied to us, and killed us, and led us by the nose."

"Go on." The tie went into one trouser pocket, cuff links into another. He began to roll up his sleeves, revealing powerful wrists and forearms shadowed with dark hair.

Lucy leaned against the wall. The pain pried into her shoulder, her wrist. *I'm going to die,* she thought, *before he gets a chance to kill me.*

"I know the worst lie you've ever told," she said.

"Tell me." He unbuttoned his collar and tossed it onto his coat. He looked completely human now, and Lucy could hardly bear to look at him.

"That you have no magic of your own."

He was finally still. "Why is that the worst lie?"

"Because you betray . . . you betray magic. The world, the gods, the Divine. You betray *us.* You lie . . ." She had no air left. The pain grew like a tree through her chest, down her arm.

"What do you imagine magic is, that you think I've done wrong in betraying it?"

"Life," she whispered. "You're the tombstone. You're the paving over the well."

"You know nothing of magic."

She looked at him past the sparkling darkness in her eyes and for an instant she was entirely *Lucy,* as if she had regained the fear-scattered pieces of herself just in time for the end. Her hand described a fluttering moth's circle in the air and she said faintly, lightly,

"Dying gives one a certain insight. So does living, I suppose. Perhaps I know something you don't."

"I have always considered the possibility," he said. He turned to the altar and with a movement devoid of ceremony he picked up the sword. Steel rang gently off the stone; light slid like water off the steel. "Tell me, Miss Donne. What did you hope to accomplish in Palton this afternoon?"

Palton? This afternoon? A lifetime ago.

"Breadon How. The Cold Hounds. I thought . . ."

"Yes?"

"I thought I . . ."

"You thought you could oppose me. You thought you could raise up some power I have kept buried for nine hundred years."

"No." Lucy's tears caught the light like the steel. "But I thought I had to try."

"Ah." It sounded oddly like satisfaction. He turned the blade in his hand as if he, too, wanted to see the candlelight run off its edge. "You aren't the first to think that."

"I know."

"The others all failed."

She knew.

He lifted the sword, a man in modern dress playing with an archaic toy—but he did not look ridiculous. He looked like himself. He looked like death.

"Does your heart pain you?"

"Yes." The pain *was* her heart, condensed into a pulsing star lodged against her spine.

"You might have succeeded at Breadon How, Miss Donne, although I think you would not have found the Cold Hounds comfortable allies. But you might well have awakened them. I believed it after dreaming your dream, and I think it even more likely now. But you are wrong about one thing, and your heart, Miss Donne, is wiser than you. Your heart, so full of life, knows that I am not magic. I am the antithesis, Miss Donne. I am exactly what you called me: a tombstone. For I promise you, Miss Donne, if I had one glimmer of magic in me, I would have ended this curse of a life the instant I knew my emperor was dead."

"But you killed him?"

"My emperor, the last emperor. Yes, I killed him, but it was treachery, Miss Donne, not magic. And it was not life that he would have summoned if I had not stopped him, very far from life, that magic he would have raised. Oh, I won't call it death. Not life, not death: a denial of both. But you do not understand me."

"I want to. Tell me . . ." But the pain clenched, her pulse stumbled, racing at the edge of a fall.

"Ah, but it is not your understanding that I need. Put out your hand."

Lucy was aware of the sword he held as she was aware of her exhausted heart, her stuttering blood, but she had come too far for petty defiance. She held out her shaking hand and he pressed the sword's hilt against her palm.

"Take it," he said. "Hold hard."

Her hand clenched in instinctual response as he let go, so she did not drop it, but the point chimed when it struck the floor. The blade was heavy, the leather-wrapped grip warmer than her own chilled flesh.

The Marshal of Kallisfane knelt on the floor and began to un-button his shirt.

"No," Lucy said.

He ignored this so completely the word might have been a burning wick, a drop of wax. He took the neck of his undershirt in both hands and tore it to bare his chest. He seemed to diminish at every stage, smaller and smaller, now showing bone as well as muscle beneath the pale skin.

"Just here," he said, pointing, as if she might have missed it, to the thick crosshatch of scars between his nipple and his breast-bone.

Lucy used the sword's weight to drag herself away from the supporting wall, though her heart beat like a bird crushed be-tween icy hands. Pain tasted like a new penny on her tongue.

"How many times . . . ?"

"Oh, many." He spoke as if he still stood over her, as if he were not half-naked on his knees. "Not always in search of death. Men have needed to test me, to be sure of who or what I am."

"And you want this?" The point of the sword jittered across a memorial stone, struck a spark from a date of birth.

"Call this," he said, "my test of you."

She put her free hand to her own breast, as though the pain she felt there was the pain of those terrible scars.

"Here," he said, and he lifted the sword, cutting his fingers on the edge as he aimed the point at his heart. "Lean your weight against the hilt, it needs no more than that."

The star behind Lucy's own heart bloomed in sympathy. She let go the hilt, and though he tried to hold the blade, it pulled itself out of his grasp, cutting his palm, ringing like a bell on the floor. Lucy fell to her knees. Her hand traveled the distance between her heart and his. She felt his scars, his warm and living skin.

"I pass your test," she whispered on the last of her breath. "I am not you."

Then there was no more light, no more air.

No more pain.

The envelope containing a left-luggage claim check was collected from the mailbox in the train station not long after the Palton train pulled away from the platform. It was sorted that day and delivered to Graham's flat the next morning at 10:12. Graham, however, was not there to receive it. He had interviews to conduct, an article to write, and an argument to have with his editor after he handed in his copy. He stopped for a drink and a bite to eat with some of his colleagues, and finally reached his flat around nine—early for him, but after the argument he was in an unsociable mood. So an early night for once, and for once, only the one drink. He unlocked the street door, fished his mail out of its box, and sorted through it as he climbed the stairs.

Lucy's handwriting stopped him cold three stairs below the landing.

Lucy, Lucy. He hadn't thought about her all day, and yet here she was. A drink of beer, a touch, a kiss. He could feel her mouth against the corner of his mouth, her lips warm and mobile, as if they shaped a thought even as she kissed him.

Graham shook himself, finished the climb to his flat and let himself inside. With Lucy's letter in his hand, he saw the place as he would if she were here: dusty, not too untidy, but uncared-for, unloved. Somehow all his things acquired a sepia tone, regardless of their original colors, as if a couch or a lampshade could fade like a plant for lack of attention. He turned on the desk lamp, which at least afforded kinder shadows, leaving the letters on the desk while he shed his coat and tie, pulled on a sweater, poured himself a drink. Only two for the night, so he was still ahead. Finally he sat, his desk chair creaking as he leaned back against the spring, and picked up her letter again. Her handwriting, elegant but hard to decipher, reminded him of her gestures, her hands.

He realized he was reluctant to open the letter. Love note, brush off, the research notes he was waiting for? He turned the envelope in his hands. Cheap, mass-produced, a far cry from the heavy rag of her usual stationery. He tapped it edge-on against his desk, feeling the shift of several folded sheets inside. Research notes, he decided, and did not know if he was relieved or— Well, but he did know, didn't he? Because he didn't believe in the love note, kiss or no kiss. He wasn't sure he believed in the kiss.

He took a drink, tore the envelope, shook out the letter and a claim check, a rectangle of red pasteboard that lay on his inky blotter, the only spot of color in the room. He let it lie, unfolded pages.

My hero, here is the story no one wants to know . . .

He read it once distractedly, remembering their conversation in the pub. His scorn, he remembered that, and her face, delicate and tired. He remembered that better than he remembered her words. *Proof,* she had said, and, *I can prove it.*

He threw the letter down, poured himself more whiskey, paced, muttering, around the room.

Then he read the letter again, forcing his attention onto the points that could be verified: parish records, newspapers, police reports.

He paced again, glass in hand. "I don't believe it." And, "Come on, Lucy! Magic isn't *news.*"

An imagined Lucy said, "The systematic murder of university professors isn't news? The manipulation of the Crown to the detriment of rural villages isn't news?"

"I don't believe it. Not a word, Lucy. I don't."

But it could be checked. Some of it could be. University records, harbormaster's logs. He emptied his glass and started for the drinks cabinet, then changed course for the desk.

"What bloody train? Where the hell did you go?"

The claim check stared up at him. Left Luggage. Skillyham Station. Hours: 6 A.M.–Midnight.

He glanced at his watch, snatched up his coat and his keys.

❖ ❖ ❖

Whirr, whirr, click.

"Benbury oh-oh-nine-three."

"Could I speak with Miss Lucy Donne?"

There was a pause, a most definite pause, and a deepening chill. "Who is calling, please?"

Something was wrong. "A colleague at the national library. We were doing some research together and she has some materials I need. If I could speak with Miss Donne . . . I know it's early . . . you can assure her I will be brief if she is otherwise engaged . . ."

Another pause. Then, ominously, another voice. "Sir, Miss Donne is not available. If you give me your name and a telephone number and address where you can be reached, I will be sure to pass the message along."

Graham hung the receiver gently on its hook, breaking the connection. Then he set the telephone on the floor, where it kept company with his typewriter, his dictionary, his mug full of pencils. Lucy's papers covered his desk, sheet after sheet of foolscap, typewriter bond, notepaper and envelopes and scraps, a drifting sea of her handwriting that threatened to drown the desk. She kept meticulous record of her researches, but it was in no sort of order at all. And yet the sheer mass of it was compelling. Whatever one thought of old wives' tales, the whispered glories of the magical past—and he had stored up a far-ranging argument on that score—it was difficult to deny that the Marshal of Kallisfane was actively at large in the world, working toward some goal.

Or did he have a goal? Could all of this be, what? The senile boredom of a very old man? The directed service of an agent of the Crown?

There were more possibilities the farther away he looked from Lucy's obsession with magic, but he couldn't deny the weight of her research. He wanted to argue it out with her. He wanted her to lead him through the chaos, form an argument, defend her conclusions—*convince* him if that was what was in the cards—but most of all he wanted her to be here. After a night of reading about death, disappearance, suppression, manipulation, he was all too ready to read bad news into that brief conversation with whomever it was that answered the telephone at Lucy's house. Especially that second voice asking his name, his telephone number, his address. Why his address, where there he was talking on the telephone? Was it because, with the newly automated exchanges, it was more difficult to trace a call? And do upper servants really "pass messages along"?

My train is leaving, I must fly—

Fly where, Lucy, damn you? And why?

Oh, Lucy, Lucy. What the hell am I supposed to do with all this?

What do you do if you have a story no one will believe?

The answer did not come so glibly this time. He sat with his elbows holding down a drift of paper and his hands clenched before his mouth. What do you do if you have a story you don't dare to tell?

"Because if you're right, Lucy . . ." If you're right about even half of this—forgetting the magic for a minute—don't you see what you have here? Not just the Revenant, but the police, the army, the church, the very Crown! And even if you ducked the whole boiling lot of them, who the hell else is there left to tell? The common people? The general public who go to church, who believe the police keep good citizens safe, who would be scared pissless if you told them you were bringing magic back into the world? The truth is, Lucy, you could publish a book and give it away on the street corners, and if the king said it was all for the good of the bloody realm, they'd believe him. They would say, thank you, Mister Revenant, sir, and toss the book on the fire, and you could kiss your hand to whatever it is you're looking for, justice or the cure for moral outrage, because you know what, Lucy? *They might be right.*

If magic is real. And if that's what the Marshal of Kallisfane has been doing: keeping magic out of the world all these years.

And if you're not just being a coward, Graham Isles, Mister Newspaperman.

My hero, here is the story that will destroy your life, your career, your every cherished illusion about yourself . . .

He bundled her papers back into the portfolio. Shaved, changed his shirt. Went to work.

He was not surprised to find a message waiting for him, directing him to his editor's office. Even if last night's dispute had not spawned fresh points of attack, he was late. He *was* surprised to find one of the crime reporters lying in ambush outside the editor's door.

"Just remember, Isles, you talk to me before you go anywhere."

"What?" Graham's attention was still more on Lucy than the world. "Go where?"

"Nowhere, until you talk to me."

Graham shut the office door in the man's anxious face.

"You took your time," his editor said. "Drowning your sorrows?"

"Research," Graham said shortly.

"Well, I've a bit more for you to do. Lucy Donne. You've heard, I suppose?"

Graham experienced the curious sensation of blood leaving his face as he went pale. A tightening, a cooling. "Heard what?"

"She went missing two nights ago. The family was keeping it quiet, figuring she'd turn up on her own, I suppose, but now the police have issued a bulletin. We've got a friend in CID who will tell us what comes of it—a dog's breakfast of bus conductors and ticket sellers so far—but no one's getting in to see the family. But you worked with her quite a bit, didn't you? Something in the way of being friends?"

"Something in the way." Graham worked his tongue in his dry mouth. Do they think . . . what do they think?"

"Reserving their opinions for the moment, but you can suppose they lie somewhere between scandalous and dead. What do *you* think? You know her. Inside information will win your employer's approval, affection, and possibly a wee bonus on the side."

Graham saw that last scribbled line. *My train is leaving, I must fly–* Had she just played into the Revenant's hands, leaving everyone a trail that went nowhere? Or had she successfully escaped his notice—and gone where?

He shook his head. "Sorry, I don't have a clue. Actually," he added with perfect honesty, "I'm stunned."

"No boyfriends that you know of? No fights with the family? Storming off to leave them stewing and make the papers who cried havoc look like silly chumps when she comes home in perfect health?"

"That, no. I think she has a very high regard for her family, in her way." In her off-hand, defended, too-sensitive way.

"And no, er, lover's quarrel?"

His editor's feeble attempt at delicacy told Graham volumes about the rumors circulating in the newsroom this morning.

"Not a chance."

"No coppers here, son."

"I've bought her a drink or two, but that's as far as it ever went. Look," he said, a little desperate in the face of skepticism, "the last time I saw her she told me a story about the Marshal of Kallisfane. I mean . . ." He shrugged, put out his hands.

"A funny story?"

"Not particularly."

His editor nodded, accepting this as proof of the absence of romance. "Well, if you think of anything. In the meantime, what about getting in to see the family? As a friend and colleague, I mean. Offer them the resources at your disposal."

"Do you mean the paper's resources?"

"Well, we wouldn't mind posting notice of a reward for information received, especially if it came with an exclusive interview with the mother. That might open the door for you. Also keeping in mind that she did work for us, even if she was freelance and, well, an amateur. We owe her our support." This was said, not with self-righteousness, but with the tone of a newsman trying a subhead out loud.

Graham felt a quickening, the conception of an idea. "If I had a note on the publisher's letterhead?"

His editor scratched his chin and said he would see what he could do.

❖ ❖ ❖

"Are there any more questions, Mr. Isles?"

Sir Roger Donne picked up the paper knife on his blotter and set it a little to one side. It was the ninth time he had made that gesture in the course of the interview and it was starting to obsess

Graham. He made a mark beside eight other marks in his notebook.

"Sir Roger, you have been very forthcoming."

Though in fact, Lucy's grandfather had not said any more than a hundred other anxious relatives Graham had interviewed over the years. *She's a good girl, really. She'd never stay away if she could come home.* And sometimes they were right, and sometimes they were wrong, and the one was as likely to crush a loving family as the other. *We're just praying she's all right, wherever she is.*

"Then if that is all." Sir Roger put his hands on the edge of his desk, preparatory to rising.

"There is one other thing." Graham hesitated, as he had been hesitating all along. He felt a flash of empathy for Lucy, remembering again their last conversation: her tentative opening, his scorn.

Sir Roger frowned into the pause. "I hope, Mr. Isles, that you and your superiors are sincere in your offer of help. It would add enormously to the pain and distress of Lucy's mother if old scandals are raked up out of the past, and it would do no good whatsoever. I'm sure I can rely on you in this matter."

"No, it isn't that. I mean, yes, sir, you can rely on us to be discreet." Although if the old man thought the tabloids weren't going to disinter the scandal of Lucy's fatherless state, he was more naïve than Graham supposed.

"What, then?"

"Are you aware of the nature of Lucy—of Miss Donne's research?"

Sir Roger's scowl deepened. "I was under the impression, Mr. Isles, that my granddaughter was providing background material for your newspaper articles. Are you suggesting that her work for you put her in some kind of danger?"

"No! Absolutely not. I was referring to her own private research."

"Lucy is an amateur historian. An intelligent and erudite young woman. And I can assure you, sir, that her 'private research' has no bearing on the case whatsoever. She reads books, sir! No young woman has ever disappeared because of reading books."

"Even if the books she reads lead her into a pursuit of the Marshal of Kallisfane?" Graham kept his eyes on his notebook, as if it was just one more question to make a note of, but eventually he had to look up into Sir Roger's silence.

For the first time Graham saw some family resemblance between Lucy and her grandfather, a ghost of her fragility and pallor, a reflection of her steady, unreadable stare. Sir Roger lifted a hand, touched the paper knife. Pushed himself away from the desk and stood.

"Come with me."

Sir Roger took him to the library, and it was a long walk through grand rooms, useless unless you were giving a party for three hundred friends. The library would have seemed just the same, as empty as a stage between shows, except that Graham had seen Lucy handle books, had seen how they spoke to her hands as well as her mind. Thousands of volumes, and any one of them might have come alive to her touch, her fingers slipping through their pages as if paper were fur, as if books could purr. For every window bay they passed he felt a jolt of anticipation, as if she might be standing there perusing the shelves, but she never was. Her absence persisted all the way down the room.

The table at the end bore a desk lamp, a blotter pad, a box of paper, and a neat stack of books. This tidy set-up obviously had nothing to do with the mad profusion of Lucy's papers and Graham gave it no more than a glance. He turned to Sir Roger, waiting for him to explain, but Lucy's grandfather gestured at the table.

"Here is my granddaughter's research, Mr. Isles. A perfectly unexceptional genealogical study of her grandmother's family. Please, have a look."

Graham picked up a book from the pile. It was a ledger, a handwritten parish register, a record of births and deaths. He gave the pages a desultory ruffle with a distinct feeling of heat growing beneath his collar.

"Take your time," Sir Roger said. "There are some notes there, too, which you are welcome to read. You see, I want you to be absolutely satisfied on this point, Mr. Isles, because when your article appears in the newspaper, I want there to be no doubt in anyone's mind that my granddaughter is a perfectly innocent young woman. Which you should already know as well as I, if your claims of friendship have not been grossly exaggerated for the sake of this intrusion into our private affairs."

The heat rose into Graham's face. "Are you suggesting that research into the Marshal of Kallisfane would *not* be innocent?"

Sir Rober rocked back on his heels. "I am telling you that this is all there is. Lucy did nothing to deserve her fate."

"What fate?" Graham said, anger giving his reporter self full rein. "Do you know what has happened to her? Do you know where she is?"

"No! Of course—"

"So what fate do you think she *would* deserve if she had been studying the Marshal of Kallisfane?"

Sir Roger's face was as red as Graham's. "This is an outrage! I let you into my home only because your superiors assured me of their desire to help us find Lucy—"

"Do you want to find Lucy?"

"Of course!"

"Then why are you lying?"

"Get out!"

"Why are you covering up for the Revenant?"

"Get out before I throw you out!"

❖   ❖   ❖

The story about Lucy's disappearance ran without any mention of the Marshal of Kallisfane. Not because of any interference from on high, but because Graham had written it that way. It had seemed the only reasonable thing to do. His editor would never have agreed to print unfounded allegations of a public figure, and to found the allegations on Lucy's research, unconfirmed as it was, would have been at best premature. There is still time to tell that story, he said to himself. But it was harder to say it to Lucy as she stared at him from the printed page. The paper had copied a studio portrait that made her look like a woodland fawn.

Graham paid for an uneaten meal and took the paper home with him; another early night, though he made no resolutions about the whiskey waiting for him in his flat. He was turning his key in the lock of the street door when a friendly voice said, "Mr. Isles? I wonder if you could give us a moment of your time?"

He turned, his keys in his hand, just in time to see the black motorcar pulling up to the curb.

❖   ❖   ❖

In the Castle of Kallisfane the silence persisted. It was impossible not to be conscious of it, of the way a footfall or a word only threw it into sharper relief. Impossible, too, not to think of museums, mausoleums, tombstones, tombs. And so Lucy did think of them, but they were not gloomy thoughts. She felt as light as a hummingbird among the mourning wreaths, a petal on the breeze. The fact that her heart skipped and bounded like a puppy tumbling down a flight of stairs, the fact that her breath came in sips and gasps, the fact that her hands were icy and her lips were halfway numb: these facts were simply irrelevant. She was alive, alive in the Marshal's stronghold, alive and on her way to talk to him again.

She had to sit on the stairs to rest halfway down. Her guide, the thin balding man who, in her other life, had taken her arm in a train station and warned her not to make a fuss, waited patiently, cleaning under his fingernails with the thumbnail on the opposite hand.

The castle was disappointing at first, as the oldest castles tend to be, being small and cramped and dim. But age exerts a subtle fascination, most of all in the ancient place that is still inhabited. Lucy the historian thought of the famous men, the legendary men, who had trod these floors, who had passed through these doors, who had ridden out from these walls to impose a new order on their collapsing world.

The Marshal's order, Lucy, don't forget. The Marshal's chaos, too.

The Marshal's library was a pokey warren of badly lit rooms, old castle offices knocked together with shelves built to fit the awkward walls, and books and papers crammed in every which way to fill the shelves. Lucy the book hound was drawn like a nail to a magnet, but the scholar in her was shocked, even offended. Did the Marshal of Kallisfane, the embodiment of living history, have so little respect . . . ? But then she remembered the dead and vanished scholars, herself included, and felt a little pulse in her gut that had nothing to do with her damaged heart. Of course he had no respect. Respect, for history and for historians, was the very last thing he would have.

He met her in the largest room.

"Sit there," he said, gesturing to a chair by the door. "It would be better for you if you don't come too close."

Lucy had to believe him, with her blood scampering through her veins, but it didn't trouble her. He took all her attention. Was this what it would be like to be in love? The shape of him, the glance of light across his shaven cheek, the arch of his brow. The movement of his chest beneath the shirt and jacket and tie. The lightless eyes that woke a tremor in her skin. Not love—fear, in fact—and yet . . . was there something of desire, some kind of desire, here? Or was it only that deceptive intimacy of being here with him, of knowing the scars that lay behind the armor of his suit?

"I wish I knew your name," Lucy said, breathless and fey.

"That isn't necessary." He was dismissive, faintly ironic. For some reason it made her laugh.

"No, I'm just curious. But I do wonder why I'm still alive?" She had lost the rhythm of breathing and had to snatch after air when her words failed. "But maybe that doesn't matter either. Maybe I'm only curious, a curious ghost, you must know so many."

The Marshal of Kallisfane looked at her a moment, his eyes black in shadow, then pulled a chair away from the desk under the window and sat down facing her from across the room. (The room darkly walled in books, with a too-small rug on the stone floor, a window cut through thick walls, a paraffin heater exuding its peculiar oily smell. Lucy would only notice these things later, when their memory cast a shadow on her mind.)

"You said a thing to me last night," the Marshal said. "You said magic was life and I was its death, keeping it out of the world. I wonder why you think you know this? I wonder how you could know."

"Then you're curious, too. Such curious hauntings . . ." More air, and a stab at humility: "I don't, of course," except she spoiled it with a shrug and a coiling gesture with her hand. "Well, maybe it came to me in a dream."

"Magic was life and death, once. We used to say, the fires of creation, the breath of the gods. They did, the wizards and the priests. I was only a soldier, of course, I made my sacrifices and held to my oaths, no more than that. Most of us were like that. Magic was part of the mysteries, part of the world. The Cold Hounds of Breadon How were no different than the ice storms that blow out of the mountains in the north. They were the same. Their victims were the same. Living and dying was what humans did. Life and death was a matter for the gods."

It *was* like love. Lucy lay back in her chair, pinning her pulse with a thumb on her wrist, watching his dry, spare mouth shape his words. Oh, to say *you* to this man. Oh, to hear him say *we* and *I*.

"Caedemus was insane, but only in the manner of his kind. Wizard, priest, emperor's son: the godfire was in him—like a disease, you would say now, but then it was expected, desired even, it was the mark that made him heir. Not that he had powers," the Marshal added distastefully. "He *had* nothing, none of them did. They were not gods, only men . . . and women, some of them, like you. You need to know this. You will need to understand."

Oh, to hear this man say *you*. Lucy's heart found its rhythm as it quickened.

"They had nothing—*he*—had nothing," the Marshal said, speaking still of the emperor he betrayed. "He was no more than a door through which magic could sometimes step into the world. And he knew it. Being a little madder than the rest, he saw it clear. And being a little madder than the rest, he sought to change that fact, to change himself, to change the world. To become magic. To transform the human world of living and dying into the world of the gods where life and death stand still, where life and death are one . . . The perfect world, he called it. I was a soldier. He was what he was: a wizard, an emperor, insane. I have never understood what he desired. But what he tried to bring into the world. What he tried to make of the world . . ."

Lucy was nothing but the sight of him, the sound of his voice. She hung suspended over his hesitation as if it were a chasm in the earth.

"I know what it would have made of the world, because I know what it made of me when I killed him. Death and life: death *in* life. Perfection. The tombstone you saw in your dreams. And that is what I have been keeping out of the world these endless years. That is what I have been keeping out of the human world. Myself, writ large."

She thought of him as he had been without his armor. She thought of him in the chapel, on his knees, her hand on the warm scars over his heart.

She thought of her studies. She thought of her letter to Graham. She thought of herself, and dared to ask, "The dreaming spring of Galburgh? The prophetic seals of Belmouth? Is that lifeless, deathless perfection?"

"It is magic."

"But then—"

"Is that," he said, "a gamble you would take if you were me?"

But Lucy's mind was already skipping down another path of logic. She laughed, incredulous, stunned. "Why, then you are a god!"

"No," he said, an absolute negation.

Lucy, not believing him, laid her fingers against her lips and stared.

"No." He rose, with the first restlessness she had seen in him, and then stood, self-restrained, as if pacing were too alien a concept—too human a concept—to pursue. "Believe me. Understand me. I am a tombstone, I am a closed door, nothing more."

"Keeping magic out of this world. Or . . . this other thing, this perfection."

"If they are not the same thing."

"If?" Lucy whispered, incredulous all over again. "If? Don't you know?"

"I have wondered," he said, and stopped. "I have wondered, from time to time."

Lucy went cold, and then more than cold, thinking of what he implied. To take on such a mission, such a burden—not only the long years, not only the murders, the lies, the kings held under his sway, but the destruction, the erasing from history of the whole world he had been born to—*and then to doubt*. The chasm between them was deep, and filled with hell, and in that moment, terribly, terrifyingly real.

"When one such as you comes along," he said to her, "an open door yourself, with a mind prying at every door I have ever closed, digging up every spring I have ever paved over, I do wonder."

"No, I . . ." Lucy's voice trembled with tears. "I only . . ."

"Wondered?" A perfection of irony. "You were only curious, I know. But perhaps you understand my dilemma now. To release what my emperor summoned would be to allow the end of everything, the end of life, an end without ending, an end with no hope of beginning, an end without even the hope of death. And yet. And yet."

"And yet," Lucy said—oh, to hear this man!—"And yet, what if what you are keeping out the world is life? 'The fires of creation, the breath of the gods.' "

"It is not such a terrible world, this world that I have made."

"No. It isn't, no. No, but . . ." Trembling on the edge of the abyss.

"But could it be better? But could it be that without magic it is as dead as that other world would be, as dead as I am, could it be?"

"But do you have the right to have made it anything at all?"

He stood with his back to the window, looking down at her with his lightless eyes, and she felt again the weight of the sword in her hand.

"No right," he said at last. "Only the necessity to save . . . do you understand, Miss Donne? It was the necessity of the moment, the desperate need to stop my emperor before he brought about the ruin of the world. And I have been stopping him ever since."

"But not knowing!" she cried, and was not sure if she was crying out in empathy or argument.

"Ah, but you still do not understand me. He was an open door, once upon a time. Like any wizard. Like you, and all the other open doors I have closed. Even if it is magic that I have been keeping out of the world, to let it back in might be to let *him* come again, some time, in some form, when I am not there to stop it as I stopped him before."

"Do you mean his ghost or his idea?"

"Either!" He turned away from her, and by that she knew.

"If that sufficed to lay your doubts I'd be dead now."

"I am so tired!" His voice broke; he bent an arm across his chest as if to protect himself from further scars. "Gods give me aid, I am so tired."

Lucy hung on his silence, afraid, but it was the fear of awe at what he had given over into her hands. Finally she realized that the silence was hers. "What do you want me to do?"

❖ ❖ ❖

The black car conveyed him to an anonymous building that was, if one unwound the tangle of streets, not far from the royal palace. A small, unnumbered door let him into a corridor lit by bare electric bulbs, stark and dim. Graham could feel his courage fading like old wallpaper, and it didn't help that his escort, a hulking young man with a face like a plowboy, moved him along by the simple expedient of stepping forward and assuming Graham would proceed to get out of his way. Graham proceeded, a wry internal voice telling him *you're in trouble now, mate* even as the sweat came out on his palms. Anger guilt fear . . . and Lucy. Lucy very much on his mind.

"Just here, Mr. Isles," said the oversized plowboy, rattling open an accordion-fold lift door. They went up, the lift bobbing and swaying in its shaft, and exited into a corridor where there were new runners on the floor and the light bulbs had frosted glass shades. Coming up in the world. The plowboy knocked on a door and pushed it open without waiting for an answer.

"Mr. Isles, you can't know how glad I am—how relieved I am to make your acquaintance. Thank the Divine you're here." Not a tall man, but a bulky one, his body fronted by a robust belly and his face obscured by jowls. Neither handsome nor famous, but Graham knew who he was, at least, he had a vague notion that crystallized as the man drew him into the room. Barrimond, senior bureaucrat, quiet power in the Ministry of State. Releasing Graham, he smoothed his hand over the glossy hair painted over his scalp and offered Graham a drink. Nothing to be offended by there, and in fact Graham could have used one, but he didn't like the assumption that had the plowboy already clattering amongst a tray of decanters.

"No," Graham said with deliberate lack of courtesy. "Why am I here?"

A small pause, a look of calculation in the fat man's eyes. "Yes. Perhaps it is a trifle late for the amenities. I should apologize for sending an invitation you could not refuse–and yet–great heavens–here I am not even offering you a chair. Please." He gestured.

Graham sat where indicated. Barrimond sat behind his desk. The plowboy propped himself against the door. *All in our stations,* Graham thought.

"I'm glad to see you're a direct kind of man, Isles," Barrimond said, "though I should say I'm not surprised, having read so much of your work–read and admired, I should hasten to say. I also believe–indeed, I am relying on it–that you are capable of discretion, a much rarer thing in a newspaperman. I take this evening's article about poor Lucy Donne as an example in point, because you and I both know how much more you could have written."

"I don't know what you mean," Graham said, more or less automatically.

Barrimond looked at him, then bent to haul open a drawer in his desk. "I suppose that if I want directness from you I should be honest myself. Always the best policy, really, though I'm afraid I owe you a kind of an apology. Or rather, since we are being driven by necessity, not so much an apology as an expression of regret. Your privacy and your person have been a little impinged upon, but I trust it will be made clear how important–and really, we could have done much worse and been justified . . ." Having been talking with his hand in the open drawer, Barrimond now dragged out a heavy object and laid it on his desk. It was Lucy's portfolio, stolen from Graham's flat. "For example, we could have simply turned this, and you, over to the Marshal of Kallisfane. As I think you know."

There is something painfully ineffectual about sitting in the face of an outrage, so Graham stood, his pulse beating in his temple. But although he was angry—almost as angry as he was frightened—his thinking was clear and he knew he was only making a show. When the oversized plowboy stepped away from the door, Graham sat back down and raised his eyes from the portfolio to Barrimond's face.

"You might as well turn me over," he said, fairly calm. "Why not let the old man do his own dirty work? He certainly doesn't seem to mind."

"No, indeed," said Barrimond, though the plowboy made a noise suggestive of irony or dissent. "But this is a rather unusual case. I take it you have in fact read . . . ?" He patted the portfolio.

"Some of it," Graham said, as if he could at this stage still hedge his bets.

"A remarkable piece of work. Truly remarkable. Miss Donne must be an interesting young woman to know."

Graham felt his temperature rise, but he said nothing. He had no intention of discussing Lucy with this man. Barrimond, however, seemed bent on discussing Lucy with him.

"A highly interesting young woman, and in other circumstances, in another field, no doubt an asset to us all. But in this particular instance . . . No, I'm afraid our Lucy has been stirring up some murky waters. Very murky—and to be frank, extremely dangerous. I wonder if you would be glad to know she is still alive?"

Graham's heart seemed to shrink, leaving a dizzy cavern in his core. He still said nothing, but he doubted his reaction went unseen. Barrimond went on finger-tapping Lucy's portfolio, almost caressing it, but his eyes never left Graham's face.

"Yes. A relief to me, too, of course, although something of a surprise. And I hope you understand me—it's crucial that you understand me—that although the *fact* that Miss Lucy Donne is still alive is a great relief to all of us, the *circumstances* are a matter of extraordinary concern, and not only for Miss Donne's sake—though she is not, I assure you, far from my thoughts at any time.

No, the consequences for her . . . But then, you see, the consequences for us all . . ."

To Graham's relief, Barrimond finally took his hand off Lucy's portfolio, knotting his fingers together as if he physically captured his thoughts. "It occurs to me that I have skipped a crucial question. I asked you if you had read Miss Donne's research. I did not ask you if you believe it. Really a crucial question, Mr. Isles. I wonder if you can answer it honestly."

"Do I believe in Lucy's research?" Graham said, stalling for time.

"No, Mr. Isles. Not, do you believe in her research. Not, do you believe in *her*. I want to know if you, having studied the evidence, agree with Miss Donne's conclusions."

"I've read her notes, but without having verified her facts—"

"They have been verified. You have my word on it. Factually, Miss Donne is in most respects entirely correct."

"Why would you verify that?" Graham said on a burst of skepticism. "Why aren't you bending over backwards to convince me the other way? Why the hell are you bothering to try and convince me of anything at all?"

"Because we need your help, Mr. Isles. We need your help very urgently—to head off unmitigated disaster—and to save Miss Lucy Donne."

❖ ❖ ❖

But did Lucy want to be saved? She was aware of her perilous situation. The Marshal of Kallisfane had made it clear.

"You held your hand from me once," he said, "and if you failed that challenge, perhaps you won another, even so. I will grant you that. But it has only won you yet another challenge, and this one you may prefer to lose. For as you held your hand from me, so I will hold mine from you, to let you live and do as you will. Would you bring magic back into the world? Would you wake the old gods, the old dreamers and the ancient dreams? I will hold my hand in the hope that you might also summon the death that has long eluded me. And if you fail to open that door, no matter. You can serve me in other ways, in my house here. I have kept other scholars so. And so you might win your own life either way.

"But do you open the door on that other world, on that dead and deathless perfection that made me what I am, it will be otherwise. I will destroy you and all of your blood unto the ninth degree, until even the name of Donne will be erased from the world.

"I tell you plainly: this challenge, you might prefer to fail."

Yes. Indeed, yes. So a sensible woman might have hoped for rescue. An even more sensible woman might have given some thought to escape. But was Lucy a sensible woman? To live in his house, to plunder that library of stolen history, to plumb the depths of that ancient mind! The rewards of failure were rich, even if she would be a prisoner, dead to her family and her friends. Except perhaps for Graham Isles, who had inherited all the breadcrumbs that had marked her trail to this end. That was a thought to pull her up sharply. As far as Graham was concerned, she would not simply disappear.

Did that matter? By his own declaration he would not pursue a story no one wants to hear. He would only know.

And, a sinful inner voice added, he would never know that she had settled for failure. He would never know she had refused to try for the greater prize.

So it must have been that voice, rather than the thought of Graham's opinion, that roused in her a hot and prickly blush of shame.

❖ ❖ ❖

As it happened, Graham was also none too sanguine about the thought of a rescue. Or rather, he thought rescuing Lucy from the Marshal of Kallisfane sounded like a fine idea; he just wasn't sure what role he was expected to play. Even after it was explained to him by Barrimond and the plowboy, it wasn't clear in his mind. "Persuade her," they said. "Make her listen to reason." But surely the telling point was whether or not she was in the Revenant's clutches? It seemed to him that the sensible order of proceeding was to extract her from her prison and *then* make her see reason. "We need to get her out quietly," said the plowboy, "and for that we need her cooperation. And for *that,* we need you. Right?"

Right, said Graham, though he said it with hidden irony, as if he could humor these men until they started to show some sense. Yet playing along had him riding in the back of the big black motorcar somewhere on the wrong side of midnight, dressed in imaginary armor and clutching a cardboard sword, on his way to rescue the princess before she could be sacrificed to the dragon. Though in fact, the idea seemed less absurd now, rushing through the cold, black night, than it had in the bureaucratic comfort of Barrimond's office.

"Sacrifice!" he had said. "Are you insane?"

"No," Barrimond had replied, "but the Marshal is."

"Well," the plowboy said, "say he has his moments. He's an old man, you know, and old men do have their moments. Most times he runs on the rails right enough."

"Yes," Barrimond said, "and the point is to get him back on the rails as soon as possible before any damage is done."

"Remove Miss Donne," said the plowboy, "and remove the temptation, like."

The temptation to do what? Suddenly there was no more time for explanations. It was down to the car and out in the night, and the sound of the engine droning back at them from the dark-windowed houses, and the quick sharp fire of the whiskey from the plowboy's flask. And then the city fell away into the dark.

Morning drew a mist out of the winter-wet ground. Lucy was out early enough to see the rising sun wrapped in a ball of foggy wool. She was weary, but a lifetime habit of nervous energy won out over the condition of her heart–if its jackrabbit thumping was an injury and not just a symptom of her confusion. She walked out into the valley of Kallisfane without a thought for her health; but her walk was of necessity a thoughtful invalid's stroll.

Kallisfane Castle could be found on any map, though there were some odd discrepancies. Did the road cross the Fernsey River above Mimmenbrook or below? Was the castle on the southern spur of the Starsey Hills, or was it more southwesterly? But all the maps agreed there was no valley behind the castle, nothing but a blank space or a ripple as of hills. This morning the mist seemed to be conspiring with the mapmakers. A haze against the sky, a creeping whiteness against the ground, it erased colors, blurred edges, muted sound, as if this valley, the heart of the Marshal's demesne, might in the next moment efface itself entirely from the world. Or perhaps it had already done so. Perhaps where Lucy walked was no-place, no-time, nothing but a memory in the Marshal's skull. A fading memory, all that was left of the Empire-that-was.

And yet the black mud sucked at her shoes. Puddles bright as mirrors cupped in worn paving stones reflected her face, the edge of a wall. The thrushes singing in the woods that guarded the hill-tops sang like the first springtime in the world.

In the valley lay a city. A city of white stone, all in ruins, though the mist filled in the gaps of fallen domes and tumbled walls, teasing the eye with long-lost grandeur. There had been a wide avenue here, palaces rising behind their colonnades, a statue, perhaps, on that great stone plinth that divided the way. Lucy sat there a moment to catch her breath and scrape the mud off her shoes. Her poor not-very-sensible shoes. They would never be the same again. Lucy sighed and pressed her hand over her heart, as if that could calm the queasy race and lag of her pulse. When she was walking, the valley seemed perfectly quiet except for her own footsteps, the ring of distant birdsong chiming with the sunlight far above the fog, but now the silence was alive with hidden drips and scrapes and soft muddy sounds, as if the mist had grown feet to follow her with. But of course she likely was being followed by one of the Marshal's men. Walking away was not one of the options he had offered her.

Well, let them watch! she thought, a nice show of courage that did nothing to dispel the prickle creeping down her spine. She rose with a too-casual glance around and continued on. The ground mist was lifting above her head, hiding the sky and the tops of the surrounding hills, but here and there a shaft of milky sunlight broke through.

And where is she going, our Lucy, strolling on a misty dawn in early spring? At the end of this long avenue, where once the legions paraded and the wizard-philosophers strolled, lies the imperial palace. The Emperor Caedemus's palace, where one age was killed and another was erected on its grave. But she is only going there to appease her curiosity, to think . . . perhaps to decide . . .

The black motorcar stopped at an iron gate and the plowboy got out to talk to the guard. Graham lowered the window on his side, hoping the shock of fresh air would rouse him from the stupe-faction of the drive. It was dawn, damp and cold, and Graham started to shiver without feeling any more awake. The real world was hot coffee, a razor, his own bed. He could not fathom what he was doing here.

The plowboy got back in and the motorcar pulled through the gate, wallowing in the ruts of the drive.

"Where are we?" Graham said.

"Kallisfane." The answer was curt. The man himself was pale with sleeplessness, stubbled and grim, and Graham had to admit that he looked more soldier than plowboy.

"You're one of the nameless regiment, aren't you? One of the Marshal's own."

The big man grunted what was probably an affirmative.

"None too loyal, then, are you?" Graham's mild tone took the edge off the provocation.

"We're sworn to serve the Crown, same as any other regiment. And we serve the Marshal, too, believe me. He's his own worst enemy, when he gets to thinking on the past."

"How so?"

"Feels the weight of the years, like. The burden of his responsibilities. Well, you can imagine it, can't you, after all this time? Wanting to let it all go?"

"Yes. But I don't see what that has to do with Lucy Donne."

The plowboy-soldier kept his eyes on the road past the driver's shoulder, but Graham had the sense of an intelligence working behind that homely face.

"We reckon he thinks he can use Miss Donne to bring us all back to the way things used to be. Bring us all back to the days when he was an ordinary man, d'you see? Return the world to the way it was, and maybe return himself to the way *he* was . . ."

"But *how* will he use her? Use her how?"

"They was grim and bloody times–" He interrupted himself to say to the driver, "Take the east fork." The car turned. Graham caught a glimpse of the castle rearing up to their left, already falling behind. Where were they going? Graham started to ask, but the plowboy was talking again.

"People don't know what it was like in those days. They have these romantic notions that it was all storybook adventures and poetry and folksongs–people like Miss Donne, who think the Marshal's a hard man doing a bloody job. Well so he is, and a good thing, too. Do you have the least notion of what this world would come to if he left his post? It'd be chaos. Your worst nightmares can't even touch what it would be to let the old gods walk again."

Graham was not immune to direful predictions, not when they echoed the fears that Lucy's work had raised, but still he persisted. "You haven't said what part Lucy has to play in all this."

"She's the sacrifice, man! Haven't you been listening? She's the life that opens the door the Marshal has been keeping shut all these years. She's the bloody key. Here," he said to the driver in the same rough tone, "park here, we'll have to go the rest of the way on foot."

"What—" Graham began.

"Right," the plowboy said, all soldier now. "We may just have a chance to take her away with no one the wiser until we're gone. The aim is to get her to come quietly back to the car, and that's your job. Say anything you need to—she's in danger, you're here to take her home—be a hero to her—"

"But—"

"Wake up, will you? We're saving the girl. We're saving the damn world!"

"But *why me*?"

The plowboy leaned to put his big face in Graham's. "You know the background, you know the girl, and I don't have time for arguments with men who don't know where their loyalties should lie. All right? There's men here who serve the Marshal before the Crown, and I can't take them all on, not if we're going to keep this quiet. You cooperate with me, you get the girl to cooperate with me, and we just drive away, no fuss, end of story. All right?"

The big man swung himself out of the car. After the briefest hesitation, Graham followed suit. But in that half-second pause, he had time to wonder what would happen to them after he had persuaded Lucy to cooperate. Were they going to be sent home and trusted to keep their mouths shut? Graham thought of Lucy's portfolio, all the stories no one wanted to hear. He climbed from the car into the misty morning. Birds were singing somewhere in the fog.

❖ ❖ ❖

The palace was roofed with mist, walled with air. Grand steps of once-white marble were broken and half buried by the fallen columns of the portico, but Lucy found she could pick her way between the disarticulated pillars, up the shattered stair. For the first time, as she scuffed her muddy shoes through the mold of windblown leaves, it struck her as odd, how lifeless the ancient Fane was. No moss to blur the carvings on the broken capitals, no grass to carpet the stairs, no bird-flitting or mouse-scurrying nearer than the treed battlements of the enclosing hills. *The end of everything,* he had said, *the end of life, an end without ending, an end with no hope of beginning, an end without even the hope of death . . .* As if everything could just stop, Lucy thought. Stop, freeze into crystal, her breath and blood, the air, the mist and the birds in the trees and the trees themselves. Like a book, she thought, a story captured between the covers, beginning and end all there, simultaneous, undifferentiated, a beginning never begun, an ending that never ended, the perfect story, unread, ideal. Yes. She did not at all understand what the Marshal had said about doing magic, or being magic, or the difference between them, but this she understood, the perfect, the completed world.

But the blood moved through her limping heart, the air moved into her lungs and out again, warm enough to make steam. She breathed out again, a deliberate puff, for the pleasure of seeing it hang for an instant in the milky brightness, and then went on into the palace. Her footsteps echoed around her, hinting, with the mist, of companionable ghosts.

Did he ever come here, the self-named Marshal of this place? *He* would have ghosts. In these rubble-mounds he would see the shape of rooms, the fountained courts and lucent tiles and stone-filigree walls. Or would he? How long had he lived here as a mortal man, a soldier and then a captain of soldiers? Twenty years? Thirty? A scant handful of decades to set against the long centuries of ruin. Perhaps he wondered, as she did, which were the rooms of state, which the private apartments, which the emperor's own room where he had been stopped in the very act of summoning the end of time. Where he had been betrayed, killed by a trusted hand.

Here, where a pillared arch still stood, though the room beyond was adrift with shattered roof tiles and the pale stones of the further wall?

Here, where the broken roots of columns still marked out the line of a shady cloister?

Here, where a fountain's bowl fell into petal-shards like a teacup dropped just so in the center of the yard?

Here, where footsteps echoed, pat-patter-pattering even though Lucy was standing still.

Or maybe it was her heart, she thought, with the hum of invisible bees in her ears. She lowered herself to the flat top of a column's tumbled capital. Its leafy carvings sloughed away a skin of rotten stone under her fingers, crumbs of past beauty sifted into the dirt beneath her feet. The walls were mostly intact here, giving a shape and a sense of enclosure to the small courtyard, but the misty ceiling was lifting away, thinning against the blue sky. Sunlight, still diffused by damp, brightened the many shades of white of all the naked stone, walls, flagstones, fallen columns, broken bowl. There was even a ghost of color on the walls, rose and blue and ocher, scabrous as lichen if lichen could have grown in this place.

This dead place . . . save for the drift of the air, the far birdsong, the dripping of condensed mist from the many lips of stone. And the footsteps. Lucy was almost sure, despite a long silence that conjured up again the humming in her ears. The blood seemed to shrink away beneath her skin, leaving it tingling and cold. But of course, she knew she was being watched.

Yes, there, the unmistakable grit of shoe leather over dirty stone.

Sunlight found its way through clouds and mist to sparkle in the rainwater cupped by the shards of the fountain. Warmth pressed through the damp tweed of Lucy's jacket, and as though the sun confirmed something she already guessed, she was abruptly convinced that there was no magic here, neither in the place nor in her, and that all this morning held for her was an early walk and a mild sort of farce, grown men sneaking about in the wake of her curiosity. Rather like the new parlormaid who hovers outside the drawing room door, holding her breath and fidgeting in her shoes, unsure whether she should go in to fetch the tea tray if there was still someone in the room. So Lucy thought, and she called out a cheerful, "Hullo!" which startled her in spite of herself, it had been so quiet before she spoke.

The silence itself seemed to be startled. Then an answering, "Lucy?" came cold and clear through the stony maze, and more footsteps, forthright ones, and then—she was dumbfounded, having refused to believe the familiarity of the voice—Graham Isles appeared in the archway on the sunny side of the court. He peered against the brightness, pale, stubbled, thoroughly disheveled, and said her name again, in as questioning a tone as before.

"Lucy?"

"Graham! But what—how on earth—" But then she remembered the portfolio, left for him a thousand years ago in the Left Luggage Office of Skillyham Station, and was silenced by a rush of guilt.

Graham glanced behind him before he crossed to where she sat. "I've lost him, I think. Or he's lost me. Listen—"

"Who?"

"Can you come? Right now? Right away? The driver's still with the car at the foot of the valley, but I think, if we climbed the hills, they don't seem very steep, we might manage to go very quietly all on our own."

He was looking around him as if he expected policemen with whistles, huntsmen with dogs. He was out of breath, and his shoes were even muddier than hers.

"Graham." She caught one of his hands, hot and damp with sweat. "Stop a moment. Please explain. Where have you come from, who are you talking about, where do you want me to go?"

"There's no time," he said, but his hand closed around hers and he hunkered down beside her where she sat on her carved and crumbling stone. "Are you all right? I didn't expect to find you wandering about on your own. You look awfully pale."

So did Graham, but in the sunlight his eyes were the same dark amber as his favorite beer. A lovely color, in fact, which Lucy had never noticed before. He was otherwise entirely himself, and wonderfully alive and real in this—now that he was here she could think it—dreary graveyard of a place.

"Not exactly on my own," Lucy said, "but on a long leash, I think. Graham, I know why I'm here, but I haven't a clue where you come into it. Did they find out about the notes I left for you? Was it the Marshal's men who brought you here?"

"Yes, but not on his orders. Listen, they seem to think there's something dangerous about you being here. I mean, not just dangerous for you, but for everyone. Damn!" He looked around again, his hand tightening on hers. "There's really no time. I'm supposed to help get you away from him, but I'm not sure I like our chances much better once I have, so I thought, if we could slip away without them . . . We should *just go,* Lucy, and save the talk for later."

"But I don't"—*want to.* She bit off the end, but her hand had gone limp in his grasp and the telepathy of touch must have told him. He stared up at her.

"They said he's going to sacrifice you. To raise the old gods. To bring the world back to the way it was."

"They're wrong!" she said fiercely, and twisted her hand out of his. "Whoever 'they' are. They're completely wrong. It's the other way round, it's exactly the other way . . ." She balked, catching a glimpse of something she hadn't quite seen before.

"Which other way?" Graham said, impatient.

"He . . ." Lucy balked again.

"Listen." Graham reclaimed her hand. "Lucy. I think we should just go. We should just get out of this, this whole thing, whatever it is, just get the hell out and—"

"And let everything go on as it has been."

"Yes! Holy fires and all, Lucy, do you hate this world so much you want to bring it crashing down around our ears?"

"No!" Lucy was shocked.

"Do you want to die for that?"

"But I'm not the one—And it's *change*, it's not—"

"Let's just go." Graham stood, pulling Lucy to her feet. "Lucy. Please. Let's just go."

She was caught, by the desperate pleading in his voice as much as by the hard grip of his hand, and it seemed as though that instant was the deciding one, as though, if she had not hesitated, if she had just moved, or spoken—but it was only a seeming. She could have changed nothing in that moment. It was only a pause before all the rest that was going to happen, happened. She looked up at him, at Graham, who was burning with impatience and determination, and then someone stepped into the archway on the sunny side of the courtyard. They looked. One of the Marshal's men, the big young man who had escorted Lucy off the train.

"Oh dear," Lucy said, feeling a guilty lick of humor at being caught.

"Oh damn," Graham said, in another tone entirely, and he pulled at Lucy's hand, turning, trying to move her, put her behind him, she wasn't sure. In any case, she stumbled against the fallen masonry she had been sitting on, and it broke, or something did, a crack that shook the air, and Graham was pulling her, very clumsily, so they both half-fell to the ground.

"Damn!" Graham said on a gasp. "Lucy. Go. If you can." But his hand was still holding hard to hers, and somehow, perhaps through that same telepathy, she realized he was shot, he had been shot by the large young man who carried, not a book, but a gun.

Lucy looked up at him, but he was already dead. The Marshal of Kallisfane withdrew his sword with a meaty sound, and the large young man, looking stupid in his dead man's surprise, fell in a heap to the ground.

"Treachery," the Marshal said in his ordinary voice. "This is a good place for it."

Graham was falling, too, a slow continuation of the motion that had put them on their knees. His mouth was open as he fought for air. He still held Lucy's left hand very hard in his right. She used her free hand to grope under his jacket until she found the small hot hole in his side. His breath seemed to be stopped wetly in his throat, but still he managed to speak.

"I loved you," he said. "I never said. I never said."

His grasp weakened. Lucy clutched his hand hard, as hard as she could, pressing it with both her hands against her side, but still he let go, he let her go. She leaned over him to catch his gaze, but she could not, he was gone.

She was very conscious, in the silence, of the beating of her heart. If she had stopped the world, one minute ago, five minutes ago, an hour ago, he would be alive, forever and always. Graham. Who had loved her. If she had. If she had only known how.

"Perhaps now you are ready to try again," the Marshal said. His sword was smeared with blood—not dripping, only smeared, like her hand.

Would she say no because Graham who had died for her would want her to? No. She would say yes, yes, because only *yes* would end the deadlock of a thousand years, the deadlock that had killed him and all the untold others. Yes.

She was very slow, but he was patient. It was hard to let go of Graham, but it was really time she wanted to hold, and she could not, the moment was past. She stood, and looked at the Marshal, and wondered what he had really stopped, what impulse had died in the last emperor's brain. He tried to hand her his sword over Graham's body and she waved him brusquely away, back toward the broken fountain. But when she had followed him there she took the warm hilt again in her hand.

Her heart pounded out a fierce and primitive rhythm. If there had been words for it, they would have run something like, *you won't stop me, you won't bury me, I won't let you end me here.* The great weight of the Marshal's presence could not stifle it. She did not know what it was. Not magic. Perhaps only life in the face of death.

He knelt, as he had in the chapel, his eyes narrowed against the sun. Looking down, as she had looked down at Graham, Lucy saw his eyes were not black but brown, a dark tea-colored brown without red or gold to lighten them. He opened his shooting coat and shirt to bear his scarred breast. Lucy set the sword's point there and stopped, seeing how her heartbeat trembled in her hands.

"Tell me your name," she said.

He told her. She drove the sword home.

He choked once, as Graham had, and died.

The world changed.

My Life as a Swan

by Tanith Lee

Tanith Lee has a rare gift for mingling the macabre and the sensual. Her award-winning fiction includes The Birthgrave, Companions on the Road, Dark Dance, East of Midnight, Drinking Sapphire Wine, Red as Blood *and many other novels and stories, as well as shorter fiction contributed to* H. P. Lovecraft's Magazine of Horror, Weird Tales *and other genre periodicals.*

Her most recent work includes the last of her Lion Wolf Trilogy: No Flame but Mine *(Tor-MacMillan) and several stories scheduled to be published in 2008 by* Isaac Asimov's Science Fiction Magazine; *Wildside Press plans a two-volume short fiction collection,* Tempting the Gods: The Selected Stories of Tanith Lee. *Her novella "Strindberg's Ghost Quartet" will be published in 2008 by Tor Books in my anthology* The Ghost Quartet.

Tanith, who lives on the southern coast of England with her husband, writer and artist John Kaiine, is a great lover of theatre and music. This is reflected in "My Life as a Swan," which was inspired in part by Tschaikovsky's "Swan Lake" ballet.

1

MY FATHER DIED. That was the end of us, my mother and me—she too old and I too young, so we counted for nothing. Bitter was the cup of my youth. Never shall I try to recapture the beginnings of my human life.

But neither, ever, even in the silver hell to which I shall fi-

nally fall, can I forget when first I saw him: Hrothgar, the Enchanter. My Fate.

❖ ❖ ❖

The dark lake spread so far, and was like a sea, or so I thought,
then. For of course, I have never seen the ocean.

Others, who had beheld such things, compared the lake to
an iron mirror. Black, yet polished and therefore reflective, it
stretched from the skeins of trees, tumble of rocks, away and
away.

The sky was dusken. To the east, several of the bird-white
stars were beginning to show. And I, the stupid one, a woman yet
a child of perhaps seventeen years—for how could I then, or can I
now, be sure—stood on the brink, staring out towards the coming
night.

How slender and determinate, however, the night.

It sped towards me. I realized, in fear naturally, since anything unusual was probably a threat, that a part of the darkness
had come away from the fastenings of the sky. It had wide wings,
and a body with a curious shape, a face, and two eyes that were
stars. These stars were not pale, but red.

Obviously I had been instructed in the idea of evil gods and
entities. And, evidently, I had taken such ideas into my mind.

So, during those moments, I turned to run.

One wing brushed my head. It seemed to comb the very top
of my skull. I felt the contact of it all through my scalp, and
through my hair to its ends.

But it was warm, *living*. It was vital yet caressive. Oh, what
had I known? Many blows and scratchings, wicked words, and
the tongue of a whip. This was unlike any of these.

In wonder I gazed upward, and as it sailed on along the hem
of the darkness, the great owl, whose eyes were forges of red
molten gold, glanced back at me.

I fell in love with it, the owl. How not? Of them all, of all things, what else, *who* else, had *looked* at me? Who else—what else—had *I* to love?

❖   ❖   ❖

Soon there was discussion of the owl all along the lake shore. The two villages talked of it, and all the cots and hovels scattered about. Owls were birds of ill-omen. Their cries indicated bad news, tidings or warnings of death. They were the familiars of witches. Worse, perhaps, they skimmed other birds and small game from the forests, that was there only to feed men. Such a large owl, too, some of the men said, might pick off even hares, even a lamb. For they had watched the owl intently by that time, as it was flying in the dusk of night or dawn. Never had so great a flying creature been seen in this locality. The wing-span, they said, was wide as that of two full-grown men placed head to foot.

In fact the owl became ever larger and more terrible, in their talk, as the days fell from the month.

Meanwhile it was heard crying, in the strange sombre pipe of its voice, above the woodcutters' hutment—and next morning a man let slip his axe, and his arm was cut open to the bone. He would never work ably again. Also a young woman had heard the owl three nights together, calling from the trees by Second Village. On the fourth evening she bore a stillbirth.

The hunters came together. They would go out with bows and knives, fire at the owl and bring it to earth, where they would kill it. They would burn the body, but offer the tawny smoky feathers to the hunter god.

So for several sevens of days they went after the owl, shot at it with bows, even thought once they had winged it—but never brought it down. Never killed it at all.

And then simply it went away. It was no longer seen by anyone, and not heard once. The summer began to vanish, too.

A child wandered off and failed to return, and they blamed

this on the deep lake, or an early wolf. No blame now for the owl of ill-omen. Almost, it was forgotten.

Although not by me, for I mourned it, in my helpless and powerless way. I had lost most things or never had them. To mourn, then, was my sole luxury.

❖ ❖ ❖

And I dreamed of it. I was used to dream of its touch, and of its flying away from me, and looking back with its fiery eyes. As if it called me to fly up in the air and to follow it. But where? And how . . .

❖ ❖ ❖

My mother's hut lay back from the shore, many steps up into the trees, as if to hide itself, poor, lonely, unworthy hovel, from the more deserving people round about.

It was a sorry shack certainly. Half the roof was down, and in the coming winter only the snow would seal it when the world froze. My mother did not stay in the hut with me by then. Since two years ago she kept outside, under a pine. I had had to ask a man of First Village to help me dig the grave, as I had not the strength to make it deep enough so the wolves, or other beasts, should be unable to get in at her. And she had had a morbid dread of that. I paid him with fresh rabbits from the traps and went hungry a little while. I hated trapped meat in any case. I would much have preferred to kill outright and swift, but none had taught me the skill. Only sometimes I managed to catch a lake fish and smash it dead instantly on a rock. That was better. I could eat that if I must.

The man had told me actually, he would settle for something else. I was surprised he wanted me for that, but I was young and put his lust down to my age. I told him I had an ailment there, it would be wrong to risk infecting him. He said I was a filthy bitch, dug the grave and took the rabbits instead.

All those years I had remained a virgin. My mother had said I must, and examined me now and then with her bruises of fingers. She whipped me often as a child. Then, when she was too old to do that, she said I must whip myself, it was a good thing to do, the gods liked it. So I would pretend, taking the whip off among the trees, striking it on things, and groaning. If she wanted evidence I showed her marks made from berry juice. Her sight was dim. She was satisfied. After her death I put the whip in her grave, thinking she might want it elsewhere. But sometimes in the winter storms I imagined I heard it slashing inside the wind, doing her penance, or seeking for me and mine.

❖ ❖ ❖

The owl had been gone thirty days and nights and a stray premature snow had come down. I was digging the last gourds from the hard ground. I looked up in the bloodless past-noon light to see a man treading through the forest towards the lake.

Due to the twists of the path between the trees, I saw him oddly, first from the back.

He was tall, or looked to be, though not as tall as some. Yet how he moved and held his body, which was lean and graceful, made him seem the taller. Long black hair, thick as poured honey, hung over his shoulders, and it had a mellow colour in its blackness, too, when the sunlight altered. The sun came out as he turned along the track. And then I saw him sidelong. His face was not like any I had ever seen. Not among men, nor even among the old carved images of the gods. Yet his face did seem to have been carved, *fashioned* more than randomly produced from flesh and bone. A straight nose he had on him, and a high bone in the cheek, and a high noble forehead off which the dark hair ran. Then the path brought him round and he was full face. His brows were arching and black, his eyes deep-set and black also. He had a beautiful mouth, slim and couth. There were no such mouths among the men I had met by the lake. But he was unlike any of them anyway, and in one further curious manner. For I could see he was older yet young. By which I mean he might be some ten years older than I. Among the lake people, either they were young, or then suddenly they grew old. Their faces and their bodies became too spare or heavy, crumpling and crumbling as if a loose earthwork sagged and came down. There is no middle country for such men, nor women either. But this man, he was both older and young. And his face, his throat, even his body as he walked, even his hands, were fine. His face was full of the knowledge of wisdom. His age was this, too. For every year he had lived, perhaps for every instant, he had learned.

Then he walked by the hut, and he glanced at me. The slant of the sun lit a moment red in the dark of his eyes. His look was playful. His clever beautiful mouth partly smiled. He said to me nothing at all. But his eyes said, *Do you not remember, then?*

And after that he was past and gone, his boots wounding the thin white skin of the snow.

When I could no longer see him for the trees, I went out and stood looking down at the marks his boots had left, till the sun slid behind a wide-winged cloud.

Generally I had little to do with the villagers in the social way. That is, I very seldom sought them, while they avoided me. Now and then I overheard, or glimpsed one or other, or some group of them at a slight distance, and then normally I would turn aside where I could not be seen, even back into the hut, if I was near enough. Part of me, though, now longed to go down into both the villages, to look about and try to find if he, the man I had watched on the path, had gone there. Yet such an act had no point. Even if he had entered the villages, he would never have stayed. What had he been? Some traveller . . . a strange traveller, however, who travelled not only on foot, but apparently without any baggage. Nor had he seemed to be armed in any way. I had noted neither a knife nor a stick in his possession. His clothes had been ordinary, I thought, some rough tunic and leggings, cloak, boots. Yet I was unsure, really, what he had worn, and whether the garments were sturdy or impoverished. I had only noticed— *him*.

The next evening I went out over the crackle of snow to set a rabbit-trap up by the big white birch. Lightning struck this tree when I was only an infant, I could remember the terrible crack and flash, as if the sky had split. Rather than destroy the tree, the lightning made it stronger. Now it towered on the hill above all the rest.

As I was kneeling there, a man spoke quietly behind me.

I nearly sprang from my body. I was well used to being wary, and knew the usual sounds both of animals and people if they approached. This one, whatever he—it—was, had made none.

What had he said? He said the words again. "Leave that. I've two here already."

Then I jumped up and round and saw it was the man I had seen the previous day.

There could be no mistaking.

I could not speak, had forgotten language.

But he held up before me a pair of large brown rabbits, both fresh slaughtered, their necks loose. They had been killed, each of them, with a single clean blow.

"You'll like this better," he said, "I think."

I said, "I haven't any money to pay you." I barely knew, though, what I said.

And he said, "Did I ask money? We'll share the meat, you and I."

I thought I had gone mad and was imagining this, as sometimes I *did* imagine things, and did think myself mad. Was I frightened? Yes, quite an amount. But I did not shake from fear, although I shook. Turning again, I bent and undid the trap and left it lying, and looking back saw he had walked down the slope towards my hut, so I must go after him.

At the door he waited. Less courtesy it seemed than some other, more savage thing.

I did not believe he was truly there. Once I went in at the door he would vanish. He was an illusion of the forest, or some elemental.

I should fetch an amulet, put it between him and me. Did I have any?

After a second I went into the hut and he walked in after me, and put the two rabbits down at once on the log that was my table.

Not knowing what to do, I took my knife and set to work, my hands trembling as all of me did. There was a spinning at my centre. I did not know if I hated or liked it. He only stood, and watched me.

When I had botched up the job of getting off the fur and jointing the carcasses, I put the iron pan on the fire, and threw in some herbs that I kept to dry by the hearth. He watched that, too. But when I picked up both rabbits he said, quietly, as before, "Cook yours. I will eat mine raw."

Then I knew he was unhuman. It is unlawful to eat raw meat, the gods forbid it to men, even I knew that.

But I put the larger of the skinned rabbits back on the log, and dropped my own portion, if mine it was, in the pot.

I thought then I had better offer him a drink. I had only water, or the thin beer I brewed as my mother taught me.

So I offered, and asked what he would have.

Then he smiled at me.

His smile burned me like a flame. And his eyes, that all this while I had not quite met, black as the wood of the forest, did they burn, too, and worse? "Look there."

On the log stood a tall grey jug. I had never seen it before. And there seemed to be blood in it. Why not, if he ate his meat raw?

Then he held out a shiny grey cup to me, and the blood, too, was in that. But I realized quite well there had been nothing in his hand a moment before—empty, his hand. And the cup was not grey but old metal, silver. And it was full of red wine, that the high classes and the priests drink only.

"Taste it," he said. I only stood there, and then I found the cup was in my hand, not his, though he had not stretched out to put it there, nor had I taken it. "Why," he said, "is your hair that shade?"

I heard myself answer from far off, as if I were really in the corner among the shadows. "When I was small, it grew out white." So it had, about a month after the lightning split the birch tree. As if the lightning had run also into my hair.

"Your hair shone on the shore," he said, "like the moon fell there. Your skin's as white. But your eyes are black."

I had never seen in a mirror to know the colour of my eyes. I wondered if they had *not* been black before, but only altered to it since having been looked at by his.

And all this while he looked at me.

None ever had, except my dead mother now and then, when she poked at me or whipped me.

His eyes were like the black lake. But they would not let you drown in them. They lured you in only to push you weightlessly away, only then to lure you back again.

He was an Enchanter. Of course by now I knew. A red glint of the departing sun had stayed caught under the black of his hair, and in the black water of his eyes.

And I could see myself reflected in his eyes after all, tiny and pale, like a water-bird that drifted on their surface.

We shared the wine, passing the cup back and forth, or rather the cup moved from me through the air to him, then back to me. I could taste the fire where his mouth had scorched the rim. The silver jug meanwhile had less and less wine in it, as we emptied the cup two or three times over. Then the jug was full to the brim again. Yet no one had poured from the jug, or refilled it. We said nothing else, and then the rabbit in the pot was savoury and done, and I put it on the log in the wooden dish, and the dark bread to one side.

We sat, he on the other log, I on my heels on the floor.

He tore the uncooked rabbit in three and ate it without ceremony, but also without any uncouthness. He ate the eyes and tongue, and the bones too he ate, I heard them crunch between his teeth. Even the teeth of the rabbit his teeth crunched and he swallowed them, those teeth of the rabbit.

Perhaps I ate. I think so.

The wine was sweet and strong; I had never tasted wine before. Perhaps, I thought without much awareness, this was *not* wine, anyway.

The shadows deepened in the hut, but the fire kept bright and warm without any attention. And then four moths came in and perched, one against each of the four walls. They were little double flying flames. He must have made them, or summoned them.

All his meal was gone. Not a trace. Instead a tawny, barred feather lay on the log. This feather did not amaze me.

"I'll tell you my name," he said. "Hrothgar. Say it back to me."

I said it back to him.

He did not ask my name, I had none, not really, just some scrap my mother and some of the villagers called me by. It had never been mine, and for myself I had never invented one.

"I will call you," he said, "Otila. It's a lucky name."

I should have asked him why he gave me a name, and a rabbit to eat, and wine. Why he sat here.

He said, "Well, now I'll be on my way."

I said nothing. On the walls the lights faded. The jug and the cup were gone. On the dish were only the bones of the cooked rabbit that perhaps I had eaten, and a crust of the bread. No feather lay on the log.

Outside something called through the darkness with a wild unholy bubbling note.

I had the impression of shadowy flight, and twice red amber fire, heartless, soulless: two eyes. Was I still reflected in them, still swimming on their surface like a water-bird? I seemed to feel myself for a moment carried up into the sky, and all the night opening around me like a limitless roof stabbed with stars.

When I woke the night was nearly done.

I lay by the table, with my head on my arm. It was cold and the fire was out.

❖ ❖ ❖

I put four young winter cabbages and some of the gourds into a sack, and some of the thin beer in the leather skin. I walked down with them, which took perhaps an hour, and into First Village.

A horrible place. Seldom had I been there, but the muck of it had, apparently, never quite been rubbed off from my mind. It stank, too, of men and their dirt, and ill-kept beasts. Grey, tusked swine rooted in the alleys that were presently floored with hard snow. Smoke rose from chimney holes and murked the pale sky.

People rambled about, seeming busy and important in that slack aimless way they have, that way I have never grasped—either its reason, or how to pretend I am the same and so pass as human.

The upper village, built on an earthen terrace and now paved white, had the gods-house, a long low wooden shack. I went by and tried the mortal houses with my wares. I had never bothered with the lower alleys. I thought he would not be down there.

Six days had passed since the night when we ate the rabbits, and he ate one and its teeth.

In all the nights I had heard the owl call only once.

Yet I knew he had not left the vicinity of the forest, still haunted it.

Of course, he might be anywhere. But then, why not here?

As to why I *sought* after him I had no idea.

When had I *ever* had one? It was only that seek him I did.

He had told me his name.

At some of the doors where I rapped with my knuckles, they shouted me away. One, a rough-haired woman, came out, snatched up and threw a clod of hard snow at me. It glanced off my hip.

Then I turned a corner, and a man walked up and bought two of the cabbages and took a drink of the beer. He gave me a brown misshapen coin—not often had I beheld true money.

When the man was gone I put the coin in the pouch in my skirt, and looking up I saw an old humped man, unlike the other, crouching along the street. Deformed, with a great broken hill seeming to rest on his back, his grey hair straggled down like cord. Less grey this hair than silver. And looking up and out, from his face all bones and ridges and age-lines that were like knife-cuts, *his* eyes. It was him. It was the Enchanter.

Having sought him and found him, now I stood powerless and speechless on the snow. In that narrow crowded space between the walls of rotted houses, he moved up to pass me. He was bent so much his head reached only to my breast, but his eyes laughed at me, cruel black as the lake of drowning, where my image had swum. "Oh, so you stirred yourself to look for me, then?" he said.

But before I could answer, to agree or deny, round the shank of a wall he went. And going after, he was gone. As I had known he must be.

So I went away, back through the village, lugging the heavy sack and the skin with me, not seeking custom, getting none.

I had seen him, and been seen.

That night in the hovel I made my own magic.

Did I know what I did? *Know?* I *knew* nothing at all.

❖   ❖   ❖

I threw torn bits of my hair on the fire and splashed my blood on it from a shallow cut I made across my arm. I called his name, on and on. I wept, too. I wept because I was lonely and had nothing beautiful, even if I did not know I was alone, nor did I understand what beauty was.

And I cursed him later, when the moon rose and not a sound in the forest, not a shadow, not a feather.

In the end I lay on my back on the floor and put my hand between my legs, as sometimes I had since childhood, somehow discovering that not all touches there must be painful, obscene, deathly and meaningless.

The fire came off the hearth, with my blood and hair and tears in it, and burst in my body, and I screamed, and yet his name still was in the screaming.

Then I fell asleep, and in my sleep dreamed the owl had entered the room and stood on me, its claws planted on my breasts like hard bone hands, and with a dead hare in its beak.

When I woke, stiff and sore at sunrise, there was a tiny scratch on my left breast. But perhaps *I* had made it by accident.

The fire, though, had not gone out. It blazed. There was wood in the middle of it burning. And on the log table was the hare, headless, bloodless, boned and peeled of fur, all ready for the pot.

❖　❖　❖

"Where's the old cripple with the humped back?"

"Ah, he's to the out-farm." This, from some man.

It was his woman who demanded, suspicious and glaring, "Why'd you ask it, white-face girl?"

"I have a pot needs mending," I replied.

For by then, here in Second Village, and three hours' walk from the hovel, I had heard tell of the old fellow with grey hair, who could heal the animals of sodden feet and the rash, and also mend household items.

I had come all this way on this occasion without anything to sell or barter.

"White *scut*!" spat the woman, as I went off.

The out-farm was a holding up a hill, with the skulls of foxes and even three wolves hung on cords, to clack in the wind and scare off others.

The poor sheep huddled by the bare trees, plucking at a bundle of dried grasses left there for them. Their coats were thick, but winter came, was arrived.

Was this the first I ever felt any pity? Even for myself I never had. Only variable hurts had I ever felt, and not known what to do with them.

He was with the sheep, too, the old cripple man that was Hrothgar the Enchanter's disguise. I saw what he did.

He must have told those in the house not to watch, frightened them with some sorcerous formula. The gods know what.

He was straddling the sheep, and for a moment I thought something else went on, as it does here and there. But no. Clamping them between his thighs with a strength and control few men, even when young, could call on, he made much of them, stroking and patting them, and singing words whose sounds did not *resemble* words. Each animal was let go from his clutch, glowing. Then they shone, in the wet white sun, like the palest gold—a metal then I had never seen.

I stood by the fence, and he paid me no attention. Nor did he shout I must go away.

In the end he was done, and all the sad sheep were shining and frisking about. *Then* he came crouching over to the fence posts.

"Why follow me?" he said.

"To see you." I was bold with exhaustion, and also amazement, and—gladness. I liked how he had made the sheep better.

"Well. I'm seen."

"Visit me," I said, "this night."

"So forward," he said. "Not tonight. I have things to steal tonight."

Now I was really astonished. Why need *he* steal?

"What?" I said. And stupidly, or maybe not stupidly, "I have things you can steal, too."

"Oh, you do. But think of this. Hrothgar steals also from himself."

Then–he did send me away.

I cannot describe how he did it. Did he ask or tell or command me to go? I found myself back among the trees, walking into Second Village.

I felt leaden as if the mud and snow and filth weighed me to the earth. Yet also, how curious it was, alight and clean.

❖ ❖ ❖

In the iron tub I washed myself and my hair with water that was chill, for I could only take the edge from its cold with the heated panful from the hearth. A little stream ran behind the hovel, not quite frozen. I had carried off so much I had thought I would drain it dry. In my mother's time we had used this tub on only a few occasions every year, and then always she first, so I washed myself in water already shallow and thickened from her cleansing.

After the bath I did not want to put on the clothes I had worn. I found the other garment, the long shapeless, colourless dress of coarse wool that had been in our family, so my mother said, since my great-grandmother's time. It was for the use of any female who must go to the gods-house, to swear hand-lock pledge, or answer for some misdeed, or show a baby to one of the gods. It fit me well enough, but at first I thought I would take it off, for it itched. But then the wool seemed to settle.

I combed my hair by the crackling fire, drinking a little of the beer.

I said to the sparks as they flew up, sizzling at the wet drops that dashed from the comb, "If you won't come to me I shall curse you properly. I know how to do it." I did not know. There had been little cunning, or craft of any kind, in my family. Yet at this time I felt a sudden power on me. It was the power of desire, which I recognized but had no name for. Except, it had *his* name. "Hrothgar," I said to the fire. "Tonight you will come here. Or I shall break your wings and you'll die."

Only the madness in me made me say such things, to threaten an Enchanter of such might. Love drives out fear, they say. Or makes fear only the servant of love, and both fools.

But he did not come. Oh, of course he did not.

❖ ❖ ❖

A light woke me.

I could not, waking up, think where it might be from. There was no moon, and clouds were all across the stars.

The fire was out. I had smothered it down to keep the wood for morning.

Usually by night in winter my bed was cold, but I was used to that. Now my bed was warm.

I turned and looked into the source of the light, which was his eyes, the whites of them so clear, and the dark lit within like two black lamps that hold a russet fire.

Did I have the sense to be afraid?

Yes.

But I put out my arms and my hands and took hold of him.

Under the cover of the old wool blanket and the older pelts, he was bare as I.

He laughed. Musical, his laugh. Never had I heard a laugh like music.

"It seems you expected me."

"I cast a spell to make you visit."

"So you did. But was it worth, your little spell, more than a shriek or a single tear?"

He was warm, hot as flame, and smooth as metal–yet not like

that. The lightest hair ran over his breast–feathers–running to a gradual, denser fur along his belly, thick at his loins, thick as the rich hair on his head.

"How quick you go," he said, amused.

But I would not stop.

I cared nothing. Perhaps I did not reckon him real at all, but a dream, a phantom come to me in sleep, to give me what life never would.

Unlike the front of him, his back and backside were naked, and hard smooth nearly as marble, though then I did not know what marble was. Yet malleable, too, for muscles moved in his back and chest and all his body, fluent as I have felt in feral animals.

Then I felt the rod of his sex tap against my thigh. I could not help but touch it, clasp it. It was like a separate thing, large and strong, a beast itself that I had interested and that now quested, blindly yet sure, coming to find me out even as I tried to discover him, while *he* lay there on his side, and only looked at me, re-moved.

I had once or twice seen the things of men, if never wanting to, been shown them. They were ugly, wrong-shaped, foul and sense-less. But this of his was not like that, and itself coaxing and eager, and I wanted, having put my fingers on it, not to let it alone.

But then gently he slid my hand off him. And I thought I had angered him, and was also myself angered–as how had I ever been angry or dared to be?–but instead he roped me with his arms and drew me in.

I lay held fast against him as his kisses opened my mouth.

What is this pleasure? Pleasure then exists–there is joy in the world–

No, it is not pleasure or joy. It is some state that has no name, as none of us have names, even when named. Even he does not have any name.

Nor is this any world I have known, and no one has known it. Or, if ever they have, not as *I* do.

This, is *mine.*

Mine, his long back, his hair, his skin, his taste, and the thrust of him that breaks me undone and spills my blood on the straw mattress under us. Mine, the sense of his wings that bear us upward. Mine the little cry of pain, and then the cry of delight, and now mine, too, the wings–the wings–and I alone am flying upward, straight through my body and his, and through the wreck of the roof, and out into the clouded darkness of the night.

Which is where next I find myself. In the night sky above the forests, flying to the slow drum of wing beats, and truly they *are* mine, and truly all things are altered.

❖ ❖ ❖

When I lived by the other shore, I was brought gifts. I had a velvet gown, dark blood-red, and a necklace of dull grey-green stones that were, I learned, polished emeralds. I had silk shoes, too. And boots with fur for the winter. And a cloak of fur, and a mirror, not of iron but burnished silver, and in that mirror I lost myself, for it was no longer myself I saw there, by whatever name I went. For it seems I had thought of myself one way, and even *his* descriptions of me had only added themselves to my comprehension of self. But she in the mirror was a stranger. I remember, too, in the mirror her hair turned to darkness, and her red dress to black.

That night, after he took me and tore me and had me and possessed and ruined and remade me, I was changed. And soon I glimpsed the whole width of the black water of the lake, below.

Miles of it there are, whole days and nights of journey and time. It is a sort of sea, though tideless, but then no one had ever told me of sea-tides and I only heard those things mentioned in the place where I later lived, on the farther shore, and most of them from him. That is, the *other*. I do not mean Hrothgar. Hrothgar taught me nothing, thereby everything.

❖ ❖ ❖

Below, on the black mirror of the water of the lake then, I see my white reflection, and high above I am, close to the misty moon, which has come out of cloud and sheens the sky, the earth, and me.

I see myself reflected there, far down on the lake, just as in the mirror of his black eyes.

A pale water-bird, flying.

For I fly.

❖ ❖ ❖

I fly.

I *feel* the tug and pull of the muscles in my body, the white wings that lift and sink and lift again.

Power.

So *strong.*

And this—is myself.

Otila—so he called me. Then maybe that is the true name of what now I am as first I fly.

I know my shape, for once long before I have seen one.

Not an owl, a predator of amber and red and flame.

I am white as the snow, as my riven hair that the shock of the shock-struck birch turned ashen.

My long smooth throat stretches.

From sideways eyes, black as the lake, I see two sides of everything, and both sides make one for me, one thing, that finally, at *last,* I understand.

I am a swan.

A swan.

I am a swan.

2

Waking, I thought I had dreamed it all. And then I saw the reed-bed that stood out on the water. Everything was grey and rose in

261

the sunrise-twilight. The dead and frozen reeds stuck up sharp as long knives, and rattled with the dawn wind.

And I sat on the shore, where trees came down to the water. But this was not the part of the lake I knew. And I did know that area of the shore quite well. It was where I came to catch fish, and where, too, now and then, reluctantly I had seen village men also fishing, or the woodcutters chopping down a tree.

But this, though, here, was a secretive place. It had been curved in by an arm of the land, and hooded over by the low-hung trees in their weight of dead snow.

As the light grew more clear, a smudge of constant smoke far along the shore revealed where must be one at least of the villages familiar to me.

I was miles away.

Having decided this, I stood up, shaking myself. I was human enough, no longer an avian creature. What had happened then? I had told myself a story in which Hrothgar became my lover, I had reached the peak of pleasure . . . then slept, or entered some other stranger state. During which, it seemed, I had walked far around the rim of the lake, believing all the while I flew.

I stared out.

The water was silkily ruffling, pleating and unpleating. It was now not very dark, only reflecting the filmy pinkness of a lifting sky.

Not quite meaning to, perhaps, I pictured the swan I had been, as if I had witnessed her arrival here, rather than accomplished it, sailing in on the air, skimming the water with extended feet, settling in a surge on its cool, unstable constant, that held no coldness for any part of me, next swimming with deft swift little kicks, until reaching the shore—

I had stepped off on the land, and after a moment was a swan no more.

Yet—and now I noticed insanely for the very first—I was naked. I had left my mattress and walked here, and lain down and slept here, on the bare earth, bare and white as *it.*

Why had I not died? Should I die now, of exposure to the deep white cold, since finally I had *realized*?

I did not *feel* cold. The atmosphere, the ice under my soles, they were only cool, like the water.

I took a step and oh–

Again everything changed.

Between a pair of heartbeats I had become the other. Now I walked, still two-legged, but balanced on a different centre, and at an altered angle. I blinked and my doubled vision drew together within some miraculous gem in the middle of my brain.

Like a thrown spear, light and sure, yet heavy and potent with the power of essential velocity, I ran and launched myself skyward.

How huge, that sky. I did not think of magical, holy spaces, or gods who might dwell there, up behind the layers of the light. I thought only of flying.

But even so, nothing was lost on me, the wisps of cloud dissolving to the west, the tiny flecks of smaller birds.

Below now, the water shone a silver mirror. Again I saw from shore to shore. Clusters of life were dotted here and there. Deer were feeding on bark, a savage pig was trotting between the stems of trees. Little ungainly boats unseamed the fringes of the water. Fish glinted, too, deep down, these seen by me in some way I cannot describe. I had no caution or doubt at flight, as I had had none in the darkness. I did not think or feel, or reason or *know* as a human does. Although some nebulous invisible cord must still have bound me to what I had been, and would be again.

I made my landing some quarter mile from the area of my mother's hovel, at the place I had gone formerly to fish.

Swooping low, alighting on the ripple-floor of the lake, I fished once more. I snapped up the shiny trophy and broke it clean of pain and horror in one faultless snap. Down it fell into my long dense body, under the firm pads of flesh and snow feathers. Bones, too, I ate. I drank a little of the lake.

Two men were out along the shore. In my human guise I

would have known them, but now did not; they had no interest for me, were like rocks that moved about. To be avoided, discarded. Only after would I recall.

One pointed to me. They paused, anxious lest I take or disturb anything they might want. But they did not attempt to kill me. There was a law everywhere in these regions against the killing of such birds. Even I had known, only lords might hunt swans, pluck, eat them. The swan did not know, and cared nothing. Men were rocks.

I turned away, floating among the brown grasses decaying by the water. Dipping my head I saw my reflection, but it meant nothing wondrous or significant. It was the normal state of my life, to see myself, as flying was. I thrust my long neck deep in the shallows, and fished again for a water plant.

When I stepped this time ashore, I trampled my way up between the pines. And here it came to me I was a woman, and so I became one again. And then, though I felt no harm at all from the cold day, and no one else was about, I fled to the hut, got inside, and slamming the rickety door, let down the bar, and leaned there on the timbers. I wept. I had and have no grasp of why. Or, if now I do, it is redundant.

And soon anyway I made up the fire and put on some beer in the pan to warm. I had eaten and needed nothing else. Nor was I thirsty, and still not chilled. Yet I required the beer, as I did the clothes I slung on myself, and the comb I pulled through my hair.

❖ ❖ ❖

It is impossible for me, sensibly and convincingly, to detail how it was for me to change my shape, either from woman to bird, or back again.

There was nothing tangibly physical in the transference. No muscle or sinew stretched or worked oddly, my breathing did not seem to become alien, nor the beat of my heart quicken. My hair—or feathers on me—did not stir. I experienced, after that second time, no transitional sense of occlusion or perspective. I was one being. Then another. I *melted* from one condition to the next. It seemed to happen only with a slight overview, something to do with my whereabouts or my consciousness when on land or water, or looking at such external or internal things. I was never, even so, to alter to a woman when on the wing high in the air. Nor half drown as a woman when adrift on the lake. Nor either did I ever change to my form of swan when inside a human habitation.

I felt no sorcerous impulse, and no coercion. It was not some spell or curse he had put on me. I believed initially, and long after again I believed, it was my own gift that somehow I had found. And even as I sat by my human fire in the hovel thinking of it, less frightened than puzzled, nearly sad, I did not really think we had joined in sexual congress. There was no trace of him left in the hut, and despite the burnt mark of blood on the mattress, I guessed I had imagined him. *That* therefore had been the dream. To shape-shift was the reality, and all my own.

Here then began my life as a swan. Or, should I say, as a woman who might become a swan—at will, presumably, a swan who likewise might re-become a woman. Some will envy me, I know, some fear me, and some hate. And many will not credit a word.

Hrothgar I did not see again for the thirty-three days of that long winter month.

Snow fell thick.

I became a swan as the mood or reverie took me. Which was quite often. One day I was humanly gathering blackened berries as a condiment from the shrubs up among the birches, and heard ducks calling as they sheered over the water. I let the berries fall and next moment found myself–my other self–running, leaping from the path among the thinner trees, springing upward and gliding free. The bluish tawny ivory of my beak was striped, I think, with the congealed juice of the berries. I had been chewing some. I did not return until the next frozen dawn, and by then little animals, or ice, had consumed the shrivelled fruit.

As a human, too, I continued impervious to the temperature. My hair had thickened, and my skin seemed to be more white. My hands did not chap or split in blains.

Sometimes I found one of my own blanched feathers lying by the doorway of the hut. Once I found one in my own hair.

One morning, too, I saw, near the hut, the tracks of a solitary wolf. It had drawn close, then sped away. I never saw it, but suspected it had seen me fly down, after which the rest had alarmed it.

Did I rejoice in my talent?

Of course. My life had been till then walled in.

Sometimes, when a woman, I sat by the hearth and domestically mended my garments or broke wood for the fire. I thought I must use my genius for flight to take me to those distant shores I had, by now, so often observed from the air. But at this era I never, when a swan, was tempted to do that. For, as a *swan,* I had slight concern with it. I preferred the nearer verges of the lake, even if I ranged somewhat further afield than ever I had as a girl. The shallows were perfect for feeding, plants still to be reached with my long and supple neck and selective beak. Even when ice formed like paving at the margins, I did not swim so much out away from shore. And sometimes, as a human, I took the axe and smashed the ice, so that I, the swan, could sail off more easily and briefly.

Sunrise was pale yellow now, sunset dark red, and the sun looked old.

Some had said the sun always slowly died in winter, returning as a fresh new orb between the midnight and dawn of a single early day of spring.

Did all things alter their shape, being and nature? Aside from birth, old age and death, of what else were mortals capable?

And did I miss the presence of the Enchanter who had so curiously enchanted me?

When a woman I missed him. I thought of him by night, if in the hut, and skillfully conjured for myself the pleasure I had now determined I never received from his body. Should I remember him I yearned after him, *burned* after him—but in the most inchoate way. I had other concerns. I had other employment.

When a bird I thought of nothing but what I did. *I,* the swan, was paramount.

Is it of interest that, as a woman, I always recollected my swan-life vividly—while as a swan, I more and more forgot my human form?

For after each excursion I examined what I had seen and done. Always it thrilled and excited me. The peculiar grieving I felt at first was all dispelled. And as it was only in human form that I could *humanly* relish my swan-times, I was no longer isolate, or dully sullen during my mortal life.

❖ ❖ ❖

The owl began to perch, high on the lightning-stricken birch tree.

I heard it. I heard him.

The cry now was particularly cruel and heartless, a deviant demonic cry that made the hearth fire crawl down under the wood.

I did not go to see save once. It had been full moon that night, and the owl a black shadow on the pallid tree, and its own shadow reeling as it raised now one fretted wing or the other, with a single sudden ignition of red eyes.

Was I ensnared?

Maybe. I was unsure.

I knew besides I could not keep the Enchanter out, should he choose to enter the hovel. He had come in through wall or barred door or too-narrow window in the past. It abruptly seemed to me, only now, that I had not dreamed our union. Or, if only a dream was all it was, then what called in the tree was only an owl.

As a swan, I had never flown where the owl was. Nor did I ever note the owl. Did I not then, at all, recall Hrothgar when I was a swan? I cannot say, even now. How curious, how bitter.

No more snow descended, but there was an early morning—I had just come into the hut—when the frost that formed was so fearsome it had turned the world white-black, with crusts of tin. Things died everywhere about, or were already dead, and the old dying sun dragged itself out of the east the colour of stale bladder-water.

That was the hour he returned, Hrothgar.

I had just started the hearth to life. I put on the beer to heat, and saw him entering through the wall.

Through the wall, as I had suspected he could if he wished, he idled into the enclosed room. And as he came in, he was changing, owl to man, that very second.

So I saw, for he showed this to me, what I, too, no doubt, resembled and was, in that metamorphosis that seemed to me, once it had happened, only inevitable, almost rational.

The owl was no longer quite a creature—but more like a mantle the Enchanter had put on, one that wore threadbare instant by instant, and frayed off from him. At first, too, it seemed the mantle of the owl was larger than a man, a giant, but as rapidly it vanished, it grew also less. *Its* body then rivered away through *his* body, leaving momentarily an impression of itself. So I saw a naked man with feathers on his skin, the knotty wood-like bird legs branched down through his own, its claws turning to vapour against the bones and muscles in his thighs. The wings of the owl, its head, went last of all. Then he was, for a single heart-beat, a man *masked* as a bird, his black eyes looking through its golden ones, the wide wings ranging out behind his back. But after this, he was solely a man. And from his nakedness only a rusty down of its eclipsed feathers drifted to the floor.

This act took no more than it would be to count to seven or nine. Yet it had seemed to last many minutes. Ever after when I thought or think of it, it will seem to last an hour or longer.

I did nothing. What could I do?

Except I gazed at him. I had not before seen him clad only in his body, since in the other undream visit, when he deflowered me, we had lain in the dark. I had only *felt* of him.

Seeing him I desired him. And I knew we had been lovers. For the desire was greedy, practiced.

Where I knelt by the fire, his shadow fell.

I looked away from him, and put out one hand and touched the shadow, at the centre of its loins, and watching only the shadow, saw the shadow weapon raise itself at once, engorged and ready. He had been quiescent before. Then I turned and glanced back at him in the flesh, and he had not roused, the blade of his sex lay sleeping.

"Well, Otila," he softly said to me, "if you can provoke a shadow by fingering it, don't you think you will be able to wake me as I am?"

He played with me, clearly.

"As you were," I said, "you were the owl."

Then for the moment of a moment, the mask of the owl glared down at me from behind his face, this time its golden eyes *inside* the black of his own.

And then—he was clothed. Fully dressed, like one of the richer travellers I had seen, if rarely, in leather and good wool and furs.

I knew I could never have made garments for myself out of the thin air, even though I might become a swan.

The beer was heated. I got up, and taking it to the log-table found two cups of earthenware standing ready to receive it.

When the beer poured it was hot wine, blond in colour, and with a scent and taste of spice.

He drank, and so did I.

269

"You never thank me," he said, "for my gifts. Aren't they to your liking?"

I could not answer. It seemed then I must accept my shape-changing came only from him. I knew without he told me. Had always suspected, no doubt, and so hidden it from myself. Lacking him I should be nothing once more. What payment did he demand?

"I never thought them gifts," I said. "I thought you pleased yourself. If I am gifted, you make me your debtor."

"Why should I do that?"

"You pray to a god of sorrow and darkness."

He smiled. "I pray to nothing. I'd not waste my time on it."

"Why," I said, "are you here with me? Why have you–*gifted* me with–this magic that–makes me–another creature–?"

"Oh," he said. "That little deed. Did *I* do *that*?"

And then there was the movement of his dark furs and hair, like a cloud, and I dropped the cup but it never reached the floor to shatter. It must have disappeared. He had hold of me, bent me round in a painless twining, so I let go even of the ground under me.

We were on the mattress, where I had not-dreamed we were before.

Now the sere light of winter day poured through the narrow windows, the broken roof, all over us.

How thoroughly he investigated me at this meeting. He *sampled* all the country of me. His tongue was like a wolf's, burning and harsh, then limpid between my legs. This was horrible, then a wonder. His sharp teeth nibbled my flesh and ran along my cheek, and bit away little snippets of my hair. He ate my hair, swallowed it. His face was full of thought as he did this–I saw it plainly in the light. He licked all my skin also, leaving behind a scent of fire and frost. When I slid my hands over him now, sometimes I felt the quills of feathers under *his* skin as perhaps he could, under mine. Several times he mounted me, and twice turned me and had me that way, from the back. Once he lifted me onto the smooth tower of his blade, and danced me there, I with my head thrown back, crying.

Light dripped on over the room, moving from one end of it to another.

I had no space to be afraid, barely even to be surprised. I knew that what we did was unholy. The pleasures of it were very great. But at the bursting climaxes of each action my body still did not change. It seemed I did not need to shape-shift here, having learnt how during our first congress, and having done so independently since. Our confluence now was simply for itself.

In the end, the last light had dripped all away.

We had not spoken ever once our flesh began its dialogue, and only I had made true sounds.

I lay motionless, sore and shining in my inner parts, my breasts scorched where he had suckled at them. My bones had flowed to melted tallow, and did not harden. I could not any more think of a life where he did not lie here beside or beneath or upon me.

As darkness, without any warmth of a sunfall however drained, began to soak into the hovel, I spoke his name.

To my ears tonight it had the noise of the quills of feathers brushing against harsh stone.

But he had already left my bed. As the blacker shadow came in and in, he clothed himself again in that. From the table he picked up the remaining cup. It still smoked with heat, though poured six hours before. And he drank it dry, as he had drunk my body, and my thoughts.

I did not believe he could go away. Or if he did, he would return to me.

Meanwhile, of course, I knew he would leave me now forever.

Nor could I say anything, other than his name—*Hrothgar*... *Hrothgar*... feathers, feathers against stone, stone—

Exactly when he went out of the hut I was unsure. He remained in human form certainly, but out through a wall he must have passed.

It was another spell on me, as it had been that time when he dismissed and sent me from him in the other village.

Only many minutes after was I able to realize I might get up.

Standing in the doorway I glimpsed, in fading dreary dusk, something great and black that winged off across the trees, over the unseen water below.

As if I *had* asked, and been answered, I knew very well he had flown to the farther shores of the lake. I knew he was gone. Only the winter would stay with me. I wept by the fire and my falling firelit tears shone red as blood, glamorously bright as gold.

Even in rejection and lament, I knew I should follow him. The swan, I thought, knew that. To follow is a natural thing. Seasons follow each other, and sun and moon, and beasts and birds. And mankind follows each some other also, through birth and life and love and death and silence. It is how we exist, moving always on, even into emptiness, one behind another. There is no choice.

It is how we exist. And how we perish.

3

The place where first I lived, on the lake's far, other side, was a box of broken stones. It was, I believe, the shrine to an ancient god. No one cared for it now. Nor did I. I made now and then a superstitious sign of respect at the old granite block which, probably, had been an altar. But I sensed no presence. There was nothing left in that space either to be entreated or feared.

No human beings came there ever. New gods replace old always, and are often jealous.

It provided me a roof and walls—despite their rents and lapses, stronger and more secure in fact than those of my mother's hovel.

Besides, anyway, I never now felt the cold injuriously. I had arrived on that bleak snow-shore at sunfall a swan, and moving up from the water—where I had found in the mud small shelled creatures that I ate—I became a woman, naked as before, and the icy dark fell on me like the softest of soft rains.

Even so, inside the shrine I discovered some pieces of sacking, and cobbled them together with yarn and a long hooked needle left in a stone cupboard by someone. This then was now my clothing. In the cupboard, too, was a broken lamp, but I made it burn from a store of sticky black oil left by, while the fire itself I struck with a shard on the altar. These things are not so difficult to accomplish, when one lives as I had.

My flight over water to get there was of a different sort.

It began, as I said, in passionate desperation.

But, once I had changed, though the abstract motive to follow remained constant, it was charged only with a kind of complacence.

Which left me, as the white wind came driving from the winter's core, and struck my wings. Then I must battle as I never had, nor could I have done when human. Many times I was cast down as if by violent fists, to the midst of the lake, far from all land. Below me I could keenly sense the alien depths of black water. Not a single island broke the surface, only thin rifts of ice floated free from shores which, in the beginning, I could no longer make out on either or any side.

After a score of attempts I rose again and rejoined my war with the wind. Until thrust down again, and again. Night and day passed.

How long the fight lasted I neither knew nor cared. My strength lessened but did not fail. But I must fly low. At last I sighted the perimeter of the other land, through darkness, as the wind itself began to weaken. I alighted, ate, came ashore, and by then the wind was dead.

Yet maybe I had need, in the shrine, of my cobbled-together

mortal comforts—shelter, garment, lamplight—in no physical way at all. But only for their normalcy.

❖ ❖ ❖

I was there a long while.

My life was uneventful, apart from its one iridescent and enormous sorcerous ingredient.

As does the least of humanity, I lived, just as I had previously. Sometimes humanly I even caught and killed fish from the water, and cooked them on a makeshift hearth I constructed in the shrine. Sometimes I went up into the forest of larch and birch, and found branches and cones for the fire. As I always had.

I did not try to brew beer. I had here no means to do it. Perhaps I thought, when spring returned, I would gather wild salad among the trees, and later in the year berries and sloes . . .

People I *never* much thought of. Never needed.

People, to one such as I, were unreal, irrelevant, important only in their threats and unkindnesses. Another race, presumably greater and more valued than my own, whatever race mine was or had been. The Enchanter was not human, however, to me. I thought of *him.* I thought of him so much and with such desire, both of my heart and my sex, but also of such emotions as I possessed, that for me he grew almost present, nearly tangible, there in that box of jagged stones.

I believed always still I should find him, yet did not any more seek him. Sometimes I dreamed of him, too. He was at his most actual then, there with me, mine.

But when I was a swan, then I was one of the winged race, the race of flying spirits. And even if Hrothgar, as an owl, was also, too, of this divine people, I did not think of him save as some detached, ascendant being, omnipresent, omnipotent, therefore forgettable.

❖ ❖ ❖

Spring did come back. It has seemed to me it always does. Though one day I may be proven wrong.

It flooded among the trees. The darker were overtaken by the greener. Flowers opened on forest floors. The reeds sliced from their mummification, they tore wide their dead encasing, each with a green lance.

When a swan, I grazed on the tough bright grasses that now filled the meadows inland.

I saw no other of my avian kind. But one afternoon near sunset, I heard the crying of swans away along the shore. I had never heard this in my life, either life. Indeed, before I received my enchantment, I had seen a swan only once, and that far out along the lake.

What did hearing this crying wake in me? Not so much, though I knew it instantly, and was for a moment alerted, intrigued—partly *drawn*. As the noise of humanity would conversely have made me, human or swan, seek cover.

There dawned a day of liquid light when I paddled steadily over the lake, feeding in the shallows, but venturing out a little to deeper water after the friskier fish. I travelled quite some distance from the shrine and up the shore-line then, further than I had ever gone in the winter. So I came to a spot where willows, translucent yellow, trailed to the lake. Beyond a thick bank of reeds, glancing sidelong from the tiny snails I feasted on, I saw the nest.

As with their calling I had, I knew the nest at once. A swan's making.

None were there. And what I should have done, had I come on my other kind in that instant, I can never know.

But I slipped in nearer, dividing the reeds, food forgotten.

It had all the vacancy, the nest, of neglect, of abandonment. Why, having built it, had they gone away?

Then I was near enough that, dipping my long neck, I beheld the empty vessel was also filled. Six objects lay within it. In my human mode I might have taken them for smooth stones, even strange large sullied gems of some sort.

But I was a swan. I lifted myself up into the nest, and stood there, gazing on what remained. Two of the egglings were dead, their faint pulse of sentience ebbed away. Four, lying close together as if for company and consolation, retained their inaudible beating of thin life.

The nest was spiky with snapped reeds and twigs, on some of which unborn buds had expired, ciphers for the other unborn deaths that came after.

A swan, I did not ponder. And I cannot, even in this, present my feelings. I was only sureness and decision.

I placed myself gently, thoroughly, my lower body set down and enfolding, and warming, the egglings. How cool and *alive* they felt to me now. Gradually, as I sat there, I was conscious their pulses modulated, grew attuned to mine. Now all five of us sang together. It was *like* a song, like music. There *is* music. In the voices of birds and animals, of rain and the flicker of leaves, in laughter. Or, in the Enchanter's laughter there had been, that single earlier time.

The day went over, a golden wing, a scarlet one, a silver one, one black—as night.

They and I kept rhythm together. Waking and sleeping.

At some time during the dark, turning a little, carefully, I tipped the two dead eggs from the nest. They fell into the water and sank, leaden with their necrosis. Heartless, I. Indifferent, rather. I was a swan.

❖ ❖ ❖

Yet—did I conserve and choose to nurture these beings from some mindless *human* urge? Had his possession of me made me aware that I might have borne a child—children? Was it, for me, in some

276

deepest recess of my brain—far deeper than any dungeon deeps of the lake—that these creatures would stand for our non-existent progeny, a proof that he had taken me and I him? To me, at this later time, it seems it may be so. But I can never swear to it.

❖ ❖ ❖

I did not leave them, save for a moment now and then, to dipper up for myself swift food from the lake margins. There was by then an abundance, and as the spring went on and the warmth began, insects swarmed flying even in among the reeds where I sat. I was able to feed myself with ease, snapping glittering jaws-full of them from the air. In the nights moths visited me to die, meat and nectar. I dined on them, while nightingales whirred from their throats of loose pearls.

My swanlets hatched one by one.

The first of the two males came out like a warrior, cracking the shell, barely assisted by me. Then the two females, more insistent and busy, more *thorough.* The second male tapped and tapped like a minuscule hammer on his cell-wall, till in the end I freed him with a light skimming blow of my beak.

They were speckled and grey as cobwebs, bemused and foolish. They tumbled about. I brought them plants to eat and bullied them into the water, which they were afraid of—until in, when they fell into a deep love with it. They worshipped the lake, staring down at their reflections, which evidently the water had created for them, to make them know themselves and become happy.

I sipped small flies from the air.

My children followed me along the line of the shore.

❖ ❖ ❖

Summer bloomed.

I had not been human by then for more than three months.

Did I recall my humanness? Or him?

I recalled . . . something. Something. What? I do not know.

But *they* were bigger now, long-necked already, their dusty, spotted sheaths under-patched by the promise of pure white.

How I loved them, but it was love by another name and nature.

The first male was certain and strong. The two females were by turns serious or playful. The last of them, the second male, younger than the others by half a day, was placid, and more slow. If he had been a mortal son, I now believe, I would have thought him due to enter some temple of a mild god, for he was quiet, and clove to me more than did the rest.

I taught them by example, as a parent always does. They learned and began to fend very much, and ably, for themselves.

I remember an evening, when I was solitary, and feeding in the long crimson of the afterglow, and stars burned through the sky. I saw my children meandering some way off, a chain of starry whiteness. They were suddenly fledged, all but the finest last residue of their feathery down. They were nearly grown, no longer mine. I never minded that. But in those moments the last one came back to me over the evening water, calling very softly. He swam about me, butted me in the side. He was now almost my own size, and must grow to be a fraction bigger. He rubbed his long head under mine. The velvety, scratchy perfection of the touch remains curiously with me as a human woman. It was a caress, I think, I know, although at the time I did not notice it as such; then it was only a greeting, an avowal. He would, I do suppose, have become my lover, since I had no mate. They pair for life, so I have been told, swans. Then the moon rose, also swan-white. A swarm of spangled dragonflies cascaded by. We raised our beaks, he and I, and supped, while the final fire smoked out in the lake.

❖ ❖ ❖

And now a man, this other *he*, enters my world. This one is very different from Hrothgar—who anyway I cannot state was mortal.

His name is Signian, which at first I could not pronounce. But then, during that renewal of my human life, I found great awkwardness with speech for a while, and even with the simple acts of walking, and standing, becoming seated, or lying down. I had been only a swan by that hour for almost five months.

❖ ❖ ❖

They approached the shore with a stealthy and studied tenseness. They were very loud, thundering through the trees and shrubs, storms of leafage and small branches bursting about them, and flies swirling up, and little birds in a clatter of frenzied wings.

Then they stood along the border of the water, all facing out towards the wideness of the lake.

Human–they were human things. I did not recollect what they were, yet I shied from them, and so my children, too, flinched back. Unrecognizable but steeped in some awfulness: they stank, they were too colourful in their green and brown clothes meant to conceal them, and raucous in their cunning stealth.

What I did now my children would copy. I stood upright and raced along the lake, flaring my wings, propelling myself skyward in a collision of breaking water and undone light.

Then they did as I had, my two sons, my two daughters.

White as secret truth, we seared from lake to sky, our fire of wings spread like sails, our necks stretched. As we rose and fled we were already forgetting the vile things on the shore.

It was a summer noon. So sheer and shining, faintly tinted with red. The season was ending, the time of falling leaves drew near.

I heard then the music of humanity. Like sick harps. A twisting strummed note, over and over. A twang.

In the air all about me, more little birds. How sharp and narrow they were. So slender, their beaks made of flint, and feathered only at the tail–*wingless*–

He made no sound. My son. My lover who was to be.

The arrow from the man's intelligent bow had pierced his sun-white throat.

He fell.

I saw him fall. White leaf out of season.

Ah, then I was a swan no longer even in middair, or my mind no longer was a swan, nor my heart.

I veered about.

Past me, reckless and unreckoning, my other three air-borne children rushed, rising on into the light, leaving us behind, celestially gone.

But *he* sank downward, fast as a stone.

There. I saw him meet the land, directly where the human things stood. I saw him smash, shattered, and untrue. A lie. His feathers scattered, like fresh snow.

No. I was not a swan any more. Though still I kept the shape of one. For I, too, dropped towards the men, oblivious of their twanging kill-harps.

There is this, of course, had I been a woman exactly then, never would I have dared—surely I should have run away. Nevertheless as my feet hit and scalded and broke the reeds and water, already my physical alteration was erupting from me. A swan, I had reached the shore. Next instant I was a woman, naked and white, her hair flying, her arms raised even then like wings, her neck arched, racing towards the hunters and their bows, murderously hissing her rage and grief—

And they darted away. Some of them were shouting, one screaming. They ran, for they had seen a demon, a bird translated abruptly into woman's form.

Only one man stayed. Rooted to the spot either with terror or surprise, I will never know, nor will I ever care.

For when I reached him, and brought forward my beating wings to shatter in turn his bones, my neck and beak to tear him into bits, a weighty darkness came from him, and covered me up. Was this, too, sorcery? No, only his long cloak, that he had swept off and over me.

Could it be that, even at such a moment, he found my public nudity unsuitable? The gods he and his revered were strict and disapproving. Perhaps that then, but mostly I believe now he was afraid, and meant to distract and net me, like the flying thing I had been only a breath before. He credited, too, all that he had seen. Swan to woman. Where his huntsmen would come to say they had been mistaken, or seen nothing odd, this one would always grasp the fact of my transformation. He liked such ideas. In childhood, he had been told stories of them.

When the cloak smothered me I was lost. I rolled on the earth in its folds–it stank of his kind–retching and shrieking, trying to rip myself free with teeth and nails, all that was left to me as armament.

At last my consciousness went out.

They came and picked me up, for he had called his followers back by then. They picked up the body of my dead son also. But I was spared seeing this, spared knowing quite then that he was taken next to the kitchen of the great royal house, slung down, stripped of his plumage, and cooked for their table. It was surely these beasts, too, who had slain the birth-parents of my other children. Being of the high human class, it was allowed them even by the gods, particularly those pale, prim gods they kneeled to, that they shoot with arrows, pluck, roast and devour swans.

For a while I lay like the dead, in a little building devoted to the female god of their pantheon. I was tended there by the veiled faceless women who served this deity.

No doubt they expected violence of me when I revived, for I had been bound to the hard couch. But I was no longer passionate or volatile. I had been returned into my former self, cautious and nervous, cringing and placatory. Though I had some trouble in speaking the human tongue for a while, I quickly came to understand it again. This, despite the differing accent and mannerisms of the priestesses, and presently the other humans who appeared. I did therefore exactly as I was bid.

Each of the priestess-women recalled to me my mother. They

were ignorant, sly and spiteful, authoritarian—and cringing, too, as I was once more. And they would regularly beat themselves for penances. Sooner almost than all else, once I had woken, been bathed and clad, they took me to gaze on their goddess. She was an upright, slender, shapeless stone, stood on an altar, and veiled over as they were, but for a fine golden crown set where her head must be. The women were the ones who boastfully educated me in the rich substance of gold. The Prince's mother, they said, had donated the crown to their goddess-house.

As I was so obedient and docile, and even acted out praying, once they advised it was best I should pray, they seemed better pleased with me. They asked my name, and when I managed to tell them it, that is the name Hrothgar gave me, the only one I could now recall, they were both pleased *and* sullen. Apparently they thought the name meant I was, notwithstanding other evidence, of high birth, perhaps even royal myself, though foreign. This was Hrothgar's joke, of course. To give me such a name. Or had he foreseen I should require it later? Again, I do not know, nor shall I, now. I think it does not count.

The leaves were dropping in the woods, and on the yard where I was put out to sit on sunny days, and sew long shapeless garments of the order.

Here, too, he visited me after some nineteen days.

Signian. I had been told his name as well by then. *Prince* Signian. Son of a dead lord and the lord's still-living wife, the Princess Orjana.

When he came into the yard, the priestesses fluttered.

He was thought very handsome. So it was continually announced.

He had long yellow hair, wide shoulders and a strong stocky frame. His eyes were narrow and light-coloured in his broad, sun-browned face.

Perhaps he was handsome. To me he was ugly. He reeked of his sweat and eating, of kennels and closed rooms. Of murder. It had been his shot that pierced my son and smashed him on the earth. And he had eaten of him, too.

Now he sat and looked at me, deep in my black eyes, black enough to resist him, as the lake mirrors, but conceals what lies beneath its surface.

The priestesses had heard the tale of my shape-shift. I could discern, despite their faultless belief in their goddess, they did not believe *this*. The young men had been hunting, when they drank deeply. The shadows had deceived them then, some trick of mid-day summer light. The priestesses would not quite say this, but they knew it to be so. And they only liked him more, their darling Prince, for his little fallibility. That he had faith in magic meant, too, he kept his faith in the miracles of the gods. Which could only be virtuous and benign in so noble a master.

He asked me if they were kind to me in the goddess-house.

Naturally I said they were.

He asked me if I yet remembered where I had come from, anything of my past—for already the women had asked that, and I had said I had no memory at all before I woke here. To him I gave the same falsehood over.

Then he put his hand out, and stroked and fingered my hair, that my first lover had compared to the moon.

After this Prince Signian left me.

But the next day I was taken, under guard, to another house, one which belonged to him and was very different.

❖ ❖ ❖

As the winter came back, I was growing used to the new phase of my life.

I hated it, it goes without saying. I was in despair.

This may seem very peculiar. I had never had much, and lacked all comforts save the most basic, and those wrested by me from a harsh environment. But I would gladly have taken my old life on, more than gladly if I might have gone back into its last stages, when I had been a bird, and had my children. Had my son, my lover.

Now, in the grand lodge just inside the wall of the Prince's town, I was given every material thing that might be wanted or wished. Fires burned hot for me, lit and maintained by servants. I had a wooden bed with linen pillows, and pelts of bears and wolves. I had a blue gown, and later another the red of blood. I could wash and bathe myself in warm scented water whenever I chose. There was food, meat and white bread, and wine to drink. After the first thirty days, he gave me a little silver ring to wear on my thumb. He said I should study it, and think how the silver circlet of my quim ringed round his manhood. To begin, I only wore it when he came to see me. Then he grew petulant, and after this I wore it always.

I was a prisoner. I do not exaggerate. I would not take on my other form, for I could not fly the house. And why was this? Something so paltry. I was never let out, always in some kind guarded, indeed watched, women to walk behind me, men to undo doors. Only into a tiny garden might I go, and that always accompanied, among the clipped bushes soon salted with snow. To get beyond the outer doors was not allowed. He had told me straightly. I was too precious, he said, too necessary to him to be risked. I had no memory, was frail. In the spring perhaps, he said. Then he might take me up into the town to see its stupendous sights of lofty buildings and gloomy byways. Even there I should, I knew, be trapped.

Yet, as a swan, I could escape instantly—Ah no. The answer to the riddle has a terrible simplicity. A swan must run and launch itself into the air, its body large and wings so big. Unlike the smaller birds it cannot spring straight up, even from the ledges of the wider windows. Even in the little garden, where there was no space to run at all. I had no *room* anywhere to begin my flight. It had been the same in the goddess-house.

I dreamed of flight, that was the sum of it. In dreams the roof blew off and the inside walls collapsed. Then I evaded my jailors, dashed through the levelled chambers without impediment, leaped and spread my wings—and was gone.

He had a story he told me, that I had been under a spell, locked into the form of a bird by an evil Enchanter. But his love—that is, Signian's love for me—had broken the sorcery.

❖ ❖ ❖

I do not say he loved me.

I know he lusted for me, or rather perhaps for what he had seen I was. He often remarked on the whiteness of my skin, my uncanny hair.

He did not take me until I had been examined intimately by an old woman, brought in by one of the priestesses. I loathed but was not unprepared for her disgusting investigations. I had had my mother to put up with in the past, after all.

But I knew the examiner would soon find I was not a virgin, and would this put off the Prince? For of course I knew also *why* I was being examined.

No one, however, said anything to me of my state, until Signian appeared that evening.

He gravely gazed at me then, as we sat before the great dinner that had been laid for him and, I suppose, for me—I barely touched it—amid the blazing forest of candles.

"I've been informed, Otila, of your misfortune. I shall not be the first with you."

Should I seem startled, shocked? Contrite? What use? I had, anyway, no heart for the game.

I said, "That is true."

"*Sir,*" he said softly, kindly. "You must always call me that."

"Very well."

He sighed and ate more of the greasy meat, chewing and frowning with thought. At least the dish was not of roasted swan.

"Otila, I recall your memory has failed you, yet do you have any notion how this came about, that you lost your maiden-head?"

Modestly I kept my eyes on the table's red shawl, trimmed with beads. "Sir, it is my one dim memory."

"You were forced?" he asked, hopefully it seemed—but whether from stricture or prurience who could say?

"I was wedded."

Where this lie had found its origin I stay unsure. It entered my brain, slipped out upon my tongue.

"Wedded?" He had laid down the joint. He must be enraged or perturbed, which was it? I had already seen he had only a lim-ited number of expressions, and one might often have to serve the purpose of two or three moods.

"Yes. My father gave me to a man. The gods witnessed our union. We were together a little while—I forget how long . . . and then—then, too, I forget."

"*Sir*," he instructed, absently now. He thought once more. He said, "Your husband—was it *he*, do you think, who aborted you from being one of the gods' creatures to a spiritless bird?"

"I can't say, sir."

"Yet you were wedded. And you recall no other detail—even his looks—his name?"

I shook my head.

He banged the table with his fist. On their bronze spikes, shaped like the branches of thin trees, the candles trembled warn-ingly.

I said, "Sometimes—I seem to think—he was tall, and dark-haired . . ."

What else, of course, could I summon. The Prince resettled himself.

"I must speak to the priests. Your previous union must be properly dissolved. It's unlawful I bed another man's wife. Unless I have killed him in battle."

Maybe I had trusted I could evade his carnality if I made out

I was that, a wife. Really I think I had known he could convince himself, always, of some acceptable path whereby he could gratify his needs.

In any case, after he had eaten he drew me to the bed in the corner, pulled my dress both down and up, wadded my flesh and bit at my breast, before cramming his piece inside me. He was a fair size, and would have hurt me if I had not been undone. He demanded little of me but compliance, though now and then instructed, as he had instructed me to call him *Sir,* to tickle or pinch him here or there. His wants were minimal. Yet he rode some while, a slow and lumbering journey during which he grunted, and at the climax of which he gave a tiny squeal.

He had me only twice, and was quicker the second time, if less vocal.

My distaste was really beyond words, even thought.

I can compare it only to the unpleasantness of certain bodily reactions, a short flux of the bowels, or vomiting. It was vile, but unimportant. Meaningless in the scheme of my severed life.

After that congress a servant brought me, the following day, the silver mirror, wrapped in silk.

This in some ways was almost worse than his utilizing me. To gape for the first at my own clear image, and know her for a stranger—more a rape even than Signian's. *He* had not touched, I thought, my soul.

Oh, I was a swan, a swan. I had looked at my reflection then and known it for my own. A swan.

Beyond the lodge, the town climbed ungainly up the hill to a terraced palace. From the highest window of my prison I could see this grandiose and insignificant dwelling, his home, where he lived with his mother, the Princess. The palace was constructed of hefty stones, and banners tipped with metal flailed about its roofs. The town itself was morose and dirty. The sort of pigs that wandered the village streets, ambled here also, through filthy alleys and along the wider lanes—that were less than the width of the lodge's main chamber, and frequently blocked by refuse.

Outside the walls of this extended jail of a town, the forest had been cut away, for reasons of defence.

Further down the trees began again, around a broader road, up which wagons and carts, and even boats mounted on wheels, sometimes toiled, and men and women trudged.

Last of all, about a mile off, I might see the lake.

Long hours I spent at the window, staring out. My mind spread its wings and spurred me from this alien body I did not recognize, and fanned away, away.

I never thought of the Enchanter Hrothgar, at the window when I watched the lake. Never once, I am prepared to vow before any god, even the unkind measly gods of Signian's town.

Only in my room, when Signian was gone, after I had washed his slime and reek away from me, only then did I think of Hrothgar. And I cursed him. I wished him in agony and dead, or in some molten pale hell, to which the worst of the wicked are consigned.

But I dreamed of him most awfully after Signian's visits. As if that thrusting bulb of meat had stirred me up to lasciviousness in turn for my other, occult lover.

I never dreamed of my dead son. Never fantasized as to what *our* love-making might have been, the rasp of feathers, flare of wings, a land-flight. As a woman, I could not picture—let alone experience—what that could be, only that it must and would have happened, and that then, from him, my lover the swan, my own true progeny would have been born, laid like ghostly opals in our nest, brought by us to life.

Spirits of the air.

❖   ❖   ❖

The winter scraped and sharpened its scythes on the four winds and mowed down the year. In the town, the palace, even in my prison, we must celebrate, now the longest month of the cold season was done.

Seven little house statues had been brought out of Signian's people's gods, six of them shapelessly male, and one a version of the shapeless veiled goddess I had been shown in the goddess-house.

They were lined up on the great hearth-lintel, given crowns of gilded straw, and candles lit to them and ribbons hung over them—as if for infants who must be kept amused. Boughs of evergreen, lugged in from the despised wood, were raised along the beams, with painted wooden bees on strings, to ensure plenty.

I was sent the red gown. And when Signian arrived, he delivered to me, in person, in a long box of carved wood, the necklace of polished emeralds.

He often harangued me now with a history of his ancestors, all of which I forgot instantly. He spoke of travels, too, not his own, I believe, and so had taught me something of items and materials, jewels and sea-tides, for these things lingered in my mind—they were not human, therefore perhaps retainable. Now, he told me this:

"These emeralds are a minor treasure of my house. My father gave this necklet to his mistress once. But she died, in childbed—only a daughter. My mother, the Princess, thinks it seemly now I award it to you, even though you've borne me no children yet, and the old wisewoman—" he meant the old woman, who now examined me always once a month—"says you are still not in that condition."

What could I say to this curious speech? I thanked him, of course. Ill-omened jewels, formerly dragged from the coffer of one dead. And he wished me fecund? I knew in the heart of my womb that it was my shape-shift that would deny always any human child, wanted or not. Just as I had come to be sure I could bear the children of swans. After he had laid me and finished, and gone away, I considered Signian's second speech to me that night. I was to be presented to the Princess Orjana. She had said she must judge me fit for my apparently enduring role as her son's plaything. So I was to go up to the palace. To the stone heap on the hill.

4

Complex preparation preceded my entry to the palace. I was soaked in a bath of honey and curd, laved in scent. I fasted for a day, drank only water. My hair was washed and dressed in six long plaits. I was told I must call the Princess *Royalness*. They clothed me in the red garment. I was not permitted to walk, as I had not been permitted when brought to the lodge. I travelled in another closed cage, this on wheels, drawn by two small horses thick with hair, in the manes of which bits of gold were wound, just as bits of bronze and silver had been wound in my plaits.

"I have been hearing tales of you," she said, the moment she was seated, and the others had withdrawn to the ends of the long, chill room. One there played a stringed instrument, perhaps further to obscure our words. The Princess motioned I might sit on a stool. I did so. "My son supposes you were enchanted under some spell, which his care of you has broken. Can this be true?"

"I don't know, Royalness."

"No. They say, too, you recall nothing of your past—only

some hint you were wedded, or think you were. Or is that merely a little fib, to hide an immorality?"

I said nothing. I gazed only at her hands, which lay together in her lap like two discarded yellowish gloves. They had mentioned to look too often in her eyes would be an impertinence.

She also was an old woman, but old in a manner I had never, until now, ever seen. Hers was a *preserved* age. Her parchment skin and skull-like face had been rubbed with unguents and lightened with powder. The thin wither of her lips was touched with soft rose. Her hair, grey where mine was white, had been burnished to a shine and intricately dressed, and she wore a little circlet of gold in it, reminding me of their ghastly faceless goddess.

"Well," she said, "my son is fond of you, and you please him. For now, therefore, it seems best you live here with us, in the high house. One day Signian must marry. He will choose two wives. Then it will be necessary for you to go away, perhaps even from the town. But don't be downcast. Though your heart will break, you will be respected among our people for your service, and will receive, in addition, a small amount of money, to keep you till your death. Any offspring you may produce will likewise be maintained. He may gain a good position either in the Prince's guard, or the god-houses, wherever it is judged most suitable. A daughter can gain, if diligent and couth, a station among the lower ladies here, a nurse to the children or somesuch. You see. We are fair enough." Still I said nothing. What must I say? Something, apparently: "I trust you're grateful," she suggested, "for my care of you?"

"Thank you, Royalness."

She refolded her thin, flaccid hands.

"Meanwhile, I should like you to tell me how you think it is my son, usually so sturdy in his commonsense, credits he witnessed your change from a white swan into a woman?"

Jolted, I stared after all into her deadly face. Her eyes were narrow and pale like his. But—unlike his—full of a dire, nearly sub-human intelligence.

"Royalness—how can I know? I remember nothing of it—"

"Yet you remember a wedding to another man. The priests here will dismiss any possible prior union this very evening. Do you accept such a thing?"

"Yes, Royalness."

"Of course. My son must be preferable. You are not quite an imbecile, I think. But now I shall tell *you* something of my own." She leaned forward slightly. Was she so eager? I felt I would recoil, but knew I must instead keep motionless, and now was expected to meet her eyes. "My son was told, when a child, stories by his nurse, legends and ancient tales. In you he believes he's glimpsed something special. But naturally you are nothing of the kind, only a young woman with strange colouring, and a mysterious, shall I say, past. Be thankful, Otila, if such is your name, at our sophistication. But let me warn you, too. *I* have heard such myths of transference and shape-shift, when a girl. I do remember one particular old yarn . . . a maid that a prince fancied, who crept every night out of his bed to a burial-mound, and plucked the plants there, and wove them into a dress that, if putting it on, made her become a wild swan. But they discovered her and knew her for a witch, and burned her to death, so not the slightest morsel of her, flesh, hair, nor bone, remained. Do not, Otila, however flighty or forgetful your mind, lead me to imagine *you* are a witch."

I sat, caught in the trancing, lizard-like glare of her eyes.

It transpired I need say nothing now.

"One further matter," the Princess Orjana added, sitting back. "You will have your hair darkened. And your skin, a little. You are too unusual. Oh, he prefers you pale, but my son always heeds my advice. Certainly *you* will do so."

She sent two of her women. They stained my hair with a stenchful paste that stung my head, and turned my tresses, as the women called them, black.

It was powder I must use on my skin.

They powdered my face and neck, my hands, to show me how I must go on. Now I had a tawny skin.

My mouth they tinted with a red salve, not rose but carmine.

When he came later, and pushed me over on the bed, he decided aloud that I stayed pale below, both flesh and hair. He seemed to like this discrepancy. He took me twice, as only the first time had he, and made louder noises. He told me after I would not mind this changing a little, to delight him and to avoid undue comment in the palace. He said I must own, his mother was wise. An outstanding woman. He hoped one day he might find a wife to help him who was half so clever, but he doubted it. And then he commented that he liked me very well for being only simple, a creature of the senses. But then, I was really a swan, was I not? Only he, like a god—*that* he did not quite say—had converted me back into a human thing.

There, in the lodge, I had neither physical space nor mental space to race and spring and shape-shift and be free. I could not even cry out and be left in peace. Someone slept by my door, some arid woman. Servant, jailor—

But the next day following the interview with the Princess, I was carted off again to the palace, and put into a pair of chambers inside the round flank of a tower.

It was a fortress, the palace. It was thought I needed, here, fewer guardians. The palace women who were meant to serve or contain me, besides, were always slipping away about their own business. The single guard in the place beyond the outer door liked to drink deep. He often slept. Yet he had the knack, too, of fully waking always at those times when the Prince arrived.

Outside the window of the room in which my bed was set, I could see only sky and a long area where a roof extended. It was long enough, perhaps, if I could only step out on it, I might race and transform and fly. The window, however, was a little too thin for me to pass through it, either as woman or bird.

I began to starve myself.

When one of my supposed attendants remarked that I left my food untouched, and out of date the old woman examiner came to poke my openings for signs of pregnancy, I next burnt each of my meals on the fire when I was briefly alone, leaving my plate empty enough, as if I had eaten my fill.

But also, alone, I did what I had done before. I tore off pieces of my hair—now black, but with roots like ice, and flung them, too, on the flames. I used the blunt table knife to release drops of my blood. I called to *him,* to the other *he*–to Hrothgar, the Enchanter.

I lay on my back and stroked my inmost part, but found now it was like a fine instrument dulled. It could yet be musical, but no longer fully answer.

Even so.

I had summoned him back to me before.

I, even *I,* who counted for nothing, I had brought him into view like my shadow.

He would not know me, I thought, if he beheld me now, black-haired and swarthy, in my blood-red dress that the silver mirror showed much darker.

I do not know why I had not properly called to him before. Perhaps only I had been sure he would never hear me, or if he did he would refuse me. As if I had not, till now, suffered enough to give my outcry credentials. As if my soul must shrivel and my heart bleed, before any might notice my plight.

Each day, alone, I tried to squeeze out through the narrow window. It was almost possible, that was the worst of it. If it had been less so, doubtless I would not have tried so desperately, so repeatedly.

But I had always been slight, and starving only made me weak, very little thinner.

One night I dreamed the walls melted away from the

window-space and enlarged it. I dreamed an owl flew over the sky beyond, which was slate-blue with dusk of dawn.

Waking with actual dawn, I smelled the spring, sheer on the dark stone breath of the palace.

That morning I was restless. Signian had gone off again to hunt, as he did, and might be away several days and nights between. I went out of my rooms and walked about the byways of the palace, those that were allowed to me, the two women padding after me like sulky wolves who did not want the prey they tracked.

People whispered as they passed me in the alley enclosures of passageways. They had always done this, but now their mutterings were pronounced more clearly—I was meant to hear, it seemed. I was the Prince's whore. A foreign woman. I had been a wife, but the priests of the seven pallid gods had absolved me of that, so I could lie with their matchless Prince in lesser sin. What more could I crave than such happiness? Though some of them reckoned I would be damned despite the priests' efforts, punished after death. Signian, of course, was blameless. I had seduced him. Some said I was a sorceress . . .

When the dark filled my window that evening, I heard an owl hooting far off in the forest, more than a mile away.

I visualized *his* eyes, looking at me, black then red-gold, through my fire.

By now I thought I barely remembered his face. Yet it at last occurred to me my falsehood of a wedding, to a dark-haired man, perhaps paraphrased his sexual acts with me and mine with him, which were as unlike the procedures of the Prince as *I* now was to my former self. I pictured Hrothgar's advent here, disguised as an old, hump-backed man, and how I would tell Signian that see— here was my husband—I recollected him now I looked at him—an evil sorcerer—Oh kill him, Sir, destroy him! Save me from his clutches.

In my sickly fasting sleep, unheralded deep pleasure erupted inside my body. I woke dazed, and tried again to force myself through the narrow window. But could not, and now was certain that for every wisp of flesh my fast had shaved from me, a further chunk of stone had added itself to the embrasure. My sulky wolf-women found me lying there. I was ill for many days, during which the foul old woman examined my blood on the linen sheet. She told me I had miscarried the Prince's seed and was a worthless dunce, but she would not tell him if I would give her a present. So then I got up, staggering and mad, and, picking up the silver mirror, I flung it at her head. It knocked her over, shrieking, and the wolves ran in and I laughed as they and the guard carried the hag out. I kept saying she must have the mirror, it was silver, and I wanted her to have it as a gift for her kindness to me. I did not know if she had lied, thought she had. I do not know either if she recovered from my present. None spoke of it. She never came in to me again.

After the event anyway all is blind, dumb, deaf, and nothing once more, for a while.

❖ ❖ ❖

Hrothgar the Enchanter appeared at the palace in the shortest spring month of eighteen days.

❖ ❖ ❖

There was a noise I heard, ringing round and round the shell of the house.

From my clamped rooms I could see nothing, only roof and sky.

In the corridors outside there seemed to be unusual activity, and then this lessened. One of the wolves went to ask the sentry, at the outer door of the apartment, if he knew what went on. When he did not, sat there with his pot of wine, she and the other stole off and left me.

I had no interest in the sounds in that house.

But then, I had not seen the company come up the road from the shore. Some lord rode foremost on a jet-black war horse, and behind him twenty grim-faced men, some mounted and some pacing in step. All of these wore dark plates of mail and carried honed weapons, but the lord himself wore heavy silk, and a cloak of the white and black furs of mustelids. A sword was at his side even so, sheathed in velvet, leather and gold.

His hair was black and chased, as his sword was, with fine strands of aging silver.

Signian had come back from his hunt by then. He waited in the larger hall to meet with this unlooked-for caller.

Who entered, and stood, lean and silent and tall, of a daunting authority almost appalling in its unspoken, latent power. He must be some mighty lord indeed, this man, or war-leader, doubtless with hordes to follow him. Where then were the rest of them? What did he want of the peaceful and pious town?

"You have a woman here," the stranger said, in a flat and unimpassioned voice. "She has white hair and dark eyes."

Signian seemed at a loss. The filled hall fidgeted and murmured.

The stranger said, ungiving as the bone mask of the moon, "She is my wife."

I was told these things. They were described to me in some detail, when Signian slammed unannounced into my cell. It was shortly evident he blamed me. I had put on him some *allure*—so he called it, not daring quite to say I had enspelled him, for strong men had now come to claim me, and besides this Prince was not so puny a woman could ever work full magic on him.

He ranted about the war-leader, and his black horse, and his dire guard, who waited there, beak-nosed, their eyes smeary glitterings behind the curious vizors of their helms. Feathers were fixed thickly on their helms and cloaks, he told me, all black.

They had, these men, a distasteful odour, perhaps of ancient un-wiped blood—

From what Signian recited, I thought that it *was* no other than Hrothgar. Who else would come here for me? Yet I did not entirely believe it. I felt neither relief nor hope.

When the Prince shouted I must remove the red and put on the other, insignificant gown, the bluish one, and that I must also take off the silver ring he had given me, since it might offend my husband, I did what he said at once. His eyes on my body, briefly bare between the garments, held no arousal.

His desire was only to have me gone.

"I have sworn to him, this man, I have kept you here for your own protection, and treated you always with respect."

I did not reply.

Signian added, abruptly almost as if he fawned on me, "See then, my girl, you won't want him to hear, will you, how you loved me so. Best say nothing of our meetings. I've held my tongue, to protect you. And he seems to accept you are still his wife, in deed as in name."

I did not ask of Signian what state—spiritual—legal—I was *truly* in, since his priests had rinsed the former marriage off me before their disapproving gods.

Nor did Signian inquire if I was glad my unremembered spouse had come to get me back, nor either if I thought I might after all *recognize* my spouse. He did instruct me that the Princess, his mother, advised that I should greet the man joyously, as was proper.

With my recent illness, I had lost the savage and bitter fantasy of turning Signian against Hrothgar from spite. In fact, inevitably, given these circumstances, it would have proved both unwork-able and immaterial.

I felt, as I say, no hope. Yet deep within myself did happiness begin to force up from the soil of my misery? Must I then disguise it? Or was I afraid? Should I disguise *that*?

I did not know. All was greyness in me.

As my wolf-women, the pair of them shivering in apprehension of the Prince's wrath and the threat of the invader in the palace, conducted me to the hall, I could think only of my dead son, the swan, my white darling with his long, strong, slender throat that the arrow pierced, his feathers broken on the shore. And I wept, how quietly.

Signian noted this.

He said, uneasy and approving together, "Yes, tears of delight at seeing him. But be careful he doesn't think they come from any shame—any abuse I meted out to you."

❖ ❖ ❖

The moment I entered the high and echoing hall, with all the Prince's arrogant people huddling at its bannered walls, and Hrothgar, of course Hrothgar, standing at the centre of the wide stone floor, his minions—they were not human and barely looked it—poised at his back in their black feathers and mail, my tears dried and left my eyes like pits of fire. He spoke to me only a handful, not even that, of words. "Come here to me," he said. And so I crossed the floor and went to him. It was so ordinary, I might once again have dreamed it all, but it was real.

Then Hrothgar turned to the Prince, and his mother, Orjana. Signian stood like a pole. She sat upright on her gilt chair, not a hair uncombed, only her limp hands now gripping, like claws, the chair-arms. She was quite terrified, I saw. More deathly grey than the places within me.

"You have been generous to my lady," said Hrothgar. "I would wish to reward you. I'll send something to you, befitting your acts. Please receive these gifts, though you deserve far more, as the payment of my debt."

Although he looked unlike himself, and yet exactly as I had known him, in the way such things are known, I recalled instantly on seeing his face, his body. His hair even lined with the silver of faked age, and his face with a fakery of lines, yet . . . I never knew him either. I had never known him. In another past we had met, not he and I—another than he, another than I. He was a stranger also to me. But we went together from the hall, unhindered, his men-who-were-not treading behind us. Outside one lifted me on to Hrothgar's black horse. It was accurate to say the creature—both guard and horse—had a feral smell—the smell of a large bird that lives on carrion. We rode away from the terraced palace, down the hill, out of the town walls, back into the forests below, towards the edges of the lake.

5

Certain was it he would never, now, possess me.

He did not.

Nor did he speak to me, had not even when I rode with him on the horse. After those first words, *Come here to me,* his silence.

By the shore he dismounted, and one of the non-men again assisted me and set me on my feet.

Then Hrothgar whistled very low, and along the lake a sort of raft came drifting. By then it grew dusk. The raft was like a slice of twilight cut free. It slid in to the land, then stopped and waited there. He indicated, by a swift, not ungracious gesture, that I should step onto the raft. I did so. I thought he would leave me there. Set me too adrift. Instead he stepped lightly after me, and at once the wooden thing—or whatever type of thing it was—moved off again, and away, scudding now briskly out on the lake, into the dark.

Behind us, a great clattering of wings.

A thick, fluctuating shadow swirled over, and on into the east, letting fall as it passed countless black feathers. They had been crows, men and horses both. Nothing remained upon the shore but for the trees. And inland, unseen, the town and palace of the Prince and his mother.

Some many miles along the lake, the raft swam back in against the shore.

None had pursued him, nor would they find us now.

I was ashamed. As if I had been truly wed to him, and deliberately joined in sex with another chosen lover.

I could say nothing, and he did not speak to me.

A fire sprang up and burned with a curdled heat. Little lights, like moths, evolved on the trees. Beer smoked in a round iron pot. He dipped in a metal cup, and gave me the drink, without a touch of his skin on mine.

Should I try to explain what had happened? Why had he come to save me from that prison, if he did not know me innocent of blame?

Not once had he looked at me. He stared into the fire he had created. Later he drew a loaf of dark bread from the ashes at the fire's rim, broke off a piece and handed me it. Gods can do such things, make men from birds and birds from men, call fire out of the ground and baked bread, beer or wine or water from the air. And the gods are always cruel. We are nothing to the gods. Or perhaps they think us cruel to them, we fail them so often, have no magic of our own to enthrall them, disappoint, and finally die. Oh, we die.

❖   ❖   ❖

"Let me tell you," he said, after the full moon rose, "how I came to be a worker of spells, what your kind call an Enchanter. How the ability of shape-shift was mine."

I gazed at him.

In the naked moonlight all traces of age had vanished from him. And I knew, though the evil mirror was no longer mine, that this was not so for me. I should look the elder now.

So he told me, still not once resting his eyes on me, that he had grown up in a sprawling town, not quite unlike the dungeonous heap of Signian. At thirteen years old, he was sold as a kind of servant, to a man said to be talented in healing and the minor arts of sorcery.

But the man was a cheat. He taught Hrothgar many knacks of spurious magic and quackery, that might seem to do good, but did nothing save deceive.

Hrothgar learnt these things, having no choice. The man beat him if he was inept, or even when he was not.

"His brain had rotted," Hrothgar told me. "At last it did not concern him whether I was able or incompetent, servile or trustless. One night he beat me, on and on, using for the task a great staff he kept, normally, for his pretence of magery. It had the head of an owl."

He paused. "At length," said Hrothgar, "I lay on the floor of his house, dying, I have no doubt. And he, to rest his tired arm, went pottering and muttering about, cursing and kicking me when he had to step over my body on the ground."

Hrothgar knew at that hour also that he died.

Of course, by then he did not care, wished only quickly to be gone.

And then—he was.

"Out of myself I lifted, on great red wings."

The shape-changing had come to him in brutalization and agony, and in death also, very likely. He did not remind me that I, otherwise, had become the swan in the throes of pleasure he had gifted.

Hrothgar flew out and off his body and circled the villainous healer's dirty room. The man watched, his mouth gaped open. "His horror," said Hrothgar, with neither passion or rage, "was a vision to me. An education I had never, till then, received."

Hrothgar, as an owl, put out the old man's eyes, then eviscerated him with his claws, and left him there. Next, flying up to a window just broad enough to allow escape—for an owl's method of flight is that way easier—with one wing Hrothgar tipped a candle off its spike.

He left the house to burn, the town to burn if it would.

"I suppose my own human body would be burnt up with it. But I was dead, and this my newest life. It suited me. You'll believe, I had never enjoyed my wretched slavery as a man."

A long way off, high among great trees, he watched and saw the scarlet smoke above the town. Then he flew on.

As an owl he lived a great while. Years, he thought, though keeping no calendar, he never afterwards learned. He became a man again only when he saw a young woman that he fancied. It was not, he told me, myself. And I saw he did not say this to be harsh to me, merely to be factual.

When returned to the human form, he was full-grown and strong. Besides, he had acquired the talents of magic. He could accomplish much.

"Every useless lying conjur of my former master's—in me became reality. It seems I knew what should be done, and therefore could do all. Like the sun will know when to rise, and when to set. And perhaps it knows this from watching other suns, in the time before time, that only seemed to do it."

After they had made sexual love, the girl he had taken and brought to ecstacy, changed into a bird. She might then alter at will and as she wished, or even to amuse Hrothgar. Later, some years later, the same skill was born in a young man that Hrothgar lay with. These two were the first lovers. But he had had many lovers since then.

It seemed to him, he told me, that he did not cast any spell upon them. Did not *infect* them with his sorcery. Instead, they themselves had attracted his notice and his desire through that very unknown, yet potent ability of shape-shift, carried dormant within their bones.

So it had been, too, he said, with me.

When he told me that, I wept again. I could not help it. It was a foolish jealousy, in part. For he had never especially valued me as a woman, only noted and wished to let out my other self, the swan—which locked up inside me, must have cried out to him for rescue. Yet, too, that inner life of mine, the swan, had been the best for me of all my existence. My *true* life. My *only* life.

I thought, if I had continued among the reeds of the lake, mated with my perfect, adopted son, borne others of our breed, I might have forgotten him, Hrothgar. And maybe that was how it always was. How it had been for all those others he had *fathered* of themselves. Even ultimately for him also, the Enchanter.

But he looked over at me when I cried my tears. For the first, and steadily.

"Otila," he said. His face was neither cruel nor kind. "Yes," he said. "Weep."

My soul knew what he meant by this. My soul then wept. Tears that were like fiery liquid glass ran out of my eyes. But my ignorant mind understood nothing. Until he drew close, and held me as the best of fathers will. And told me why I cried. Told me why I should, from that minute, inside the silence of my soul, cry forever, until my useless mortal time is worn away.

"To be this other, this true self, we must steal from ourselves. We must rob ourselves of humanness, and glory in the theft. So I, so you, Otila. For our humanity is also a thief." So he said, that night.

The gods decree it is a crime for humans to kill themselves. Even in extremity they must labour to survive.

By this it seems they wish further to punish us.

Maybe they are only sorry that we become dust after life, and so strive to keep us animate.

Or else we are fire and stars after life, and they are envious, and grudge us.

I discovered, when several of my years had gone by, that he did send rewards, as he had said he would, to Signian and the Princess, his mother. These were not gold or jewels. Signian, who bathed very seldom, took a bath that next summer, and was sinisterly drowned in the metal tub. He died thrashing and calling in front of his steward and servants, who tried frantically to save him. Something weighted him beneath the water, they said, struggle as he and they would to hoist him out. Orjana died of grief, or I have heard a tale she hanged herself. But self-murder is forbidden, as the killing of swans is forbidden, to any but the royal class.

❖ ❖ ❖

"I can afford you sexual love," he said. "If you want. But you'll find only ashes in it now. We are no longer of the same tribe, you and I, Otila, my poor Otila. All that, for you, is done."

It was love, anyway, that had destroyed me.

Not any love for my Creator, Hrothgar the Enchanter. No, it was my other love. My son—my lover—

In fury and despair I had run ashore, changing as I went from swan to mortal woman, and shown myself like this to the Prince who had slain my love. I had thought it was the courage of the swan that made me do this. But it was not the swan. It was my human fury and my mortal anguish, those sins which, though they may make us brave, we are ever warned of, for they destroy us.

He had no name, my son. Nor I, as a swan.

We had no need of names.

We had had no name even for love. For love is beyond all namings as all true things must be. Such is the most real nature of magic. It is *met* with, not taught or learned. It is ourselves. But these—we lose.

Hrothgar it was told me that, despite my own view, I had

acted not as my actual self, who was a swan, but as my other, in-grained, thieving *unreal* self. A mortal thing. And by doing this, I smashed the enchantment. Gave everything away. And so the hunter captured me. And with his poisoned and filthsome and ir-relevant sexual acts, he confirmed my wreck, scorched out of me what truly, truly only I *was*—as no fire or acid could have done. Had I been struck by whitest lightning, like the birch tree whose paleness changed my hair, or by the flaming spear of some down-falling star—or by the wrath of the gods themselves—I could not have been separated from the creature of the air, the spirit I had been. Live or dead, a swan I must have stayed.

And a swan, I would have mourned my loss, my beloved. I would have mourned him. But not been stripped of my *self.*

Never now could I shape-shift any more. Never would I be-come again a swan.

All that while in the hell-house of the Prince, I had deceived myself, making out I was constricted, kept from change and flight by walls of stone. As I was. But the stone was my heart.

And there is no mourning, either, as no penance or sweet-ness, that can bring solace for the loss of self.

There is no world in which to live thereafter, either this or an-other.

There is nothing. No thing. None.

And He? Hrothgar's action of seeking me in the palace, of set-ting me free, even of punishing my two principal jailors, his former action, too, when he had killed the man who beat him—were these not the revenges and honour of a human man? I said no word of them to him, as already now I knew. For him it had been different. For he had gone *through* the lightning and the star, the wrath of gods—he had died, was dead. His body burned but he, having be-come his true self, might do as he wanted. He was an Enchanter. If of the same tribe, as he had said, he was of the royal class. A Prince. Having gained a privilege that could not be mine.

And he also, having told so much, said of this no word. He read my heart. My untaught lesson was over and complete.

He held me through the night, my father the Enchanter. I felt no hint of feathers under his tactful skin, no shift of wings at his back. In his black hair no redness shone, even from the clear fire. His eyes showed nothing amber, golden.

I thought of the black crows he had liberated, and with a dull start of the horses, too, from which he must have liberated the selves of birds–perhaps not in any way of sex, but more as I had seen him do with the sheep whose fleeces glowed . . . What birds, then, would the sheep become?

But I recalled mostly the black crows, how they flew away into the moonrise. I thought of my three children who had lived, and who winged also away.

And I thought of my death, which now was all the life I had.

From one prison I had come. Yet out into the vast prison of the earth I must wander. Wingless. Alone.

When morning began, soft as flowers, Hrothgar left me and walked away. He showed me no sign of anything but his male humanness. I recall the path twisted there. I saw him last, as at the first, from the back.

There was even drink that stayed hot by the fire and a crust of the dark bread, as at our former meal. They did not vanish until I spoke to them, and said I would not eat or drink. And then I wept again, for with their going, the end began.

These were my last tears.

I have shed none since that can be seen. My weeping is tearless. What, after all, have I to do with water? It shames me that I breathe–for the gods know now, I can have nothing ever to do with the air.

Let me have only the earth. Or fire.

They are still mine. Burn or bury me.

❖ ❖ ❖

Twice ten years are gone since that morning by the shore. I dwell far inland of the lake. I do not see the water. I whore for my food,

if ever I want any. My hair, that was made black in that kennel of
a palace, grows out now grey, as with the Princess it did.

Sometimes, in the blundering and unmusical assault of man-
woman congress, I feel a faint fluttering at my womb, as if the
soul of a bird flew there, trying to come in, to make itself within
me, to be born of me. But I am barren, and now old.

In the winter dawns, above this ramshackle village of scav-
engers and thieves, sometimes I see swans fly over, not white
but black on the golden sky. Then for the splinter of an instant, I
spread my wings, and am among them. But this is not what occurs, and indeed, I never dream of it. Nor of the Enchanter. Nor
ever, ever, ever of what I would wish to dream of most. My life.
My life as a swan—

What Tune the
Enchantress Plays

by Peter S. Beagle

I am especially pleased to present new fiction by one of America's finest fantasists, Peter S. Beagle, who was born and raised in The Bronx, just a few blocks from Woodlawn Cemetery, the inspiration for his first novel: the amusing, poignant ghost story, A Fine and Private Place. *"I originally proclaimed I would be a writer when I was ten years old," he recollects. "Subsequent events have proven I was either prescient or even more stubborn than suspected." His subsequent novels and stories include the acclaimed* The Last Unicorn, Tamsin, The Innkeeper's Song, Lila the Werewolf, *"Come Lady Death," and many others.*

He has also written numerous teleplays and screenplays, including the animated versions of Lord of the Rings *and* The Last Unicorn, *plus the popular "Sarek" episode of* Star Trek: The Next Generation. *His nonfiction book,* I See by My Outfit, *which recounts a 1963 journey across America on motor scooter, is considered a classic of American travel writing. He also writes poetry and lyrics, and is a singer and songwriter. His story collection,* The Line Between, *released in 2006 by Tachyon Publications, includes the long-awaited coda story to* The Last Unicorn, *"Two Hearts," which won the 2006 Hugo and Nebula Awards for best novelette, and was also nominated for the World Fantasy Award. For more details on his career and upcoming titles, see www.peterbeagle.com.*

"What Tune the Enchantress Plays" is set in the same world as The Innkeeper's Song.

AH, *THERE* YOU are. I was beginning to wonder.

No, no, come in, do—it's your lair, after all. Tidy, too, for a demon. I'd do something about those bones, myself, and whatever *that* is, over in the corner, that smelly wet thing. But each to his taste, I say; you probably wouldn't think much of my notions of décor, either. Gods know, my mother doesn't.

Ah-ah-*ah,* no bolting—don't embarrass us both on such a pleasant evening. Sit down, and let's chat a little, you and I, like the old friends we practically are. Well, we might as well be, don't you think, as long as it's taken me to track you here. You're very good, you know. *Sit.*

Now.

You're good, as I said, but as shortsighted with it as all your kind. Whatever possessed you to come to Kalagira, when you could have been happily ravaging Coraic, or the fat, juicy villages around Chun? Didn't you know about Kalagira?

Forgive me—that was most rude, and foolish as well. Why expect a demon to be aware of one small southern province, tucked away beyond the Pass of Soshali, when so few humans are? Let me enlighten you, then. Kalagira is a country of *majkes:* witches like my grandmother, sorceresses like my mother . . . and the occasional enchantress, like me. There are certain differences worth note, but we will come to that. There is time.

There is time, until moonset.

At moonset I will sing to you, as I sang you here—oh, yes, that was my song you followed, with its whispers of blood and rapine, its bait of helpless victims, so close. At moonset I will sing another song, and you will go wherever it is that such as you go, when ended in this world.

Meanwhile, we will talk, because it amuses me, because it passes the time, and for one other reason. I shall tell you of my first encounter with a creature like you. Perhaps it will amuse you in your turn.

Well, it was not quite like you, really, that first demon of mine. If *demon* is what it truly was—it was larger, and rather more . . . majestic, excuse me, and definitely more powerful–but I run ahead of myself. Bide, Breya Drom, bide. The moon is still high.

Well, then.

Not all Kalagira women are witches or sorceresses–far from it–but there has been no male with such power born here in the entire history of the province, as far back as the old tales tell us, or the chronicles go. What is known, and known well, is that if the men of Kalagira cannot themselves work magic, still they are its *carriers,* if you understand me. A Kalagira *maj* who marries a local man will invariably find the knack–as we call it–making itself felt in all of her girl children; while one who weds Outside will see it come to an end in her own line, never to reappear. For that reason, Kalagira magic stays in Kalagira. In the oldest and most powerful families, it may have run true for five, six, seven generations, or even more. This can lead to old rivalries at times, old grudges.

Do you have males and females, your kind? I've never been certain. Well out of it, if you don't, but it's the sort of thing I wonder about in the early mornings, when I'm trying not to wake.

Do you have parents? Do you have children?

No?

Then attend, please, for these details matter. My mother's name is Willalou. In her time she was the most powerful sorceress in Kalagira, though today she spends her time gardening and translating the later poems of Lenji. My father is Dunreath, the potter. They live together in the house he built for my mother. She was powerful enough to have brought it into being with a chant and a gesture–a single scribing in the air–but he would never allow it, and she was wise enough to leave such matters entirely to him. You may not know this, being a demon, but it is not easy, in Kalagira or anywhere else, for a proud, skilled man to be with a woman like my mother. But they loved each other, always, and they have lived well together.

One evening, when I was perhaps five years old, my father brought home a small boy.

He brought him home under his arm, squirming and snarling like a trapped *shukri*. I remember as though it were yesterday: the fire smoking, and the smell of wet wool; the rain—little more than a mist—sighing against the windows, and my mother rising from her loom, saying, "Dunreath?" And me, asking loudly—quite loudly, I fear—"What is *that*? Papa, what is *that*?"

"It's not a that, dear," my father answered wearily. "It's a he—a very dirty he—but I can't tell you his name, because he won't say." He looked at my mother and raised his bushy eyebrows slightly. I loved his eyebrows.

"His name is Lathro," my mother said. "Lathro Baraquil." The boy's eyes widened, but his mouth remained almost invisible, so tightly was it shut. "He lives with his Aunt Yunieska and her son Pashak, and he needs a bath. He needs two baths." My father put the boy down; my mother held out her hand, and he went with her, mutely still, but obediently. My mother had that effect on people.

I heard them talking that night, and was surprised when my father asked, "How did you know he was Yunieska's boy?" Didn't he realize that Mother was magic, and knew everything?

"He's her nephew," my mother answered. "I've seen him in the street now and then, filthier even than this sometimes. That woman has no business with a child, none."

"Cleans up well enough," my father said. "I had no idea he's got freckles."

My mother laughed softly. "He's very brave, too. He *looked* at me when I put him in the tub—Dunreath, I don't think he's ever had a bath in his life, not an all-over one. He must have thought I was going to drown him, but he gave me that *look,* and then he stepped into the tub like a prince. There's definitely somebody under all that dirt."

"I wasn't planning on keeping him," my father said quickly.

"I just thought maybe you could clean him up a little, find him something to eat, and shoo him off home. I'll clean the tub."

My mother did not answer for a time, and then not directly. She said only, "I'm going to speak to Yunieska the next time I see her." The way she said *speak* made me giggle, but it made me shiver a little as well.

That was how Lathro came.

He stayed two days, that first time, hardly saying a word he didn't have to, but behaving with a kind of silent grace and courtesy that must have been natural to him; he certainly couldn't have learned it from his aunt and his cousin. On the third day he got into a fight with my older brother Jadrilja, and disappeared for very nearly a month, which is difficult in a small village like ours.

But then he came back.

I found him myself this time, standing in front of our house, balanced on one bare foot and scratching it with the toes of the other. He looked at me, looked away, and mumbled the first words he ever addressed directly to me, "I come for a wash."

Jadrilja was more than ready to pick up his debate with Lathro where our father had halted it, but that didn't happen for a good day and a half; and by that time I had noticed that Lathro Baraquil's brown eyes stood forth with a rich warmth disconcerting in that fierce little face. My own eyes are green, like my mother's; my father's are almost black, like those of all the men in his family. I had never seen eyes like Lathro Baraquil's eyes. I still haven't.

So it began, long and long before either of us was aware that anything was beginning. It was much like inviting a wary, untrusting feral animal first into the yard, then a little way up onto the veranda; then into the house, if only by leaving the door ajar for the creature to choose as it will. First Lathro came, as he said, only for a bath, and once in a great while for my mother to trim his thatch of thick brown hair. Then he began to arrive, more and more, at dinnertime, for my mother to stuff him like a Thieves'

Day piglet. She was not a particularly good cook, no more than
I—magic never provided a proper meal for anyone—but Lathro
never complained.

And in time he began to come for me.

I knew it, accepted it, and gave it no further thought beyond
our pleasure in being together. We wandered, raced, climbed trees,
told each other stories; squabbled on many occasions, made up
quickly, and often fell asleep on a hillside or under a tree, piled together as warmly and innocently as puppies. And when Lathro
fought with one or another of my brothers—he simply could not
keep from it—they had me to deal with as well. Utterly disloyal, but
there you are.

Was I aware that one of us was heir to power such as the
other could never possibly know, merely by virtue of being born
the right sex? I suppose I must have been, but I cannot recall it
making the least bit of difference or discord between us. It might
well have done so, as the years passed, if I had paid the heed I
should have to my mother's grimly patient attempts to instruct
me in shapeshifting, in spirit-summoning, thaumaturgy, rhymes
and songs of lore, and all the other arts I was condemned to master. But surely even a demon can see that I was fatally happy as
I was. I had my mother for any magic I needed, my father for
those moments when I was sad for no reason that I could put a
name to . . . and for all the rest I had Lathro Baraquil.

We must have seemed a strange pair to many, even as children. I was considered beautiful from my earliest youth, while for
his part Lathro grew up plain—beautifully, beguilingly plain—and
stubby with it, being no taller than I, ever. His best features, to the
outside eye, would have been that tumbly brown hair that I loved
to comb (useless as the effort was), and those brown eyes, kind for
all the wide wildness they held.

He grew up strong as well, much stronger than could be
imagined at sight. At fifteen he was working at Jarg's smithy, han-
dling such tasks as holding the back of a haywagon up for as long
a time as it took Jarg to replace a wheel or improvise an axle. I re-

call seeing him turn with his bare hands a frozen bolt that old Jarg couldn't budge with a sledgehammer and a bucket of grease. Lathro hurt his right hand badly doing that once, and I healed it on the spot in a way my mother had taught me when I happened to be actually paying attention. I was proud of myself then.

If my parents thought us too close in those days, I never knew about it. My belief is that they still saw us as children, and Lathro as family, or the very next thing to it. At all events, they made no objection to the hours we spent together, and the only time my mother ever became annoyed with us was the day when I saw five of the village boys harassing a blind madman, snatching away his crutch so that he fell, and then breaking it over his shoulders. I ran to tell Lathro, who came down on them like a storm out of the Northern Barrens. Two or three of them went limping around on crutches themselves for some while.

Unhappily, these very ones happened to be the sons of the wealthiest merchants in our village. Their fathers descended on Jarg, insisting that Lathro be discharged immediately; and from his Aunt Yunieska they demanded he be given swift and merciless punishment. I can still see their puffy, bearded faces, red as vultures' pates, and hear their voices splitting with fury, and the spittle flying. As I can still feel Lathro's firm, gentle hand in mine as we looked on.

My mother put a stop to it all, as I knew she would the moment I saw her approaching. The merchants fell silent before her gaze, and I realized—for the first time, really—that they were dreadfully afraid of her.

She said to the merchants, "If I had seen what your sons were at, I can assure you, there would not be one of them who got away from there on less than four legs. Quite possibly six." I had never heard her voice sound like that. She said, "Count yourselves fortunate, and go away. Now."

They went away, and my mother turned on me before I could cheer her triumph. "Child, what on earth possessed you to place Lathro in such jeopardy, doing your work for you? You know who you are—you could have run those boys into the next shire with three words I taught you long ago. You are a stupid, stupid girl, and I am ashamed of you."

I hung my head. I muttered, "I am ashamed, too, Mother. But I was afraid. I did not think. I ask your forgiveness."

"Breya is *not* stupid," Lathro said. "She is *not.*"

As angry as my mother was, that took more courage than attacking those five fools. My mother ignored him, seemingly, but her voice softened. She said, "My daughter, after me you are already the most powerful woman in Kalagira, whether you know it or not, and there will come a time when you will be far more powerful than I. Others can afford not to think; you never can, or you will do great damage. Do you understand what I am saying to you, Breya Drom? And why I say it?"

I nodded. I whispered, "Yes."

My mother turned to Lathro, and she actually smiled slightly. "Boy," she said, "inhumanly dirty and hungry small boy, you cannot conquer all the cruelty in the world by yourself. Not even you." She patted his cheek then, and turned away. Over her shoulder, she added, "But there's no harm in trying. I'll say that for you."

Was it with that last light glance that she understood what was between us, Lathro and me? I will never know, and she will certainly never tell me. Not even now.

What I do know, for always, is that on that very same day, Lathro Baraquil kissed me for the first time.

It was a clumsy kiss, as unruly as his hair, and it stumbled blindly over my face for what felt like a lifetime before it found my mouth. I was just as awkward: the two of us like blind newborn kittens, scrambling through a forest of fur toward the nipple—toward life. It was so sweet that I wept as though my heart were breaking, and poor Lathro was terrified, thinking that he had somehow hurt me or frightened me. But I reassured him.

And where to from there? What did we whisper, what did we promise each other? What gift did we exchange to seal our troth?

And again, what did my mother know before we did? No business of any demon's.

When the time finally came to speak I never told my mother, "Lathro Baraquil has my heart." I was much too clever for that, well knowing that she could have crumbled the notion like stale bread with a few gently scornful words, and blown the fragments away with a look or a gesture. What I said was, "Lathro is my heart," which was the truth.

But Willalou my mother was more clever than I by far. She embraced me immediately—not the least moment of hesitation, mind—and cried out, "My dear, my Breya, I am so happy for you—*so* happy!" Thus she caused me to lower my guard, to ease my anxiety regarding her reaction to my news; and, indeed, *almost* to miss her wistful little sideways murmur, "But a bit sad for myself . . ."

I didn't miss it, nor was I meant to. With a suddenly lurching heart, I demanded, "Sad? Why should you be sad?"

My mother smiled valiantly. "I'm sorry, darling. Do forgive an old woman her self-indulgence." She sighed deeply, perfectly. "It's terrible of me, but I have to say it, forgive me. It's the children, you see."

I wasn't prepared. I was ready for a lot of things that she might say, but not that. I said indignantly, "Children? And why should there not be children?"

Oh, Mother. Clever, clever Mother. No sorcery of any sort: not even that thing she did with the fingers of her left hand, out of sight by her side, to change someone's mind. No, she merely let her eyes fill slowly, and stepped back, still with her hands tight on my arms, and she whispered, "My dear, my dear, didn't he tell you?"

This time it was no lurch, but a freezing drop, as though through a gallows trapdoor. "Tell me *what*?"

"He didn't tell you he was from Outside? He really didn't tell you? He was very little when they came here, Yunieska and

Pashak. From Chun, I think, although it's hard to remember . . . maybe I mean Oun, I'm not sure. But anyway."

I said, "I don't care." She didn't hear me. I couldn't hear myself.

She drew me close now, saying, "Darling, darling, you mustn't blame the boy. Think how frightened he must have been at the thought of telling you that if you married him you could never have children of . . . our sort. I certainly don't blame him, and you *mustn't*."

"I don't," I said, louder this time. "Oh, I don't." Then I ran away. I could feel her looking after me—one always can with *our sort*—but she did not call, and I did not look back.

Lathro was not at the smithy—I could tell that from a good distance by the silence of the forge. I hurried on by, and found him mucking out Dree Shandriladze's livery stable, as I had thought he would be. No one ever accused my Lathro of not knowing the meaning of real work.

He looked up as I entered the stable, and I could have wept without shame for the pure joy and welcome in his eyes. The next moment, I did weep, for he raised a hand in warning, saying, "Wait, Moon Fox—" such was always his pet name for me—"wait only a moment, while I make this midden-heap fit for your feet." Then, after laying down every board and bit of sacking he could find, he strode to me anyway, scooped me high in his arms, and carried me over to the nest of straw bales he had made for us when he began working there. We held each other, and I breathed his breath and burrowed my way under his arm, and asked, "When did you know?"

He had no idea what I meant. Lathro never lied, not to anyone. I told him the truth of his Outside birth, and of his coming to Kalagira as an infant, and he took it in as flesh parts before the candor of an arrow: I even heard the soft gasp as it went home. Then I made him make love with me, there, for the very first time, with half a dozen coach horses looking on, because it was all I knew to do to comfort him.

In time, when we could at last distinguish the beating of his heart from my own, he said, "Breya. You have to leave me."

I stared at him. There was no answer in me. He said, "You come from a great line of *majkes,* and you will grow to be the greatest of all that line, as your mother said. Am I to be the cause of that line ending with you? I love you better than that, Breya Drom."

"And I love you better than my grandchildren," I answered him. "What have they ever done for me?" I meant to make him laugh, but clearly failed. I went on, "I am not responsible to my *line,* Lathro. I am responsible for my *life*–our life together. For the rest of it, I could be as happy here, right here with you, as anywhere else in the world. I would never ask for more than this– cleaning stables, rubbing down horses, currying them, loving in their good smell. This is happiness for me, Lathro, don't you understand?"

He quieted me with a finger across my lips. "Beloved, this is contentment, nothing more. I haven't your education, but I know the difference. I am no one, son of nothing, and always will be. But magic is part of what you are–you could no more abandon it than step out of that beautiful tea-colored skin you wear so well. And with no daughters to pass it on to, and they to theirs–"

"What if I married someone else, but only had sons? The magic would end then just as surely."

"But at least they would be Kalagira men, such children, able to pass the knack to their own daughters if fate so willed. Ours could not."

"It wouldn't matter!" I tried to hush him with kisses, but he put me aside. "Yes, it would, Breya. Yes, you would live in joy with me anywhere–a stable, a woodcutter's shack, a swineherd's one-room hovel–I know that, how could I not know that? And you would never think for a moment of envying the life of another person on this earth, or of using power to make us more than we already were together." He kissed my fingers then, slowly, one by one. He said, "But children . . . grandchildren . . . great-grandchildren . . . all without magic, never to have it, none of them—look at me, Breya, and tell me you would not ever regret your choice. No, straight at me, there's my girl. Tell me now."

Unlike Lathro, I am a very good liar. Daughter of Willalou, how should I not be? What is all magic but lying, a grandly ruthless reshaping of reality to our purposes? I lied you here, did I not, singing to you of slaughter, luring you with your own hunger? But I could not lie to Lathro in that moment. I wanted him to be wrong, with all my heart . . . but I was not certain, so I lowered my eyes and turned away.

"There's my girl," he said again, and there was more love and understanding in his voice than I could bear. I took my leave of him as soon as I could, and he did not try to keep me, though I wanted him to. Love as we might, I was a long time forgiving him for knowing me.

We did not see each other for some while after that. My doing.

Nor did I have much to do with my mother and father. I stayed in my own quarters, speaking to no one, eating hardly at all, creating small, spiteful enchantments that shame me today, for their pettiness as much as their malice; and generally *sulking*— I can find no kinder word for my behavior, and I have tried. Something was so, and its so-ness stood between me and my heart's desire; and though I willed it not to be so, it was more powerful than my will.

I did much of my sulking in one shuttered storeroom, perhaps because of its particular air of dank misery, perhaps merely because my parents always knew where I was, and what I was doing, and could come and find me there doing it, if they really wanted to. Only they had better not try.

Dunreath chanced on me when he came into the storeroom looking for the ingredients to a glaze he had not used in years. He might well have missed me, huddled silent in a corner as I was; but, blundering in the darkness, he stumbled over me, letting out a yelp of startlement. He is a big, absent-minded sort of man, my father, happiest at his wheel and kiln; but he does know about love, and at a glance he had my measure.

"Child," he said, awkward as a troll at a tea-party. "Child, Breya, don't, please. Don't cry, Breya." And he patted my hair with his rough potter's hand.

I wasn't crying then, for a wonder, but that clumsy touch opened the sluicegates in earnest. I fell on his chest, wailing loudly and wildly enough to deafen the dead. My father held me, whispering whatever lame comfort he could, stroking my neck and shoulders as though I were clay to be petted and kneaded into life.

"Girl, don't weep so," he begged me. "Don't weep, I can't bear it. I like the boy myself, always did, and if you want him so much, you should have him, that's the way *I* look at it. To hell with our line, we've known magic long enough. Your mother would have married *me* if I'd been born Outside, everybody knows that. What bloody difference, hey?"

Is there giving in marriage among demons? If that is so, then maybe—just maybe—you understand something about my father's loyalty. If I knew anything about Willalou, it's that she would never have married a man who was not from Kalagira. My mother loved Dunreath more than anyone, but she loved her heritage more, for good or ill. And Dunreath knew it, but loved her enough not to say so. There is more magic in this world than magicians dream.

"I wish men could be *majkes*," I told him when I finally stopped crying. "I *do*, I wish I could give Lathro my knack. He'd be so good—he'd know the right way to use the power, and I don't, and I don't *care* that I don't. Mother's determined to make me into a great enchantress, but it's not what I want. Doesn't what *I* want matter to *anybody*? Can't I ever be ordinary and happy, like a man?"

"No, love," my father answered me. "No, you can't be—and if you could be, you wouldn't like it." He went back to holding me then, and I went back to weeping. At some point he said, "Breya, you're a hawk, born to soar, born for the heights. You were never meant for the barnyard."

And I remember wailing, "I'm not a bird—I'm human, I'm *me*!" and running away to find Lathro, with my heart wild in my throat and my eyes blind with loneliness and dread.

By instinct, I looked for him neither in the smithy nor the stable, but at the moribund *dika* tree that had been our meeting place since we were children. It was dying then, and it is still stubbornly dying now; but our pet superstition was that our presence—and, in time, our love—was all that kept it putting out the occasional blossom or pale sprig of leaves. It is where I would have gone.

But he was not there, under the tree. He had vanished completely, from the village and from my days, leaving not a trace of his passage.

There are certain obvious advantages to being a *maj* of any sort. One is the ability to track down almost anyone you really set out to find. But nothing that I tried worked. And even Willalou, when I went to her, finally threw up her hands and said, "Daughter, wherever he may be, he has passed beyond my reach. Which is a worry by itself, as much as his being gone."

"Yes," I said. "How thoughtless of him." If my words sound harsh and unfilial . . . well, remember that I was trying not to shatter into very small fragments. I said, "I will find him, Mother."

My mother said, "You will not."

I stared at her. Dunreath had spoiled me shamelessly, with no slightest regard to its effect on my future character; and while Willalou was sterner, I had known all my life that her *no* truly meant *not now, don't bother me, try me again in a day or two.* But in this moment her lips were thinner, her eyes harder, than I had ever seen them. Protest dried up on my own mouth, and I actually backed away from her.

She said, "Wherever that boy has run off to is no fit place for you. Not as you are, gifted beyond my imagining, and vulnerable as a newborn. You have disregarded my instruction all your life, shirked every lesson you could manage to avoid, studied nothing you found boring—and where are you now? Not only would you be useless in any peril when I am not by to rescue you, but you are utterly powerless to aid the one you claim to love. Tell me I am wrong, my daughter. I want to hear you tell me I am wrong."

She had never spoken so to me in my life. There was nothing for me to say; and if there had been, I would have known better than to say it. I waited in silence, staring down at the intricacies of my sandal straps, until she finally ran out of rage and breath more or less together. She said, "So. Now, at bloody last, we begin."

And so, indeed, it began: that insanely intensive course of training in everything that should have been woven into my bones and brain before ever I had need of them. My mother was absolutely pitiless, driving me without rest for either of us, constantly humiliating me to tears, whether over the nursery-simple rhymes that can confer invisibility, locate water in a desert, or heal a fatal wound; or when I, for the hundredth time, tangled up one of her fiendishly complicated invocations with another that was almost identical. She drilled me endlessly in the doggerel chants, phrases, and rituals of a dozen languages, all seemingly unrelated, that could, even so, be fitted together in a remarkable number of different ways to produce strikingly varied results. We battled through the night many a time, I and this terrible woman with my mother's face: me with my mind turning to watery curds, and she haranguing me without cease, barking, "I taught you that when you were seven years old—or I thought I had—you should know it in your sleep. Where is your head?" To this day, I still hate that contemptuous question with no answer. "Where is your head?" over and over. "*Where is your head?*"

Fortunately I learn quickly, when I learn at all; fortunately also, I have an ear for music. This is crucial for an enchantress, as it is not for a witch or a sorceress, since so much of our power lies in song. My mother has a perfectly good voice, but much preferred to recite her spells in a decidedly flat, plain manner—always while *moving*, letting her body sing the magic. But if I could not sing, I might as well be a witch in a cave, growling my incantations over a greasy, smoky fire. (Meaning no disrespect to Grandmother, who was actually a cheerful, sociable soul, like most witches.) As it was, Willalou sang me hoarse, day on day, night on night. "No, do it *again*–can't you hear where you lose the rhythm? *Where is your head?*"

Five endless months. Nearly six. I am grateful beyond words that the memory blurs. It was coming on autumn when my mother finally announced, with no preamble, "Well, I've done what I could. You're still the poorest excuse for a proper enchantress I've ever seen, but at least I'm not quite so feared that you'll put a spell on yourself, or call something you don't want when you're trying to summon Lathro." She paused for a moment, and then added quietly, her voice that of the mother I knew for the first time in forever, "Which, by the way, would *not* do. Do not ever try to bring that boy of yours to you by magic, despite all temptation. Do you understand me, Breya?"

Her eyes were dark with urgency, as I have only rarely seen them. I said, "I understand your meaning, Mother. But not your reason. Why not?"

My mother hesitated again, longer this time. She said finally, her voice uncharacteristically muffled, almost mumbling, "Because it will alert the Being he has gone to seek. And may have found by now."

I gaped at her. She went on, increasingly defensive, "He came to me the very day before he ran off. He wanted me to know–though he swore me not to tell you–that he was away in search of a creature he had heard tell of, powerful enough to change fate and make *maj* of an ordinary man." She paused a third time. "Even a man of Kalagira. He thought such a change might help him carry magic for you, even Outside born, and would not listen when I warned him of the terrible price the Being would claim."

There is a difference between being truly speechless and not having the air to make the sound come out. I felt as though I had been struck in the stomach, having had no warning and no chance to brace myself. I said stupidly, "A creature."

"A Being," my mother said. "It was old when your grandmother was not yet born, and its power is not of this world. I believe, if it so chose–"

"A *maj*." My voice was rising slowly, like floodwaters. "You think Lathro has gone to this–thing–to be magicked into the knack, so that he and I might perhaps have . . ." My mother nodded, looking guiltier by the minute. I whispered, "And you tell me this *now*?"

"It would have done no good before. You would have hared off straight after him, and you no more suited for such a quest than a–a *chicken*!"

"All this time," I said. I was cold with fury, shaking uncontrollably. "All these days wasted going over and over this stupid spell, that baby rhyme, the Three Theories–"

"–which you should have *learned* as a baby–"

"And all the time, Lathro going further and further away, *disappearing* . . ." I couldn't speak any more; it was language disappearing now. I turned and walked out of the house. My mother said nothing, and did not follow.

I left the next morning on Belgarth, the warhorse my father had accepted in payment for a great floral vase, so huge as to require three handles, that he had created for a lord's wedding. Belgarth was getting on by then, and grown fat with inactivity; but I had learned to ride on his king's couch of a back, and we were fond of each other. Besides, he always smelled wonderful, like a dew-damp hayfield warming in the morning sun, and his chestnut hide set off my coloring to perfection. And yes, *majkes* do indeed think about such things, like anyone else.

Dunreath made no objection to my taking his horse, but he looked so wretched that it hurt my heart, and I would have turned back then, if I could have. When he held me, I whispered, "I'm sorry," which I could not say to Willalou, even when she held my stirrup while I mounted, and we bade each other farewell. Nor did she ask forgiveness for what she had said and done, but only stood at Belgarth's head, tall and beautiful and dry-eyed, looking straight at me. She said, "I have no counsel for you, and only one suggestion. Accept it or not, as you choose."

I waited, not speaking. My mother said, "All I know of this Being that you and Lathro seek, is that it is in some way bound to running water. Look for it near rivers, brooks, the smallest streams, search where running water is used by men—in mills, in tanneries, canals, weirs. And if you go north, towards Chun—remember, Lathro may have been born there—seek out a river town called Mulleary, and a woman named Dragine. We were acquainted long ago. If anyone in the land knows where this Being can be found, it will be Dragine." The way she held my gaze with her own was as near to an embrace as makes no matter. "Goodbye, then, my daughter," and she stood aside to let Belgarth pass.

I did not look back as I rode away.

I had never been beyond the borders of Kalagira, nor even close to them. I had never been away from home for longer than three days. Yet here I was, journeying alone into what, for me, was wilderness: the country roads winding more or less towards Chun, so ill-kept and overgrown that half a dozen bandits could be crouched within arm's-reach and you not know—and beyond those, the bare hills surrounding Fors na' Shachim and the Queen's black castle. Belgarth wasn't much concerned with scenery—he's all for tiltyards, short, lumbering charges with murderous clashes at the end of them—and he wasn't happy with stony little roads overhung with brambly vines. Yet he strode on gallantly all the same, a warhorse ever, war or no. There would have been little forage for him, in the normal way; but I made certain to bring rich grass to birth unseasonably, wherever we made camp, and water pooling out of stones. And yes, it *was* my mother who finally hammered that smallest charm into me—and yes, I *should* have learned it at the same time I learned to dress myself.

It seemed the most practical thing—grudge it as I might—to follow Willalou's suggestion and seek out the Dragine woman. I had no notion of what a Being—and did that signify demon, lamia, *yaroth,* or some other monster?—powerful enough to turn a mortal man into a *maj* might look or be like, and if there was someone who did I had many questions to ask. I heeded my mother's hint about running water as well, and set out to trace the course of everything flowing south of Fors na' Shachim. Of course it was a completely absurd notion—was that a laugh? Does your kind actually make a sound to express amusement?—but I was frightened for my man, and certain that nothing was beyond one as much in love as I.

Yes, that *is* a laugh-sound, isn't it? But as dark and distorted as you are.

Often I let Belgarth choose our road—why not, since all horses, left to themselves, will go toward the smell of water, and all paths were the same to me so long as they headed eventually toward Chun? Meanwhile I practiced my spells, like any novice, as we covered the country foot by plodding foot: singing to mark earth and stone and the air itself, to keep us from wandering in circles or unwittingly doubling back on our trail.

As for what I would do when I at last saw Lathro Baraquil's face, I had forced myself, days and miles back, to banish such imaginings altogether. I might—or might not, even after Willalou's improvised disciplines—be a match for the Being I sought; but even if I were, that was no guarantee Lathro would choose to return home with me when I found him. What if he had not yet found the Being, but insisted on continuing the search? Or what if he had already become a *maj* and considered himself far too grand now for a scab-kneed childhood playmate? Too many unknown factors; nothing to do but trudge on, singing.

We kept almost entirely to the mountains: since so many of the streams and rivers of this region spring up there, it did seem to improve the odds at least somewhat. But we might as well have been seeking roses in the Northern Barrens, for I encountered no smallest trace of Lathro, nor of the Being I was hunting so steadfastly. I learned not a thing from the rare traveler, and nothing at all in any of the few villages in which I stabled Belgarth and passed the night. Yet I could not rid myself of the *awareness* of both of them, the conviction that they were somewhere nearby, whatever my training, my observations, or my inborn senses told me to the contrary. The heart is not the infallible guide it claims to be, but it does get a few things right now and then.

The nights were turning seriously chilly, and Belgarth was even showing early suggestions of a winter coat, when we followed a swift, restless little river into a town called, not Mulleary, but Mul*deary,* rather larger than any we had come across in some while. I asked if a woman named Dragine lived there, and was told that she was visiting in a distant village, but would return in two days' time. Belgarth and I spent those days doing little else but eating and sleeping. I had been running for nearly two months on nothing but vague memories of rest, real meals and a proper bed; and for all that happened in Muldeary, I will remember it as the town in which I *slept*. And took baths.

Dragine arrived at dawn of the second day, walking briskly out of a dust storm that drifted away when she told it to. She was a tiny creature with a face like a spiderweb and hair so black you could hardly see it, if you understand me. I caught up with her crossing Beggars' Square, where the homeless of Muldeary are fed every morning, and began to introduce myself, but she kept striding on without even looking at me until I said, "I am Willalou's daughter. Willalou of Kalagira."

Dragine stopped in her tracks then, and I saw her eyes for the first time. I had expected them to be as black as her hair, but they were a tawny brownish yellow, or yellowish brown. She peered at me—I suppose I should say "up at me," small as she was, but somehow it felt as though our eyes were on a level—and she said, "I know your mother." Her voice sounded like sand blowing against the sides of an empty house.

"Yes," I said. "She told me not to leave Muldeary until I had seen you." She started to turn away, and I grabbed at flattery to hold her attention, adding, "She speaks well of you."

Dragine said, "You are a liar," but she said it indifferently, as though she were already tired of me. "I never could abide your mother, and she never had anything but contempt for me. Why are you still bothering me?"

"Because my mother told me you had knowledge to fit my need." Dragine did not reply, but she did not walk away, either, or turn her strange eyes from mine. We stood there together in Beggars' Square, and I told her about Lathro Baraquil.

Her expression never changed, nor did her tone. She looked me up and down for a time, then shrugged very slightly and said, "Come to my house tonight. Ten minutes to midnight, no sooner." She never mentioned where her house could be found, nor did I think then to ask her for directions. Whatever she actually might be—witch, sorceress like my mother, or even a true enchantress—in her presence I had trouble thinking at all.

I took Belgarth out for a fast trot, bordering on a canter, and spent the rest of the day searching for someone willing to tell me where Dragine lived. It was an interesting experience: none of them recoiled in obvious terror at the idea of revealing her location, and yet somehow I came away from none of them with an exact address. In the end I had to employ a finding spell, which is so childishly simple that it always gives me a headache. But I was there precisely at the appointed time, and I came on foot to show respect, though it meant a long walk.

It was an ordinary house she lived in, neither a mansion nor a hovel: it might well have been the home of an honest and energetic farmwife, one who spent great amounts of time scrubbing and polishing worn kitchen flagstones that would never come quite clean. I remember that it smelled of old fires, and that the river ran near enough that I could see its banks from the front yard, and hear its rambling chatter as I stood on the threshold.

Lathro Baraquil opened the door to me.

Do your folk have hearts? Do they serve another purpose, as ours do, besides hurrying the impatient blood along through your veins, if you even *have* veins? Mine stopped—just for an instant, but completely—and then it surged to the size of Belgarth, so that my chest could not nearly contain it, and with a cry the Queen must have heard in Fors na' Shachim, I threw myself into Lathro's arms. I think we mortals must each be allowed one moment like that in our lives. I don't believe we are constructed to withstand two.

For the sake of accuracy, however, I must admit that I threw myself against Lathro's arms, not into them. He made no effort to embrace me, but only stood still, looking not into my eyes but over my shoulder, his own eyes empty as eggshells of feeling. He did not know me at all; and what stood in his place, in his clothes—I had made him that shirt; *made* it, not conjured it—I could never possibly know.

He did not recoil, nor thrust me away. He stood still, staring over my shoulder at the night, with every treasured bump and bone and angle of him turned foreign, after years of being as much my own as his. I babbled his name, but it had no more effect than the sound of the stream. Nothing in him knew me.

Beyond him Dragine waited, her face as unreadable as ever, but her eyes glowing like the eyes of a hunting *shukri*. She said, "He has been here for some while, waiting for the Being to be called. I myself, however, have been waiting for you."

I pushed past Lathro to confront her, demanding, "What have you done to him? Tell me now, or I will kill you where you stand!" Eighteen and gently bred up, can you imagine me saying such a thing to anyone? I have not even said it to you, although the moon is on its way to setting.

In her voice of blowing sand, Dragine answered me, "That would be wrong and foolish of you, since it was not I who set this spell upon him."

I could not respond. I simply stared. Dragine said, "It happens with humans. They often desire something so greatly, for so long, that with the proper push they cannot remember why they craved it in the first place. So it is with your man—he was in this state when he found his way here. Only if he came from where you did, I suspect there was little *finding* on his path. He has been here quite some time." She paused, watching me take that in, and then went on. "In the end, it is your doing, even more than his."

"*My* doing?" The absurdity of the claim outraged me, but it frightened me as well. "How can it have been my doing?"

Dragine pointed at Lathro, standing completely motionless, not even blinking. "When you told him that you two could never marry, because of his being an Outsider, what did you *think* he would do? You say you have known him since childhood—what did you *think*?"

I could hear my mother's *"Where is your head?"* under my own whispered reply. "I never told him that. I would never have . . ."

"No? Well, someone did." Dragine's yellow teeth bared their tips in a smile of mean delight. "And that same someone directed him straight here, to me. What do you think of that, Breya Drom, daughter of Willalou?"

There was a taste of copper in my mouth, and a distant braying in my ears. I said, "My mother set Lathro searching for you? I don't believe it." But I did, I did, even before Dragine answered me.

"I would never dream of lying to you—I am enjoying the truth far too much, little witch-girl." She was beginning to laugh, like a sandstorm gathering strength.

Strangely, the contempt in the word *witch-girl* cleared my head, leaving me more coldly, stubbornly rational than I had been since I left home. I said, as haughtily as I was able, "I am no witch, but an enchantress, as you well know, and the daughter of one who could crumble you and a dozen like you into her soup." The laughter grew until I could actually feel the sand against my skin, like tiny blades. Beside me, Lathro showed no reaction at all, his entire attention focused on nothing I could see or imagine. His eyes had not met mine squarely since he had opened Dragine's door to me. I said again, "Tell me why you hate my mother so. Because she doesn't know, I'm sure."

"You think not?" Dragine's laughter did not return; rather,

she looked at me with something almost like pity. "She told you nothing she did not *have* to tell you, did she then? Nothing?"

I had no answer for her. With no further word, she turned and led me—and silent, obedient Lathro, too—through the house to a curious place I'd not noticed from outside: neither a room nor a yard nor a veranda, but a plain high-walled space open in part to the sky. The walls were white and bare. There were no chairs, or even cushions, to sit on; the only distinguishing feature of the area was a small pool, ringed round with large stones, carefully arranged. There was no moon that night, but the stars were reflected thickly in the pool, darting like bright fish, as the current from some hidden inlet stirred the surface. I could see my shadow in it, but not my face.

Dragine squatted on her heels, and gestured to me to do the same. She did not look at Lathro, who stood by, hands folded in front of him, staring away at nothing. She said, "I was born in Kalagira. I grew up with your mother. Did she tell you *that,* at least?" I shook my head. "Well, so it was. And as you and this one here—" she jerked a gaunt finger at Lathro—"have been to each other, so was I with your father. Dunreath the potter." When she spoke his name she closed her eyes, barely for longer than a blink, but I saw.

"Were you promised?" I could not imagine her young with Dunreath—the bitter spider-lines gone, the tawny eyes innocently yearning—but my folk take handfasting seriously, and I had to know.

Dragine looked at me for a long, cold time before she replied. "Breathe easy, witch-girl, your father never deceived me. We were close to promising—he even spoke of it, a time or two—but I was shy still. I was shy . . ." Her voice had grown soft when she spoke of Dunreath, almost wistful; but it turned to blowing sand again with her next words. "Then came your mother."

Oh, perhaps you can see it; perhaps you can take my word for my young father's first sight of a maiden Willalou. Dragine must have seen the vision in my face, for she said, "Aye, there was never a day when I could match her for beauty. Nor for power, either . . . not then."

The last two words were uttered in a near-animal growl, and I could hardly catch them, but I did. I said, "And now?"

Dragine smiled fully for the first time, granting me, as though by a flash of lightning, an instant's glimpse of the girl who had had every reason to believe that Dunreath belonged to her, with her. She said, "I was not born a *maj,* or to a gifted line. There has never been so much as the feeblest barnyard witch in my family, search as far back as you will. How should my potter not have been drawn to such a face, such a gift, as Willalou's? No, I blame him not at all, your father."

"But my mother must take the blame for everything," I said, "every misfortune that has befallen you since you lost Dunreath to her. Even before then, am I wrong?"

"I blame her for being exactly what she is, no more: for knowing that what is not hers is hers to take. Do you feel that unjust, witch-girl? Too bad. I also honor her for making me what I am." The smile thinned, curling into the newest of new moons. "The Being your foolish man seeks draws no line between one sex and another. It responds simply to desire. To need."

"Such as yours," I said, and she nodded. I said, "But it could not bring my father back to you. He loved my mother on sight, loves her still. Nothing could have changed that."

"The Being gave me a greater gift." Dragine's voice was surprisingly gentle, almost dreamy. "Shall I show you?"

She raised both arms, crossed them at the wrists, pointed at me with both pairs of middle and index fingers, and spoke a rhyme that Willalou had drummed into my head so hard, so often, that I knew to drop flat on my belly as two gouts of fire, shaped like dragon heads, leaped from Dragine's fingertips and shot past me, hissing like full-sized wyrms. Ordinarily such sendings burst within seconds, harmless as Thieves' Day crackers; but these doubled on their sizzling trails and came racing for me again. There were eyes in those tiny fire-faces, and they saw me.

But I know a rhyme worth two of that, and I sang it, rising to a crouch—sang it back at Dragine, not at the dragon-heads, and they promptly popped like milkweed seedpods, and were gone.

I stood up slowly, glancing sideways at Lathro as I did so. He had not moved, nor did he appear to have noticed what had taken place. I said loudly to Dragine, "*That* was what your Being taught you? *That* was worth a slice of your soul? You ought to ask for your payment back."

Dragine was breathing hard: deep animal inhalations—such as you breathe now, in the darkness, waiting for the moon to be gone. She said, "The Being has no interest in souls. What it took in payment for my new power was my ability to love, for which I had no more use in any case, nor ever would. I have no complaints. See now!"

And with those last words—and a few others—she Shifted, and on the instant it was a great *sheknath* who stood in her place: hindquarters higher than the mighty bowed forelegs, jaws and chest and shoulders still muddy from digging out its most recent meal. It rose on its hind legs and roared at me, but I sang my mother's favorite old lullaby, and it dropped down and promptly went to sleep. Dragine was some little while regaining her true shape, and she was not pleased when she finally managed it.

"I will not fight with you," she declared. "I did not summon you for that, but to watch you lose your man to a fantasy, as I lost mine. It lasts longer than destruction, grief does. As you will learn."

Whereupon she made a sign before Lathro's face. The eager life came back into his brown eyes to break my heart, but he never looked at me, only asking Dragine, "Is it time? Has the Being come at last?"

"Soon, boy," she answered him soothingly. "Very soon now." Her eyes were full of triumph as she looked back at me, saying, "You see how it is? He has no care for you, nor for anything but his desire. The memory of Willalou's daughter has vanished, making you a ghost to him, and any dream of your future together just that, a dream, long slipped away with the morning. Nor will being made a *maj*–oh, yes, the Being will certainly grant his wish–bring him home to you, no more than I will ever have your father back. So here we both are, abandoned forever by our loves–" and this time the smile was as joyously murderous as a rock-*targ*'s skull-baring grin, just before it strikes for the throat or the contents of your stomach–"and all of it, *all,* due to the devices of the clever, wicked woman from whose wickedness you spring. Do you understand me at last, witch-girl?"

"No," I said. "I will not. I will not understand you." Rather than listen further to her, or to myself, I turned desperately to Lathro, saying, "Love, love, here I am, your Moon Fox, your Breya. Can't you see me, don't you know me at all?" I even shook him a little, grasping his shoulders, to no avail.

His eyes were warm and alive, as I have said, but I was not in them. Whoever he saw standing before him, shrilling like a locust, it was not I. He spoke for the first time, saying, with some wonder in his voice, "You are so pretty. I never imagined the Being would be pretty."

I choked on my own sudden tears, and Dragine laughed in purest delight, sounding almost like a happy child. "Nay, she's no Being, boy, she can give you nothing you need, my word on it. Come, we'll call now, you and I."

She moved to the edge of the pool, spread her hands over the star-fish shimmering in its depths, and spoke to them too rapidly for me to catch more than a few of the words. They were in a tongue I had heard my mother speak: it is very old, and there are some bad stories about its origins. Lathro joined in the calling, briefly and stumblingly, as Dragine's voice rose to a kind of shrill croon, not loud, but *high,* high enough that it disappeared at the end, like a lark or a falcon climbing out of sight. I wanted to cover my ears, but I didn't. A moment later I very nearly covered my eyes, because the surface of the pool gradually began to swirl counterclockwise, right to left, gaining speed until the sound of its spinning echoed Dragine's uncanny wail. It no longer looked like water: first it was black stone—then starlit spiraling diamond—and finally it was jeweled smoke, sparkling pale-blue smoke, whirling slowly into shape, like clay on my father's wheel. A figure began to rise out of the little pool.

It was man-shaped, but not a man. I never did determine what it was, or even what it chose to resemble, so sinuously and playfully did it sport from form to smoky near-form. At one moment it might have been a sort of hornless goat, dancing on its hind legs; but step closer to the pool, or consider it from another angle—or simply *wait*—and it seemed an enormous head, with black wriggly-wet things like eels where its teeth should have been, and that head was dancing, too. Or let a small pewter cloud hide a star or two, and behold then a dead tree, its skeletal boughs aswarm with glittering, watchful stone eyes; or again you might suddenly be staring at a great almost-butterfly, burning as it whirled, yet never consumed, though its blaze dazzled even Dragine's eyes. She turned from it to stare at me, and though she said nothing, yet I heard her in my mind, her silent laughter echoing within me.

"She arranged it all, witch-girl. She set your man all afire to get rid of him . . . then set you to find him, after training you up to face the Being who comes when I call, as she well knows. A Being who has more power than she ever dreamed of having, for all her hopes, all her craving . . ."

When the Being spoke out of its flaming, shifting whirlwind, it addressed itself directly to me. Through all its constant transformations its voice remained the same: a deep, deep buzzing that I heard along my spine and in my cheekbones more than in my ears. "There will be no confrontation between us, Breya Drom, because there is no reason for such a thing. You have already lost any battle there could be."

"Have I, then?" Compared to that voice, I sounded to myself like a little girl refusing to go to bed. But I was profoundly weary, and deeply frightened, and more stubbornly angry than either. I said, "Whatever battles my mother had in mind, she will have to find someone else to fight them. All I came for was Lathro Baraquil."

"And all *he* came for, he has already found." The Being extended what was momentarily a hand toward Lathro, and he *hungered* toward it–that is the best word I can find–reaching out with his whole self, but I pushed his hand away before they could meet.

"We are going home," I said. "Lathro and I."

The Being chuckled. It had slowed its spinning–a dizzying effect by itself–and was regarding me out of a single eye in the flat face of a creature a bit like a furry fish. It buzzed. "Tell *him* that, girl." Lathro looked as though he were about to jump into the pool: not to gain any gift from the Being, but to join with it, to become part of it, as he had been part of me so long ago. The Being said to him, "Ask and have, Lathro Baraquil."

Behind me Dragine laughed once, a single bark, bruising my ears. "Yes! Ask and have, boy. Ask and have!"

And suddenly it was all too much for me–too much and too little at the same time. All of it, all: Lathro's dream of carrying magic . . . Willalou's shameless machinations . . . Dragine's vengefulness . . . my own idiot journey in pursuit of my useless fantasies . . . the Being's benign disregard . . . even being called *witch-girl* one time too many. Suddenly I wanted no further part of it, even if it cost me my one love. "Do what you will," I said aloud, though none seemed to hear me. "Do what you please, I'm done." And I turned my back on the lot of them, and I walked away.

Nor did I turn again, not until I heard the Being's insect-whirr once more, "Ask and have of me, Lathro Baraquil," and Lathro's voice, that I had first heard mumbling *I come for a wash,* saying now, loudly and boldly, "Then I ask for the full powers and abilities of a true *maj,* and I ask further–"

But by then I was singing.

I have no memory of making that decision, or of choosing the charm I sang. It has only happened so for me once or twice since.

What I do remember is that Lathro went mute on the instant, and that Dragine whirled, wrinkled lips drawn back, furiously chanting a counterspell that I warded off easily with a gesture. That made me overconfident—I was young, after all—and I was not prepared when the Being struck at me with . . . with what? A spell, was it? A cantrip of some sort? A hex, even? Did the Being know any of those words, did it think in those terms? No matter: my brain was too occupied with careening from one side of the universe to the other, and I could not find my legs and arms. There was a howling in my head.

I stood up—somebody did, anyway—and saw that the Being had flowed into the form of something that might have set out to be a clawfooted, stinking *churfa,* and changed its mind halfway along, for the worse. It said, "Give over, Breya Drom. Go your way and leave me to mine, and your man to the way he has chosen. What he pays to walk it may not be what Dragine paid—but in any case, he is lost to you. Give over, child. Go home."

I might have done just that, had Dragine not squalled at that moment, "And tell your mother we are quits when you get there." Her face was as savagely satisfied as though she had been making love all night long.

Lathro was silent still, but not staring worshipfully at the Being now. He was looking directly toward me, and it seemed to me that there was at least *something* like recognition in his face—something surfacing that was near to being my Lathro. I dared not think any further than that.

Not that there was time for it, since I had no illusions that the Being's words meant truce; they certainly didn't to me. Lathro was coming home with me, whether he wanted to or not—his desires had just become completely irrelevant. Dragine aimed a second spell at me: a spiteful thing that would likely have cost me a few years in beetle shape, had she managed it, but I batted it back at her like a featherball, such as children play with, and kept my attention focused on the Being. Willalou may indeed have decoyed me to its den and its acolyte to destroy it; my only concern now was to keep it from destroying me. Nothing in my body was working properly, except my blood, and that was up and raging. I took a deep breath, began walking directly towards the Being, and I sang as I went.

Not until I began that song had I truly known I was an enchantress, for all my proud disdain. Do you understand me, huddling there, as far from me as the walls of your lair will let you, with your red eyes counting the minutes until the moon is gone? It was one of the many things I had never bothered to learn, you see. I knew who my mother was, for good or ill, and that my power descended from her, and from my mothers before her. I knew that Willalou was a sorceress, and that a sorceress thinks about magic—with great care, in most cases. But an enchantress *is* magic, *is* what she does: an enchantress dwells in a place, not without thought, but beyond it, somewhere on some other side. And I hadn't known that, for all my mother's harping on how much greater than herself I was born to be. Some things cannot be known, only experienced.

With that song, with those charmed notes leaping up out of me like children—for all I knew at the time, the only children I was ever likely to have—I came of age.

The Being had reverted to the whirling cone of pale-blue smoke that I had first seen rising out of the pool. I felt its enormous blasts of heat and energy hammering at me, and I know most of them connected somewhere, but it did not seem to matter, it seemed to be happening very far off, to someone else. The song I sang was our family's ancient war chant: few beyond the family have ever heard it, and nobody sings it but us. I knew the Being could not have heard it before.

The song built up momentum, like a sling whirled round and round the head until you at last let go. When I did, with the last stanza, the recoil—there is no other word—lifted me and hurled me across that open space, helpless as a new-hatched canary in a cloudburst. It slammed me first into a white wall, then tumbled me straight into Dragine's pool. I seem to remember the water tasting somehow burned, but I could be wrong. I was drowning at the time.

It was a shallow little pool, but you can drown just as easily in inches as in fathoms, and I wasn't even conscious enough to lift my head out of the water. Lathro it was who picked me up, and then put me down carefully and dried my wet clothes as best he could. He whispered *"Moon Fox . . . Moon Fox,"* over and over as he did so.

The Being itself was out of the pool, stumbling near me—almost over me, as I sat up—on absurdly pink pigeon feet far too small for the hulking, unwieldy form it appeared to have been trapped in by my song. I cannot adequately describe that shape: it had something of flesh to it, but more was quite simply wooden, or almost wooden . . . and there was, about the face, if that is what it was, a sort of . . . No. No. All I know is that it was dying, and blind, and that I felt sorry for it, for the Being, whatever it had so nearly cost Lathro and me. And when it managed to buzz out, *"I have had my price, all the same . . ."* before it toppled and crashed down, there were tears in my eyes. I did not understand what it had told me, not then.

Lathro took my hand without speaking. I said, "Well, there goes your chance at magic. Perhaps you'll forgive me one day."

Dragine was on her knees beside the fallen Being. After a moment she reached out slowly to touch the blind face, that face that I cannot portray any more than I could the look in her eyes. Lathro took my own face between his hands, as of old, this time so gently and timorously that I could barely feel it. He said, "The question is whether you can forgive me. I only wanted to be a proper match for you, Breya."

I stopped him, and not gently. "And just exactly what have you been to me since we were five years old? Can you honestly imagine me partnered with anyone else in the entire world? Anyone?"

"No. No, I never could, you know that. But then our children—"

"Bugger the children!" I picked that word up from Dunreath when I was quite small, and he was having a bad day with his pots and jugs. "If my line's knack comes to an end with me—well, so it does. Too many *majkes* in the family, anyway, and not enough blacksmiths." Bruised and hurting everywhere, I was yet holding him so hard that I was having as much trouble breathing as he was. I said, "Home. We are going home now."

Strangely—or perhaps not—Dragine showed me no rancor for having caused the end of the Being; indeed, she showed nothing at all, but only crouched on her heels by the great dead thing, still touching it now and again. Once, when she looked up and saw me staring, as I could not help doing, she said in her desert voice, "It was my friend. Go away."

So we took the road home to Kalagira, the two of us astride Belgarth, who carries double easily, though he complains vigorously in the mornings. It took us a long time, but we didn't mind. There's little to tell of that passage, except for a moment I do like to remember, when I suggested proudly to Lathro that he had but to say the word and I could surely make our journey a great deal easier for everyone involved, and perhaps even eliminate it altogether. What's the good of being an enchantress, after all, if you can't show off for your beloved once in a while?

But Lathro refused. He said—and I have it still in my head, word for firm word—"Breya Drom, through my foolishness we have already missed too much of our time together in this world, and risked all. I will not lose another minute of you, another second, for good or ill, ever again."

When we reached my home, I asked Lathro to stable Belgarth for me, and he nodded understandingly. "You'll want some time alone with your mother. Of course." I watched him walk away with the old horse, and felt my heart floating after him. Then I left my shoes at the door, and went in.

She was practicing on her *kiit* in her workroom; I could hear the music as I came along the corridor. Her hands are not quite big enough for the full-sized instrument she insists on using, but she plays well all the same—I loved to have her play me to sleep when I was small.

She spoke to me before I had even reached her workroom. "Welcome, daughter. Welcome, my pride." No one catches Willalou unaware: and what I now was she would have sensed two villages away.

She put down the *kiit* and came swiftly to enfold me, but I held her off with a raised hand. How strange that did feel, evading my mother's embrace for the first time in my life. I could hear the comforting old sound of Dunreath's wheel going, deep in his own studio, and was desperately glad that he was not present. I said, "We talk."

She stood straight now, as always, and looked into my eyes and shrugged slightly. She said, "I did what was necessary. No more, and no less."

"I think not," I said. "I think bloody not."

"The Being is dead. There will be no others, and so no witches or sorceresses who should never have been *majkes*, not ever. Dragine had no power in her before her desperate bargain, and she is broken now, no danger to anyone. You did these things, not I, and it is a little late for qualms and regrets. As though you had any need of them."

I had to fight off the appeal of her smile, exactly as I had had to deal with Dragine's spells, except that this was much harder, and took much more of me. I said, "You manipulated everything. *Everything.* You goaded Lathro into running off to make himself worthy of me, thinking that would be the end of him—and then you put me through that whole charade of *training*—"

"Charade?" My mother spat the word out, genuinely furious; no elegant play-acting here. "I saved your life, ungrateful idiot! You would be dead now—or worse, much worse—if I had not forced you to become what you were supposed to be, what I had come to despair of your ever bothering to be. I made you an enchantress, my daughter, which was more than your inheritance or your own nature could have done, and what matter if I used all the world to do it. Will you give me the lie, then?"

Rage can often make plain, homely people beautiful, or almost so. It does not have the same effect on beautiful ones like my mother. I said, "It was poor Dragine, and the Being itself, who made me an enchantress. You made me a tool." I fell silent for a moment, because my own anger suddenly had me by the throat, and I could barely breathe with it. "And I could have stood that— I could have endured it all and still trusted you, and loved you— but for the look of my Lathro when he opened Dragine's door and did not know me."

My mother had the grace not to speak. My mother has a great deal of grace.

"You ensorcelled my love," I said. "You *dared*," and how I got that word out, I will never know. "Lathro was under your spell from the moment he left this house and set off to find the Being, as you had charged him, bidding him forget me. But you had not counted on the strength of his love; he was throwing off the charm before ever I defeated the Being." I actually smiled at her then, so proud I was of Lathro. "You should have known better, Mother."

There was no surrender in Willalou, no smallest yielding; I would never have expected any. "When I was training you, I knew that it might one day come to this—that if you survived the trials for which I was preparing you, you would return with mastery enough to punish me for deceiving you. Do it, then. I did what I did, and unlike you I regret none of it. Do as you choose, Breya. Don't dally, girl, *do* it."

I think she may very well have expected death, but I could not do that to Dunreath. So I did something else instead.

She never lowered her eyes from mine as I sang three words that stripped her power from her, leaving her as mortal as my father, as vulnerable to the world as Lathro's first kiss had made me feel. She took a single long breath—then went back to her chair, picked up the *kiit,* and began to play again.

We have not spoken since.

And, yes, if it could possibly interest a demon, I regret that. But it was to be expected, for the Being's last words were spoken truly. I did pay a price that night in Muldeary: I lost my mother. At need an enchantress can deceive anyone or anything but herself, but no spell in my throat could ever hide the truth of Willalou from me, no matter how much I may sometimes wish it.

So here I sit now, in your lair, watching the moon over your spine-crested shoulder, and feeling the quickening inside me. Not even Lathro knows yet, but I am with child. Actually, I think I am with children, for I can already sense the doubleness, though it is too soon for them to be much more than two breaths. Daughters, I hope, though *majkes* they will not be, neither of them. They are Lathro's children. That is magic enough.

The moon is down and gone, and it has come time for me to sing you to your end—or, for all I know, your beginning—in some demon afterworld. It seems a pity, after having spent this night telling you things I have never spoken of to another human, but there it is. You can only be what you are, with that nasty fixation of yours on other people's livers and hearts . . . and I can only be myself. It has cost me what it has cost me, but I am an enchantress, which is different from a witch or a sorceress, and I have more lives to guard than just the two I carry. You do understand? I would truly prefer to think so.

Goodbye, demon. Goodbye.

KNIGHT OF THE WELL

BY PATRICIA A. MCKILLIP

Patricia A. McKillip is primarily known for her fantasy novels both for adults and young adults. Her YA novel The Forgotten Beasts of Eld *won the first World Fantasy Award in 1975. Her other YA works include* The Riddle-Master Trilogy, The Changeling Sea, *the SF duo,* Moon-Flash *and* The Moon and the Face. *Among her adult fantasy novels are* Winter Rose *and* The Tower at Stony Wood, *both of which received Nebula nominations.* Something Rich and Strange *was accorded a Mythopoeic Award, and* Ombria in Shadow *won both the Mythopoeic and World Fantasy Awards. Her short stories include "The Kelpie," which appeared in my 2005 SF Book Club anthology,* The Fair Folk, *which won the World Fantasy Award. Her latest novel is* Solstice Wood, *a contemporary sequel to* Winter Rose*—and her new work,* Od Magic, *won the 2007 Mythopoeic Award. She lives in Oregon with her husband, the poet David Lunde.*

Even by the standards of originality set by the other stories in A Book of Wizards, *"Knight of the Well" is a truly sorcerous nonpareil.*

THE KNIGHTS OF the Well came last in the royal procession into Luminum. Their barge was pale green and ivory, the colors of the river; their standard was blue and stone gray, for water and for well. Their surcoats were cloth of gold, their cloaks white for foam, for the moon that drove the waters, bid them come and go. Their hoods were black for the secret dark from which the well bubbled out of the earth, also for humility. Their faces were all but invisible. The city folk crowding the banks of the Halcyon River to watch the parade of brightly painted boats carrying Kayne, King of Obelos, and his court to the summer palace in Luminum, cheered and flung flowers at the still, mysterious figures in the last barge. The procession heralded both the beginning of summer and the ritual, old as Luminum, which would honor and placate the waters of the world, most particularly the waters of the Kingdom of Obelos.

The dozen knights had been standing for hours, it seemed, though the procession had shifted from horses and wagons to boats just outside the city. No one dared move. The small, colorful barge was balanced to a breath, five men on either side plying their gilded oars, the oar master on his narrow perch keeping their time with a brass gong and hammer. The knights were supposed, by the city folk, to be contemplating their awesome function. Most were indeed contemplating water: the last one who had moved impulsively, at the nip of a bloodthirsty insect, had nearly thrown them all into it.

Mingling with the flow of water, the golden drip of sound from the gong, the drift of voices from the other barges, the distant roil of shouts, cheers, scraps of music from the crowds, was the murmur of memory the knights passed to one another, trying, as they always did during this part of the journey, to pinpoint why the water-mage had chosen them.

"One of my ancestors was found floating among the reeds in a shallow pond just after she had given birth to a child with webs between its fingers . . . family lore has it she fell in love with a water sprite."

"My grandmother flung herself over a cliff into the sea. Her body was never found, though she left her shoes at the place where she jumped. There were prints in the earth beside them that were not quite human."

"There is a lake on our land in south Obelos said to be inhabited by water creatures of a most extraordinary beauty . . ."

Garner Slade, who had been a knight of the king's for three

years, and a Knight of the Well since the previous year, recognized most of the hushed voices that came from under the lowered hoods. Not all of the men were knights of the court; a few he only saw at this time of the year: those who left their lands and families at the mage's bidding. The young man who spoke next Garner recognized as one of them only because he bore the standard that fluttered over their heads.

"I drink water," he said a trifle hollowly. "Sometimes I wash. Sometimes I just stand in a good rain instead. I don't know how to swim. I don't even like water. I'm afraid of it. I'd trade this standard for a beer in a moment. So why would the mage have picked me?"

He had a moment's sympathy. Summer was no further away than a change of expression on the moon's face, a richer hue in the gold that fell freely out of the blue. Even now, heat clung to them as heavily as cloth, beading their faces with the sweat that lured the tiny, malignant pests.

Then came the inevitable: "Clear your mind of such distractions or we will fail in our task. Contemplate water; allow it to flow into your thoughts, your blood. You will begin to know it instead of fear it. Take care what you say in the same breath as the word, for water will hear; you will offend."

And the crops, Garner thought, will wither on the vine. The sea will open the gates, plunder the ships in the harbor. He blinked salt out of his eyes and contemplated the floating market, the swift, narrow boats drawn close to the banks, decked with flowers and bright ribbons in welcome. The procession was passing through the heart of the city. Ancient stone river houses, interspersed with equally ancient thatched cottages whose garden walls were moldy with bygone floods, offered intervals of shadow cast by the sudden jut of high roofs. Then light, as the rooftops dropped. Then again the welcoming shadow.

Garner's cousin, who had been a Knight of the Well longer than any of them, and who liked the sound of his voice, was still proffering the benefits of his experience. "Our minds must be as waters flowing into one another, pellucid and free of the twigs and sodden leaves of earth. The debris of language. Water speaks; we must listen. Water hears; we must beware."

"I can't hear," Garner murmured finally.

"What?"

"Over the debris of language. A word the river is saying."

Edord paused. The pause was weighted with significance. Garner heard the standard-bearer's breath quiver with suppressed laughter. The oar master, reprovingly, struck the gong a sharp, meaningful stroke. Edord began another word. From the bridge arching across the river just ahead, someone tossed a handful of flowers into the boat.

Garner looked up. For that moment, his face was visible to the world: his dark hair and eyes, his restless, brooding, quizzical expression. He revealed himself as human within the hood, within the solemnity of his status. The young woman who had thrown the flowers flashed a surprised grin at him. The standard-bearer gave a sneeze of laughter, bending to conceal it. The barge rocked; the gong gave a hiccup between beats. For a moment oars flailed; the knights froze. The shadow of the bridge fell mercifully over them.

Then they slid again into light, water lapping with little, agitated river-words against the boat. Garner, standing stolidly, could feel it under the soles of his boots: the thin, thin boundary between wood and water, between dry and wet, between profoundity and disgrace.

Even the standard-bearer was silent, the long pennant whipping reproofs into the air, which was stirring suddenly as the river quickened to meet the sea.

Edord opened his mouth.

Garner tried to shut him out, his fair-haired, handsome, humorless cousin with his irritatingly reedy voice that made Garner want to swat at it, as though it had wings and would bite. Edord was the oldest of the twelve, and entirely confident of the mage's choice of him to help balance the powerful, mysterious forces of earth and water. Her choices were varied; at times they seemed wildly arbitrary. Garner, for instance, would not have chosen himself. Despite his good intentions, he was more prone to muddying the waters than placating them. The standard-bearer, affected by nerves and fearful of water, seemed inexplicable. But the mage's ancient, sunken eye, weirdly nacreous, had seen in them both something she needed.

The blunt, craggy walls of the castle guarding the jut of land where the river met the sea revealed themselves above the houses, inns, and warehouses along the tangle of city streets. The pattern of the oldest streets in Luminum resembled a wad of thread that had been shoved into a pocket and forgotten. Some said the early roads followed animal tracks, others that their loops and switchbacks were an attempt to confuse the floodwaters, the raging winter tides. Across the Halcyon, where land was diked and drained of marsh water, the younger city was flat as an anvil. Sea walls, gates and sluices, canals and locks, added over the centuries, had tamed much of the flow, trained it into fields and, more recently, into pipes. But even on the most tranquil of nights, no one completely trusted water not to possess a will of its own. The impulses, secrets, history, the sprites and elementals who swelled beneath its surface, were understood most completely by the mage, who spoke all the languages of water. The rulers of Obelos would sooner have left a sea gate open to a wild winter tempest than neglect the Ritual of the Well.

There was a flourish of brass as the trumpeters in the high walls saluted the king. Edord fell mercifully silent. The castle walls were shrugging out of the city, growing sheer, stark against the blue sky and the sea. Garner could see the stone sea walls curving along the path of the river to front the tide. Tide was turning now, tugging the boats along with it. Ahead, the king's barge began to angle toward the royal dock, along which so many banners and standards and pennants flew that, in a better wind, they might have lifted the dock into the air.

The oar master spoke, slowing the ritual barge until it wallowed, waiting for those ahead to disembark. It took a while. The canopied stairway up the bank to the back of the castle was crowded with courtiers. The oarsmen plied oars expertly, pushing against the tide, then letting the boat creep a little closer as a barge pulled away. They emptied quickly; no one lingered on the dock after the long journey from the west, and all baggage had been left on the wagons coming down the coast road to the castle. Garner's thoughts drifted. He stared at the flowers at his feet, not daring to look up, knowing that his eyes would search for a phantasm, a dream. Petals the color of bright new blood reflected a sudden bloom of pain in his heart. She could have written, he thought. She could have sent word to him privately at the king's winter court, instead of word traveling carelessly from anyone to anyone before it reached him. He hadn't realized, until then, that in her eyes he was just anyone as well. In spite of himself, he raised his head slightly, looked up from under his hood to search the knots of courtiers along the stairs. The scallops along the windblown canopy hid too many faces; he could not find her. He lowered his eyes, found her face again in memory.

Much his return to the summer court mattered to her now, she with her betrothed with his great barking brass horn that bayed so deep it could have drawn whales to the surface to mate with it. She with her head full of water pipes and fountains. No room now for one who had loved her since she was six. Garner made an incautious, despairing movement. The barge shivered; an oar caught a crab, splashed.

"Peace," the oar master pleaded. "Peace. We're nearly there."

"Peace," Edord echoed abruptly, jarringly, "is what we must impress upon the waters of Obelos with our minds, our breath, the rhythms of our hearts. From us it will learn; from us it will—"

"Oh, give it a rest," Garner shouted, exasperated. Somehow he was facing his cousin, not an easy thing to do in a boat crammed with men. Turning, he had shouldered a couple off-balance; they reeled into others; the barge rocked one way and then the other. And then the great crowds on both sides of the river watched with astonishment as the Knights of the Well staggered out of the sides of their barge and tried to walk on water. The wallowing barge scattered its oars, then its oarsmen. The oar master, clutching his gong, fell in last and disappeared entirely as the barge flipped over on top of him.

Garner, descending among the riverweeds, thought he should just settle on the bottom with the snails and stay there. But someone was descending faster than he was within the streaming thicket of weeds. The standard-bearer, he thought in horror, and kicked hard upriver toward him, losing both his boots to the tide. A school of tiny fish flashed past his eyes; it was suddenly hard to see. What he thought was a cloak seemed darker, a cloudy gray shadow fading into the green. He pushed downward. Someone else's falling boot careened off his shoulder. The cloak, billowing and flapping in the current like a live thing, seemed empty as he grew closer, and it began to rise. So did he, with relief, tearing the clinging water weeds away as he pulled toward the light and air and churning bodies above him, beginning to hear his heartbeat in the surging wash of his blood.

He saw the cloak again, suspended in a long, motionless shaft of light. Still it seemed empty, his eyes told him as he passed it. It twisted slowly among the weeds, the hood turning, turning, until its limp emptiness, shaped by the current, opened to Garner's transfixed gaze.

He saw the face in it.

Breath bubbled out of him. He caught himself desperately before he took in water, felt the aching impulse all through his body. Still he hung there, treading water to keep from beginning the long, slow, irrevocable slide, unable to look away from the strange eyes, shell-white and expressionless in a shifting face as green as waterweed.

A struggling mass of boot and wool and limbs came between them. Garner, started again, lost the last of his breath. Then he recognized the standard-bearer, trailing bubbles and looking terrified. Garner reached out, grabbed his hood, and drove them both, with a couple of furious kicks, to the surface. Coming up under the overturned barge, he bumped his head on the edge of the oar master's seat.

He held on to it, heaving for breath. The standard-bearer grabbed hold of an oarsman's plank. Garner, his vision clearing, found himself face-to-face with the indignant oar master. They were surrounded by the swirling cloaks and churning legs of men outside clinging to the bottom of the barge. The weltering tide pulling them toward the sea, the constantly shifting weight on the barge bottom, made breathing difficult for those caught under it. The oar master, gripping his gong with one hand and an oarlock with the other, looked as though he wanted to shove Garner back under the water himself.

"What," he barked, "possessed the mage to choose you?"

Someone outside hoisted himself higher up the barge bottom; the plank the standard-bearer clung to dipped abruptly. He inhaled water, coughing; flailing again, he seized Garner's hair, pushed him briefly down.

Garner hauled them both up again, answered between his teeth, "My cousin would say that I exemplify the chaotic aspect of water."

"Which it is your duty to guard us against!"

"Then the mage must have made a mistake."

"Impossible!" the oar master snapped unreasonably.

Garner rolled an eye at him, still grappling with the standard-bearer, whose sodden hood had slid over his eyes, blinding him. "Then she didn't," he said succinctly. He saw a pair of legs kick away from the side of the barge, and then another. The empty barges must have come to their rescue, he realized with relief, and added, "I might be your greatest hope."

The oar master snorted, inhaled a sudden splash as someone tried to turn the barge over and failed.

"Let go," Garner urged the standard-bearer, who had a death grip with one hand on an oarlock and with the other on Garner's hair. "They've come to help us."

The young man shook his blind head mutely, emphatically.

"Just leave him," the oar master suggested, and vanished under the side of the barge.

Garner treaded water and waited, wondering if the oar master would bother sending anyone to rescue the pair of them.

A little later, as he sat dripping in a fishing boat that had come out to help with the rescue, he saw Damaris finally, on the dock, talking to his sodden cousin, who was gesticulating forcefully. Green she was wearing, the soft pale green of the waterweed dangling over Edord's shoulder. He would be making very clear to her exactly who had caused the Knights of the Well to become one with the river, of that Garner had no doubt. He sighed noiselessly, regretting the absurd incident, except for dunking Edord. Then, beneath the weave and break of light on the water, he saw the strange, rippling underwater face again, the pale eyes alone unmoved by currents, looking back at him within the waterweeds.

He blinked. The face or the memory of it vanished.

One of the water sprites, he guessed, drawn by the odd commotion in the river. The mage would know its name. He raised his eyes from the water again, and saw Damaris and Edord turned away from him, walking up the steps to the palace together. He watched that green until it disappeared within the walls.

In the small, private chamber allotted to him by his rank as knight both of the king and of the Well, he found his baggage and his young squire Inis, who had been attached to him, presumably to learn from Garner's knightly example and experience. Sweet-tempered and capable, he was too polite to comment on Garner's dripping garments, simply helped him out of them and handed him dry clothes. He looked more doubtfully at Garner's bare feet. Garner's family could trace its lineage, in the northern mountains, back past the naming of Obelos. But what with one thing and another, including some disastrous battles with a reigning monarch or two, whom Garner's ancestors considered usurpers, the family had lost its wealth over a century ago.

"Your boots, sir?"

"Water-logged," Garner answered tersely. "The river ate them."

"Your best boots?"

"Yes."

"Well," Inis said, rummaging. "There's your shoes in here somewhere. Ah, and here's your old patched pair of boots, right under them."

Someone pounded at the door.

It was not what Garner expected: his annoyed cousin, or worse, a summons from the king. It was the impossible, what he would have chosen if he had a say in the various possibilities knocking on his door. It was a request from the Minister of Water for his immediate presence.

Lady Damaris Ambre.

Dazed, he put on the boots Inis handed him and followed the messenger.

The minister was in her official chamber, a lofty corner room just beneath the battlement walls. The side casements overlooked the vast gardens behind the castle, the cobbled path leading down the back of the hill to the city below, with its eccentric tangle of streets cautiously edging closer and closer to the river where it curved around the sudden upthrust of land. From the adjacent wall, the view was of the harbor, the sea walls, the immense gates that protected the inner harbor, the brilliant, unending sea. An enormous table filled most of the room, covered with papers with seals and ribbons dangling from them, letters, lists, meticulous drawings of water projects, maps, schedules, sketches of everything from plumbing pipes to gargoyle-headed water taps. A tray holding cups and pitchers of wine and water stood swamped in the clutter like a drowning island.

Damaris had thrown a black work robe over her gown; its sleeves were shiny with ink stains. The long, white gold coil of braid at her neck was beginning to sag, too heavy, too silken for restraints. Leaning over some paperwork on the table, she looked up as Garner entered. The sudden flash of green, the color of river moss, under her heavy, hooded eyelids and pale brows, took his breath away.

She gazed at him a moment, her ivory, broad-boned face the way he remembered it from childhood, open, curious, just beginning to smile. Then she remembered what he was doing there, and the smile vanished. She straightened to her full height, nearly as tall as he, slender and so supple her bones seemed made of kelp.

"Garner," she said in her deep, lovely voice that cut easily through any flow of water or words, "your cousin told me you nearly sank the ritual barge."

"I was told by rumor," he answered recklessly, "that you were betrothed."

"And that has what to do with half-a-dozen gilded oars that went sailing out to sea, and which must be replaced before the ceremony of the fountain?"

"Fountain?" he echoed bewilderedly, wondering how she could be thinking of such mundane details. "What fountain? Of course I didn't mean to overturn the barge."

"Then why did you?"

"I was provoked—"

She held up a hand before he could go on; helplessly he watched a familiar dimple deepen in her cheek as her lips compressed, then quickly vanish. "Never mind. I don't need to know. The water-mage wants to see you. You can explain to her."

Heat surged through him, then, as he remembered the precise moment. His mouth tightened; his eyes went to the sea, where a gull as white as Damaris's brows angled over the dark blue water.

"I was looking for you," he said bluntly, and felt her go abruptly still. "You drew my eyes. You always did. Since I first saw you coming so carefully down those same steps when you were a child, and so was I, come downriver to court in my uncle's company, just docking where you were about to step. You wore green that day, too, and your hair was in the same braid. We met there on that dock. Ever since, I have looked for you there. I was looking today, though I have no right." He looked at her finally, then found her face as stiff, her eyes as distant, as he expected. "My cousin was lecturing. I lost my temper, and unbalanced the boat. For that, I'm sorry. Is this what I must tell the mage?"

Color flushed over her, swiftly and evenly, from collarbone to brow. "That it was my fault?" she asked with some asperity. "Because I forgot—no, because I didn't know how to tell you?"

"No. Of course not. Let's blame Edord."

"I don't understand. What has Edord to do with this?"

"He opened his mouth," Garner said dourly, "at the wrong time."

She studied him a moment, a line as fine as gossamer above her brows. "I love Lord Felden." Her voice had softened; her eyes shifted away from him briefly. "I discovered that he loves me, too. His music has always enchanted me. We have much in common."

"His horn and your pipes?"

She met his eyes again. "You and I have been friends for many years. Can we keep it that way? Or will you swamp boats every time you pass that dock?" He couldn't answer. The unfamiliar secrets within the green, the fine, clean bones beginning to surface in her face since he last saw her, rendered him wordless. She made a sudden, exasperated gesture, trying to brush away his gaze. "Stop that."

"What?"

"Stop looking at me like that. Just stop looking at me. Garner, just go away."

"Why," he asked her with simple pain, "could you not love me like that?"

She swallowed, whispered, "I don't know. I don't know. Maybe—you were too much my friend. My brother. Maybe nothing more or less than that."

"Damaris—"

"No," she told him firmly. "Go. The mage is waiting for you."

"How much of this do I tell her?"

She shook her head slightly, picking up a piece of chalk, worrying it through her long fingers. She didn't look at him again.

"I think she must already know. She sent for you through me. Now I understand why. Whatever she wants with you, it won't be about the mistakes and mysteries and messiness of love, but about the waters of Obelos. Go and find out."

So he did, feeling as shaken as if he had been bellowed at by the king.

❖ ❖ ❖

Someone opened the door. Damaris, staring blindly at the chalk in her fingers and contemplating the messiness and mysteries, flashed a wide, incredulous stare at it. But it wasn't Garner back again with his obstinate, tormented eyes to demand impossible explanations from her. It was a stranger, gestured in by a footman.

"Master Tabbart Ainsley, Minister," he murmured.

"Yes?"

"The composer from Sucia."

She blinked. "Why didn't you take him to Lord Felden?"

"I couldn't find the musicians, my lady," the man explained apologetically. "Everything is chaos with the king's arrival. Master Ainsley said he wrote some water music, so I brought him to you."

Speechless, Damaris gazed at the composer, who looked miserably back at her. His face, framed by windblown chestnut hair, was colorless as curds; he swayed a little under the weight of her regard.

"You are welcome," she assured him hastily. "Please. Sit down."

"Thank you," he said faintly, and the footman closed the door. Master Ainsley crept into the nearest seat, which was her drafting stool, and dropped his face into his hands. Damaris, alarmed, poured a hefty cup of wine, brought it to him.

"Are you ill, Master Ainsley?"

He lifted one hand, eyed the wine glumly, covered his eye again. "I could be cheerfully dead."

"Ah," Damaris said, enlightened.

"In Sucia, I was dragged up a canal in a barge. And then floated down a river along with some goats and chickens and a great many noisy children. When we finally reached the ocean, I thought, with all that blue space, it would be peaceful."

"But no?"

"But yes." He came out from behind his hands finally, and winced at the sight of the sea in the window. "But how could I enjoy it? The ship tossed me this way, threw me that; my bed fell down; my dinner came up. I was never so happy to see land. Your port looks so calm. It barely breathes."

"We struggle for that," Damaris told him a trifle grimly. "That's why we celebrate our victories so lavishly. And why you're here."

The young man reached for the wine, took a cautious sip. The damp fungal sheen on his face brightened to a healthier shade of white. He looked slight but muscular within his untidy traveler's garb; his eyes, going seaward again, had a blue-green hue much like it.

"Look at it," he said bitterly, nodding toward the spiky forest of masts rising over waters separated and calmed by sea gates and walls. "Somewhere among those stripped tree trunks is my torment. Now they hardly move. Like ships in a painting."

"Would you like to rest awhile?" Damaris asked him with sympathy. "Lord Felden is one of the musicians, as well as the director of the court orchestra that is to play your music. I'll find him; he'll know where you'll be lodged."

He smiled at her, a fleeting but genuine effort that brought even more color into his face. "If I'm not needed, I think I would like a walk first. I've been so confined these past days. Perhaps you could direct me to the object of your celebration? I would like to be sure that my music is suitable. I've only seen and heard this wonderful fountain in my imagination. And you know how different they are, all the voices of water."

She found herself smiling back at him, trying to remember what Beale had said about his music. She made a sudden decision, removed her work-robe. "I'll take you there. I want to be sure it will be finished in time, that there are no unexpected problems. I'm afraid you must continue to imagine the sound of it, since the water won't begin to flow until the day of the celebration. Nor has it been seen except by invitation. It's been shrouded in mystery for weeks."

The brisk walk through the royal gardens and out the back gate revived the composer even more. By the time they descended the gentler northern slope behind the castle and reached the streets he grew animated, viewing with energy and curiosity the flower boxes in the windows, the brightly painted doors of houses and shops, the costumes of other visitors. He brought to Damaris's attention tapestries from his own country in a shop window, and stopped now and then to exclaim over one or another of Luminum's renowned arts: delicate glass, lacework, water clocks of elegantly painted porcelain.

"You tell time by water?"

"Everything in Luminum is translated into water. It is the first and last sound we hear."

He made another of his fitful stops at the far end of one unusually straight street, glimpsing another blue horizon, another thicket of water traffic. He turned confusedly, walked backward a pace or two, gazing at the castle on the cliff around which the river curled. "Is Luminum an island?"

"Only on three sides."

He righted himself, gestured down the street. "And that?"

"The Halcyon River."

"More water," he breathed, making Damaris smile again.

"That, we worship. It waters our fields, our animals, our city.

We dedicate monuments to it, build shrines, offer gifts to those who dwell in it. Your music will be among those gifts. It is finished, isn't it?" she asked practically, and was reassured when the composer nodded.

His eyes were on the concealed object in the square ahead of them, where four streets ended at a broad bed of cobbles. Flowering chestnuts shaded the people hurrying under them as intently and single-mindedly as fish pursuing dinner in the deep. It was a motley mix at this end of the city, where ancient cottages shared the waterfront with houseboats and barges flying pennants of laundry, and the market boats darted and hovered like dragonflies over the water to sell a loaf of bread, a dozen oranges, before they flitted away to answer the next summons along the bank.

As they grew closer to the hidden object, Damaris heard the sound of hammering. The shrouds, great lengths of sailcloth, bulged briefly and oddly here and there, poked by mysteries within. The work must be finished, she realized, pleased. The scaffolding around the fountain was being dismantled.

"Minister," murmured the guard, rising from the stool on the cobbles where, with the aid of a book, he was defending the shrouds from entry. There was a shout from within; a sudden ridge in the canvas marked the path of a falling plank, which narrowly missed his head. He ducked, breathing a curse. "Are you sure, my lady, that you want to go in there?"

"You're wearing a helmet," she answered briskly. "Go in and tell them to stop for a moment."

The guard slipped between shrouds. Another plank clattered down; they heard laughter among indignant shouting. Then all was silent. The guard reappeared, held apart the shrouds for them.

"Be careful. There are perils everywhere."

There were indeed, Damaris saw: downed tools, swaying planks hammered half free, clinging to others by a nail, the rubble and dust of the sculptor's final touches to his masterpiece. He was still there, tinkering with the very top of the fountain, while he knelt in the basin below it. He grinned down at the minister, saluting with a brush, half his face masked with marble dust.

There were four broad basins, all scalloped and festooned with carvings. The largest, at the bottom, was a twenty-foot platter of pale yellow marble veined with cream. Three mermaids rose to their scaled hips out of the water in the center of the basin, their upraised arms holding the second basin, smaller by five feet. The exuberance of their poses, their alabaster breasts and dancers' arms, was mitigated by taut muscles the sculptor had chiseled to surface beneath the smooth skin. He knew how hard they worked to hold that ton of marble. Their serene smiles made nothing of it. The basin they held was sea green. Three porpoises, slightly smaller than the mermaids, danced upon the surface of the sea, balancing on their noses the third basin, a pale sky blue. A single rosy fish leaped out of its center, a carp by the look of the sinuous fins, standing on its tail and bearing the highest basin on its head. That carried the emblem of Obelos: the white fluted pillar with the water-blue orb upon it. The carp basin also held the sculptor, who was carefully cleaning the ring of holes in the orb, out of which water would rain in a perfect halo to overflow its basin and cascade into those beneath it.

Master Ainsley, who was staring at the massive stonework, closed his mouth with a click of teeth and lowered his head. The sculptor, blowing softly into the holes, had an ear cocked, Damaris noticed, toward their voices.

"Big," the composer pronounced finally, and added, after considering the matter, "Very big."

"As you noticed, we have a lot of water. Will your music be up to the task?"

"I think"—he paused again, finished cautiously—"I think so. I hadn't expected anything so ornate. I've seen such work in the courtyards and gardens of the rich in Iolea, but never so far north in a city square surrounded by chestnut trees . . . the water will come from the river?"

"No. The source is the pure water of the Well itself. Water was guided from the underground river into a large holding tank; from there, pipes were laid across Master Greyson's hops fields, with concessions for use as irrigation, along a stone archway across the river, and then buried beneath the banks and run under various gardens and streets, and finally the square. Once the fountain is open, the water can be piped into houses all around the square. So you can see why we planned such an elaborate celebration. Many in Luminum still get their water by lugging a bucket down to the river."

She gazed at the great conduit head, the fountain, with satisfaction a moment longer, remembering months and even years of discussions, plans, legal contracts over property, endless papers she read requesting funds to pay for directors, engineers, pipemakers, ditch-diggers, shovels and hoes and wheelbarrows, the ceaseless trail of problems into her office, annoyed citizens, leaky pipes, stolen equipment, miscalculations, and miscreants.

All finished. Even the carp standing on its tail seemed to be smiling . . .

A halo of water shot out of the orb the carp carried. In a heartbeat, the sculptor's face and hair were drenched. A mask of wet marble dust opened its mouth in a silent, astonished O. Damaris, her own mouth open, noted dazedly the single clogged hole in the orb. The water, oddly striated, filled the smallest basin quickly and began to run over its scalloped edge in three orderly cascades around the frolicking carp and the sculptor.

The sculptor shouted an incoherent word that freed Damaris from her transfixed state. She drew a sharp breath and whirled.

"Where is the engineer?" she demanded of the staring workmen.

"What is it doing?" Master Ainsley asked confusedly. "Should it be running now?"

"He went up to the castle to see you," one of the workmen told her. "Said he needed to check something. I thought that's why you came here."

She was silent, pulling a vision of the project plans out of memory. The water had filled the carp basin and was flowing cheerfully down among the dolphins. The sculptor, on one knee in the water and clinging to the carp, was groping for a ladder behind him with his foot. It careened as he kicked. The workmen caught it, steadied it for him. He descended finally, cursing ceaselessly, wet as the carp.

"Go down to the river," Damaris said to one of the men. "Make sure no one is in the discharge drain, and that it is covered. When this starts gushing out the flow will be strong. And you—"

"Why," the sculptor demanded, interrupting his own steady stream, "is the water that color? It should be coming directly from the source waters of the Well."

It was, Damaris saw with horror, turning as brown as mud, or worse: as streams running beneath schools sometimes turned in summer when the water grew shallow and the waste from a hundred students tumbled into it from their simple wooden water closets.

The guard was peering through the opening now, drawn by the noises of water and the sculptor. "Stay here," Damaris told him tersely as his eyes widened. "Don't let anyone in."

"What—"

"Don't say a word about this to anyone."

The composer asked helplessly, grimacing at the murk. "Should I revise my music?"

"Of course not." She seized his arm, tugged him away. "It's a temporary problem. A bit of soil in the water main. Most likely. The engineer will fix it easily. Come back to the castle with me; we'll find Lord Felden so he can begin practicing your music."

"I wrote water music, not mud music," he muttered with one last incredulous glance at it before Damaris pulled him out of the shrouds. "Maybe your Well is running dry."

Damaris closed her eyes briefly. Behind them, she caught an unexpected glimpse of the mage's eyes, the swirling hues of mother-of-pearl opening to look at her, and she felt the skin prickle painfully at the nape of her neck.

"Not possible," she told him adamantly, hurrying him along the ancient, colorful, bustling streets. "Human error. The engineer will find it. All will be well. You needn't mention the incident to the musicians. It might weigh heavily on their playing and your music."

"Water," he sighed. "It plagues me still, even on bone-dry streets. Is it cursed, this fountain?"

"I hope not," she breathed. "We would be forced to revise our lives."

"But it is possible?" he asked so shrewdly that she could not answer, only rush him even more ruthlessly uphill until he had no breath for words.

Within the castle, she delivered him gratefully into the care of her betrothed.

"I've been looking for you," Beale Felden told Master Ainsley. "They told me you had arrived and vanished."

"Lady Ambre kindly took me to see the fountain," the composer answered, and did not elaborate, to Damaris's relief.

"Ah." Beale smiled at her amiably but absently. She could almost see the notes and instruments, the faces of musicians crowded behind his limpid blue eyes. As he, if he noticed, might have seen the pipes and conduits in hers, as well as something of her terror. Fortunately for her, he was not particularly perceptive. That was one of the reasons, along with his fair hair, his amiable temper, his ancient title and wealth, that Damaris had permitted him to court her. He added to the composer, "The musicians are all eager to meet you and see what you've brought us to play for the ceremony."

"I only hope it will be suitable," Master Ainsley sighed; his own eyes seemed to fill with visions of mud.

"I'm sure it will be wonderful," Lord Felden answered. "This will seal your reputation in Obelos." He bore the speechless composer down the hallway. Damaris watched them a moment; Beale seemed to be doing most of the talking. She turned away. She couldn't guard every word the composer said, and, anyway, Beale, if alarmed, would be convinced by the simplest of explanations. A little dirt in the conduit pipe. Easily flushed out. He wouldn't think to wonder who had started the appalling flow in the first place.

She found the engineer pacing as she entered her office; turning abruptly, he nearly bumped into her. They both spoke at once.

"Did you see–?"

"Have you heard–?"

They stopped, studied one another's perturbed faces. The engineer, a lean, muscular, balding man apt to grab a shovel and leap into a trench if work on a project seemed slow, asked tersely, "Is it about the fountain?"

"Yes. Yours?"

"Yes. I was at the river, early this morning, making sure the discharge drain was completely clear before the guard-gate was locked over it. You remember where it is? Parallel to the conduit at that point where it arches across the river near the central bridge–"

"Yes."

"It was just near my head, coming down off the stone archway. So I could hear what was going on inside."

Damaris blinked. "Inside."

"The conduit pipe."

"Nothing," Damaris said after a moment. Her voice shook. "Nothing should have been going on inside the conduit pipe. Why are you here? Why are you not checking the pipe at the source?"

He gazed at her, his brow furrowing. "For what?" he demanded. "What did you see?"

"A great deal of very murky water coming out of the fountain. Isn't that what you heard? Water in flow?"

"No," he said soundlessly. Then he cleared his throat. "I heard voices."

"What?" She stared back at him in horror. "Someone inside the pipe?"

"Singing."

"Inside the pipe?"

"And laughter. Some banging—"

"Children," she whispered, her fingers icy.

"They didn't sound like children. And I couldn't understand a word. Sometimes the pipes themselves seemed to sing. I sent one of the workmen to the Well to check the cap over the conduit pipe, make sure no one had broken the locks on it."

"If any one had opened the cap to enter it, they would have drowned long before they crossed the river. No one would be laughing."

They were silent again; their eyes slid away from one another, neither wanting to glimpse the doubt blooming there.

"Mud," the engineer said heavily.

"Or worse. I couldn't tell. At least it didn't smell. But where could it possibly be coming from? What did the workman say?"

He shook his head. "The cap was sealed in the water as we left it. Nothing seemed amiss." He paused again, asked her diffidently, "Any word from the water-mage?"

"No. Not for me, at least."

His face loosened slightly. "An accident, then, along the pipeline. I'll have the workmen follow it, check for wet or sinking ground. I'll take a look at the source myself."

She nodded briefly. "And your voices?"

"Echoes from somewhere else, they must have been. The river was misty at dawn; I couldn't see clearly . . ."

She drew breath, loosed it silently, and met his eyes again. "That must have been it. Let me know immediately if you find anything."

He bowed his head, left her listening to the bewildering silence from the water-mage.

The water-mage stood listening as well.

In the rocky, sunken cave where the water ran up out of the secret earth, Eada was little more than a bulky shadow in her black skirts and the veil that hid her long silver hair. She might have been a boulder in the jumble of rock that had broken and cascaded down around the Well so long ago that the shards were growing together again, grain by grain, century by century. The water filled its ancient, rounded pool among the stones with only the slightest tremor at its heart, the little flutter in the center of the pool that spoke of the unseen treasure of water buried deep beneath, in perpetual night. Seemingly without end, it pushed itself up into this silent cave with its little circular roof of sky and light; it gleamed a greeting, then passed into darkness again, down a narrow, shallow bed of stones, pushing more quickly now through its ancient waterway to find the light again, beyond the cave, where it bubbled up and pooled beneath the open sky.

That pool was where the city dwellers came to worship. They brought gifts, dropped wishes into it in the form of coins or words written on thin strips of metal. They crowded around it during the ritual, under the first full summer moon. The knights ringed the Well beneath the ground; the king stood on the earth above, drank water from a gold cup, and dropped coins and jewels the color of blood into the wellspring. Near the natural pool above, and fed by it, a great marble tank had been built, a pretty thing surrounded by broad walkways, flowering vines, fluted pillars with little fountains perpetually offering water to the worshippers. Beyond it, the water flowed free again, very briefly, offering itself to insects, mosses and reeds, birds and wild creatures before it dove underground again, vanished back into the dark. Around this open water, the city dwellers watched the ritual, flooding beyond their human boundaries once a year to honor the mysteries of the Well, and to drink, after the king, the pure water out of the earth.

The water welling up out of the underearth made no sound. The water welling up out of the underearth should have made no sound.

The mage, standing in the shadows, kept listening for silence from the sunlit pool. An ancient, familiar silence there should have been in that cave, as old and peaceful as the dark. Instead, there were half-words, like water emptying down a drain; there were hisses, a gurgle like a laugh that echoed against the walls, a sudden splash that left no ripple behind it. The language of water, she recognized. But who spoke? What was said?

She heard a step in the low passageway that led from the well to her dwelling. The walls echoed suddenly, as though a stone had spoken. Eada looked quickly into the water, saw nothing but the insouciant reflection of the sky.

"Mistress, the knight is here," Perla said. She was a slight young girl, the daughter of a market-boater, used to the vagaries of water, who had come to peer into the cave one day and stayed to give the old mage a hand with this or that. She might have been part water sprite, Eada guessed. She feared nothing that poked its head unexpectedly out of the Well, and didn't mind running errands between the underearth and sky.

A hesitant step in the stone chamber beyond told Eada how far the knight had gotten. Her odd experiments, her trifles, had slowed him in her workroom. She played with water in all its forms, even ice in its season. In tanks, she kept strange fish and other river creatures Perla and her friends found; she studied most for a moon or two before she sent them back. Scholars and witches from all over Obelos sent her the odd instrument, the unusual crystal that might interest her.

Perla was hovering, looking, with her pale hair and scant, restive limbs, like she might sprout wings like a dragonfly if she touched the earth another minute. "Shall I stay, mistress? Or shall I go buy bread?"

"Go," Eada said, shooing the sprite away. Eada found her slow way around the stony edges of the pool, and down the passage into her chambers. They were roofed above the earth by domes of stone and wood studded with crystals that caught the daylight and drew it underground in mellow, shimmering shafts. Entering her workroom, the mage found that the knight had indeed been slowed by her playthings; he was toying with a tiny windmill on the table, turning its blades with his forefinger.

"Better to blow it," Eada suggested, and he started.

"I wasn't sure it worked."

"Try it."

He blew gently. The slats turned; the mill wheel, driven by the cogs and pistons within, drew up water from a shallow pan, flicked it into a chute that fed it neatly into a pot of basil.

The knight grunted, almost smiled. But he wasn't in the habit of it; Eada could tell by the clouds that gathered immediately to engulf the simple moment of pleasure. The mage reckoned that she had not been that young in at least a couple of centuries.

He looked at her silently then, uneasily. Well he should, she thought. Living in the water-cavern, she had become a shapeless, bulky thing: a boulder with legs and great slab hands. Her neck had vanished somewhere; her white head balanced on her shoulders. Strange colors had seeped into her eyes from what she had seen. Witch-lights, Perla called them; they fascinated the child. But Garner Slade was not a child; he had a good idea of what was worth fearing.

"Did it speak to you?" she asked, and his eyes widened. He was quick, though; she'd seen that when she chose him.

"No. It only looked at me." He hesitated, ventured a question. "What was it?"

"Something that wanted you to see it. You," she repeated with emphasis. "Garner Slade. Your eyes."

"How did you—how did you know?"

"I was watching, in the Well. I'm mage, so I can do such things with water."

"And you saw—"

"Everything. I see through all your eyes." The knight opened his mouth, then closed it, a red tide rising in his face. "That's how I choose the knights," Eada continued. "I must be able to see. The young man who thinks he dislikes water sees it with such clarity . . . and your cousin loves it, though he might have trouble loving anything human."

"I'm sorry," Garner blurted. "I'm sorry I lost my temper."

"Ah, but look what you found. Look what you saw. Something is wrong in the water world, and we need to know what. Since you were the one to look trouble in the eye, you're the one to help me. If we have offended the water realms, if some strange mage is churning up things better left on the bottom, if the kingdom itself is in danger, we need to know." She turned without waiting for him to answer. "Come."

Perversely, now that she wished to show, to illumine, the Well made no sound; not a ripple or a chuckle disturbed it. The bright face of the pool was blank and still. She waited, the knight a breathing shadow beside her. No one even glanced up from underwater to see who was there. Finally, without comment, she led him back into her workroom, where she rummaged through her books and manuscripts. The knight, looking confused, finally spoke.

"Was there something I should have seen?"

"I couldn't see anything either," she said absently. "They're teasing our eyes; they knew we were looking. They were whispering and laughing all morning before you came."

"Who?" he asked bewilderedly. "Who?"

She showed him.

"I drew these on my travels all around Obelos, when I was young," she said, turning pages slowly in the bound book she had made of her sketches. "I wasn't even a water-mage then. I didn't know that's what I wanted to be. I only knew that I never wanted to be far from water . . . Some of these have been given human names. Others are seen so rarely they have no names in our world."

Many she had drawn from memory, a brief glimpse of the face

within the waterfall, among the flowers along a brook, the shadowy creature swimming with the school of fish. Others she saw clearly; they had human names: the kelpies, the water nymphs, the naiads, and nereids and undines, the mer-people. Some spoke to her in various ways, touching her with pale, webbed fingers, showing alarming teeth in warning, singing to her, beckoning. There seemed a different face for every stream, every pond and branch water. She drew as many as she could find. Some stayed to watch their own faces flowing out of her ink jars onto paper. They knew their human names, and had learned to speak to humans for their own purposes. They did not consider Eada entirely human. They didn't try to entice her underwater or into their arms. They questioned her, gossiped about other water creatures, told her where to find the shyest, the most secretive, the wildest.

They spread her name throughout the water-web of Obelos. When the dying water-mage in Luminum searched for his successor, he heard the water speak Eada's name and summoned her.

"And that's when I finally realized what I am," she told the speechless knight, who was staring at the wide-set eyes and languid mouth of the face peering up from under a water lily. "Now you know what you'll be looking for."

He came to life again. "What?" he asked huskily.

"That one will make you forget your own name when you look at her."

"What is it you want me to do?"

"I need your eyes. I need you to follow the waterways of Luminum, looking for such as these. Look into every rivulet, every puddle, every rain barrel, every place where water gathers. See what you can see. You'll be my eyes; I'll be behind yours, watching, listening. I must know what is troubling the water creatures. Go swimming if you have to. That worked for you earlier."

"The creature seemed more inclined to let me drown than talk to me."

"Well, some are like that. Just do your best. I'll help you in any way I can. We need answers before moonrise tomorrow, or the Ritual of the Well will become the disaster your mishap on the river portended."

"That soon," he breathed.

"And let Damaris know what I've told you to do."

He gazed at her, seeing what she knew he would. "Must I?" he asked a little explosively. "I'm the last man she wants to see. She's the Minister of Water and you're the water-mage. Shouldn't you tell her?"

"I'm hoping you will," she only said. "Be careful of teeth, and don't fall in love with anything water-born."

He drew breath, debated over any number of replies. Then he loosed it with a huff and a toss of his hands, and made his way back out of her caverns and across the threshold of day.

❖ ❖ ❖

Faced with another encounter with the annoyed Minister of Water, Garner found the most labyrinthine path possible back to the castle. Follow the water, the mage had instructed. So he did, beginning with the irrigation ditches along the broad fields beyond the river. Seeing anything in them but gaudy insects and weeds seemed unlikely. The sudden glimpse of a splintered darkness beneath the surface made him start; his horse gave an uneasy snort. Then he saw the blackbird swoop past him, its shadow flying behind it in the ditchwater. The ditch ended at a canal with its sluice gate closed. He rode along the canal for a while. Nothing disturbed the water; nothing spoke. He watched it carefully, remembering that the mage watched as well. Remembering, too, the lovely eyes beneath the lily pad, he could not help looking for them among the clustering green on the still, sunlit water. But nothing beckoned; nothing lured; the only face he saw in the water was his own.

Nearer the river, he dismounted to thread his way at random through the streets of the city. On that side of the river, they fanned evenly away from the water toward the fields. The cross-streets, cobbled with fieldstones, were equally straight. Except for the ancient houses along the bank, this part of the city was newer, tidier, and, he discovered, eagerly awaiting the pipes that would connect it to the massive conduit from the Well, send its water flowing into the houses.

"The minister promised us water by the end of autumn," a tavern keeper told Garner, who had stopped to peer into his rain barrel. It was positioned beneath a clay gutter-pipe; water poured out of the wide mouth of an ornate, hideous face that, despite its chipped nose, reminded Garner of one of the sprites in the mage's book. He gazed with interest into the water. But nothing gazed back at him, with or without teeth. "They have to wait until after harvest to go digging up the fields. I've waited years, but it's hardest to wait that one more season." He paused, watching Garner curiously. "Something your lordship wanted?"

Garner nodded, realizing what. "A dip into your barrel?"

"Help yourself."

Garner filled the cup dangling from its chain, drank, felt the sweet rain branch through him in all its secret rills. *How can I possibly?* he wondered tiredly. *How can I find what the mage needs? I might have just drunk the answer down.*

"They say the Well is as pure as rain," the tavern-keeper commented reverently. "We'll hear it singing from that fountain across the river in a day or two."

Damaris had said something about a fountain, Garner remembered. He let the cup drop. "Is it important, the fountain?"

The man cocked a brow. "Where have you been?"

"With the king at the winter court."

"Ah. Those with pipes and without take their water from the river, even the king. No telling what you might find in it, especially toward the end of summer before the rains come. The fountain will draw its water from the Well itself. Can't get much cleaner than that. Straight out of the bones of the earth . . ."

"Where is this fountain?"

"Just across the central bridge, up the street and in the square.

Nobody's seen it yet. It'll be unveiled and let run after the Ritual of the Well. That'll be something to celebrate."

Garner left him gazing with anticipation in the direction of the square. He continued his meandering way through the streets until one led him to the river, ending at the dock where the market boats loaded their wares. There he could see distant chestnut trees where the streets ended, and the smudged blur of part of some huge thing standing among them, the unwrapped gift to the city. He debated crossing for a closer look. Then he envisioned the Minister of Water with the same impulse at the same time, and the two of them running into one another under a tree. Not only would he be forced to give Damaris the unpleasant message from the mage, he must present her with the last thing she wanted to look at: his face.

He turned instead, went downriver toward the sea, and the place where he had seen the water creature.

That side of the river was wilder, thinly populated; the city tended to cluster around its stronghold and its bridges. Here the fishing boats docked, coming and going with the tide. Here the river quickened as it curved around the headland, broadened to meet the sea. A massive watchtower guarded the castle across the water. Garner had spent some months in it when he was younger, learning how to use his weapons. There was little river traffic now. The fishing boats were still out at sea. The royal dock where Garner had so ignominiously disembarked that morning still ported its pennants and scallops, but the few barges tied there were all empty.

Garner dismounted at the river, stood watching the water while his horse drank. The bank was low there. The water of the little inlet lapped softly along mossy tree roots and tangles of bramble and wildflowers. Afternoon sun lay gently on the shallows, a rumpled cloth-of-gold, stirring languidly in the backwash of deeper currents. The pennants fluttering like colorful leaves across the water drew Garner's eyes. He saw Damaris in memory, several years earlier, coming down those steps to welcome the returning court. Garner, who had accompanied one of the king's knights as his squire, had been transfixed by the sight of her. She had grown quite tall and slender over the winter. She moved like water, he thought. Like kelp, every frond graceful, swaying dreamily to the slightest touch of tide. He felt the moment when her eyes met his. She laughed and waved; he could only stand there, forgetting to move even after the barge had docked.

He drew a soft breath, forced his eyes away. No one stood there now, and anyway, all her welcomes were for someone else. Lord Felden, with his wealth, his horn, his absent-minded humming, his amiable disposition. He gave all his passion to his music, Garner had heard, when news of the betrothal reached the winter court. His mother, who reigned in his rich house south of Luminum, must have reminded him that no amount of copious outpourings of beautiful music would transform itself into an heir to his title and fortune, no matter how hard he blew.

Her eyes met his.

Garner started, feeling the implosion like a silent lightning bolt all through him. Those eyes, as green as river moss, watched him just above the surface of the water. Her pale hair floated all around her like the petals of some extravagant flower. In the next moment he caught his breath. It was not, could not possibly be Damaris, silent as a wild thing, her nose under water, and from what he could see, naked as an eel.

A river creature, he realized, his pulse quickening again. Sunning in the shallows, breathing water like air as she gazed at him. He wondered whether, if he spoke, she would vanish with a twist and a ripple, like a fish.

But he had to risk it. "You startled me," he said.

She lifted her face out of the water then, revealing a familiar, charming smile, a slender neck, the curves and hollows of her shoulders. He wondered if her skin was that golden everywhere.

"I know," she answered. Her voice was light and sweet, a purl of water. She raised her fingers; he saw the webs between them, delicate, iridescent. She pushed lazily at the water, the light. "Come join me."

"I don't dare," he said somberly.

"Then I'll leave you."

"No—don't do that."

"Then come in with me. We'll talk."

That face drew hard at him, so familiar, all its smiles for him, promising all he wanted.

"You're a dream," he breathed.

"So? Don't you take pleasure in dreams?"

Don't fall in love, the mage had warned him, *with the water-born* . . . She was there, he remembered, starting again. In his head, watching out of his eyes. He sighed noiselessly, relieved to have the choice made for him.

"The water-mage sent me," he said carefully. "She wonders if we have offended the water-folk."

She flicked water toward him again, not answering, only looking at him out of that face she must have pulled out of his thoughts. Was her true face, he wondered, what he had seen under the water that morning, watching him?

"If we have, tell us what to do to make amends."

She smiled, raising both hands out of the water, fingers stroking the air like wings, beckoning.

"I'll show you . . ." he heard, but how he couldn't imagine, for she had already vanished.

He stood a moment longer, waiting for her, feeling a curious emptiness, as though it truly had been Damaris and he had turned away from love.

Damaris, he reminded himself, or the mage did, urging him along. Reluctantly, he mounted again, rode to the watchtower dock to summon the ferryman.

A dozen market-boats had ventured down that far; they swarmed around the dock, selling bread, strawberries, cheese, ale and savory pasties to the men in the tower. Garner bought some meat and onions skewered on a stick, and roasted on a little brazier balanced on a shelf on the prow of the boat. It seemed precarious, but fire rode easily over the swell and dip of water. The boatman, his face seamed with an endless labyrinth of wrinkles, lingered at the dock to thread more meat and turn his skewers.

Garner, watching him as he ate, asked impulsively, "Have you seen anything strange in the water?"

"Strange? You mean like mermaids, such?"

"Anything out of the ordinary."

The man shook his head. But his mouth widened into a gap-toothed grin at the same time; he chuckled soundlessly, waving a skewer at the bees. "Only what everybody saw this morning."

Garner felt himself flush, but pursued the matter anyway. "What?"

"You didn't see? It happened near the bridge, where the market-boats are thickest. A man in one of the fancy houses along the river pushed his head out of the vent in his private water-closet, crying that something was in there laughing at him. Then the water-closet slid right down his wall and into the river. For a few moments, we all thought it would float at the head of the king's procession. But it stuck in the mud and got pulled ashore before the king had to see it. The man came out cursing his leaky pipes that had rotted the wood. But a water pipe wasn't what terrified him. You could see that in his eyes."

"What was it, then?"

The old man shrugged. "Water-sprite, likely," he said calmly. "They get frisky sometimes just before the Ritual. We make our living on the water; we've learned to placate them, leave gifts in the river—flowers, beads, floating candles, little carvings—so they don't toy with our boats. But I've never seen them go that far before. Up pipes and into someone's house."

Garner finished his meal hastily, disturbed, and rode to the shallows beside the dock, where the ferryman, a lean man with his head hooded against the wind, sat alone on his raft, watching the currents.

"Between tides," he remarked cryptically. "Easy journey."

Garner led his horse on; they were the only passengers. The ferryman glanced up and down for traffic, then gave a cry. High-pitched, inarticulate, it sounded across the river like some wild water bird calling to another. At the royal dock a giant spool began to turn. A pair of ropes attached to the front of the raft rose slowly through the water to the surface and tautened. Another spool turned on the watchtower dock, loosing the raft cables. Garner felt it begin to move.

The ferryman plied his pole, kept the raft from drifting. Garner stood stroking his horse, watching the great stone pile loom above them until it filled the sky. Its shadow slid over them, mid-river.

"She get the message yet?" the ferryman asked, shifting his pole.

"She—" His thoughts had strayed; he couldn't imagine what they were talking about. "The water-mage?"

The ferryman flashed him a glance. "The mage. The minister. Either." Garner stared at him. He looked back, long enough this time to give the knight a clear view of his spindrift face, his shell-white eyes. The ferryman smiled then, a quick, tight smile. "Guess not."

The cables on one side of the boat snapped, whipped the water with a vicious hiss. Garner ducked, clinging to his horse's reins. On the other side, the rope dipped underwater, pulling the raft down with it. He felt his boots fill again with water. The raft tilted like a door opening into the riverworld and he went through it for the second time that day.

Beale would not go away. Damaris, desperate to find her engineer again and inquire about the fountain, kept seeing her betrothed in her doorway, no matter how many times she paced around the table. His pleasant, thoughtful voice went on and on; his eyes, seeming to follow her spiral path, saw nothing disturbing in it; walking around and around a table must be simply what she wanted to do.

"Chairs," he said, "for fifteen musicians. The little gilt ones. To be placed, I think, beside the fountain and facing it. The music is, after all, a gift to the fountain. Don't you agree? The king, I believe, is planning to step out of the royal barge near the square and proceed up one of the streets to the fountain. I'm not sure who else will make up the procession. The musicians, of course, will not come down by water. The Minister of Ceremony has not yet decided exactly when to unveil the fountain: before or after the king's arrival. In either event, the musicians will already be there. I don't think I've told you this: Master Ainsley plays a very sweet flute and will be joining us to perform his own composition for the first time."

Master Ainsley, Damaris thought, chilled. Who must still wonder if he'll be playing mud-music.

"Beale," she said desperately.

"Not to leap ahead, since there are so many details to consider, but I am so much anticipating our journey after the celebration to my estate, where you will finally meet my mother. As I've told you, she's much too frail to make the journey to Luminum."

"Beale."

"She is eagerly awaiting our arrival. So is my sister, who used to be one of the king's musicians until our mother's health—"

"Beale!"

He stopped, seeing her finally, his fair brows raised. "What is it, my love?"

"If—if there should be—if something should go wrong—"

"What could possibly go wrong? You're intelligent, wonderful, young enough to bear twenty grandchildren for my mother, your family and history are impeccable, you look like a water-nymph, my mother will adore you."

She closed her eyes, tried to keep her voice steady. "I meant with the fountain."

"The fountain. What could go wrong with the fountain? You

let the water flow; it comes out the holes; we play. Simple as breathing."

She opened her eyes, saw, over his shoulder, a bad dream coming toward her down the hall, its bare feet squelching watery footprints on the marble. She gave a hiccup of astonishment, and closed her eyes again, hoping it might go away.

"Beale. Excuse me, but I must find my engineer."

"There is such a charming analogy between the holes in the fountain, and those in our instruments," he said with sudden enthusiasm. "Don't you think? One flowing water, the other music; both necessary for life, I would argue, though no amount of music would—now, I wonder, could an instrument be fashioned that could flow with both water and music at once? What would it look like? Surely—"

The face of the nightmare was beside him now: the Knight of the Well running water like a leaky pipe. His dark eyes were furious, but that she understood. It was the fear in them that brought her fingers to her mouth. Be careful, she pleaded silently to him. Be discreet.

Beale turned; even he must have felt the exudations of emotions and dampness. He stared, amazed, at the knight. "You seem to be dripping."

"I fell in the river," Garner said shortly, and otherwise ignored him, holding Damaris's eyes with his disquieting gaze.

"Again?" she said through her fingers.

"The ferryman tossed me in. This was after I spoke to the nymph—"

"Stop," she said sharply, and, to her relief, he veered away from that.

"I have a message for you from the water-mage."

"Nymphs and water-mages and Knights of the Well," Beale murmured. "Sounds like a tale that should be set to music. Does it not? A small, perfect cycle of compositions—"

"Beale," Damaris interrupted explosively, "I must hear Eada's message in private. Please."

"Oh." He glanced with surprise at the doorpost against which he leaned. "Of course." He moved himself, but only to advance with a touch of deliberation into the room, where he positioned a kiss firmly on the cheek of his betrothed. "Come and tell it to me when you're finished here." He left finally, passing Garner with a careless nod and a laugh. "You must tell me your nymph story in more detail later. Don't forget."

"Come in and close the door," Damaris said tightly. "Don't drip on my papers. Tell me what the mage said."

"Something is wrong in the waterworld. She sent me searching everything from ditchwater to the river to find out what. She told me to tell you this."

"She did."

"Do you think I wanted to come back here?" he demanded. "To interrupt your intimate conversation with Lord Felden? To make a fool of myself drenched and barefoot in front of you both?"

"No," she admitted. "Anyway, it wasn't very intimate. Anyway," she said more firmly, "what did you mean about the ferryman? He had an accident, taking you across the river?"

"It wasn't an accident, and he wasn't human."

"Oh," she whispered.

"He sank the ferry deliberately. I nearly got kicked by my horse flailing in the water before I could grab its mane. We swam across together. I didn't have a chance to question anything among the waterweeds. I lost my boots. Again. Whatever is going on among the water people is becoming dangerous to humans."

"Well, did you find anyone to ask?"

"I asked the water nymph. She just looked at me out of your face and refused to answer."

Damaris felt behind her for the edge of the table, held on. "My face," she said faintly.

"You had been on my mind," Garner sighed. "I think she– whatever it truly was–must have seen it in my thoughts."

"I see." She chose words carefully, as though they were stones across a swirling current. "You didn't–I've heard such nymphs are–are difficult to resist."

"Of course she was," he said bluntly. "But I also had a water-mage looking out of my eyes, and after this morning, I was wary of going anywhere near you. Or anything that looked like you. I didn't want to come here now. But I'm beginning to be afraid for Luminum."

"Yes." Her fingers tightened on the wood. "So am I. We had what looked like muddy water coming out of the fountain earlier today. Before anyone had uncapped the conduit pipe at the Well."

He gazed at her silently, some of the anger in his eyes yielding to bewilderment. "Do you have any idea why?"

"Because we have run pipes out of the Well itself?" she guessed. "But we began the project years ago, and nothing has bothered us until now." She paused, eyeing his plastered hair, his sodden clothes, his naked feet. "Garner, be careful. They seem to be using you as a–a conduit for their messages."

"Yes," he said quickly. "The ferryman asked me if you had gotten it."

"What?"

"The message."

She felt the blood leave her face. "He said that. If I had–"

"The mage or the minister," Garner amended himself. "I assumed he meant the Minister of Water. Maybe not." He moved restively. "I need to get out of these wet clothes and continue my search. Do you have any suggestions? You know the waterworld as well as any human can."

"I'm beginning to feel that I don't know it at all . . . I may understand more after I speak to the engineer. But, Garner, what will you do for boots?"

He shrugged. "Steal a pair from my cousin."

"Be careful," she said again, and he looked at her a moment, silently.

"You be careful, too," he warned, and followed his own soggy path back out.

Soon after that, she received the first message from the engineer. He had checked the conduit-line from fountain to Well, and seen nothing amiss. But something, he assured her, was. On that disturbing note, he ended, but she didn't have long to wait before the next messenger came, and the next. Garner's was not the only sodden body to appear in her office. Sprites had invaded the water pipes of Luminum, and they showed no respect, not even to the king, whose luxurious water-closet, fitted with cushions, scented linens, and bowls of flower petals, had somehow popped its ornate taps completely off to spew river water all over the carpets. There were similar disasters throughout the city, in those houses and inns fortunate enough to have private systems. The harassments extended beyond pipes, Damaris learned. Fishers found their boats immobile in mid-current, or completely overturned. Sluice gates between canals and irrigation ditches were randomly opened or shut, causing herds of pastured animals to find themselves shank-deep in water. Mill wheels ground to a halt for no reason anyone could see. Damaris, fearing for the dikes, sent riders out to check for breaches. The harbormaster came himself to tell her that a dock had floated out to sea.

"Why," she demanded incoherently of him, "can't they just put it into words? Why must water speak for them?"

"I don't know, Minister," he sighed. "I'm only hoping the seagates don't start talking."

Beale wandered back in the midst of all this to invite her to the rehearsal, after supper, of Master Ainsley's music. She stared at him incredulously, then remembered what he was talking about.

"Music. Yes. For a little while. But Beale—"

But he was already leaving, trumpeting, in his resonant baritone, what must have been the horn section to Master Ainsley's piece.

She saw Garner again finally, taking his place belatedly among the knights in the hall for supper. He was still alive, and he looked dry; other than that she couldn't draw conclusions. She watched him, hearing Beale only when he stopped speaking. Then she would shift her attention quickly back to him.

"Beale," she said carefully, during one of his brief silences. "Are you aware of the water problems in the city?"

He shook his head. His eyes, she realized suddenly, were on the knights' table also. "You seem distracted," he murmured, in a rare moment of discernment she could have done without.

"I am," she said quickly. "I have been hearing all day long about disturbances, restlessness in the water."

His face cleared; he asked with a sudden chuckle, "You mean the king's water-closet?"

"Yes, that, too. And—"

"I heard they had to bail out the royal bedchamber before the water was stopped. You keep staring at that knight. The morose one with no manners."

"He's a Knight of the Well, on the water-mage's business. I need to talk to him after supper. I'm beginning to be very worried."

"Oh," he said complacently. "Is that all. I was beginning to think—no matter. It's probably just a storm."

"What?"

"The weather seems to be changing. I heard the wind rise as I came to supper. An early summer storm, nothing more; it will no doubt blow over by morning." She opened her mouth just as he pushed back his chair and stood up. "I beg your pardon, my dear, but we have so little time to practice. You will join us, won't you, before too long? You must hear Master Ainsley's composition; it is wonderful. The voice of water itself . . ."

She had to wait for Garner until the king and his nobles rose from the dais table; then the knights were permitted to leave. Garner, watching for her, came to meet her as the elegant court swirled around the king to welcome him. He looked exhausted, she thought, as well as a bit wild-eyed, haunted by sprites.

"Anything?" she demanded.

He shook his head. "Nothing that makes any sense. Fountains

refused to flow, or poured like waterfalls all over the streets. Rain barrels overflowed as though they were fed by secret springs. Public water-closet doors stuck fast; I helped tear several open to free those trapped inside. Pipes leaked; people were chased out of their houses by water."

"Did you meet any other water creatures?"

"I heard them singing out of buckets people dropped on their way back from the river. I searched along the river, and on my way to the Well. But, perversely, they hid from me."

"You saw Eada again?"

"I tried to, but she was nowhere to be found, either. I saw your engineer."

"More than I did," she said grimly. "Did he have any messages for me?"

"Only that he could find—"

"Nothing amiss," she guessed, and he nodded.

"He told me to tell you that the fountain was clean, completely dry. The scaffolding is down; the debris cleared; the work is ready to be unveiled."

"If we dare," she sighed. "Well. That's something."

"A trick," he suggested somberly.

"Maybe. But if anything goes wrong, it will go wrong first tomorrow night at the Ritual of the Well. They won't wait for the water-music the day after." He was silent, so completely baffled, she saw, that he had forgotten to be angry. She added, "At least you didn't fall in the river again."

"Maybe I should," he murmured. "Maybe I should go back, find that nymph with your face and listen to what she has to tell me."

"Lies," Damaris said succinctly. "Like her face."

He was silent again, blinking at her out of heavy, bloodshot eyes, as though he couldn't remember the difference between the minister and the nymph. She shifted abruptly; he raised his hand to his eyes, rubbed them wearily.

"I'm too tired to think. I'm going to rest a little, for as long as the mage will let me."

"Let's hope the night will be more peaceful than the day."

She went to the music room, where the musicians, Master Ainsley, and Lord Felden sat on their gilt chairs in ranks according to their instruments. Beale smiled at her, pleased.

"Welcome, my lady. We are just about to go over it again."

Damaris sat down. He lifted his horn and nodded his head. As they played the first light, charming flurry of falling water droplets, she heard the storm begin.

A summer storm, Beale had said. Warm, noisy, clearing by morning. But nothing was predictable that day, not even water coming out of a tap. Damaris left as early as she could, throwing Beale an apologetic smile without quite meeting his eyes. In her office, she studied the tide tables. Rare for a summer storm to be destructive. As rare, she thought dourly, for a water bucket to sing. And that night the moon was nearly full, the tide would be high, and late, and everyone would be sleeping as it rose . . .

She made her decision, wrote a note, affixed her seal of office, and sent it to the harbormaster.

Close the sea-gates now.

The mage heard the first falling notes of rain on the river, on the sea. She was a shadow beside the Well, night-dark, motionless as the ancient tumble of stones around her. Her blank gaze was fixed upon the water. She saw nothing; she saw everything. Her mind was a fish, a ripple, a current running here, there, everywhere: through pipes, along ditches, in ponds, canals, down the river flowing to the sea. She listened, wondered, watched.

Snatches, she heard: underwater whisperings. Brief as the gurgle of water down a drain, some were, and as coherent. But she had been water-mage for many decades. She understood the ways of water creatures, and many of their words. When she

didn't understand, she went farther, her mind seeping into another like water, filling every wrinkled crevice of it until she saw,
she spoke, she understood.

What she guessed at last amazed her.

Her surprise cast her thoughts back into the still old woman
she had left at the edge of the Well. For a long time she sat there,
contemplating the fragments of this and that she had pieced together. A word repeated many different ways, an odd detail washing up against another, an underwater face seen through as many
kinds of eyes as were in the water, now a colorless blur, now a
bright, startling mosaic of itself repeated in a single eye, now as
nearly human as it could get . . .

"Well, I never," the mage said in the dark, and a little later,
"All this fuss . . ."

The Well turned suddenly vivid, bone-white, as though the
moon had fallen into it. The mage gazed at the water, astonished
again. Then the thunderbolts pounded all around her, trying to
shake apart the boulders. She drew fully into herself for a moment, hearing the rain hiss down through the open roof onto the
Well; then she felt it. She grunted; her thoughts slid back into the
water. She rode the river current down until down became up as
the salt tide pushed upriver. She borrowed bodies, then. There
were many, she realized, and all swimming against the tide, making for the sea.

She saw it as they did: the massive gates across the harbor,
sluice gates lowered, hinged gates fashioned to open outward
with the outgoing sea and close fast when needed, with the help
of the incoming tide. The tide had barely begun to turn, but they
were already shut.

She came slowly back to herself, feeling as though, between
rain and river and sea, she must be wet as a puddle. She whispered, as she pulled herself to her feet, balancing on one stone,
then another, "Good girl."

She moved through the torch-lit cavern of her workroom,
into the chamber beyond, which had a bed, and a hearth, and

warm, dry clothes. She put them on, and moved into the tiny kitchen. She found Perla there, windblown and barefoot, stirring something savory in a pot over the fire.

"The knight came, Mistress."

"Did he?" She warmed her hands, remembering him like a dream: the knight looking into her cave, she seeing nothing out of his eyes. "Did he leave a message?"

"No."

"What are you doing here, child? Didn't you see the rain coming? You should have scampered home."

Perla answered only with a brief, wild grin at the thought that storm should be something to avoid. She brought Eada a bowl of stew, bread, and some late strawberries. The mage ate absently, mulling over what she had glimpsed underwater.

"Who's to say?" she inquired finally, of nobody, she realized. The child had gone somewhere, maybe home, maybe out to watch the lightning. "Not I," she answered herself, and rose with sudden energy to clear the table. "Not for me to say . . ."

For a long time then, she sat beside the Well, half-dreaming, half-dozing. She heard rain dripping off reeds and waterweeds, dimpling ponds, sighing in gusts over the restless sea. In her thoughts, or her dreams, she allowed herself to be carried along by impulses. They went against the tide, she realized: push against flow, drive against mindless drag. Mute and innocent as a polliwog she went along, seeing little beyond a silken, singing dark running against the tide. Then the tide caught the shadowy travelers, sent them swirling, tumbling in its grasp, flung them toward stones, toward the moon. They melted down, fingering themselves between stones, slithering, flattening themselves, easing around, sliding under vast slabs of wood, finding ways through the heave and swamp of tide, clinging, climbing, up and over, into the calm on the other side.

And then they began to push back at the tide.

Eada woke as though she had heard, across the city and river and fields, the sound of moored ships banging recklessly against the wharves, straining at their cables, masts reeling drunkenly, swiping at one another.

She opened her eyes, just as she felt Damaris, in her own bed, open hers, stare into the suddenly chaotic night.

Damaris, the mage said to her. *They have opened a gate.*

"I can hear it," Damaris said aloud. The mage, riding her mind, looking out of her eyes as she sprang out of bed, felt the cold stones under her feet and the slap of wind and rain as she pushed a casement open.

In the harbor, ships and boats heaved and tumbled on a tide that was trying to tear away the wharves. Some, anchored in deeper water, had already begun to drift, meandering a choppy, heedless path toward other ships, toward warehouses and moored boats. Little rain-battered blooms of fire moved quickly along the harbor's edge; some met to confer, parted again; a few vanished, doused under a wild burst of tide.

The great harbor bell in its massive tower began to boom a warning, accompanied by the high, fey voices of ships' bells careening madly in the waves.

I'll be right there, Eada told the Minister of Water, and was, quick as a thought, far more quickly than any of the Knights of the Well her thoughts had galvanized awake along the way.

The tide was still dancing its way into the open gate, which trembled mightily under the onslaught, but couldn't bring itself to close, locked, as it was, in the grip of many invisible hands. The sprites recognized the mage, who was barely visible, and who looked more like a battering ram than herself. She wedged herself against the gate and pushed back at them: an enormous snag caught against the gate, her feet its root ball in the sand, her head and shoulders its broken trunk rising above the weltering. She could hear the hisses and whispers in the rain, the spindrift.

"You'll have to sort things out another way," she told them. "Drowning Luminum will not explain anything to humans."

The longboats were casting off from the wharf, rowing against the tide. Some of her knights were among them, the strongest, the most fearless, straining against the surge to reach the gate. Their boats rode low under the weight of huge chains, which they would lock into the iron rings on the inner side of the gate, so their pulling could help the tide push it shut.

If the water-mage could only coax it free from the stubborn grip of the waterworld.

She saw, in a vivid flash of lightning, the world out of Garner's eyes as he rowed.

The sprites have gotten hold of it, she told him. *That's what you must pull against.*

She gave him a crazed glimpse of the formless swarm inside the gate jamming it open. Eada felt their strength pitted against her power. The power of persuasion would be even stronger, she thought, if only she could think of what to say.

And then she knew.

How they understood something shaped like a battered old tree trunk, she wasn't sure. Maybe they just picked the impulse and the image out of her head. *Take what you want at the Ritual of the Well,* she told them. *Until then, let the city be.*

The gate shifted; the tree trunk slid. They were gone, she realized. Vanished like the last thinning rill of a wave into sand. Water pushed the gate; the men pulled their chains, plied their oars. The trunk, angled sharply now, and underwater, prodded at the gate as it moved a few more feet. The gate closed finally; tide built against it, but could not enter. The tree trunk, finally level, floated to the surface and vanished as well.

Garner, standing at the prow of one of the longboats, struggling with wet, numb hands to unhook all the chains from the ring, nearly fell overboard yet again when the mage appeared beside him. She freed the chains easily, and passed them back into the boats alongside them. Garner stared at her, worse for the wear, she noted, thoroughly soaked again, and just waking as from a nightmare.

"What happened?" he asked hoarsely. "We couldn't budge that gate."

"I made a bargain."

The boat lurched, turning; he tumbled into a seat, took up his oars. Eada sat in the prow on the pile of chain; the knight's incredulous eyes were telling him there was no room, between him and the pile of chain, and the sea, for anything bigger than a broom straw.

"Or a shadow," she told him.

"What?"

"I need you to do something for me."

"Now?"

"Well, no, not exactly at this moment. When it seems appropriate. You know far better than I how these things go."

He pulled his oars, blinking rain out of his eyes, as though, if he could see her more clearly, she might make more sense. "Exactly what kind of bargain did you make?"

"We've got something they think is theirs. I told them they could have it back at the Ritual."

"And you want me to—"

"Find it." She put a weightless hand on his shoulder, patted it. "Don't worry. Just go along as you do. How do humans put it? Follow your heart." He stared at her, his mouth hanging open to any passing wave, as she nodded. "Oh, and tell the Minister of Water what I've just told you. That's all."

Above his head, she saw that the winds were busy shredding cloud, uncovering stars, and then the glowing moon, which illumined the tattered roil, turning cloud to silk and smoke before everything blew back into black.

"But I have no idea—"

"Magic," the mage breathed, enchanted, and vanished.

❖ ❖ ❖

Garner fell into the sea and woke.

He pulled himself out of the dream of dark, cold, weltering

water, and blinked at his squire, who was reverently examining the ceremonial garb.

"For tonight, sir," he told Garner, who needed no reminding.

He sat up, holding his head together in both hands, while pieces of the extremely early morning's adventure came back to him. What had the mage said to him? Something he was supposed to find? Something he was supposed to tell Damaris . . . he groaned softly.

Inis murmured sympathetically, "A short and noisy night, sir . . . at least you didn't lose your boots this time. My boots." He brought Garner a cup of watered, spiced wine, and added, "Your ritual tunic has a couple of stains on it, but only in the back, and your cloak will cover them. Everything's dry, now."

"Let's hope it stays that way," Garner muttered. "See if you can get me a pair of boots made by this evening, and you'll have yours back."

"Yes, sir," Inis answered simply, having grown used to the vicissitudes of knightly endeavor, especially Garner's.

"Do I have anything decent left to wear? I have to talk to the Minister of Water." He saw the rare trace of anxiety cross his squire's face. "Have you been hearing tales?"

Inis nodded. "From everywhere in the city. And even in the palace. Your cousin, Sir Edord, was found climbing into the well near the stables yesterday. He said a woman was calling to him, and he had to rescue her. He fought, but they managed to pull him out before he got far."

Garner, musing over possibilities, breathed, "Pity . . ."

"Sir?"

"The mage spoke to the water creatures last night while we were having a tug-of-war over the sea-gate. She made some kind of truce with them. Things will be much quieter today."

"And the Ritual?" Inis prodded shrewdly.

Garner shook his head, completely mystified. "All we can do is trust that the mage knows what she's doing."

He couldn't begin to guess what Eada wanted him to find. All he could do was send a page ahead to request an interview with the Minister of Water, and hope that the mage had revealed a few more details to Damaris. The Minister of Water, summoning him immediately to her office, seemed neither surprised nor displeased to see him. She hadn't slept much, either, he guessed; her braid was becoming unraveled and her eyes seemed huge, luminous.

"Eada told me to give you a message," Garner said.

"Another one?" she marveled. "Why doesn't she speak to me?"

"I have no idea."

"She wants you to speak to me," Damaris answered herself promptly. "But why?" She gazed at him, as perplexed as he; he restrained himself from taking the braid she was picking apart out of her restless fingers, and folding her hands in his own to calm them.

"I don't know. She said that we have something the water creatures think belongs to them. She promised that, if they left Luminum in peace until the Ritual, they could claim it then." He paused. She was absolutely still now, her eyes lowered, her fingers motionless. "Oh," he added, remembering, "and she wants me to find this thing. Whatever it is. Do you have any idea what she's talking about? Where do I begin to look for this nameless, vital thing?"

She raised her eyes finally. "Why you?" she asked again, her brows crumpled, her tired eyes trying to look so deeply through his that he wondered if she were trying to find the mage in his head.

"Because we have known each other most of our lives? Because I can hide nothing from you, so if I know something that will help us, you will know it, too? Because, despite all my blunderings and rashness, there is nothing I wouldn't do for the Minister of Water? I don't know. Is any of that likely?"

She swallowed, looked down again, quickly. "As likely as it is unlikely."

"What should I do?" he pleaded. "Where do I begin? It must

be something that the water creatures want badly, judging from the ways they have been harassing us."

"And why now?" she wondered. "What's different now?"

"You're betrothed." She stared at him. "I'm sorry," he said hastily. "I'm sorry. It was the first thing that leaped into my head. Of course, that has nothing to do with water."

"Garner—"

"You have every right to please yourself, and I have no right to torment you about your decisions. I promise I will stop. Just tell me where to go, what to look for—"

"I don't know!" she cried, so fiercely that he started. "I don't know. Garner, just go away and look for something. Anything. I have to think." He opened his mouth. She shook her head wildly and he closed it. "If I think anything useful at all, I will send for you, I promise. I promise. Go."

So he went, following the paths of water as he had the day before, hoping at every moment for a whisper from the mage, a message from the minister. Both were silent. So were the water people, he realized as the day passed. Water behaved like water in pipes and buckets, stayed mute and did not sing. Fountains splashed with decorum; sluice gates remained as they were set; mill wheels turned placidly. Everyone waited, Garner felt.

But for what?

At dusk, he returned to the palace to dress. Inis gave him new boots, buckled his sword belt and brightly polished spurs, pinned the bright silver disc of the moon that drew all waters onto his cloak. They joined the other knights and squires in the yard where the procession was forming behind the king.

The townspeople lined the streets, carrying torches and drinking vessels. They were subdued, murmuring, laughing only softly, for the Ritual was ancient, vital, and, the previous day had warned them, by no means predictable. After the king, his consort, his courtiers, the royal knights and the Knights of the Well with their torch-bearing squires had all passed, the townspeople fell in behind them. The procession grew slowly longer and longer, a river of people flowing down the twining streets of the old city, past the shrouded fountain in the square and across the bridge to the broader streets that changed, beyond Luminum, into the wide, rutted, uncobbled wagon roads between the fields.

Garner rode silently, his eyes on the gentle uprise ahead, already marked by torches thrust into the earth around the opening above the Well. It was growing very dark. The pillars and walkways of the outer pool were lined with fire as well, where the city folk would gather to drop their gifts and wishes, and dip their cups to salute the moon. The full moon, rising in leisurely fashion out of the sea, had been following the procession for some time, arching higher and higher among the stars. By the time the king and the knights gathered around the Well itself and began the ritual, the moon would already be regarding its own perfect reflection in the water beneath the earth.

The king reached the hillock finally and drew aside. Courtiers, warriors, and city folk all waited, while the Knights of the Well dismounted and filed underground through the mage's doorway. Eada drew them one by one to their positions around the Well. No one spoke, not even Edord, who usually had some appropriate exhortation ready for the occasion. Even he looked apprehensive, Garner noted, after his adventure with the nymph in the stable well. Garner himself wanted nothing more than to drown himself in the nearest tavern until dawn. He had found nothing; neither mage nor minister was speaking to him; he foresaw nothing but disaster.

The king's face appeared in the water beside the moon. He stood above them on the stony crown of the hill, alone between water and moon; torches on either side of him illumined his face. He would address the Well, giving thanks for the generosity of its waters, pay tribute to the moon that drew such pure waters out of the earth. Garner heard a quick intake of breath beside him, from the newest of Eada's knights. He was seeing for the first time the gathering faces of the underwater creatures, blurred, distorted, many of them paler than the moon, or tinged the colors of water.

Garner looked down at them morosely. They didn't look happy, either, the way they milled and turned in the water, flicking so close to the surface that they left ripples in the peaceful pool. If they had been human, he would have said they were pacing.

Eada murmured something incomprehensible. Water splashed back at her, an unprecedented occurrence. The king had just begun the traditional phrases, which had lengthened, like the night's procession, through the centuries. Along with dropping the first words into the Well, he dropped a handful of gold coins, and a carefully faceted jewel. They fell in a rich little shower, lightly pocking the water.

The jewel shot back out of the water, smacked him on the shin.

He stopped mid-word, dumbfounded. His face, above his golden beard, grew bright, somewhere near the color of the jewel. He looked torn between continuing the Ritual and fuming at his water-mage, who was just standing there, as near as Garner could tell, doing nothing. A gold piece ejected next from the water, struck a rock beside the king with a tiny, musical clang. Another, cast higher, was caught in mid-air. It seemed as though the moon itself had reached out long white fingers to claim it.

It was the Minister of Water, moving into the torchlight. The king stared at her, as did the knights; even the moon seemed to take more than a passing interest in the proceedings.

The king found his voice first.

"Lady Ambre," he said brusquely. "Why are they rejecting our gifts? Can you explain?"

She nodded. Garner, seeing again the green-eyed, foam-haired nymph in the river, felt his heart twist like a fish in his chest.

"My lord," she said ruefully, "I believe they want your Minister of Water to acknowledge her heritage." The king's brows tangled; his mouth dropped. "I don't," Damaris continued, "entirely understand the disturbance, but if it will ease the tensions between our worlds, I will claim my connection with both. My mother is human. My father, evidently, is some kind of water creature. Since I have no markings of the water-born, only a fascination with water-works and an ability to spend an impossible amount of time under water, I was able to conceal that side of me. Until now. Now, before you all, I claim the water-born as my kin."

The king closed his mouth wordlessly, looked again into the Well, where the accumulated coin of countless rituals, tossed lightly out of the water, caught fire as they fell, and were tossed again, as quickly as they hit the water, like a little golden rain of cheers.

"They seem," he observed cautiously, "to be pleased with that. But why now? Why disturb the entire city of Luminum over this? Why ravage my water-closet?"

"My lord, I do not know."

"Eada?"

She shook her head. "Nor I. Shall I ask them?"

"Please," said the king. But it was not his answer she wanted. The water-mage gazed at the Minister of Water, one sparse brow cocked questioningly. Damaris looked down at her silently, her face as expressionless as the moon watching over her shoulder. They were speaking to one another again, Garner realized. And about time.

Damaris came to life again, answered the water-mage with a little, decisive nod. "I'll go to them," she said. "I owe them that courtesy."

Then she was gone, gliding down a shaft of moonlight, it seemed, to fall with scarcely a ripple into the water. The king gave a cry; Garner managed to swallow his. He froze, his eyes on the thin, fading ripples crossing the moon's reflection. Nothing, he decided, could make him move; he would stand there, watching the dark water, turning himself to stone if need be, until she returned to earth.

"Where did she go?" the king demanded. "She'll drown!"

Eada patted the air, as though his head were beneath her hand. "Hush, my lord," she said. "I'm listening."

"To what?"

"To them talking. She doesn't understand their words; I must translate what I can."

"But—"

"Shh."

The king was silent finally, staring into the Well, as they all were, and then at the mage, then back at the water, trying, as they all were, with his fixed attention to raise a sign of life from it. Garner, unblinking and scarcely breathing, grasped at what he could understand of the mage's language: her quick nod of comprehension, followed by suddenly raised eyebrows, and then a mew of surprise. *What?* he shouted silently. *What?* But nothing. Yet. The knights waited soundlessly beside him, as though if they listened hard enough they might hear, within the trembling waters of the Well, the language far older than their own.

Finally, a pale, wet head appeared above the water. Damaris drew herself out onto the rocks with such ease and grace she seemed scarcely human. Garner saw the water nymph again, and felt his own powerful urge to walk across water to join her. Shifting around him, unsteady breathing, told him he would not be alone.

Then she shivered slightly and turned human in his eyes.

"Well?" the king asked harshly, unsettled himself, it seemed, by this vision of his capable Minister of Water.

"My lord," Damaris began, then gave up, gesturing helplessly to Eada. "I understood so little. Except that they were pleased that I had come to meet them in their own world."

"Yes, they were," the water-mage answered. "Very pleased."

"What did they say?" Damaris and the king asked together.

"They told Damaris that her father has found his way back to the great deep from which all things flow and to which all return."

"I guessed that," she said softly. "I am sorry. I would like to have known him. I was never brave enough to admit his existence before."

"Well, it seems that he was the powerful ruler of the realm beneath the river. He has many children, and since such water creatures like their rulers to live a long time, it is the youngest child, not the oldest, who inherits the realm. That would be you."

"Me," Damaris said blankly.

"Yes."

"But I can't—I could never—"

"Of course not. You'd not last a day underwater, which would surely defeat their intentions. But by their own customs, and out of honor to your father's wish, they were duty-bound to ask you first. To do that, they had to get your attention."

"Which I never, ever wanted," she breathed. "I only wanted to be human."

"Yes."

"So they tried to speak to me in the only language we have in common. Water."

"Yes."

"But the mage understood them," the king interrupted. "Why could they not just explain all this to Eada, so that she could tell you?"

The mage was silent, letting Damaris answer, which she did, drawing herself to her feet so that she could turn and look up at him.

"Because, my lord, they were angry with me. They wanted to do me this great honor, give me this gift from my father. But I refused to hear them. I made use of their water realm, but I gave them no honor, not even the simplest courtesy of recognition. I rejected them, pretending to everyone that I am only human. I ask your forgiveness for the deception, and for being the cause of all this trouble."

"You are more than human," the king amended gruffly, and raised his voice, to make her status very clear to those courtiers who might be forming doubts about the matter. "You do us honor to refuse a kingdom for the sake of Luminum. I would hate to lose our dear friend, and our very gifted Minister of Water."

"Thank you, my lord."

"Is that all, then?" he added with a touch of anxiety. "Can we get on with it?"

"You may continue the ritual," the water-mage told him. "They are content."

After the king and his knights had drunk from the Well, and then from the pool, Garner looked for Damaris. She was nowhere in the crush of city folk and courtiers filling their cups around the pool and drinking vociferously to the moon, the Well, to Luminum and to the eagerly awaited water pipes. He found her sitting where the king had stood, well away from the noisy crowd, gazing down at the Well. Someone was with her, Garner realized, just before he walked into the torchlight. He recognized the light hair, the deep, easy, unruffled voice, and stopped, trying, for once, to be courteous, to turn and disappear.

But Lord Felden's words unraveled his good intentions.

"Of course we cannot marry," he was saying. "You understand that, I'm sure." Damaris's answer was inaudible, even to Garner's straining ears. "I can't risk having an heir with webs between its fingers who might spend all its time in the fish pond."

"Of course not."

"My mother will understand completely."

"Yes."

There was a short silence, during which Lord Felden refused to take his leave.

"I wish I could," he admitted unexpectedly. "I've grown very fond of you. If only I were not the eldest, with the title and responsibilities—"

"But you are," the naiad on the rock at his feet said firmly. "You must do your duty. Besides, our marriage might interfere with my work, and you heard what the king said." She lifted a hand to him. "Let us stay friends."

"You're not—ah—offended?"

"No. You will continue to enjoy the benefits of my work, and I the beauties of yours. Which should not be troubled tomorrow by so much as a misplaced drop of water from the fountain."

Still he paused, for which Garner had to give him credit, much as he wished him gone. "You almost make me fall in love with you all over again," he said huskily.

"It's the water nymph in me," Damaris said evenly. "Don't take it seriously."

He went off finally, a little hurriedly, after that. Garner, motionless and awkward in the shadows, wondered if he should as well; he had no reason to suppose she would be grateful for his presence. But he took a step toward her anyway. She turned, and he watched her expression change as he emerged from the night.

"Garner," she sighed.

"I don't want to disturb you if you would prefer to be alone."

She shook her head, gesturing him to join her. She was still wet, he realized, and trembling a little in the midnight air. He took his cloak off, put it over her shoulders.

"Thank you," she said, huddling herself into it. "Thank you for noticing that I am cold. I wanted to see you."

"Really?" he marveled, sitting down beside her.

"To apologize. Did you hear any of my conversation with Lord Felden?"

"Enough," he admitted. "Are you sorry?"

"Beale offered me everything I thought would make me completely human. The wealthy noble, the title, his children—I could hide safely behind him for the rest of my life."

"Are you sorry?" he asked again.

She stared down at the reflection of the moon, which was beginning to disappear as it drifted toward the underground stream.

"I would have wronged us both," she said simply, "if I had married him. I didn't understand that until tonight. I didn't understand how little in love I was." She looked at Garner then, wryly. "You saw how wrong it was, I think. That's why you were so angry with me."

"You were angry with me."

"For seeing far too much."

He was silent, gazing into the pool. Somewhere in his idle thoughts a child with Damaris's eyes and fingers webbed with dragonfly-wings dove without a ripple into a sunlit pond.

Damaris tossed a tear of gold into the Well; the image in his head blurred, faded.

"What was that?" he asked.

"One of the king's coins. I found it in the grass."

"Did you make a wish?"

She smiled at him, untangling her feet from her wet skirt, shifting to rise. "You can have the wish. All I want now is a drink of water."

So he took it, tossing his heart into the Well after the coin, and walked with her to join the celebration.